REALM

ISBN 10: 1-934666-04-1
ISBN 13: 978-1-934666-04-3

Published and distributed by:
High-Pitched Hum Publishing
321 15th Street North
Jacksonville Beach, Florida 32250

Contact High-Pitched Hum Publishing at www.highpitchedhum.net

High-Pitched Hum
Publishing

REALM

ACKNOWLEDGEMENTS

I would like to thank my daughter, Tiffiny, who is also my editor and worst critic, my husband Jim, my father Joseph Ferreira, Karen Mockel who now believes in magic, Margaret Caywood who has the patience of a saint and was my computer teacher at Independent Living for the Adult Blind at Florida Community College of Jacksonville, Chris Pihl for her encouragement and for being there to keep me sane, Jamie Bennett for the fantastic cover art, Frank Green for the discipline, Bill Reynolds for allowing me to participate in his dream, and Freedom Scientific for developing the software program that allows me to write. Most of all, I'd like to thank everyone who enjoys this book and believes in magic.

CHAPTER ONE

Myarra felt as if her heart would burst. The unicorn had been running for miles, her belly swollen with the foal she would soon deliver. Behind her, and closing fast, were the hounds. They were close enough to smell, and their baying rang in her ears. Behind them were the hunters on horseback, and their voices rang out in the joy of the sport. She had been chased before, but they had never gotten quite this close and she was frightened. In her condition, it was impossible to outrun the pack of hounds and seeing the futility of the chase, she realized she would have to turn and fight as her strength left her. Her breath came in short grunts of exhaustion. She scanned the horizon for an advantage point from which to make her stand. It was either turn and fight, or run until she dropped and let the hounds rip her apart. Either way, she knew it was going to be fatal for her and her unborn foal.

She saw a rise in the terrain, a rocky foothill she could climb and defend herself. Changing directions, she scuttled up the rise, small rocks raining down from her hooves. Climbing as high as footing would allow she turned to face her attackers, taking in great gulps of air. She lowered her sharp horn and calculated that she could at least take out three or four of the hounds before they would overcome her. The hounds were sounding now, letting their masters know that she had been cornered and the horses' hooves could be heard in the distance. She knew the hounds would hold her at bay until their masters could spear her or shoot her full of arrows.

It was her horn they wanted; a unicorn horn was a valuable commodity all of a sudden, and her kind were hunted down relentlessly and killed for it. So many members of her herd had been lost to the hunt, and very few of them remained. She was now to be their next trophy, and she knew they would cut out her foal and take its little horn as well, as they had done before to other mares.

The hounds came up the hill, growling and snapping at her legs, saliva splashing on her hooves. She deftly caught the first hound with her horn and tossed him to the right, a yelp escaping him as he flew through the air. The second hound took his place without a care to what had happened to his pack member. He was tossed to the left. Myarra felt the strain in her neck from the weight she had to lift and throw. As she prepared to catch the next hound, she saw a group of them were circling around to her hindquarters. They would surround her, she knew, and she had very little room for maneuverability. The masters were dismounting their horses and running towards the dogs, spears in hand. She knew the end would be swift. She kicked out at the hounds behind her, almost losing her footing. She managed to connect with at least one of them, but she kept her eyes on the large hound approaching her head-on, snarling and baring his teeth. She knew as soon as they attacked her legs, all would be lost. She would tumble down and they would fall on her and tear her apart, even before their masters had reached them.

She startled as the sky turned dark and a blast of flames ignited the dry grasses around her. The hounds yelped and backed off, barking indignantly, as enormous strong talons encircled her and lifted her straight up. Vast wings beat the air furiously and she was turned in the opposite direction of the men who were shooting arrows at her. The arrows bounced off the armored wings, like so many drops of rain, and fell harmlessly to the ground. She ventured a look down to see the hounds and men growing smaller and smaller in her sight until she could see them no more, just the fires and smoke that Oberon had caused as he rescued her. She breathed a sigh of relief, as tears began to fall from her large blue eyes.

The wind cut sharply through her mane and she remained motionless. Oberon, a young dragon of well renowned bravery, had her clutched tightly to his chest as he bore her away to his lair. She felt the damp ocean air as he turned sharply into his cave, cut deep within the cliffs. He back-winged and, as gently as he could, set her down and did not release her until he knew all four hooves were solidly on the ground. He then backed off, circling the cave, and then came in for a landing. He folded his wings and turned to face her.

"My dear Myarra of the Morning Mysts, may I say you are keeping strange company of late?"

Magically, he produced a large bucket of water for her and a bed of thick fragrant hay. She drank and lay down in the hay, trying for all her might to stop the tears that were flowing freely and turning into perfect white diamonds as they sprinkled the cave floor. She shook her mane and lowered her head.

Still breathing heavily, she gasped, "Thank the Gods for you, Oberon. You saved our lives once again. That was too close this time. If it weren't for you, well, I would have been murdered by now, and my foal as well. What has happened to the world? Why are we being hunted and slaughtered? It was never like this before. Times have changed and it is no longer safe for any of us."

Oberon stretched his massive body out on the cool cave floor and watched Myarra with concern. She was right, of course; they all knew it, and no one had an answer.

"Are you going to be alright, my dear? Do you need me to contact the elves to look you over? Those hounds were pretty nasty. Did you get bitten by any of them? I should have fried them all. Let me get the griffin, Reaper, to carry up one of the elves to look you over. You're in a delicate condition, I know. How did you get separated from the rest of your herd? You know it is no longer safe to graze on your own anymore. What happened?"

Myarra bobbed her head in agreement. "I was with my herd. The hounds came out of nowhere and scattered us like a mischief of mice. There was so many of them. Some of the stallions stayed to fight, my mate being one of them, and the rest of us just ran. I couldn't run as fast as the rest, not being this heavy, and I guess the hounds realized that fact and they all took off after me. I ran as fast as I could. They chased me for miles, Oberon, and my strength just gave out." She looked sadly at the dragon.

"I think I'm alright." She looked at her legs, carefully, and nodded. "I have a few scratches from the rocks, but they didn't get close enough to bite me. I tossed two of them and kicked a few, but I really had nothing left. How did you find me out there in the middle of nowhere?"

Oberon scowled. "There was more trouble besides your own. The griffins were attacked, and I helped to give them cover to move their families. Something has to be done. We lost a great griffin today, one of the elders. The elven king had to rescue a group of fairies that were captured. One of them had her wings ripped off. I'm telling you, this has all got to stop. But now, my precious, I want you to rest. Your heart is thundering away and you're still shaking like a leaf in a storm. Have some more water. Would you care for something to eat? Please, Myarra, nothing can get to you in here and you're safe." He nosed the pail of water nearer to her so she could drink without having to stand up.

She took a drink and then shook her mane. "Thank you, Oberon. I couldn't eat if I was starving right now, which I'm not. I am worried about Knight. He was holding the dogs off for awhile. I hope he was alright in the attack. He'll be worried about me, I know. I really should go." She tried to rise to her feet, but her legs shook so badly that Oberon motioned her to lay back down.

"Myarra, you're not strong enough and far too upset to do anything right now. Lay back down and rest. I will find Knight for you, if you wish, and tell him of your whereabouts, if you promise to rest until I get back. You will come to no harm here. It is perfectly safe. It's a sheer cliff and if you can't fly, you won't get in. Promise me you'll stay and relax and try to sleep just a little and I'll go."

The tears had stopped and she nodded her head, eagerly. "Thank you. It would make me feel better if Knight knew I was safe, at least for the moment. I am so very tired."

Oberon caught her meaning and gave her a slight nod as he leapt from the mouth of the cave and unfolded his wings with a sharp snap. He caught the ocean breeze and the warm thermals lifted him higher. Soaring even higher now, he turned in the direction of the area where he knew the unicorns lived. How long could he keep rescuing everyone? The dragons, and there were so very few of them, had been running themselves ragged all over the world, trying to keep everyone safe from these insane humans. Indeed, what happened to the way things once were? The world was changing and it was becoming crueler. He flew higher and surveyed the lands. He spotted the group of humans on the road back to their town, luckily without a captured magical creature in tow. He turned and headed above the forest lands of the elves. Spotting a couple of unicorns nervously talking to a group of elves, he dove down, keeping his massive black and gold wings tucked tightly to his sides until he cleared the trees.

One unicorn bolted at his landing, then came walking back, embarrassed, once he knew who it was. It was the young stallion, Storm Wind.

"Sorry, Oberon, we're all a little on edge. We've lost one of our mares and we're trying to locate her. We were scattered by a pack of those damn hunting dogs again."

Oberon nodded. "If it is the mare, Myarra, you are seeking, she is in my den. I pulled her off a precipice not that long ago. She's exhausted and resting, but she was concerned about Knight and I told her I would find him and relay her message that she is well. Have you seen him?"

The two young unicorns looked at each other and then at the elf, Tannyn. He was tall, dressed in a drab brown tunic. His light brown hair shone in the sun, and his emerald green eyes looked sad.

"Starry Knight is with us for healing right now. Perhaps it would be better for you to keep Myarra for the night. His legs were severely bitten and he foundered while taking on several of the hounds, and he's lost a lot of blood. He'll recover, but we will keep him here until he does. It is too dangerous for an injured unicorn to venture out in these times." He shook his head.

Oberon growled in rage. "We must have a meeting. Pass the word, Tannyn. Tomorrow night, in the elven clearing, if your father will permit it. We need a representative from each of the clans in attendance. We must do something to ward off these attacks. The magical creatures are beyond suffering now. Please tell Knight his lady is safe with me as long as she needs to be, she is heavy with her foal, and it wouldn't be safe for her either. So, it looks as if I have a roommate for the time being. Storm, tell the unicorns and have a member of the herd at the meeting and contact the Pegasus and anyone else you can think of. Tannyn, would your father be available to see me now?"

Tannyn looked up, thoughtful for a minute, one hand on Stormy's shoulder.

"Let me run and see if I can find him for you, Oberon. Things have been hectic here with so many injured, but I agree, this can't be allowed to continue."

Oberon nodded and watched the young elf vanish into the trees. He stood with Stormy and his younger sister, Silver Lining, who were both stamping nervously, their ears up and their eyes darting about. It was clear that they had been sent to inquire about the mare at the elven lands and both of them were nervous away from the protection of their herd, even though it had not offered much protection today.

Storm Wind nudged his sister and she jumped. "We'll go back to the herd now, and bring the news that Myarra is with you for awhile, and that although badly injured, Knight will recover but will remain here until he is stronger. He was the strongest stallion that we have, too." His deep blue eyes looked mournful and he lowered his head. "We'll spread the news of the meeting, as well."

With a toss of his head, he was gone, his sister flanking him on his right. It was painfully obvious to Oberon that the unicorns were all in an understandably anxious state. They had been suffering the most and their numbers were dwindling to a dangerous low. It was as if these humans were trying to cause genocide, and for what reason? The unicorns were delightful creatures, warm and kind, and illusive in nature. They were in the dreams of every little girl, and were so beautiful that it seemed to Oberon you would want more of them, not cause their extinction.

He drew in a great breath as he watched the elves moving back and forth in the trees. They had been overburdened as much as the dragons. He was on the front lines, but it was the elves that were caring for the wounded. It sounded like a damn war. They had never had trouble such as this. He was still lost in his thoughts when he was suddenly aware of King Orion standing in front of him and he bowed.

"King Orion, I hate to bother you in times like these, but I'm sure you will agree with me that the magical clans need to meet. We either have to organize and fight off these attacks, or move out of

these humans' way. I have the unicorn mare, Myarra, in my den as
we speak. She would have been the latest casualty. I hear you have
her mate, Knight, with you. Their foal is soon to be born. That
would have been a whole family of unicorns that we would have
lost."

King Orion frowned and shook his head. "Transform, Oberon,
and come into my glade and we will talk." He clapped the dragon
on the chest.

Oberon transformed into human form and followed the king
into a refreshing green glade and took a seat on one of the tree
stumps that were within it. The king did the same.

"Forgive the crude surroundings. I have the infirm everywhere
in my court, as you can imagine. I can tell you I fully intend to
move my subjects from here as soon as it is possible, no matter what
the rest of the magicals decide to do. It is up to me to see to their
safety. But I think a meeting is warranted, to be sure. We can fight,
but we would rather not. It would be easier to move away. My elves
are exhausted. The injured are too many. Let us meet tomorrow
night, here in my glade. We need to find the cause of all this misery.
Contact as many magicals as you can, both the Light and the Dark,
and we'll get to the bottom of all of this. You are right, Oberon.
This cannot continue."

Oberon clasped his hand. King Orion was a strong elf, tall,
handsome and lively, with chestnut hair adorned by a simple band
of gold crowning it, and green eyes that always spoke the truth.
They parted then, Oberon transforming back to dragon form and
leaping into the air. He planned to contact as many magicals as he
could.

So, the elves were leaving. That left the rest of them without the
healers they would need. The dragons had healing power, but with
less than a few dozen of them worldwide, it would not be enough.
He was usually the only dragon in this part of the world. The unicorns had life-giving powers and had healing properties, but they
were so delicate they were the ones that were injured the most often. No, they would not be able to function without the elves. And,
what of the fairies? They worked side by side with the elves and
would probably go with them. Then the land would blight. If that
was the case, the unicorns and Pegasus would have to leave as well,

as their main source of food was the pasturelands. Of course, the Pegasus would probably return to the land of the Gods. They were the messengers, after all, and only stayed long enough to refresh themselves and take care of whatever business they were sent on. They did enjoy visiting here and it was a shame to have them go, but it wasn't safe anymore, damn it all. The water nymphs would leave with the fairies and there would be no drinkable water. That would take care of everyone else. He could see the domino effect starting already. It was just as everything else was. They all depended on each other to survive.

His den was in view now and he glanced in to see Myarra fast asleep, curled up in the hay. That was well. He thought, as exhausted as she was, she would sleep for quite some time and she needed that for herself and her unborn foal. He would continue on so as not to disturb her and head on north to the land of the dwarves and trolls. This meeting was vital. They all had decisions to make and perhaps someone could come up with a workable solution.

He looked down into the mountain passes and spotted the home of the old Druid scholar, Elijah. He was part of the old world and had lived in peace with all creatures. As his Druid clans were scattered now, he chose to live in seclusion, as a hermit of sorts. He had been disgusted with the treatment of his people and the constant wars and upheaval of the world as it was now. Oberon was beginning to know just how persecuted the Druids were and how it felt, now that his own people were in the same position. Elijah kept to himself and wrote volumes of scrolls on every subject. Oberon, on impulse decided to visit with him, if he was indeed there, and see what Elijah could tell him. As his claws scuttled to land, Elijah came to the door, a quill pen still in his hand. He raised his hand in greeting.

"I just knew something exciting would happen today. Oberon, my old friend, it's been quite awhile since you remembered to visit with me. Would you like to change into human form and join me in my modest lunch? Or, if you prefer, you may stay the glorious dragon that you are and I will come outside and you can still snatch a boulder or two, but please spare my humble home."

Elijah looked to the tops of the mountains where Oberon had eaten heartily. Dragons were notorious eaters of stone. As a scholar, he knew that. So many of the legends had dragons as killers of men and it was simply not true.

Oberon laughed heartily. "As if I would destroy your home. I recall it was me who brought you all the stone to build it in the first place. You know I could have easily snacked on that quantity of rocks for weeks."

Oberon changed again into human form and shook hands with Elijah, who held the door to his cottage open, ushering him in. Oberon sat down at the roughly carved wooden table, careful not to disturb Elijah's writings and drawings. Elijah removed his writings and put down a tankard of ale for the dragon. He pulled up a chair and had a tankard of his own.

"I can see by your face that things are not well with you, Oberon, and I know your troubles. I had a few merchants come through this way a month ago, offering to sell me ground unicorn horn for vitality, ground fairy wings for maladies of the brain, and griffin claws for ensuring victory in battle." He made a face and shook his head.

"Of course I sent them away, telling them they were wrong to offer such wares. We are in a dark time, my friend. Even you would be worth something now." He gave Oberon a sad wry smile.

Oberon looked at the pictures on Elijah's walls. He spied one of himself in full flight, labeled *Oberon the King*, and it made him chuckle. He pointed at it and Elijah smiled.

"I would have you for a king. You are the mightiest of the magical creatures and yet, you are humble to the point of coddling everyone else. Ferocious, to be sure, when you want to be. But you really are of the gentlest nature, and more importantly, you have respect for every clan, right down to the smallest of fairies." Oberon blushed at the compliment. He wasn't used to receiving them and found it rather uncomfortable.

"What good is that, Elijah? What good is being humble when we are being reduced to commodities? It seems we are on the dawning of the end of the magical world. Your people understood us. We lived in harmony with them. Why can't these new people do the same? We cause them no problems, yet they attack us every time they can. Do they want us to fight back? I could contact my dragons and burn their town down in minutes, killing everyone within it. Is that the answer? No, of course not. More people would come. Still, no one feels safe anymore and it has become dangerous. There is a meeting in King Orion's land tomorrow. We will have as many representatives from the magicals that we can get. Would you like to attend? I could fly you in for it. You would be able to answer many questions, and you've always been trusted." He looked hopefully at the scribe.

Elijah looked down at the table for a moment. "I would come if you wanted me to, but I'm afraid they would see me as part of the problem. Tensions are so high now, as you well know. I know the problem well enough, and I will tell it to you and you can tell it to them at the meeting. I'm afraid I would not be welcome."

He raised his hands and his robe sleeves dropped to reveal the blue veins of his forearms. "Oh, I know you will guarantee my safety, but I would prefer it that they think you all the wiser, not for bringing a human to the meeting, but for visiting with me and trying to find the solution for yourself and for them. You see, I do believe you would make a good king, and I would have them agree. I have been watching this situation erode for the past few years. The human population is getting denser and the overcrowding is contributing to the problem. We have different groups taking over at different intervals, bringing their own sets of laws and beliefs that they are determined everyone should follow. It is conformity that puts them at ease and anything outside of that makes them wary and hostile. I don't know why a conquering people should expect everyone to conform to their way of thinking, but they do, and therein lies the problem. As far as the magicals are concerned, well, you are all so different and you have what they will never possess, and that's the magic. They won't get it, but it won't stop them from trying."

Oberon listened attentively as Elijah put dried apples and flatbread in front of him with a dish of honey. He refilled Oberon's tankard with ale.

Sighing heavily, Elijah went on, "You have two groups that I can see are the problems. Group one tries to just take the magic from your subjects and that's where the danger lies. They think if they can just get a part of a magical creature they can transfer the magic to themselves. Ridiculous, I understand, and you know that as well, but that's where the unicorn horns are going. It doesn't matter if you have to hunt and kill one to get it. Alright, so we have those ruthless people trying to take the magic by force."

Elijah dipped a piece of bread in the honey and ate it, indicating to Oberon to do the same, which he did. It was fresh mountain honey, and in human form he found it delicious. He very seldom ate in this form, using it only when room did not permit a full sized dragon. He absently thought he should take this form to eat once in awhile, as food seemed to take on a social quality here and it was not just for sustenance as it was in his world. Different customs were not necessarily a bad thing.

Elijah, nodding at Oberon's comment that the honey was delicious, went on, "The second group of people is the religious fanatics. They are almost as dangerous as the first group, maybe even more so, now that I think about it. Their religion allows no room for magic and labels it evil. That's all magic, light and dark. It's all demons to them."

Oberon shrugged. "But we do have demons and the creatures that practice the dark magic. It's a smaller percentage of us, but we've managed to stay out of their way. They don't really bother with us, either. They deal with the people more than we do, selling them curses and spells. The people seek them out, and now they want to get rid of them? I don't understand."

Elijah agreed. "I know, but in these people's eyes there is good and evil. They don't see it as a balance as we do; their way of thinking is that all evil must be destroyed. If you have magic, then you are evil because only their God is allowed to have power, not anything else. This is a fight of conviction, too. People will die defending their God, and allow only him the magic. As they see it, you all have to be destroyed along with all the people who even acknowledge that the magicals exist."

Oberon did not move. He blinked a few times, but he was frozen in place by the knowledge he had just received. It was very clear to him none of them stood a chance against the world as it was changing and shutting the door on magic. Elijah stood up, walked around the room and pointed to the scrolls.

He looked a little sheepish as he said, "Why do you think I work so hard, day in and day out, to record everything I can? All of the magicals, all their stories and the memories of things past? I want to preserve the events and I wish I could preserve our way of life too, but I haven't been able to, not even of my own people. That's why I hide. The first thing that conquering people do is burn everything so they can start over and make the people start over as well. I am afraid I will come to that fate. It's inevitable. So, on these walls and in these shelves, are our epitaphs."

They looked at each other in silence. This was even worse than Oberon had imagined. The sound of slow hoofbeats turned both heads towards the door. A young woman on horseback was coming down the mountain pass, her dark hair blowing in the breeze. Oberon, seeing her first with his acute dragon eyesight, raised his eyebrows.

"Well, Elijah, if you think my arrival was the excitement for the day, you haven't seen anything yet. There's a very lovely woman on her way."

Elijah went to the door and strained his eyes to see what the dragon had reported. Barely making out the form, still quite a distance off, he said, "Ah, yes, that is Glynnis. She said in her letter she would arrive soon, but I didn't expect her this soon. The weather must have held up well in the high country. I hate that she travels alone, but she's strong- willed and will have it no other way."

Seeing the look the dragon was giving him, he laughed. "Oberon, I'm a scholar, not a priest. She's very beautiful, isn't she? She's a Druid and has a little magic. The healing kind mostly, and she has bewitched me, to be sure. I am not so old as to not appreciate a pretty face."

He cleared his throat, embarrassed. "She brings me supplies from town."

Oberon was still amused. He had thought the scribe was solitary by nature. Elijah's face brightened as she neared. Oberon thought to leave, but Elijah insisted that he stay and meet Glynnis.

"I'm afraid I once was trying to impress her and I happened to mention my allegiance with a certain dragon," he confessed, his face reddening. "I know she would love to meet you. You are legendary among our clan, you know."

Oberon made a face. "Elijah, what am I to do with you? Very well, I will meet the young lady, for your sake. Perhaps it will ensure you a more exciting evening?"

Elijah laughed and shoved him out of the door and they stood in the pathway, watching her wave as she approached. She jumped down without help and Elijah kissed her hand. Glancing quickly at Oberon, she smiled. It was evident that if it were not for mixed company Elijah would have given her a warmer welcome.

"Glynnis, I would like you to meet a friend of mine. This is Oberon."

Glynnis gave a curtsey. "It's my pleasure to meet you, Oberon. Are you named for the mighty dragon?" She grinned.

Oberon put up a hand to silence Elijah. "As a matter of fact, I am. I wish I could stay and talk with you more, but I have a pressing matter to attend to. Elijah, thank you for the lunch. I will not take so long in returning this time. I feel we have a lot to discuss. There is more I would wish to know. But, knowing you as I do, once this beautiful woman has your attention, and well she should, there will be no more of your concentration on the conversation. Now, my dear, if you will stand in the doorway there, and Elijah, if you would be so kind as to hold the horse, I must be leaving."

Elijah grabbed the reins and backed the horse up and Glynnis, looking puzzled, backed up into the doorway. Oberon ran several yards away and transformed with his wings extended, taking on the updraft and flew into the sky. That should have impressed her, he mused. He hoped his friend would have a lot of explaining to do, and a good time afterwards.

Glynnis' jaw dropped as she watched the man transform. Elijah kept a strong hand on the horse's reins as he tried to bolt. They watched, hands above their eyes to block the sun, as the dragon took flight. Glynnis ran to Elijah and he put an arm around her as the horse quieted down.

"Good Gods. Why didn't you tell me who that was?" She looked with wonder at Elijah.

He threw up one hand. "I did. I'm surprised you couldn't tell, yourself, from those golden eyes of his. He's been here awhile, discussing the annihilation of his magical world."

Her eyes clouded and she looked down, shaking her head. "It's the same in our village. No one knows what to do. Surely he doesn't feel threatened. A dragon of his power?"

Elijah walked the horse and tied him to the tree, removing the bit so the horse could graze. He began unloading the packs, absently handing them to Glynnis, who set them on the ground.

"Of course he feels threatened, Glynnis. Oberon never has a care for himself. It's the magicals he fears for and their way of life, and well that he should. We are all looking at the end of the magical world. I'm sure you've noticed. I do so wish you would marry me and live here away from all the troubles. You must know that with your powers, you will be a target soon, too."

She nodded. "How far can you run, Elijah? They will hunt us down just as they are hunting the unicorns. Where do we go then? There is no safe place, and I'm needed in the village. All the other healers have left in fear. I can't just leave and let people die."

Elijah took her in his arms and held her feeling the disillusionment in her that he already felt in himself.

* * *

When Oberon finally made it back to his den, the sun was setting. He hadn't planned to be away for so long, but he had contacted the dwarves and the trolls and had spread the word out to the Elementals. He could see that Myarra was up and walking around, probably starving by now, he thought, as he cursed himself for leaving her without food. Myarra was awake and looking blankly out of the cave into the setting sun. She moved out of the way when she saw Oberon heading towards the mouth of the cave. Her legs were stiff and she had been walking slowly around the cave for awhile, trying to loosen them up.

Oberon landed and immediately transformed back into human form to allow her the extra room to walk around. There wasn't much room if you had a large dragon lying in the middle of the cave floor. He walked over to her and put his arms around her neck. She shied a bit and he looked at her questioningly.

"I'm sorry, Oberon." She stammered a bit. "I'm beginning to fear humans. I'm more comfortable with you in your dragon form. At least dragons don't eat unicorns. I hear in some village taverns we are actually served as a delicacy."

She said that with resentment and her words came out sharp

and bitter. Oberon was concerned. Unicorns were never like this. They were cheerful and hopeful, always pleasant and kind. He knew Myarra's heart was hardening against the humans and no one could blame her. He conjured a brush and began to curry her, which set her a little at ease.

"I have some good news and some bad news, Myarra. The good news is that Knight, although injured in the fight with the hounds, remains in elven lands being tended by their healers and will make a full recovery. He will be given the message that you are safe. I also talked with Storm Wind and he will tell your herd as much. The bad news is that we're to be roommates for awhile, as suggested by the elves. They feel you will need Knight by your side to fare very well in these times. There is to be a meeting tomorrow night of the magicals. Hopefully we can make some sense out of what to do with the situation we find ourselves in."

He worked on a few tangles in her mane and she blinked back a few tears.

"Knight was injured, protecting me. If the elves are keeping him, his situation must be grave. I want to see him, Oberon. I want to go to the elven lands."

He stopped brushing her. Of course she would want to be with him, and in her condition, it probably wouldn't hurt for her to be near healers as well. As much trauma as she had been through, there might be problems and the elves were better at handling the situation. They needed all the new healthy unicorns they could get. He kissed her cheek.

"I'll bring you with me tomorrow when I go to the meeting and you can be with him. If King Orion allows it, perhaps you could stay with him while he recovers. A beautiful face never hinders recovery and it would put his mind at ease to know you are well. But you must promise me to just eat and sleep and rest through the night and the day until the time of the meeting. I'm sure bouncing you around in the air does you no good, so you must rest now for the trip. We want nothing to go wrong with that little foal of yours, do we?"

She bobbed her head in agreement. She seemed more relaxed now that she knew she could be with Knight. She shook out her mane he had brushed and nuzzled his face.

"Thank you, Oberon. Thank you for understanding. I know I must seem like an ungrateful, demanding mare, but I really am in your debt. If it weren't for you, I would have been killed. I don't mean to be so difficult. You have been so kind to me and I just feel terrible about my manners."

Oberon laughed and directed a spell into a corner of the cave. There were all sorts of grasses, fruits, and vegetables there now. To the right of that, he fabricated a huge barrel of fresh spring water.

"Nonsense, my dear Myarra. You've been a perfect lady. Maybe a little cranky, but we'll forgive that considering your condition and the situations you've just been through."

She whinnied and took a playful nip at him. He laughed and motioned her to the corner. "Dinner is served."

He sat at the mouth of the cave, watching the sun sink into the ocean, and listening to Myarra graze happily in the corner. He thought about his conversation with Elijah. He hadn't realized the situation was accelerating as fast as it was. They stood no chance here. Where else could they go? Everywhere, there would be the same problem. Were they to give up and die? He took a deep breath of the ocean air and fought off the depression that was setting in. Surely, there must be an answer. Suddenly he knew what he had to do.

He watched Myarra finish eating and said, "Myarra, there is something I must do before tomorrow. Will you be alright for the night here? I should be back by daybreak. I hate to leave you alone in your condition, stranded on top of a mountain, but I'm afraid it can't be helped."

Myarra stared at him thoughtfully. "I'll be fine, Oberon. I feel the need to sleep again, and my time will not come tonight, nor for the next few weeks, for that matter. I think I'll sleep sounder knowing I'll be safe. I promise to go right to bed and stay there until you return. Does it concern our dilemma with the humans?"

Oberon nodded.

She continued, "Well, then, for our future and that of my foal, you certainly should go. I place my trust in you, Oberon, and you may be the only one to see us through these terrible times. Go then, and Gods speed your flight."

He nodded at her once more, transformed into the shining black and gold dragon and flew away. Myarra said a silent prayer for his protection and thanked the Gods for his generosity. She walked over to the soft pile of hay and carefully lay down. She watched him as his shape became smaller and then finally disappeared from sight altogether. She lowered her head and slept.

CHAPTER TWO

Oberon accelerated his speed as he flew southwest to the Andes. He would see his father, Elgin, The Blood Dragon, as he was called for his deep red coloring. He didn't know why he hadn't thought of it sooner. The temperature dropped the higher he went into the mountain range. He stopped only once, seeing a mountain lake and he drank his fill of the cold clear water and ate several large boulders, enjoying the different taste of the rocks in this area. It was a nice change. He rested for a bit, and then took off, hoping his father would still be in the same cave that he remembered. Dragons seldom left their lairs, being solitary creatures.

He soared through the low clouds to the mountain peak. Shivering a bit, he fired a blast of fire to announce his presence, as was the proper custom. It made the snow sparkle and he saw an answering blast from the mouth of the cave. Once again, the mountainsides lit up with the red and blue reflections of the fiery plumes. He turned in his approach to land inside. His father had a massive cave, one that he carved out and consumed with relish. There was enough room for a dozen dragons and as he folded his wings, his father came out to greet him.

"Oberon, my son. How good it is to see you. You look fit. I hope you are here to tell me of the news of my grandson? I certainly hope so, there are so few of us left."

His father stood there with a wide grin, looking expectantly at Oberon, his one claw on Oberon's shoulder.

Oberon laughed. "It is good to see you again, Father. A grandson? Already? I'm just a mere couple hundred years old. I'm too young for a family."

Elgin grunted in disappointment and showed his son in. He pushed a few of his pile of choice rocks over to Oberon.

"Thank you, Father, but I've just eaten. What I did come for is more knowledge. I need your help. Perhaps if we can come up with solutions together, I would have more time to court, although the choices are rather slim, are they not?"

Elgin placed both feet on the ground and sat with his head straight up, almost touching the top of the cave. One of the largest dragons, he made an impressive sight with his rich crimson color and bright sharp eyes. He tapped a claw and had a look of concentration on his face.

"Well, now, there is Harmonia. She's about your age, perhaps a few years younger. She would be a suitable mother, although I hear she is a little vain and self- centered. Still, she's your best choice. She's healthy and a good fighter, from what I've heard. You might consider her. I could contact her family if you like, you know, to arrange a meeting? I do so look forward to a youngster under my feet again. There is nothing like children to keep you young." Elgin lifted his head and grinned a bit.

It seemed that every time Oberon visited his father, the subject turned to offspring. Oberon listened patiently, but children were the last things on his mind right now. He sprawled out, letting the colder stone floor cool him off. It was a long flight, and it would seem even longer on the way back, but he would not interrupt his father. He knew he was going to have to listen to this need for more dragons. He tried not to yawn.

"You know, Father, you are not so old. Perhaps a new little brother or sister for me is in order."

Elgin's eyes twinkled. "Perhaps. If we men don't get busy soon, we'll be extinct. Dragons are being killed all over the world for the blood, you know. It has fantastic healing properties, and the humans have discovered this. Dragon hunting has become the newest sport, or so I'm told."

Oberon sat up at this. "That's precisely why I've come here, Father. It's not only dragons that are being hunted."

He told his father of the massacre that was happening in his homeland. His father asked a few questions, nodded a few times, and then grew silent and withdrew into himself for awhile. Oberon waited patiently. He knew his father was trying to formulate a solution to his problem. He found himself dozing a little when his father cleared his throat. Oberon sat back up. His father gave him a sharp look.

"You can do nothing about your homeland."

Oberon's hope sank and it showed in his eyes.

Elgin raised one claw. "But, you can create your own land." He saw Oberon's confusion and made tisking sounds. "You don't remember your lessons, do you? Shame be on you, Oberon. Do you remember the dragon holes in time?"

Oberon nodded slowly, not knowing where this was going or why it had anything to do with his problem. Still, he answered, "You're talking about time travel? Yes, I know it, and I know about freezing time, but how can I make my own world out of that?"

Elgin gave a deep throaty laugh at his son's expense. "It's simple; freeze the land in a time when humans didn't exist. Now, you don't want to go back too far, not and meet your great relatives. You don't want a fight like that on your hands, but you could pick an earlier time, and a land large enough to support your magicals. You will need the magic from them as well to create a suitable frontier, you know, enough pasture lands, mountains, forests for your elves, an ocean for your Mer-people and so on and so forth. Every clan will know what it is they need. If they can't create it themselves, then you must do it for them. Some of the old Druids have a creative magic, but on the scale that you would need, you'll need all of us dragons to do it. This has been on my mind of late, as well. If you haven't bothered to go into the future, you wouldn't know the chaos that is coming. No one will be safe anymore. We all will need a place to go, or face extinction. In your land, it would just be the magicals. As long as they live reasonably, they will have no troubles at all and you'll be able to repopulate your numbers in peace. We can create a gate to the present world if you like. I'm sure the Elementals will not leave their Mother. Fairies and sprites, the same thing. At least they are small enough to hide and survive."

He drew a great breath, resting, and let Oberon think things over. Elgin flew out of the cave then, as Oberon stood thinking. He returned with a huge chunk of ice and dropped it down on the floor.

"Here, try this, it's really refreshing."

Oberon munched the ice happily, as he considered his father's words. Was it indeed possible? A safe haven for all of his magical kindred? Oberon took it one step at a time. It would take a great deal of magic, more than he had, to make it work, but in theory, other than having a few displaced animals at the time, he could find no fault in it.

"Father, do you think you could get all the dragons to agree to come to this new world, this magic realm?"

His father nodded. "They will go to the Magic Realm, as you call it. Even though they wouldn't admit it, they are just as scared as you are. Don't look at me like that. I've seen the future and you all need to be scared. Scared enough to do something about it. Isn't it strange that no one does anything until they get truly frightened, or threatened? Rest, Oberon. It's a long flight back. Talk to your magicals and I will talk to the other dragons. We will meet again and next time, we'll be ready to act. Even if your magicals aren't interested, I think the dragons should go. Don't you agree? Oh, we'll be able to come and go into the present world if we wish it, but I'm willing to put diamonds on it that once we're all there, we won't want to leave."

Oberon nodded. He did think that with the help of everyone, it could be done. He no longer wanted to rest. He was excited now, as excited as someone with a great gift to give to the people they love.

"I will go now, Father, and I will mind-contact you when we're ready to proceed. Thank you, Father. I knew if there was an answer to all this, you would be the one to come up with it."

He embraced his father and was gone in a flash. It was a long flight, with an awful head wind. The sun was well over the horizon when he finally made it back to his liar. Myarra was up and eating again and he stuck his head in the barrel and drank. He apologized to Myarra for being later than he should have been, but she looked no worse for wear and tear, and there was nothing she needed.

She greeted him warmly. "I should sleep here once a month,

just to get a decent night's sleep without the fear that I may have to bolt and run at a minute's notice. It's the best sleep I've had in a long time."

Oberon transformed into human form to give her more room. He wished he had a cave as large as his father's, but the small one he did have was comfortable enough, as he seldom had any visitors. He stretched out on the hay. The rock floor was not as comfortable when he was in human form. She watched him curiously, knowing how tired he must be and reluctant to ask him the hundred questions that were on her mind. She watched as he fell fast asleep, and she sighed and lay down next to him. She may as well get all the rest she could before going back into the hell she had been rescued from. She nuzzled his hair affectionately. The poor guy had flown himself into exhaustion just to try to find a solution to all of this mayhem. She owed him a lot. Tonight, she would be back with Knight. She missed his warmth and his gentle breathing. She would see to it he recovered, and she would lend her healing magic to that of the elves for a faster recovery. She still was disillusioned over the prospect of the future. Oberon had said the elves were leaving. Maybe they could go with them. There had to be a safe place to go, somewhere. She put her nose on her swollen belly. She had to provide a safe place for her foal to grow without the fear they were all experiencing.

* * *

King Orion prepared for the meeting in his glade. It had always been used for celebrations and events of a joyous nature. Tonight would be different. It was a sad state of affairs they were all facing now. His scouts reported there was a festival of some sort in the village and the humans were celebrating, and it looked as if they were safe enough as they doubted if the humans would leave the festival. Still, the king had his lookouts placed up in the trees all around. There would be a lot of magicals here tonight, he had said. Torches were being lit and representatives were starting to arrive.

Oberon had flown in earlier with the mare, Myarra, who had been joyfully reunited with her mate, to the relief of both of them. Knight was healing well, and she was welcome to stay with him.

Oberon seemed to be in a more jovial mood than the king had seen him in for a long time, and he wondered why. All in good time, the dragon had said.

Oberon transformed back into human form and helped to seat the many leaders of the clans, stopping to chat with each one. Some of them he hadn't seen in years. *If the situation wasn't so grave,* thought King Orion, *it would have made a great party.* He was ashamed to say they hadn't had a decent party in months due to all the attacks on the magicals. His people loved and deserved to have social gatherings and he was hoping that whatever Oberon and the rest of the leaders had up their sleeves would quash these troubled times, and they could go back to the way things used to be. He hung his head; he had no solution and by the looks of most of the visiting leaders, they had no answers either. Only Oberon looked as if he might have a plan and King Orion prayed that it would be a good one and that he would not have to lead his people out of their beloved forest and travel to, where? He had no ideas about that, either. As a leader, he felt insignificant in these times. There was just no safe place to go to, and the eyes of all his elves were upon him, looking for direction, and secure in the fact he would protect them and preserve their way of life. But could he still do that? He didn't have an answer for that either.

He watched as food was being brought out and served to the visitors. He sat on a platform overlooking the crowd. The griffin, Reaper, had flown in and once he had landed, he went right over to Oberon, talking furiously. King Orion could tell he had recently been in a battle of some sort, as he had large patches of feathers missing and a long cut on his side. He made a mental note to have one of his healers take a look at that cut. So, even their best warriors were no match for this onslaught.

Members of the dark magic arrived unobtrusively and sat away from the light magic members. They preferred to keep to themselves. He saw the changeling, Mordread, with the sorceress, Nadreyl. He did see the siren, Lorelei, looking as enticing as ever, accept a drink from one of his serving elves. Naturally, she would not confine herself to a corner. He saw Oberon kiss her cheek and thought that if it were him, he would stay clear of those man-eating teeth of hers.

Two of the fairies flew up to sit with him on the railing of the platform and he told them it would be fine for them to stay there and see from a higher point all that would be going on. They, too, had a sad story to tell him, as did everyone, it seemed. He noticed the shy air elemental, Maura, hanging overhead from the limbs of the giant oak tree. To anyone but a magical, it would only look like so much Spanish moss. He knew better and made a flower bloom right next to her, coming out of the tree bark and she winked at him with clear grey eyes.

The dwarves and trolls arrived together and it seemed the trouble had reached into the far north, with the invaders taking their members into slavery. They made their way into the glade and bowed their respects to King Orion, as they found seats and exchanged tales with their neighbors. He assumed they were the last to arrive, coming from the furthest distance. He signaled to one of his elves to blow his horn and get everyone's attention. The glade was quiet now, and all eyes were upon him.

He drew a great breath. "Thank you all for coming on such short notice. You will all be recognized in turn to speak as dignitaries of your clans. We all know the problem and to hear more of them would be more than we can bear, I fear. It is a solution that we are after, here. I know, as the king of the elven lands, my plan was to move my people out of the way of this terrorism, and yet, where is a safe place to go? I see we have everyone here tonight, both of the light and dark magics. Although there has been some trouble in the past between the light and dark magicals, everyone will be respected here in my land, as I fear it will take all of us, light and dark alike, working together to overcome this plague we are now facing. Has anyone worked out a solution to this problem?"

Knight had hobbled in against the better judgment of his healer. There was a murmur at all of his injuries. Knight was a ferocious fighter and for him to be in that condition spoke volumes to everyone in attendance, who looked on him with eyes full of compassion and sympathy. He stood silently looking around with the rest of them, his body shaking with the strain of his injuries. It seemed no one knew what to say.

Oberon took a few steps and climbed up onto the platform. King Orion smiled and introduced him, praying he would be the one to bring salvation to their lands.

"Oberon of the dragon clan, you have our attention."

Oberon bowed to the king and to the crowd. "As you can see, I have taken human form to allow for more seating." He smiled and a titter of laughter went around.

He continued, "There is no solution to our problem here, in this world, and I've been told the future is even worse. There is no more room for magicals here and there never will be again."

He paused as there were a few cries of despair and indignation. Both Knight and Reaper gave him looks of incredulity. Oberon put up his hands to quiet them.

"I am not finished. These humans are of two groups. One is selling our body parts as trophies or potions to enhance themselves. The other group is religious in nature, and not of the older Druid religion, who accepted us without question as magical beings with the same rights to exist as they had. These new religions don't allow for magic; they consider it all evil and have decreed that all creatures doing magic must be eliminated, along with anyone else that supports or even acknowledges that magic exists."

There were gasps of disbelief and frightened, hurried comments, and Oberon waited until it quieted again.

"In the past day, I have been thousands of miles to find a solution to all of this."

There was dead silence now, everyone on the edge of their seats waiting to hear a solution that they themselves could not come up with. Oberon scanned the crowd to make sure he had everyone's attention. He did.

"There is a way out of all of this torture. It's complicated at best and will require everyone's help. I'm not going to pretend I understand it perfectly because I don't, and I don't believe for one minute everyone will want to go along with this idea either, and that's alright, too. The dragons have an ability none of the rest of you possess, as some of you may already know. We have the ability to transcend time, being the oldest of the clans. We can also freeze time, as well. The dragons have a plan to choose a time uninhabited by the humans, freeze it, and make it their own. Gates to the present world can be established for those dedicated to the Mother Earth, and they would be able to use the gate to nurture her and still come back to a land frozen in time to be safe."

Heads were turning to look at each other and there were a lot of anxious faces in the crowd. Oberon knew they were all concerned about their own clans.

He went on, "We believe we can create our own world, free from the brutalities of the humans, and live in peace together, much as we are meeting in peace right here. Each clan would be welcome to change and design the land that they need, and we can claim as much of it as we all need to live in comfort. Everyone can have whatever they need and we can make it possible with dragon magic. Now, dragon magic won't do everything. The land would still have to be cared for and the water, as well. The kingdoms can be run just like they are now, and we can live without fear of annihilation. I will answer any questions I can or I will defer to any representative with another solution."

It was deathly quiet. Mordread of the dark magic spoke, "The members of the Dark do not need dragon magic. We enjoy living with these humans and tormenting them. If we want our own world, we can make a Realm of Darkness, ourselves, if we want it."

Mordread smiled smugly and looked over to Nadreyl, who nodded once. The Furies laughed wildly at that.

Oberon shrugged and said, "All would be welcome to join whichever Realm you would be more comfortable in, I suppose."

A few faces held looks of relief; the light magical creatures had always had a problem living with those of the dark. It would solve even more problems than just the original one. Mordread nodded in satisfaction.

One of the fairies wanted to be heard and Oberon repeated her question for all to hear.

"Ivy of the Fairies wishes to express that their fairies will remain behind to tend the lands, but wonders if they could be in contact and receive help from the Realm if the need arises. I would answer her that her people are very courageous, showing more bravery than those of us that will flee, once again proving that stature has nothing to do with courage, and we will find a way to support her in any way that we can."

Oberon suggested to the king they be allowed to talk amongst themselves and see if they could come up with any problems that would be better addressed with all the clans present. The king told them to talk it over and have some refreshments, and they would convene again once everyone had been fed. He leaned over to Oberon who had taken a seat near him.

"That is the best idea I've heard so far. It is really possible, isn't it?"

Oberon smiled. "So I've been told. The dragons are getting together now. They intended to do this anyway, even if the magicals weren't interested."

The king looked struck. "Who wouldn't be interested in surviving? It is very generous of your clan to offer to do this for all of our kind."

Oberon bowed his head. "As I see it, my Lord, there is no other choice."

The king nodded gravely.

Knight limped up to Oberon. "Thank you, Oberon, for saving Myarra and for saving us all. The unicorns will comply, but I was wondering if there would be trouble, as unicorns need a lot of room, naturally. We would not want to appear greedy."

Oberon patted Knight's shoulder. "I think we all know the requirements for herds of unicorns, and we would be pleased that you chose the Realm of the light magic. The unicorns will be able to design their own lands, however large they need, with pastures, trees, whatever you think you'll require. That's the beauty of it all, Knight. We can secure land in abundance. Have no fear."

Knight bowed his head and wearily let himself be led back to his original position, but leaned a bit on one of the trees. His healer implored him to return to his stall for rest, but he flatly refused and held up his head with as much dignity as he could muster in his condition.

"I will remain for the rest of the meeting, as representative of the unicorns. Our world depends on it."

The healer sighed and rubbed some healing herbs on his sore legs. Knight had good news for Myarra. Their foal would be born in a new Realm, free and safe from predators

With what everyone deemed to be salvation at hand, the mood lightened and it seemed as if everyone was talking at once, floods of relief washing over their faces. Hope seemed to conduct electricity and soon, each clan seemed to agree on a Magic Realm of their own. Only the creatures of the Dark seemed bored, but reluctant to leave. The meeting reconvened and again, the focus was on Oberon.

"Let me understand everyone. It seems as if, with the exceptions of the faries, the Earth elementals and the members of the Dark magic, all of the rest of the clans are in agreement."

There were nods and shouts of approval all around. Oberon waited a bit to make sure there were no misunderstandings.

"Then, it's agreed, and considering the attacks we have suffered," He glanced pointedly at Knight and Reaper, whose wounds were evident to everyone. "I see no reason to delay the forward progress. Now, I'm sure there will be problems; there are always problems in any endeavor of this magnitude, so I would ask the patience and constructive help of everyone. We do not need short tempers and negativity. I will contact my clan. Before you ask, I do not know how long this will take. You should make every effort to avoid the humans and keep well hidden. I suggest you all go back to your clans, after you enjoy this fine fare put on for us all by the kindness of the Elven King Orion, and prepare them for the journey."

There were shouts of elation and appreciation for King Orion and indeed, it turned out to be a spectacular evening, after all, and everyone's mood was light. Oberon leaned towards the King.

"May I have leave to examine your forest maps, my Lord? I have no desire to celebrate until the work is done. I would like to find a suitable forest in which to have a gate; one dark and thick, without too many visitors, even in this time."

The king nodded and directed one of his elves to show Oberon the direction of the map rooms. Oberon caught Reaper's eye and he made his way over to follow Oberon. The rest of the clans were enjoying the food and catching up on the gossip and exchanging horror stories of the present.

Oberon and Reaper looked at many scrolls of drawings and locations. They found one thick, almost impenetrable, forest in a kingdom to the north and Oberon was surprised he remembered it well from his trips to see Elijah. It wasn't far from there at all. It was near a small village just outside of a large castle with a peaceful noble soon to be in charge, but not yet in residence. Both Oberon and Reaper considered it a workable forest. The griffins would need game to survive and it could be brought in, or the griffins could hunt for themselves. It was bordered by the North Sea on one side, and opened up to a small village on the southeast side that Oberon knew to be a village of mostly Druids. On the far west side was the castle. Reaper studied it considerably, at length.

"I like it, Oberon. Griffins get restless and they are predatory. Of course, they can't pray on their fellow magicals, but to be able to get out into the forest and be able to fly over the sea will give them the freedom that they will need from time to time."

Oberon nodded. "The dragons are the same; although not hunters, the exercise is essential. If the gate is close enough to the cliff, we can come and go virtually unnoticed, save for a few boats, and who's going to believe a bunch of drunken sailors? It may also prove to be a benefit for the kingdom. The sight of griffins and dragons is enough to ward off attackers. If we keep the kingdom happy, we're even safer. I believe that is Druid territory, as well. The king there may profess this new religion, but I bet he's tolerant of the old world religion, too. That Druid settlement has been there for a long time unmolested, so it must be under the protection of the king."

They both looked up as King Orion walked in. He, too, glanced over the map they were studying and nodded in agreement.

"That was the forest I was planning to move my people into should we have to evacuate, and considering the latest attacks, I was planning on doing it relatively soon. It is a good place for the gate. Even elves get restless after awhile and like to interfere in the lives of humans. Nothing evil, mind you; they usually intervene for the humans' own good. But it is a change, and that forest is thick and beautiful. It is also near enough to the local pub for the elves to sing their songs and tell their stories." Oberon smiled.

"Your elves will be an essential part of the new Realm. The clan elders of the dragons may choose a desert or a blighted land to freeze for our own. It would have to be a place with no inhabitants, other than perhaps a few animals and natural wildlife. We will need the elven magic to make the pastures for the unicorns green, the forest lush and the way your elves like it. The water nymphs may be needed to clean the water and make it useable. I doubt the Mer people will choose to live in the Realm, as the sea will be so near the gate. The humans haven't been able to threaten them yet, and that's a good thing. It may be a lot of work for your elves."

King Orion smiled and motioned to the party going on outside. "My people need the practice. Most of my older elves have worked hard in securing our location here and turning it into the paradise that it is. It will be hard for us to leave it, but the elders will teach the young and they will finally get a chance to know what they're all about. They'll learn what wonders they can do. Right now, they're reaping the benefits of those who have worked long and hard before them to make our land this way. It is time for them to give back and learn our ways. The next Elven kingdom will be even more beautiful than this one. Perhaps there, in the new Magic Realm, less time will have to be devoted to the healing arts and more time can be given to their creative talents. It will be like the old times then, and not the infirmary that it has turned into as of late. Speaking of infirmary, I would like my healers to look at that wound on your side, Reaper. No sense in dying of an infection when life is about to change for the better."

He made a face at that, then shook his head and brightened. "Now, we have good things to look forward to, instead of days of anguish and misery. The elves are very sensitive to other's emotions, and lately it has been like a tomb around here, not the happy place it once was."

Oberon put an arm around the king. "We all look forward to being rid of the suffering and anxiety. I will contact the elders of my clan and it won't be long. Evidently, according to my father, they have already been planning a move, like the rest of us. It shouldn't take long."

As they walked back out into the glen where music was now being played, and it was indeed turning into a lively celebration, Mordread made his way through the crowd and begged a word with the griffin, who was holding very still at the moment; an elf was putting a healing salve on his cut. As soon as the elf was finished, Reaper thanked him and turned to Mordread.

The elven king and Oberon watched as Reaper walked along with Mordread. It was hard to tell what they were discussing. Oberon frowned.

To the king, he said, "Now, what do you suppose all that is about? I would bet diamonds that Mordread is trying to win the hearts of the griffins to join the Dark Magic." He shook his head slowly. "I know it won't work. As vicious and stealthy as griffins are, there isn't one among them who is not noble in thought and deed. We would be in serious trouble if they did turn towards the Dark. I can't believe he's lobbying. This is not a war between the Light and the Dark magics. This is the preservation of all magic. What is he trying to prove?" Oberon scoffed and gave the talking pair a scrutinizing look.

The king's attentions were turned away from Oberon as a large troll engaged him in conversation. Oberon continued walking and was making his way over to Knight when he was grabbed from behind and he felt teeth nibbling on the back of his neck. He sighed and turned around.

"Lorelei, how marvelous you look. It's been a long time since we've talked, my pet."

She laughed and brushed his blonde hair back. "Oberon. Why, you look good enough to eat."

It was an old joke between them, and Oberon went along with it. She gave him a dazzling smile.

"Now, if only you weren't a tough old dragon. I like this look on you." She ran her hands down his body. "Soft and tender, and I bet even your bones are tender, too." She squealed in delight, hugging him even closer to her and he backed her up a bit.

"You have always been so insatiable. What am I to do with you, Lorelei?"

His eyes twinkled as he looked at her. He remembered seeing her and her deadly sisters, half dressed, singing on the rocks, and luring the ships in to savage their crews.

"I know neither of us is what we appear to be, now, are we? Are you considering the Magic Realm or do you intend on taking your chances out there, you and your sisters, that is? I'm sure as long as we both know where we stand, we can amuse one another."

He raised his eyebrows. No matter how dangerous they were, they certainly were interesting and so damn beautiful in their baiting form. They were smart and cunning and very good conversationalists, and even if the rest of the magicals scorned them, well, he for one, enjoyed their company from time to time. He would land on their island and he had always been treated well, at least in his dragon form.

She wrinkled her nose at him and even that motion was attractive. He fought to get out from under the spell she was casting on him. He knew how vulnerable he was in human form and it was probably some trick of Mordread's to get him out of the way. He had never gotten along with Mordread. He was a changeling demon with a lot of power and influence.

She batted her eyelashes at him. "I doubt we would want to be confined in a world without much, ah, food. You know we like men. Now, if only the unicorns attracted young virgin boys instead of girls, we might just consider the possibilities, but as it stands now, we'll remain the same as we always have. If you go to the new Realm, Oberon, will that mean we'll never see each other again?"

Oberon accepted a meat pie from a tray being passed around and gave it to Lorelei, who bit into it while still watching his face. Oberon put an arm around her.

"It's not a prison, my love. I can come and go and so can everyone else, if they like. So could you if you choose the Light. It would just be a safe place to live without fear of annihilation. How long do you think you all will live once the church deems you demons?"

She finished the meat pie and considered what he was saying. She looked down. "I guess, then, we would go with the Dark Magic group. At least they don't look down on us the way the Light does. Now, you know I don't mean you, Oberon, but the rest of them, well, they have no love for the way we live. Even the elves, and you know how promiscuous they are. I'm surprised I was invited here."

Oberon tried not to laugh. Comparing the love lives of sirens and elves was just too funny. There was a big difference, he thought; at least the elves don't eat their lovers when they were through with them.

Knight walked up, aided by his healer. He studied the siren and gave her a polite nod. She reached out and kissed his muzzle.

"I'm sorry for your troubles, Knight. I swear if I get the chance, I will make a nice meal out of all those men."

Knight nodded. He wished Oberon and Lorelei a good evening and made his way back to the stall where Myarra had gone back to sleep once again. He snuffled her mane and stood still while his healer fastened the straps that would raise his weight off of his legs, in a kind of hammock for him to sleep in. He was thankful for all the elves had done and he told his healer so.

Oberon looked deeply into Lorelei's beautiful eyes and sighed in exasperation. "I'm afraid I have to fly. If I let you seduce me, you'll probably have a huge chunk taken out of my arm, which would transform into an injured wing, and I just have too much that I have to do, my beauty. It was so good seeing you again, though. I must make it a point to visit you all more often."

She kissed him and he felt her teeth bite his lip just a bit. She whispered, "Oberon, you're no fun at all."

He smiled and walked away from her. He did have to stop and talk to the fairies, but afterwards, he made a beeline to an open field where he could transform. He needed to get back to his father and set the plans into motion. It couldn't be soon enough, he thought, as he took wing and looked down on all the magicals gathered below him. They were his people, his friends, and the sooner he could protect them, the better off they would all be.

CHAPTER THREE

"So, tell me, Reaper, are your griffins inclined to join this magical world of Oberon's? I should think that with your clan's fierce reputation that it wouldn't be very much to your liking."

Mordread walked along with Reaper, one hand resting on his back as if they were old friends. Reaper only tolerated the act of familiarity because there were so many in attendance and, if nothing else, griffins were masters of sophistication, well breeding, and good manners. He would not offend anyone in front of so many faces. He set his beak to compensate for the ill feeling that Mordread's touch gave him.

"I'm sorry, Mordread? I really don't understand your question. What's not to like in the new Realm? Any place where we can be beyond the influence of the human world sounds like a good thing to me. We all have families to protect, and being the latest, most coveted trophy in the human's eyes only dwindles our numbers. These constant hunts and murders of our clan have left a bitter taste in our mouths for this world. We've recently lost one of our elders and it seems like the attacks go on daily. If Oberon can provide us with a safe place to live, then what would not be to our liking?"

· Mordread nodded in agreement with Reaper, but removed his hand, much to Reaper's relief, and came around in front of him to face him and talk eye to eye, although that meant Reaper would have to lower his head.

"Yes, of course, we all know of the attacks on your clan, but really, Reaper, would the griffins be satisfied without the hunt? I'm sure you will not be permitted to stalk and bring down a unicorn or two over there. Oh, I imagine enough meat could be magically provided to feed you all sufficiently. I know Oberon would not let you all starve, but the sheer lethargic state you will all be in does not coincide with your characters. I just don't see you all living without the excitement. You are predatory creatures, after all, carnivorous in nature."

Reaper eyed him, amused, wondering if he would taste good or if he would give him indigestion. After weighing the facts for a moment, Reaper decided that it would probably be indigestion for sure, and he was becoming impatient with Mordread as to what exactly he wanted to know, not that it was any of his business. If there was one thing he knew of Mordread, it was that Mordread would never bother with you unless it was going to benefit him in some manner.

Mordread stood there with his hands on his hips, taking Reaper's hesitation to answer as some small victory; perhaps he had struck a cord in the griffin's mind that living in the Realm would be dull.

Reaper startled him by thrusting his very sharp beak into Mordread's face and growling, "Yes, we are carnivorous, Mordread; ill tempered and impatient, as well. So why don't you ask me what's really on your mind or do you intend to waste my time dancing around the issues? Would we join your Dark Realm? I doubt it. I have not yet had a chance to address my clan as to all these new issues. Of course, I'll mention the fact that the holders of the Dark magics will not be in the Magic Realm with us, and in all honesty, Mordread, they will probably be pleased by that fact. Although exquisite hunters and masters of the air, we still are a peaceful clan to those who pose no danger to us. The thought of hunting unicorns frankly disgusts me. We don't eat unicorns and have an alliance with them, and always have. Now that I think about it, a vacation with meat served to me sounds delightful. As you can see, times have been hectic and the fighting has been fierce. I could use a rest. Now, if you will excuse me, Mordread, I'm expected somewhere else now that the meeting is over."

With a sidelong glance to Mordread, Reaper left, chuckling to himself. Of course he would want the griffins on his side, although he found it odd that sides were being drawn at all. They had coexisted in the same world for a long time. It was the humans that they needed a break from. The Dark magicals had held no threat to them in the past and he wondered if Mordread had sinister plans for the future.

He hopped up, limb by limb, into a huge oak and reaching the top, opened his wings and leapt into the cool night air, filled with stars and a waning moon. He would head to his homeland, the cliffs overlooking the ocean, and gather his clan and tell them the news. Nothing Mordread said would persuade him to keep his griffins here.

They had come too close to losing the youngsters to the dogs this afternoon. All it had been was a simple little hunting lesson with a few of the new fledglings. The area had been scouted out and it had looked like a perfect day for the lessons. The dogs came out of nowhere. A cry for help went up and they had gotten the fledglings up into the trees and carried away by the adults. He, personally, had fought off the dogs, bringing down at least six of them before a human showed up with a sword. He had taken a scrape, but it would be the last sword the human would wield. The revenge was sweet enough, he thought, as he caught a thermal and flew higher to glide, resting his sore wings, but at what price, now? It seemed the attacks and the resulting carnage only fueled the situation. An eye for an eye, a child for a child? It was all too complicated. Still, none of the griffins had drawn first blood on any occasion, but in answering the attacks, there had been many casualties on the human side. This made them all evil in the eyes of the humans, and a true trophy with boasting rights, to sport a griffin claw around one's neck. No, it was getting much too dangerous to remain here, no matter what the Dark magicals had in mind. Let them deal with the attacks from the humans, if they wanted to stay here. True enough, most of them were indeed in human form and could slip quietly away, unnoticed, where a griffin was just that: big and unable to change form, like the unicorns and Pegasus. Their clan numbers were declining rapidly, and even now, it was a small clan of no more than twenty. They could not afford to lose any more members.

It had been no great privilege to live amongst the humans. Of course, they would have to hunt and eat, feed their young, and the forests there could be stocked from the human world. Deer and rabbit were prolific enough to repopulate themselves. He had no worries, only relief in knowing his clan could be safe in the new world. They were the ones with the most to lose and they had lost plenty already.

* * *

Myarra brushed up against her mate, Starry Knight, nickering in affection.

"I'm afraid I've missed the meeting, my love. I've been so tired. Tell me what happened there. Did Oberon come up with any way we can avoid these attacks? I'm telling you, if it wasn't for Oberon, well, I just don't even want to think about it."

She lowered her head, remembering how frightened she had been, and her nose quivered. Knight looked at her with weary eyes and took a great breath. He couldn't reach her to comfort her, being rigged up like a fish in a net.

"Oberon and the dragons have a plan they think will work. Dragon magic is the strongest and they believe they can create a world without humans for us all to live in, in peace. If he is right, and it really is possible, our foal will be born without fear. I have to trust in that. I have no other answers and neither does anyone else. Oh, Mordread said they can create a Dark Realm themselves, but he is given to delusion and I wouldn't want to be a part of that world, even if they could pull it off. No, our hope is with the dragons, now. I've never known Oberon to brag or invent promises he couldn't deliver on, and as much as we owe him, our trust will be with him, even if he's wrong. At least he's always had everyone's best interests in his heart, and not just for his dragons, either. I've never known Mordread to be benevolent in any way, have you? "

Myarra snorted in revulsion. "No, never. I've never liked him. He's like a vulture. He just looks out for himself. I wouldn't go willingly anywhere he went. I agree with you. If Oberon said he can do this marvelous thing, well, I trust he can. He flew off to see his father today, in South America. That was a long trip. He was so tired, he came into his lair and collapsed, falling fast asleep. But do you know what? The first thing he did was apologize for being late and ask me if I had everything I needed." She tossed her head and nuzzled Knight. "He's a good dragon, Knight. I think our troubles will be over as soon as we reach this new land and you are healed. Rest, now."

She watched and sighed as Knight relaxed and fell fast asleep. She stood there, listening to the sounds of the elves talking excitedly as they cleaned the glade of the remains of the meeting. She looked up into the starry night and made a wish that Oberon could save them all. She touched her horn to Knight's head and a warm golden glow filled the stable. An extra boost of healing magic and energy wouldn't hurt him one bit.

* * *

Brodrick and Kelton made an odd couple walking along the forest paths towards their homelands. They had a long way to go and would have to stop for the night and continue on in the morning. Brodrick, an elderly dwarf, walked with determination now that he had a solution to go on. It was hard keeping up with Kelton's long strides. The troll had noticed that earlier in the trip there, and had purposely slowed his pace so the dwarf could keep up. The clan of the dwarves had been hit harder than that of the trolls and Brodrick would not even consider going home without a solution to the degradation that his people were suffering at the hands of the humans. Many had been taken as novelties, toys for the noble's children to play with. Considering how stout and hardy they were, many of the men were enslaved to work in the huge furnaces, and to dig tunnels for the castle keeps. They would come at night and kidnap as many as they could, tying them up and throwing them on their horses like so much baggage. *Gods' speed*, Oberon, he thought, and his mind was busy with rescue plans for his captive people. Perhaps the dragons and griffins could help him recover and reunite his clansmen with their tearful families. The dwarves had led peaceful lives, keeping to themselves, and now this. Their magic with rocks and minerals did them no good here.

Kelton noticed his companion seemed to be in heavy contemplation. Kelton was unusually tall for a troll and made a queer picture walking along with Brodrick, but thought nothing of it. Bro-

drick was a good leader and would go the extra mile every time
to help his dwarves. Kelton had dealt with him many times, over
land disputes. The lands of the dwarves and the trolls bordered each
other and disagreements came up from time to time, and the two
men had gained each other's respect, numerous times. They found
a suitable place to camp for the night and filled their canteens from
the creek that passed through the clearing. Kelton, with the height
advantage, used his eyesight and acute troll senses to make sure they
could relax for the night without being attacked. He felt no life
forms other than Brodrick and a few night creatures. Brodrick built
a small fire and they sat on their bedrolls, eating some of the elven
fare that they had carefully wrapped up and insisted that the travelers take with them. Kelton was especially fond of the meat pies. It
was different from the troll's usual fare of wild mountain goat. He
smiled as Brodrick handed one to him. It almost disappeared into
his huge callused hand. The thick black hair on his body gleamed
in the firelight.

"The elves honored us all with this fine food. It's a pity it wasn't
a party we all could enjoy, although if Oberon can do what he says
he can do, well then, we all have reason to celebrate. What do you
think, Brodrick?"

The dwarf was eating flatbread and cheese. His mouth full, he
shook his head until he swallowed. "That's so. I have heard of this
dragon magic, and I've seen them freeze time. It's very mysterious,
but I believe it can be done. At least, that's what I've been praying
for." He gave Kelton a painfed look and the sensitive troll gently
patted him on the back.

"I know, old friend. I know. Even if we do get this new land, we
need to talk with Oberon about getting your people back from the
clutches of those barbarians, and we will. The trolls will help, if we
can. Haven't the trolls I sent you helped to ward off the attacks?"

The dwarf nodded. "Yes, Kelton, they have made a difference
and I've declared any business out of the town forbidden, for now.
With your trolls, and limiting the people's movements, there have
been only one more taken and she had left to visit another town
against my warnings. But I don't know how long I can keep the
people there. Our people trade gems and minerals, fashion fine jewelry. I can't keep them confined as prisoners forever, and yet, just

when I think things will be safe, more are captured. We make our living by trading and selling the gems. How can we do this without leaving the village? What have we done to these people to have them treat us like animals? At least your clan hasn't had too much trouble. We can be thankful for that."

Kelton looked sad. The humans would have to go through the land of the dwarves to get to them, and one or two of his clan members had been brutally killed. Filled with arrows, they were, as if they had used his friends as target practice. He was certain his trolls would go, and he knew the dwarves would go with Oberon, as well. The trolls were mountain people. As the dwarves tunneled and gleaned their precious stones, the trolls were builders. Carving huge boulders from the mountainside, they would load their huge wagons, pulled by hefty draft horses, into towns and build the churches and wealthy people's homes, out of solid rock. Both clans were industrious and hard-working and got along reasonably well, considering they were both using the same resources. Neither of the clans had quarreled with the humans or given them any reasons to attack their villages. But these weren't the peaceful people of the older times; these were new barbarians, hell bent on claiming all the land and the people within it.

* * *

Elijah stretched and yawned as he went to the small creek to wash his face and fill the small cooking pot with water. It looked to be a beautiful day. He snatched up a couple of logs for the fireplace and went back inside. He blinked, his eyes adjusting to the difference between the bright morning light and the darkness of his little cottage. He placed the logs on the fire, lifting them gently with a rod to let air under them and get a blaze going again, not only to ward off the morning chill, but to boil the water in the kettle, which he put on a hook over it. He heard the sound of feet hitting the floor and smiled as Glynnis crawled out of the featherbed. She rubbed her arms against the morning chill and went over to embrace him.

"I'll be glad for the warmer weather to reach the mountains. In my village, it's warmer in the morning."

He gave her a smile and a kiss. "Ah, but I bet it's warmer here at night."

She laughed and gave him a playful shove. She went outside to wash in the stream. The water, trickling down from the melted snow above, in the higher reaches of the mountain, was fresh and ice cold. She splashed her face, but decided to wait for some boiled water to wash in. It was just too cold, and she saw goose bumps pop up all over her arms. As she grabbed her cloak to dry her face, she heard a loud flapping sound from above. She gave a little cry and ducked, as the huge dragon landed in front of her.

"Good morning, Glynnis. I hope I didn't startle you too badly, or interrupt your bath."

She shook her head and turned, as Elijah came out of the cottage.

"Oberon. I heard of the meeting. Tell me of the news. I talked to a troll and dwarf passing through this way, late last night. They say you have the answer to all their problems, but as they didn't know me, they were hesitant to speak with me and I can't say as I blame them." He frowned, walking over and putting an arm around Glynnis.

"The way times are, now, they don't trust anyone anymore. There was a time when they would stop on their travels and share my supper, but no more. They both looked troubled. What news do you have? Please, come in. I have some porridge on the boil and a loaf."

They sat down and had a breakfast of hot porridge, bread, and honey, and Oberon told them of the meeting. As he described the location of where he was planning to make a gate, Glynnis' eyes widened and she asked several questions to be sure she was understanding exactly where it was to go.

"Why, Oberon, if I'm not mistaken, I live in that forest. Mine is the only cottage there. It's called Griffin Forest, as the villagers have seen griffins go into it to hunt. I have seen them, myself. There is a little village, not far away, but no one wanted to live close to the forest. They say it's haunted, but it's not. My family has lived there as long as anyone can remember. We just keep fixing up the cottage and it suits us. The trolls have helped me before with some of the walls that were getting weak. I hope I can stay there. You wouldn't make me move, would you?"

She looked scared to death, thought Oberon.

"No, child, you can stay. Who am I to tell you to leave your home, to make one for us? As long as you don't mind magical creatures. You may see a unicorn or a griffin, or who knows what? Do you live alone, there?"

She nodded. "I make medicines from the plants in the woods. I've been alone since the last coughing sickness took my mother, years ago."

Elijah made a face. "I keep asking her to move in here with me and marry me, but she won't. She'll stay a few days, and back she goes." He kissed her forehead. "She breaks my heart every time she leaves."

Oberon gave him a smile, and looked at Glynnis, who was blushing. He showed her where the gate would go, using rocks as landmarks and anything else he could find handy to use as the ocean. She nodded, seeing in her mind where it would go.

"Your gate would be on top of the tower of Griffin castle, in the tower, to be exact. If you angle it right, the gate would face the ocean and you wouldn't be seen. The tower area is deserted right now. The whole castle is. I hear a noble from Rome is taking it over soon, though. Every time, I pray they will leave me in peace. So far, they have, caring very little about my little cottage. I hope this noble will do the same. If I tell them I know medicine, they keep me on. I'm not afraid of them. The cottage is so deep in the woods, sometimes it takes them years to find me, and usually when they're out hunting. If they run into a griffin, they stop hunting, and luckily, the griffins hunt in the area before my cottage, by the small stream there. That's where the deer and other animals go to drink. It's a perfect place for them to hunt. I have seen a unicorn, once, though, and a few fairies, but no one believes me. They think I'm taking too much of my own medicine, but it's true; I have seen them."

She smiled and put her head on Elijah's shoulder. "He believes me."

Oberon grinned. "Of course, he does; he talks to dragons, too."

Elijah laughed. "When are you going to construct this Realm of yours, Oberon? Everyone must be so excited, although with all the magicals gone, it will turn into a dark world, here. I can't even imagine a world without magic." He looked as if he was watching something far away.

Oberon looked solemn. "I know. I can't believe it, myself. But, what else can we do? If we don't leave, there will truly be no magic left at all. They're killing us all off. This is the only real way to preserve true magic. With a gate, we'll be able to come and go, as we please."

He touched Glynnis' arm. "The fairies are staying behind, so if you've seen them once, you will see them again, I'm sure. She's a good woman, Elijah. Fairies don't appear unless you have a true and kind heart, and perhaps a little magic, as well. Maybe you'd better try to talk her into marrying you some more. I'll vouch for him."

Glynnis got up to clear the table, hearing quite enough talk of marriage. Elijah watched every move she made, fascinated with every motion, and shrugged at Oberon.

"What can I do?"

Oberon looked at Elijah with envy. He could tell that there was a greater force working between the couple that even they were unaware of. They would be good for each other, and all three of them knew it, although they were hesitant to talk about it. The subject turned to the new Realm.

"I have scrolls and scrolls, mentioning the dragon magic, but no one knows exactly how you dragons do it. How do you just create a new world?" Elijah threw up his hands at that and Oberon chuckled.

"I don't understand it all, myself, and I'm not even going to pretend I do. All the dragons have to get together and everyone has a part of the information inborn in each one. No one dragon knows the whole procedure. It's a mystery, even to us. The elders are the ones that will initiate the whole thing. I'd like it to look relatively the same as our land, here. Basically, the same land formations as we have here. A lot more pasture land, perhaps, for the unicorns would be helpful. As far as I know, the dragons are moving now to the woods near your location, Glynnis. Of course, they will be in human form, and since the castle is deserted and you aren't home either, they should meet with very little resistance, I should think.

So, it looks as if we'll be neighbors, you and I. I look forward to it. I'm glad you will be privy to the fact as to what's going on in the forest. Perhaps we can keep the haunted reputation, and it will keep the curious away, leaving us all in peace."

Glynnis had cleared the table and came back to sit with them. She shook her head, thoughtfully. "I wish there was more I could do to help. My people are of the old clan. We've known about magical creatures, just as Elijah's people have. I, too, would be sad to see them leave, but I can understand your point; the annihilation seems eminent, and I would rather see you seldom, than never at all. If there is ever anything I can do, I would be pleased if you were to call upon me."

Oberon took her hand and kissed it. "I will hold you to that promise, my dear, and thank you. Now, as much as I am enjoying the company, and as much as I've enjoyed the wonderful breakfast, I'm afraid I have to leave for the forest. I wanted to stop by and tell you about the meeting. We will talk again soon, my friend." He gave a little bow and left through the door, transformed, and flew to the north. They watched him go, both lost in thoughts of a world without magic.

* * *

It was an undertaking of monumental proportions. There were eleven dragons present, all in human form, and all gathered around a table in the middle of the forest. A few were skeptical that it could even be done, but the elders were confident, and in the process of hammering out the particulars. Yes, they would make the mountains taller and broader, so there would be more and higher cliffs to placate the griffins. The trolls would be happy at the foot of the mountains, where they could glean their boulders. The forest areas would be thick and dense, with huge trees to accommodate the large elven tree houses. There would be plenty of wetlands for the water nymphs. Most of them had decided to remain in the true world, but they were divided in their decision and would be welcome, for those that would come. There were miles of pasturelands with clumps of trees for the unicorns, and the dwarves would thrive in tunneling into the broad mountainside. Everything looked as it should be. What an opportunity they had, to create a world custom-made for their people. Bordering the cliffs, was a huge ocean, deep and clean for the Mer people. They would leave room for expansion, of course, but for now, it would do.

It pleased Oberon that it was set up much the same as the world they were in right now, and as a matter of fact, it was a copy of it with a lot of enhancements. The old ones had chosen that same land in a time when there were no populations there, frozen it and duplicated it. Set at a different frequency, it was invisible, although taking up a parallel space, higher up. Everyone's magic was needed to make the transformation happen, and when it was finally complete, they crossed over to have a look around, even though they were exhausted. The shaman of the dragons had been in seclusion all this time, praying and sending all the extra power the Gods would give to him.

He did tell them something very interesting. He had a vision that they would be given a wonderful lake by the Gods as a gift for all their efforts in protecting their people and all creatures of the magic. This lake would have the power of healing, and would thus be called the Healing Waters Lake. It had only been a vision, but all of the shaman's visions so far had become a reality. Oberon sighed with relief. Just the thought that their efforts pleased their Gods was enough to give him the confidence that they were indeed, doing the right thing. What a miraculous gift that was. A lake that could cure.

As they toured the area, they did come across a pristine lake that Oberon knew was not in the original plan. It was located towards the end of the pasture lands and very near the beginnings of the massive forests. The Healing Waters Lake was as beautiful as it would be useful. Most of them took time out to rest in the shade of the forest trees. They drank from the lake and found it to be fortifying. Elgin, the Blood Dragon, lounged by the lake and Oberon went to visit with him.

"You know, my son, rumors are flying already, and the work has hardly been done. I've heard that the magicals want you for a king. Can you believe that? My son, the king. Oh, don't give me that patronizing look, it's true, you know. I just wondered what you thought about that?"

Oberon studied the mountains in the distance. He was proud of what they had done and was elated that it didn't take as long as he thought it would. He couldn't wait to transport their magicals to safety. He was lining up the exodus in his mind and he had little time for the frivolous thoughts of being king.

"Why in the world would we need a king? Everyone gets along just fine together, and if there is a squabble, well, they've always handled that between themselves. We never needed a king. What we needed was a place without terror. Now, we have it and all would be well. I think we should move the griffins first, as their numbers are dwindling at an alarming rate. I'm not sure who has the most young to move, but the sooner we move them the better. Then again, the unicorns have suffered enough, too, and they can't fly to get away from predators. I can't decide whether the elves or the dwarves should go next. Did you know the fairies want to remain in the old world? I hope we can convince at least some of them to come with us. Of course, the elves are quite capable of getting all the plants and flowers to grow as well, but it's just not the same without a few fairies to brighten the day."

He sat there, musing about the problems, and was deep in a decision-making process, when his father cleared his throat and looked sharply at him.

"You're very good at avoiding the subject. I'm sure everything will work itself out, as far as the order of migration. I asked you what you thought of being nominated as king."

Oberon huffed in exasperation. "I've answered that already, Father. We don't need one. We never had one before, and I really don't see a need for one now, either. Each clan has their own government and customs, laws and traditions, as it should be. What would a king do, anyway?"

His father managed to look flustered and annoyed at the same time. "Well, he would organize the Realm, just as you are doing now. Someone needs to keep order. Just because we are all magical doesn't mean we are all of good character. A rogue creature may surface, and who would deal with that? We would need someone to deal with Mordread and the Dark Realm, should it surface. You know how it will be, just as it always is when there a few different groups. Each will look to the other to do what needs to be done and nothing would get accomplished. What about territories? You know how it is, now. The encroachment issues aren't so bad in the real world, as everyone has to live wherever they can, but when they all have their own lands, they will try to get more. You see? A king would handle all those type of issues. I know I'm biased, but I do think you'd make a good king." He said the last with a bit more force and a nod of his head to punctuate his feelings.

Oberon shrugged. "So, why me? I am not the eldest of the dragons. There are many before me who could serve."

His father shook his head. "No. A lot of the dragons are remaining where they are. Oh, I suppose we will have them sooner or later, as the natural world populates itself to the point that there are no remote places left, but we are an old and solitary race, you know that. They have lived for centuries where they have and will remain. Only you, seem to be the most active and involved in the world of the other magicals. They all know you, but I hardly think they know any of the rest of us. You would be the choice, and I'll let you in on a secret, all the dragons already agree that it should be you."

Oberon made a face at that. He could see where having a king to settle disputes would prevent problems. They needed no wars in the Realm. After what they all had been through, it would not seem likely, but time has a way of making people forget.

"Why don't we cross that bridge when we get to it? There is so much to do, now. All the rest of it can wait. Moving everyone safely here is the problem at hand. Oh, good Gods, what next?"

His father turned his head and smiled broadly when he saw what had captured Oberon's gaze. Harmonia, a lovely young female dragon was heading in their direction. Oberon knew his father had hopes for Harmonia to be a suitable mate for him, but he wasn't interested at the moment, and if the truth was told, he could hardly stand to be near her. He found her pretentious and rude, at best.

She was smiling today, which was a change from her usual sour face and Oberon found it almost tolerable. She landed prettily, and Oberon could find no fault with her flying. He really could not find too many shortcomings, other than the fact that he didn't really like her. He smiled anyway; *grin and bear it*, he thought. He knew his father would make a big fuss over her and try to match-make, and he wanted to be anywhere else but where he was. He took a deep breath; it would be too rude to take off, now.

"Harmonia, it's nice to see you. What do you think of the Realm?"

She fluttered her eyelashes at him and he thought it would be more attractive if it were a pebble that she was trying to get out of her eye.

"You've done a marvelous job, Oberon."

He had to laugh at that. He did no more than his share and he told her so.

"But you were in the forefront, and your leadership qualities, well, if it weren't for you, I don't think we would have accomplished as much, as fast."

She gave him a toothy grin and all he could think was that she must be coming into season, to act so polite. He said nothing, not wanting to blurt out something he would regret.

She continued, "Tyros thinks that we should blast out our caves now, rather than wait for everyone to get here. He thinks the sounds of the blasts would be frightening or disruptive. I think it's a good idea, once everyone has rested, of course."

His eyes went to the high mountain tops. She was right, of course. Having that out of the way would be the right thing to do. It would be loud and dangerous, especially if anyone took it into their head to want to watch.

"Yes. I think that would be best. Also, we could blast out the shelters for the griffins on the cliffs, at the same time. We can always go back and adjust any cave if we have to later, but we should get the majority of it done while we are the only ones here. It shouldn't take long. Let me get a quick drink of water and I'll fly up there and have a look. It would make a nice feast afterwards for everyone, and we will be hungry by then, I'll wager."

She brushed up against him and he winced just a little as his father beamed.

"You are so clever, Oberon."

She giggled and he found that the sound grated on his nerves. He went down to the water, drank deeply, and took off without another look for Harmonia or his father.

When he reached the top of the mountains, he met Tyros and a few of the elders circling around and they had a conference of sorts, and then started blasting out the caves. There was plenty of room and the task went quickly and efficiently. Tons of boulders tumbled down to the foothills, and some into the ocean, when they worked on the cliffs for the griffins. There would be plenty of rock and boulders for stone cottages for the dwarves and trolls.

There was a lot of camaraderie that day and lots of good feelings and back- slapping. This was the first time in Oberon's memory that the clan had all united together and he thought it a glorious sight to see them all whirling in the air, colors flashing in the bright sunlight. He had to admit that Harmonia, one of the very few females, did some spectacular flying and yes, all her qualities would constitute good breeding for a son. All the other females were much older. Well, there was time to think of that once the Realm was up and running. He supposed his father deserved a grandson.

He wasn't sure at all about this king issue. He never considered it and was only half-heartedly considering it now. He thought King Orion would make a better king, but there were so many elves to command, and he doubted if he wanted the extra burden of the entire Realm.

They had all landed now and were feasting on the enormous quantities of boulders laying about, cleaning up the mess, so to speak. They decided to move both the griffins and the unicorns at the same time. The Pegasus would be next, if they wanted to go, and any other magicals that were in animal form. The humans were less likely to kill the human-formed magicals, but thought nothing of making sport of killing the animal magicals. It was all making good sense. He would return and organize the groups to be moved.

A few of the dragons picked out the choicest of caves for themselves and others returned through the gate they had constructed to their original world. His father was one of those. He had lived in South America so long now, and his cave was so high up that he doubted he'd have to move for another thousand years. His appearance every fifty years or so in that area gave the local people good fortune and reasons to celebrate. He would hate to just vanish from their lives. Oberon was a bit saddened that his father would not be one of the Realm's inhabitants, but he knew the size of his cave and there was none to compare to his cave, here.

He took one last look around, pleased at what had been accomplished. Soon, there would be unicorns bounding through the pastures, and griffins in the air. There would be loud, noisy elven celebrations, and the sounds of the dwarves digging and trolls building. He would have to remember to ask King Orion to make a few of the clumps of trees in the pasture lands apple trees. He thought that would be a nice touch for the unicorns.

He saw Harmonia flying in for a landing, and he pretended he didn't see her and took wing. That was too close, he thought, and he made for the gate. He had a lot to do and to have to stay and make polite conversation with Harmonia was not on his list of things that needed to be done.

CHAPTER FOUR

Glynnis walked Baron, her dark bay cob, through the familiar forest to her home. Baron, knowing the trail well, was light of heart as he scented the cool stream just through the trees ahead. He would stop for a well deserved drink. She loosened the reins and he lowered his head to the rushing water surrounding his feet. She led him to a small stable attached to the wall of her home that housed her fireplace. It stayed warm in his quarters, even in the coldest of temperatures. She led him in and removed his tack. She brushed out where the saddle had flattened his hair then filled his food bucket with oats and he munched happily, glad to be home. Gathering up the packs, she exited the stable and went into her home.

Carefully, she removed the scrolls she had borrowed from Elijah and put them on her desk. On rainy days, she would have plenty of reading material. She emptied all of the packs; the laundry, she would do in the stream tomorrow. Even though she missed her sweet Elijah already, it was good to be home again. There were many dried plants to prepare and grind into powder for the medicines she made. Making medicines was a tradition in the Thatcher family, passed down from generation to generation. The townspeople might call her the witch from the woods, but it didn't seem to bother them when they needed a cure the healers in town couldn't handle. She moved some of the bunches of flowers to hang upside down near the fireplace. These would dry faster now.

She glanced through her door when Baron whinnied. There was

someone coming through the woods and she went outside to see who it was. Baron acted as if he knew the scent and was happy for the company. She smiled as Father Murphy came out of the woods, leading his mule, Jenny.

"A good afternoon to you, Glynnis." He said with a wave of his arm. "It's been a glorious day so far, hasn't it?"

She reached out for Jenny and led her to a bucket of oats and water. Father Murphy came inside at her invitation and sat down heavily at her kitchen table. It was a large table, simply made out of planks of wood. She put a kettle on to boil over the fireplace.

"It has been a beautiful day. Actually, I've just gotten home from the mountains, myself. If you would have come yesterday, you wouldn't have found me."

He looked up at her. His sandy brown hair always looked unkempt no matter what he tried to do with it, but his green eyes were friendly and sometimes full of mischief, unusual for a respected member of the local church.

"Is that so? How is Elijah? I can't remember the last time I laid eyes on him. Did you bring back any scrolls of his to read? I swear, you should marry that man. I'll be honored to do the ceremony, myself, if you please."

She chuckled a bit at that and he ducked as she took a playful swat at him.

"As a matter of fact, I did bring back quite a few scrolls. If you promise not to mention marrying me off again, I'll let you borrow them when I'm through with them. I'm afraid they are all on subjects that don't quite coincide with your religion."

He raised his eyebrows at that comment and she continued, "They are all on magic and magical creatures. I know your religion believes in demons, but why don't they believe in magic?"

He smiled a little. "Now, who says we don't believe in magic? I've never seen magical creatures, but then I've never seen God either and I believe in him."

She got up and made the tea and placed a cup into his hands. He nodded his thanks and stared at her for a reply. Glyniss sat back down and in a voice that you would explain things to children, she went on, "But, Father, you have seen the magicals. Elves look very much like everyone else, perhaps a bit taller, but they are the ones who tell the best tales, sing the loudest in the pubs, and generally make people feel good about themselves, and make them want to do good deeds for each other. Like your clergy. It's very much the same. I know you've seen the dwarves come into town and trade their minerals and gems. The trolls are the really big and tall people with beards and lots of hair. Now, you may not have seen a unicorn, but I have. You wouldn't forget something like that, I'd wager, nor would you forget seeing a griffin or a dragon, but I know you've heard all the tales. I'm afraid that's all that's left of them by now. They've gone to the Magic Realm to be away from men and the people who have tormented them so. In a hundred years, I doubt if anyone at all will believe in magic anymore. It's a shame, really."

Father Murphy rubbed his chin. He was hoping she was teasing him, but he knew by the look in her eyes that she was serious, and the sadness in her eyes concerned him.

"Ah, lass, are you telling me that you can do magic?"

She made a face at him. "No. I'm not a magical creature. I make medicine, that's all. Sometimes I wish I were, and that I could heal people that are far beyond my medicine, but it's only a wish. I would have gone with them if I were. Let's see, that would have been days ago if I'm calculating it right, so they're all gone, except the fairies."

She sighed heavily and Father Murphy really didn't know what to make out of what she had said. Usually Glynnis was such a level headed, reasonable woman. He eyed her curiously, but said nothing. What in the name of heaven could he say in reply? She looked as if she had come out of a daydream and she stood up, her hands on her hips.

"So, it's your back you are needing medicine for then, or is it another malady?"

He looked at her with surprise. "So, you are a witch. I never said what was bothering me, and yet you knew."

She exhaled in exasperation. "I don't need to be a witch to know your back hurts. That's why you were walking Jenny. It became too painful to ride, didn't it? And look at the way you're sitting. You don't have to have powers to figure all that out, just some common sense. Really, Father."

They both laughed at that and she prepared him a powder to add into water to drink. She sprinkled some of it into his tea as well. He folded the packet containing the powder and put it inside his robe, nodding his thanks. He knew it would do no good to try to pay her. She never took any money from anyone and never would. People did bring her gifts of food and flowers and these she accepted with thanks. She was a good woman, and he was only teasing her about being a witch, but the talk in the town about her was ugly and he feared for her every time he overheard someone talking about the witch in the woods. He wished she'd marry Elijah, the scholar. He knew they had been an item for years, even before he had moved into seclusion to study. Having a strong man around might save her from the hurtful comments and any worthless man who would act on the rumors.

He sat back, feeling relief immediately from the powder she'd put in his tea. He was more comfortable now, and he wondered just what was in the powder. It was herbs, no doubt, as she had them hung from the craggy rock wall by the fireplace, but the cure seemed magical to him. He knew all about her, however; her family had lived in the same woods for as long as anyone could remember. They were Druids of the old clan of Druids that had eventually migrated further north from threats of persecution. Only the Thatcher women remained. It seemed as if none of them ever married, and as the older ones passed away, there was always a younger one to take up the cross, so to speak, and he was thankful for that, as no one could make medicine more effective than the Thatchers. Even though the castle was vacant for the moment, the state of the region once again in upheaval, the Thatchers remained and he was sure if another nobleman took over he'd be a fool to run this woman off of the land. They had always been employed, of sorts, as the local healer to the castle and were usually under its protection. It was a curious thing, though; even given the best directions, unless you were welcome at the Thatcher's home, you couldn't find the house. He had tried to send one of his order there to get some medicine for the bishop, who was ailing at the time, and he ended up having to leave the church and go himself. It was as if the forest itself protected the women there.

He watched as she refilled his tea and offered him some flatbread smeared with mountain honey and he accepted it with relish. He had always had a sweet tooth, and very seldom did they get honey at the rectory. She had once again sprinkled his tea with the medicine and soon he felt better than he had in moons.

"You know, Glynnis, people have been acting strangely as of late. Have you noticed? At first, I thought it was the full of the moon , but here we are in the dark of it and still people are more sinister, for lack of a better word. If all the good magic is gone now, as you say, could it be the bad magic that's left to cause so much ill, or has all the magic gone altogether? What do you think?"

She took a sip of her tea and regarded him solemnly. "I was afraid that would happen. It is only the good that has left. It was only the good magicals that were being killed. People embrace the demons, and they've stayed. I shouldn't doubt there will be plenty of evil afoot. Why do you suppose people would choose evil over the good? It doesn't make sense to me at all."

He took both of her hands and kissed them. "My dear child, if I only knew the answer to that. It's been my life's work. Although we believe in different things, we agree on the exact same. Isn't that amazing? That is where tolerance, intelligence, and understanding come in. It is the ones who are so closed-minded that they cannot accept anything on faith that are the problem, no matter what the faith is. That is why I still would like to read the scrolls and I promise not to marry you, but I would find another to do so if you wish."

The amusement and laughter was back in his eyes and his back was as good as it would ever get. He thanked her and took his leave to get back to town before nightfall. Magic or no, haunted or not, he still did not feel comfortable in those woods after dark, even with his God on his side. He would not tempt the Fates that he wasn't supposed to believe in.

Glyniss went outside and watched as he rode Jenny through the trees. She had known him for a long time and knew his heart was always in the right place. Whether he believed her or not was of no consequence. He would never repeat the conversation to anyone.

Father Murphy rode through the forest, his mind turning over what Glyniss told him. As he knew, she wasn't given to fancy. If she was right, he wondered where she'd come upon those facts. It was true enough, devilment was rampant as of late, and if what she said was true, it would only get worse. He wondered how he could warn his bishop without seeming mad and in need of a retreat. He frowned, and couldn't think of anything that would make sense to his Holiness. He sighed and resolved himself to place the problem in the hands of the Lord. It would make sense to Him and He would deal with it.

An owl hooted, its heavy baritone echoing through the woods. It chilled him and he kicked Jenny a bit to hurry her along. The sun was setting and he would rather be back on the road to town and not out in the woods with only demons left in the land. Jenny seemed to feel the same way and she quickened her pace to a trot, masterfully maneuvering through the trees towards the road. The sounds of the night were warming up as Jenny's hooves plodded through the dirt of the winding road to town. Father Murphy gave a sigh of relief as he saw the church tower off in the distance. He would make it home to his cubical before he was totally immersed in the night. He shook it off as a childish fear and scolded himself for acting silly. He had God on his side and he had nothing to fear. Except Father Johns. The elderly cleric was waiting for him just outside the rectory.

"Father Murphy, I was about to send some of the younger clerics to go and look for you. You've missed supper and evening mass. It wasn't like you, and I became concerned, with all the trouble in town."

Father Murphy dismounted and handed Jenny to one of the serving boys to take to the stable. He brushed off his robes.

"Thank you, Father, for your concern, but I assure you I am fine. I went to a healer about my back. I have mass to perform this Sunday and I'm afraid I would have been hunched over for it had I not gotten the medicine I needed."

Father Johns sniffed in disapproval. He was a tall, stern cleric with hair so grey it had turned white, and cold, unfeeling ice blue eyes. "Perhaps you should have prayed on it, first. Don't tell me you went to see that, ah, Pagan fraud in the woods again."

Father Murphy smiled. "The same, and I have found much relief there. I am more myself now."

Father Johns looked suspiciously at him. "I'm afraid I may have to go to the Bishop over this matter."

Father Murphy smiled and clapped him on the back as he walked into the rectory.

"Ah, that is well, then. Tell his holiness that Glynnis sends her best. If she is a fraud, please don't tell my back, and the Bishop will remember her fondly as she was the one who cured his spotted fever several years ago, but I think he would still remember, as none of the healers in town could cure the fever. I think he even dedicated his mass to her afterwards, saying that God had given her a great grace in her knowledge of the sciences."

Father Johns gave him a sour look as he parted from him and made his way to his own cubicle. Father Murphy sat down in the wooden chair and brought out his Biblical scrolls and read a bit before going to bed. He was hoping for a good night's sleep now that the pain in his back was gone. He was sure he'd have to endure Father Johns' scrutiny for visiting Glynnis, but the relief that she gave him was a mercy he was not about to relinquish.

Father Johns had already retired as he always did, with the sunset after evening Mass. But sleep would not come. He was disturbed a member of their order would be as complacent and foolish as to consort with a pagan of some notoriety. Just the simple fact that Father Murphy would put his trust, yes indeed, his very soul in mortal danger by not having faith in their Lord and Savior for the healing he needed, spoke harshly about his devotions. It saddened and enraged him at the same time. The devil had guided him on the wrong path to recovery and he felt he couldn't stand still and ignore that fact. It was imperative the Bishop be told and Father Murphy repent his sins before he had the gall to conduct Mass for their parishioners. How could he lead these people into grace while embracing a pagan? He shuddered. The thought was just too appalling to ponder.

After a time of brooding and praying, Father Johns did fall asleep and the forms that were waiting for him began to make their move. They were dark entities, almost invisible, with very little substance. They oozed through the slit stone window, re-materializing on the other side, like shadows dripping down the stone wall. These were doubtlets, one of Mordread's favorite creations. They were mind magics and lived to place uncertainty, fears and doubts into the minds of poor unsuspecting people of little faith.

Mordread had noticed Father Johns berating citizens in town for the most innocent games of gambling and frankly, he was tired of Father Johns' interrupting his quests for chaos. Father Johns waved guilt around like a solid steel sword, cutting deeply into the hearts and souls of the townspeople, making them scatter, cross themselves and take their minds off of all the simple pleasures the demons could relieve these people with. It wasn't as if Father Johns had a faith so watertight that he could climb upon his pulpit and preach with all the love of God in his heart. No. Nothing was further from the truth. Mordread could see his soul. It was almost as black with the evils of man as his own was, but he hid under the guise of a holy man and Mordread found it very entertaining. Mordread was bored quite often, and to find a novelty such as this was priceless. It wasn't often he found a member of the clergy he could play with and especially one who was always holier than thou. For the most part the secular order was a humble devout group that was just no fun at all. He would see what he could do with Father Johns.

The doubtlets encircled the holy Father and examined his thoughts. They'd have to work with whatever was at hand. It seemed, at the time, it was a Father Murphy and his worry that Father Murphy was backsliding into the abyss.

"Well, let's see if we can intensify the feelings," said one of the larger doubtlets.

"Oh, yes, and let's see if we can make it into a real threat to the good Father Johns and to the entire faith, as it were. Let's make it a matter of some urgency as well, as if his very life depended upon ridding this situation from their midst."

The doublet was giggling now; it was so easy to manipulate him and Mordread will be so pleased.

"I think it would help to let him think he had been called upon by God himself to take up the cross and bear this burden, alone. If we let him take it to the Bishop, it would then be out of his hands."

The other doublet agreed heartily. "Yes, I think it would take him to the edge to have to handle it himself. Oh, he'll think he can do it, but it'll put every nerve on its end to do so."

They slithered out, just as easily as they had come in, with no trace except the poison of their doubts and instructions implanted on a very susceptible brain. Father Johns would have a very dark vision this night. He moaned in his sleep, sweat beading up on his hairline and he tossed and turned, finding no position comfortable. He threw off the rough woolen blanket, finding himself first hot, then searching for the blanket again as he felt chilled. All the time, he was in twilight, needing to find that secure deep sleep. He found that he stayed too near the surface with all the worries of the day. But, in this darkness, they seemed even worse now and the refreshing sleep would not come. He lay there, muscles stiffening from the cold, but when he put the blanket back on he began to perspire. It seemed as if every muscle ached, and he could only wonder how pleasantly Father Murphy was sleeping with the spell of the pagan witch cast over him. He would rather die than have his soul in that position of damnation.

He tried to pray, but he found he could not concentrate, and to his horror, he found he was forgetting the words. He strained his brain and commanded it to repeat the prayers he knew so well, but they didn't come. Instead, he found that perhaps he would never be able to engage himself in comforting prayer again until he rid the town of the pagan witch. It must be her influence that was causing him such a misery. God commanded him to cast out the demons and by God, it would be done. Sometime after that, Father Johns was granted a few hours of sleep, but when he awoke, his body was stiff and he wasn't in an agreeable mood. He would go to confession and receive communion before his morning meal. He thought that would put things to rights.

Father Murphy rose later than usual; having the relief of Glynnis' medicine, he had slept better than he had in months. He wondered why he'd waited so long to seek relief. His mood was bright and cheery and as he had missed Mass last night, he thought to confess and receive his communion at Mass this morning. He knelt in the confessional and begged God's forgiveness for the usual sum of disobedience: nothing more serious than letting his mind wander when he should be concentrating, some thoughts of folly as he usually found more humor in the ordinary things than most of his fellow priests. But wasn't it strange that the confessional Father asked him if there was more he would like to confess? He thought about

it. He had taken an extra slice of flatbread with honey at Glynnis' home. Would that be considered gluttony? Well, maybe so, but
how would the Father have known? If you have to think about it,
then confess it, he had always been taught.

"I confess the sin of gluttony, Father. I had an extra slice of
bread and honey, for which I am repenting. One would have suf-
ficed."

He sat back, his mind completely clear of all guilt now, and still
the good Father persisted, as if he knew of a sin Father Murphy
hadn't confessed. Father Murphy caught himself before he laughed.
Of course, it was so obvious, and yet it had escaped him.

"I confess that I missed evening Mass. I was away on a visit and
I'm afraid I didn't make it back before dark. For this, I beg forgiveness."

There. Now, he had put things back on an even keel, and he
sat back, satisfied that he was in a state of grace to receive communion. The confessional Father hesitated just a bit, waiting for anything else. He had previously been Father Johns' confessor, and the
stories of Father Murphy's scandalous behavior, consorting with
a witch troubled him immensely, but he was only the go-between
for these priests and their communication with God, and if Father
Murphy felt his sins were all confessed, he had no right to add additional ones. He gave Father Murphy his penance.

It wasn't a very large order, roughly a dozen priests, a few dozen
seminary students, and some orphan boys the church was shelter-
ing. They all sat around the dining room table, taking a humble
breakfast of porridge and bread. The orphan boys were dipping
cups of water and setting them before the priests. Father Murphy
tousled the bright red hair of the freckle-faced boy who handed him
his water.

"Thank you, Red, and a good morning to you."

Red, who was really Franklin Walker, smiled with glee. He
was always a pert boy, loud and gregarious, but with a keen intelligence. His parents died in a terrible fever epidemic that had swept
through the village after the last barbarian raid. If they only took
what they wanted and didn't spread disease, that would be better.
No one grumbled about what they had stolen, after awhile, but the
people who had died of the fevers could have been spared. He liked

Red and all the other boys in the orphanage. He always marveled at their spirits. Lambs of God, he thought, and they would do their best to help these boys get an education and be able to make it back into the world that had been so cruel to them. Most of the priests either disliked having to deal with children or just ignored them completely, but Father Murphy had volunteered to teach them simple sums and reading, so he knew most of them pretty well. They were good boys, for the most part. The more spirited ones found punishment at the end of a rod by Father Johns.

He chewed on the bread. It seemed to be older than usual, but he dipped it in the porridge and washed it down with the water. Conversation seemed to be non-existent this morning but still, he felt as if eyes were upon him. He glanced up to see Father Johns glaring at him, his ice blue eyes hard and angry. Father Murphy sighed but decided to make the best of it.

"Father Johns? I have not taken your slice of bread by mistake, have I? You seem to be in quite a state this morning. Can I be of any service?"

There were a few muffled chuckles around the table. Father Johns grunted in disgust, picked up his water and drank, but his hands were shaking and water spilled on the table. The other priests looked to the source of entertainment for this morning's meal eagerly. One of the orphan boys hastily wiped up the spill and Father Johns pushed him back roughly.

"I was surprised to see you at Mass this morning, Father Murphy."

Frowning a little at that, Father Murphy, who did not like Father Johns' manner this morning, bit down on the hook.

"How so? I always attend morning Mass when I'm able, just as you do."

Father Johns pushed away his bowl in disgust. "How dare you compare your devotions to mine? I'm surprised you are not still in the confessional."

This raised quite a few eyebrows around the table; all chatter stopped and it became deathly quiet, as the audience waited for the next round. Most had even stopped eating to watch. There was nothing like idle gossip and juicy scandals to brighten a day at the rectory.

Father Murphy tilted his hands in a questioning pose. "I should hope we can compare devotions, Father, being of the same order, and all. You haven't converted to another religion, have you? I'm afraid there was a longer than usual line at the confessional and I had to hurry. I just had my usual sins, nothing of real interest to confess, although I assure you, it's not for lack of trying."

There were a few outbursts of laughter at this, but Father Johns silenced the offenders with just a cold glance.

"I am not the one consorting with the devil's concubine. My devotions are untainted, but I fear for your soul, Father Murphy. You seem to be easily misled and I feel it is all our responsibilities to guide you back to the paths of salvation before your soul is damned to Hell for all eternity." He had raised his voice, and now all eyes were glancing back and forth between the two dueling Fathers.

Father Murphy smiled and lowered his voice to try and placate the distraught cleric. "Aye, and I thank you all for your concerns. Now I understand the problem. I know you feel I should have prayed for a cure to my back complaints, but when you are hungry you take the food, and when it is a medical problem, you take the cure. I know you have no love for non-Catholics, but you do agree we are all God's creatures. I feel I was led to Mistress Thatcher's home to get a cure for my back, by the mercy of the Lord. I know of no devil's concubine, just a Druid who makes medicine that works for my back, and a pleasant enough person. She stands by her own religion, which is older than our own. If she decides to convert, well, that would be fine, but she has to follow her own heart in the matter. I would be more than happy to give her the lessons she requires should she have a change of heart."

Some of the other priests rolled their eyes and went back to their breakfasts. They all knew of Father Johns' self-righteousness and the back problems Father Murphy suffered from, and now the conversation was not of as much interest. Everyone knew Mistress Thatcher. They even bought some teas from her from time to time.

Father Johns got up and briskly walked away, saying "Blasphemy." under his breath. Father Murphy shook his head sadly. He knew this would not be the end of the conversation and he was not looking forward to continuing it. The other priests looked at him in support, knowing how hard Father Johns was on all the priests when he found any discretion at all that he thought was not in keeping strictly with the faith. They were all relieved that it was Father Murphy and not themselves that had fallen out of favor with Father Johns. They all knew how tenacious and unrelenting Father Johns could be once he climbed on his pedestal, and they were sympathetic to Father Murphy's cause.

"I would be surprised if he did not go to the Bishop with this, Father, but rest assured that I will vouch for your innocence. Every one of us has had a tea or a cure from that woman, including the Bishop, himself, if my memory serves me correctly. He will find no ally in the Bishop for condemning Mistress Thatcher, or you. I wouldn't let it worry me. Maybe he'll pray on the matter and it'll become clearer to him that he's mistaken to berate you so brutally for taking medicine."

That had been Father Roberts, a compassionate priest who'd been with the order about the same amount of time as Father Murphy, and he had always considered him a friend. It seemed they were all anxious to lend him their support and Father Murphy had never realized how unpopular Father Johns was.

"I think if it were he that was cursed with the back pain, he would think differently." Father Mathews sniffed. "He would be the first in line at Mistress Thatcher's door. Judge not, lest ye be judged."

They nodded in agreement.

Father Murphy smiled at them all. "I thank you for your camaraderie, but I fear I will be hearing more from the good Father. We don't ask our vendors what their religion is before we purchase our wine and candles, why should it be a sin to take medicine when one needs it, from one who is so gifted in the art of making it? I don't think it's the matter of medicine, as much as it is the religion of the woman. Have we all become so intolerant of the indigenous people? Her family has been here long before this church was built. We are the newer religion, so who are we to say she is wrong and a tool of the devil? She profits not, from her efforts. She gives freely of her talents to all those who are in need. Isn't that essentially our Christian principle? Perhaps there is not such a difference. Either way, I'm sure the matter will give poor Father Johns no rest. I, on the other hand, have a class to teach very shortly."

He nodded to his fellow priests and made his way through the hall. Upon arriving at the courtyard where his lessons would be given, he saw one of the more advanced seminary students trying to get the orphan boys to settle down. When they saw Father Murphy arrive, they quieted and sat down as they usually did. He walked up to Michael, the seminary student.

"Michael, how nice it is for you to join us in class."

Michael reddened a bit and moved Father Murphy off to one side.

"I was told by Father Johns that you were unfit to teach today, Father. I can teach the class, if you wish it. Are you feeling well now?"

Father Murphy frowned. "I suppose Father Johns was referring to my back problem, but I've taken medicine for it and I'm fit enough."

He smiled at Michael, who looked confused. "It wasn't your back that he mentioned; he said you needed the day to dedicate to devotions and prayer. I didn't know about your back. I can handle the classes, Father, really, I can. I'm anxious to try and see for myself. Take the day off, if you wish."

Father Murphy thought a bit on this. He certainly didn't want Michael to think he didn't trust him to teach his classes. He knew it was purely manipulation on Father Johns' part to unsettle him. He could use the time to go over some of the scrolls he had wanted to read, and relaxing his back would do no harm, either. Seeing Michael, who was so anxious to please, he nodded.

"You know, I could use the rest. It was very kind of you to offer, Michael, thank you. Let me know if any of these hoodlums get out of hand. They will be doing double lessons tomorrow, if they do."

The last he made sure to say loud enough for the class to hear, and they were making faces and looking at each other with mischief. Michael looked relieved, and in a stern voice, began the class. Father Murphy only stayed long enough to give a few warning looks and then went back to his cubical. It was such a lovely day he decided to take the scrolls out into the courtyard that bordered the road, to read. He was totally immersed into his reading when he heard a child calling his name. He looked around and saw young William McCallum hanging over the stone wall, waving at him. Tucking the scroll under his arm, he went to see him.

"William. How is your mother? Has she given you a sister or brother yet?"

The young Scottish boy wrinkled his nose and was licking a piece of honeycomb.

"Ach, no. Not yet, but Mistress Thatcher is with her now. It seems the babe is stuck, and they sent me outside." He shrugged his shoulders, and then his face brightened. "Mistress Thatcher told me she was going to see you afterwards though, so she can tell you what it is when she's through."

Father Murphy smiled. "So, the Mistress Thatcher is there, is she? They didn't send you to get a priest, did they? All is going as it should be, right?"

William nodded. "Oh, Aye. No one told me to come and fetch a priest. Mistress Thatcher just said the babe has to be turned around to go the other way, from what I heard. Me mum will be glad of it, I'm sure. She was up all night, howling, until Father went for the Mistress. I think she wants to bring you some scrolls. I told her I would take them but she said I'd be too sticky, and that I am. She brought honeycomb for all of us."

His eyes sparkled as he ate the sweet treat. Father Murphy laughed. There were four more children in the family and he had baptized every one.

"Well then, I should look forward to seeing her, and I'll look forward to baptizing either your new brother or sister."

He patted the boy's head and went back to his bench to read. William went on down the road, his hands and mouth sticky. Father Murphy wasn't sure if having Glynnis in the church courtyard was such a good idea on a day like today, but she must have read a few of the scrolls and brought them with her, knowing she would be so near the church.

The church bells rang out for afternoon devotions, which would be held before the noon meal. As Father Murphy gathered up his scrolls, he heard someone running towards him. He spun his head around in time to meet the collision of a young woman, frantic with fear, clutching his robes.

"Help me, Father, or I fear they will kill me. Hide me, quickly."

Father Murphy herded the girl under the stone archway and to his cubical. He hastily dropped the scrolls down on his desk, as he heard a commotion in the courtyard. Having the barest of rooms, he searched quickly for a place to hide the woman. He pushed her down and told her to be still and hide under his desk. Hearing men pounding on his door, he sat abruptly, hiding the girl with his robes.

Father Johns came in, swiftly, with a few of the king's guard. Father Murphy gave them his best insulted look.

"Yes, Father Johns? What is the meaning of all this?"

Father Johns' eyes looked about the room in a suspicious manner. "These guardsmen have told me that they are pursuing a witch. Naturally, knowing your affiliation with Mistress Thatcher, I only assumed that she might be in here."

Father Murphy frowned. "Is it the Mistress Thatcher that you are searching for? I believe she's in the progress of delivering a newborn babe to the McCallum family, or so says young William McCallum. I've just spoken to him, not more than a few moments ago."

The young woman under his desk shook with fright and clutched his knees. Father Murphy found this to be a rather awkward situation, but stood his ground.

The guardsmen searched the room and said, "No. It is not the Mistress Thatcher that we seek. She is under no suspicion, not that she shouldn't be, but it is a stranger in town that has bewitched some of the king's men. She ran in this direction. Let's search the rest of the church."

They stormed out, as they had stormed in, leaving Father Johns looking very foolish. He gave Father Murphy a disdainful look.

"Why aren't you at devotions?"

Father Murphy stretched, holding his back. It didn't really hurt, but he did need a plausible excuse to satisfy Johns. "Well, Father, as you say, I felt unfit. I do thank you for your kindness in procuring a substitute to teach my class. I feel as if I shall rest today, as you see, I will be all the better for it tomorrow. I'm using this time to read the gospel and examine my soul." He indicated the scrolls of prayers on his desk.

The young woman hugged his legs tighter, burying her head into his knees.

Father Johns straightened. "I see." Saying nothing else, he walked out of Father Murthy's room, slamming his door.

He remained seated until he heard the footfalls diminish down the long corridor. Then, he backed up his chair and motioning to the girl for silence, he put out his hand and helped her out.

He whispered, "All right, my dear, that was too close. Not only the guardsmen, but you strangling my legs. I don't know what sin that is, but it sure felt like one."

As she lifted her bowed head he noticed she had a bruised eye and the mark of a whip lash across her face. She was young, maybe seventeen or so, long blonde curls and sad blue eyes.

"Oh, my poor child, you're hurt. Did the king's men do that to you?"

She nodded, still shaking, and she began to cry. Father Murphy put an arm around her and patted her thin back.

"There, now, you're safe enough right now, although with you in my room, I am not. Why don't you sit and tell me what this is all about and we'll come up with a way to solve these problems?"

She sat down, one hand going to the whip lash across her face. It was red and oozing. One of her eyes had swollen shut. It was turning black and purple. Her voice shook as she spoke and Father Murphy detected a Gaelic accent. The tears flowed freely and he handed her a cloth dipped in the water he had in a basin. She pressed the cool cloth to her eye.

"Thank you, Father. I was brought here as a slave by the barbarians that stole me from me homeland. They all had gotten drunk last night and I slipped away and hid. This morning, after they left, tiring of searching for me, the king's guardsmen thought to have some sport with me that I refused. I'm a good Catholic, Father. When I refused, they said I bewitched them and I would hang as a witch if I didn't see things their way. They beat me and one hit me with his whip. I pulled away then and ran. I want to go home to me family." She buried her face in the cool cloth. "All I could see was the church cross. I knew God would save me, so I ran in that direction. I didn't mean to cause you trouble."

Father Murphy sat back in the other chair on the side of his desk and ran a hand through his hair, trying to think of what to do. His eyes rested on his dark woolen cloak, hanging on a peg. An idea had come to him, but it would have to be executed very carefully.

"I have a friend visiting me later today. She lives northwest of here in the Griffin wood. Perhaps we can disguise you enough to have you leave with her. She's quite a normal sight here in the village. She would give you shelter, I'm sure, until she can send a message to your family to come and get you. No one bothers her where she lives. I think the sooner we can get you out of the village the better, for your sake. Now, we'll have to keep you hidden until then, and sneak you out when she arrives. If you're found here, it would be my rosary, you understand."

He gave her a smile and she smiled back, relieved that there was a way for her to escape safely. He thought her a lovely girl and found it difficult to believe someone could abuse her so horribly. He noticed she held her side. More injury at the hands of the king's men. He winced.

"My friend's name is Glynnis Thatcher and she's a wonderful healer, as well. I am sure she will be able to help you with those injuries."

She grabbed his hands and kissed them, and he blushed.

"Now, then." He began standing up so she would stop kissing his hands. "I'm afraid you'll have to hide back under the desk if we hear anyone coming. Can you do that with your difficulties?"

She nodded conspiratorially. She hugged him and climbed back under the desk. He sighed heavily. How did he manage to get into so much trouble without even trying? He had said at breakfast that he tried to commit interesting sins, but he wished he could repent his boast now. But God had sent this woman to him to help; he was sure of it, and he tossed his dark cloak to her to put over her in case anyone came in. She wrapped up in it, and her eyes were so very grateful, and he wondered at that moment if becoming a priest was the wisest choice. He told her that he'd have to attend devotions and would be back.

"Rest, if it's possible, all crunched up like that, as it's a long ride to Mistress Thatcher's home."

He closed the door behind him and went into the chapel where devotions were almost over already. He crossed himself and knelt to pray. It wasn't his soul he prayed for, however; it was that Glynnis would show up and relieve him of the stowaway under his desk. If she decided to go straight home, he would have to come up with another plan, and frankly, he was too upset to think of anything. Father Johns watched him enter and he caught Father Murphy's eye. Father Murphy knelt and gave him his most devout look.

Glynnis trotted Baron up to the church after the noon meal. She was tired. It had been a long and labored birth, but everyone was well and the McCallums now sported a new son named Glen. She had smiled at that, knowing they were honoring her for all her efforts. They had tried to give her coins for her services, but she kissed the tiny baby, squeezed Ruth McCallum's hand and bid them good fortune. She left them a little tonic to regain Ruth's strength. She had been in labor for two days.

Dismounting, she took the scrolls from her pack and walked into the church and knocked on Father Murphy's door. The door creaked open. He grabbed her and pulled her in, to her surprise. She laughed.

"Now, you wouldn't be giving up your vows now, are you, Father?"

He waved his arms, wildly motioning her to silence. She stood there and jumped as the young girl climbed out from under his desk. Glynnis couldn't help it as her jaw dropped. She saw the girl's face and went to her.

"Oh, my. Who has done this to you? I know it wasn't the good Father."

Father Murphy put his hand on her arm. "No time for that, Glynnis, we have to get her out of here. She's wanted by the king's guard for witchery because she would not give in to their advances. She needs passage to the north lands to return to her family. Her name is Mary. Glynnis, I hate to ask you to take her and care for her, but you know I certainly can't keep her here."

Glynnis put the scrolls down on his desk and wrapped the cloak around Mary. She peeked out of the door, seeing the way clear, all the way to her horse, she hurried her out. She jumped up on Baron and pulled the girl in front of her on the saddle and, yanking on the reins, turned Baron back to the road and kicked him into a canter.

No sense in drawing attention by kicking him into a run. She was only stopped once as she left, and said it was a cousin of hers who was learning to midwife. She smiled broadly as she reported to the guard that the McCallums had a strong healthy boy. The guard waved her on, not really looking at the girl. Glynnis held on to the girl as she brought Baron to a full gallop. The sooner they were away, the better. The guardsmen had no love for her and if she was caught with a wanted woman, they would both be hung as witches; she was sure of it.

Father Murphy sat down heavily and put Mary's wet cloth over his face as he listened to Baron's hoof beats until he could hear them no longer. Father Johns burst into his room and looked around quickly.

"I thought I heard some noise, a knocking and a woman's laughter. What do you know of it?"

Father Murphy shook his head at him. "I did hear it, too. Maybe it was out on the road?"

Father Johns grunted at him and went to leave. "You know, you should lie down; you really do not look as if you're feeling quite yourself. As you can see, I hope, the pagan witch has done you no good after all."

Father Murphy got up and stretched out on his cot. He breathed a huge sigh of relief and said a little prayer for the girls' safety. *She has done me good*, he thought, *very good, indeed. God bless her.*

CHAPTER FIVE

All of the magicals had been moved and the Realm had begun to flourish. The elves were busy building their houses, and the trolls and dwarves were building as well. The Fairy Queen had sent quite a few of her subjects over to help the land thrive. The land had taken on a whole new dimension then with flowering trees, bushes, and fields of wildflowers. The unicorn pastures had been lined with apple trees and other fruit-bearing trees were planted throughout the Realm. Long, bright green leafy ferns grew in the underbrush of the forest and there were trees of walnut and hazelnut. Pomegranates were under the cliffs as they were a favorite of the griffins. Large water lilies and cattails were in the wetlands and the water nymphs were delighted. The fairies had outdone themselves.

Oberon and King Orion went together to visit Myarra and Knight and to give their respects to Illustra, their new filly who had been born into legend. She was born on the first night of their new residency in the Realm. A red comet had streaked through the sky and the newborn had been surrounded in the golden light. It was prophesized in the old unicorn legends that a mare would be born in a new land in a golden glow under the fiery comet. She would have curls instead of the usual mane and she would be wise. She would become the Queen of the Unicorns and it was a monumental event for everyone there when it did, in fact, happen. Myarra named her Illustra, Light of the Morning Star, and she was indeed sporting not only a curly mane, but her tail was a mass of curls as well. She had golden hooves and her horn was gold. It was cause for a celebration and the Realm had been one big happy family for days. King Orion smiled as he walked easily through the pasture lands.

"Well, it's nothing short of miraculous Oberon. This has been in legend since time remembered, yet it has never happened. Every mare hopes and dreams she will be the one to give birth to the queen, but to have it actually happen in our time, well, things just don't get much better than that. As the legend goes, she will have the power to give life back to the dead, give gifts of an extraordinary nature, have healing powers that surpass even mine, and will be a queen of compassion and wisdom. We are so very fortunate. It's an omen of the best kind."

Oberon, in human form, nodded with contentment. Things had indeed gone very well for them all. He was concerned that Myarra was delivering too quickly due to the stress of the past several days and was worried about the health of both the foal and the mare. They saw them under a thicket of apple trees, the young filly asleep by her mother's side. Myarra bobbed her head in greeting when she saw them. The little foal was unbelievably beautiful, and when she opened her dark blue eyes, Oberon could see the wisdom there already. The little filly did not start and bolt like the young ones do, but calmly got to her wobbly legs and bowed her head in humility before the king of the elves and Oberon.

The elven king bowed low in response and said, as if he were talking to an adult unicorn, "Welcome to our world, Illustra, Queen of the Unicorns. I am Orion, King of the elves and I pledge you our service."

Oberon bowed low, following suit. "I am Oberon, a dragon in human form. I, too, pledge my service, Illustra the beautiful Light of the Morning Star, Queen of the Unicorns."

The young filly bowed again. "As I am ever at your service, mighty king of the Elves and Oberon, noble dragon." She laid back down and was soon fast asleep.

Myarra nuzzled her newborn and smiled at the men. "I'm afraid she hasn't the strength yet. So many have been by to see her that she hasn't had much sleep. She surprises me with her wisdom beyond her years, and she is so beautiful, isn't she? Oh, dear, I sound like a boasting parent, don't I?"

Orion smiled at her. "And so you should boast, my dear. I have never seen a more lovely foal, and so well mannered at such a tender age. She will be a queen of extraordinary power and beauty and I look forward to serving with her."

Oberon bent to kiss Myarra and couldn't resist a gentle kiss on the filly's forehead. "She is so wonderful, Myarra. Give our regards to Knight as well."

Myarra beamed at him. "You know, Oberon, if you hadn't saved me when you did that day..."

A tear formed in her eye and Oberon brushed it away quickly. "Now, we'll have none of that. Those times are far behind us now. Little Illustra has no worries for her safety. She will grow up strong, lovely and powerful, free to run without looking behind her. All is as it should be now and I think it was destined to happen this way for us all. Perhaps if your misfortune had never happened, she would not have been born in safety. It was all the atrocities that drove us to move and move quickly enough for this angel to be born in freedom, and not a day too soon, for that matter."

Myarra held up her head then, and nodded. They took their leave of her, not wanting to tire out the mother or the new queen, and left them both to sleep under the boughs of the fragrant apple tree which was now so full of white sweet blossoms that when the breeze blew it showered them both in petals. The pasture land was a bright spring green and Oberon would remember the sight of Myarra and the new queen and save it to bring to mind whenever he was in need of a happy thought. They walked further south and came upon the Healing Waters Lake. Reaper had spotted them and flew in to land.

"The cliffs are just perfect for us, Oberon. The shelters are ideal. Expertly carved, if you ask me, with the griffins' needs in mind. You must have had nothing to do with that." He winked and Orion laughed as Oberon gave him a nasty look.

They stood on the shores of the lake. Oberon said, "It's amazing, isn't it? It was never in the plans at all. We had the river going through the forest, a few streams here and there, wetlands to keep the water nymphs happy, but we never even thought of a lake. The dragon shaman did have a vision of it, though. The Pegasus confirm that it's a gift from the Gods. Say, Reaper, you have those wounds.

Have you tried the lake water?"

Reaper looked at him speculatively. "Do you think I should?"

Orion nodded. "We haven't even thought to use it yet. It's supposed to have miraculous healing powers. No time like the present. Hop on in there, Reaper. It should cure all those aches and pains of yours, not to mention the cuts and wounds."

Reaper looked from one man to the other, shrugged, took off and flew about six feet above the lake, folded his wings and dove into it. He paddled to the shore, came out and shook his feathers. They all looked closely to see that all the wounds were gone.

Reaper gasped, "By the Gods. I feel great, and look, here and over there." He pointed to the spots that had originally been bare of feathers and had sported jagged cuts. "It's like it's never happened at all."

He looked amazed and they all turned to look at the peaceful waters, a green blue in the middle of the pasture. King Orion was amazed and he took out his short sword and cut the palm of his hand as they all stared at him in disbelief. He then took his bleeding hand and immersed it in the water of the lake. As he lifted his hand out, water dripped from his fingers but there was no sign of the cut he'd made in his hand. He smiled and nodded with satisfaction as he raised it to show Oberon and Reaper. Oberon shook his head. It was a miracle.

"King Orion, perhaps you should bring all of the injured here for a complete baptism."

King Orion nodded. "Exactly what I was thinking. I'm going now to get everyone together. Why did we wait so long to find this lake?" He bustled off and vanished into the trees.

Reaper told Oberon he was going to spread the news among his griffins. A lot of them were stiff and sore from the bitter battles they had been through at the hands of the humans. He vowed the lake would look like the most popular swimming hole before long. Oberon watched as he flew off above the trees. He saw Knight limping along and called him over.

"First, let me congratulate you on the birth of the queen. We just came from there and I must say she is a vision to behold."

Knight bobbed his head happily.

Oberon went on, "Knight, if you were to swim in this lake, I think your troubles with your legs would be over. I've just witnessed two miraculous healings right here and I know it would work for you. Have you tried it?"

Knight looked over the lake and back at Oberon. "No. I knew it was called the Healing Waters Lake, but I never realized that. I've drunk from it, but I never thought to swim in it. I didn't think I had the strength to swim back out. Do you think it would work? I'd give anything to be out of this pain and be able to run with Illustra when she's strong enough."

Oberon nodded at Knight. "I'll tell you what. Let me change back into my form and if you get into trouble, I'll pluck you right back out just as quickly. But I think it will work."

Oberon ran a few yards from Knight and transformed into the black and gold dragon. He flexed his wings. "I'll take off and circle the lake. You go in and if I see you're having trouble, I'll be right in position to help."

Knight turned his head from the gust of wind created by the huge wings. He waited until Oberon was directly over the lake, and then he inhaled and took a few tentative steps into the water. Then he went in up to his belly. Feeling the pain subside, he went in over his head and swam to the other side. He climbed back out and shook off the water. He was in no pain and his legs felt sound and strong. He pranced a bit, then cantered. In jubilation, he broke into a full gallop. Oberon watched and followed him back to Myarra who jumped to her feet, seeing Knight in a full gallop. He saw him brush up against Myarra and nuzzle the young queen. Oberon smiled as he made his way to his cave. He landed and folding his wings, laid down with satisfaction and fell asleep.

* * *

King Orion was enthusiastic as he gathered his elves together.

"I have just witnessed the powers of the Healing Waters Lake. I want all the infirm brought to its shores and immersed in the water. Its healing power is tremendous."

The elves looked at each other and grinned. They wasted no time in transporting the sick and injured to the shores of the lake. The worst cases were brought by the griffins, who had congregated along the lake shores to ease their troubles and were only too happy to help out the elves. They all watched in wonder as one by one, the injured were cured. Trolls and dwarves had arrived and they too marveled at the lake's ability to heal. King Orion was helping some of the smaller residents, a few of the hurt faries. He held out his hand with the fairy in it, cupped it, and let his hand fill with water. Most of them took flight afterwards, happy to be back into the air. It was a glorious sight and it didn't take long before a celebration was declared in honor of the lake. Someone shouted to Reaper to fly up and get the dragons but he hesitated one moment.

"While we are all here without Oberon, I would suggest to the new Realm that Oberon be made king for all his service and that every clan pledge their undying service to his judgments and position. Now, I don't mean he would be the head of the individual clans, but over us all, as the Realm. We don't know what to expect from the Dark magicals, and we could use a king to organize us all if the need arises. He has personally helped every clan here, has he not? He thinks not of himself, but for the greater good. What say you all?"

There was no hesitation on the parts of any clan. They all shouted for King Oberon, King Orion being the loudest.

King Orion said, "Get him, Reaper, and let's see if we can convince him to take the job. We will need a feast."

Cheers went up and the elves scattered as food needed to be prepared. Dwarves rode on the other griffins to go back and bring more food. The trolls lugged large tables and the unicorns took off to bring the other clans there in a hurry. Fairies lit up the trees and the water nymphs set the water sparkling with phosphorescent light. The Pegasus flew in to act as witness and convey the magicals' choice to the Gods if Oberon agreed. The trolls talked excitedly about building a great castle for him and some had already begun moving boulders. There wasn't a doubt in anyone's heart that Oberon wouldn't make the mightiest of kings.

Reaper flew into Oberon's cave, yelling for the ugly worm to get up. He hit Oberon with a barrage of insults and bad language, enough so that Oberon sat up and considered setting his tail on fire.

"I know you have been healed, Reaper, I was there and I saw it for myself, but I swear if you don't tell me the meaning of all this I will set your tail on fire. What is wrong with you, anyway? How dare you come in here and insult me for no reason, and wake me up, to boot. Smarter animals have been fried for less you know."

Reaper looked at him with wide glittering eyes. "I have to get it all out right now while I can. By the morrow, it would be treason to do what I just did."

Oberon shook his head to clear it. What was the babbling fool talking about, anyway? He yawned, showing massive rows of sharp teeth. He had no clue as to what was wrong with Reaper and hoped the Healing Waters Lake had no side effects. As strangely as Reaper was acting, he had to worry.

Reaper was laughing at Oberon's expression and he flapped over and bit his tail. Oberon grabbed the griffin then, just under the wings, and lifted him off of the ground.

"This is your last chance, Reaper. You'd better tell me what you are talking about, or I will throw a fiery clump of feathers off of this mountain."

Reaper stopped laughing and held up his talons. "Alright, alright. You have to come with me to the Healing Waters Lake. You are to be made king, unofficially of course, then we will plan a real formal coronation later, but everyone has agreed already and there's a party for you. You see? If I didn't get all my hostilities out now, you'd fry me for treason tomorrow."

Oberon looked pained and he set Reaper back down on his feet again. Oberon looked over the ocean from his high mountain cave. He sighed.

"I had heard rumors of as much. Is this what the clans really want? I don't see the need for a king, do you, Reaper? We all get along just fine."

Reaper turned serious and approached Oberon closely, looking him straight in the eyes. "It isn't so much of what they want, Oberon, although they all do really want you. But it's what they all need to feel as a Realm. To feel as part of a whole. It would be as a kingdom then, not just some place frozen out of time to live in. It's what we're all used to. It would make them feel more secure if they had the mighty Oberon as their king. We need laws and responsibilities. We need to be held accountable for our actions, both good and bad. We all need a sense of order, so to speak. We need a king we can trust and feel secure with, and that would be you, Oberon."

He stood back and bowed low. "Long live the king."

Oberon cuffed him. "Stop that."

He was still unsure, although what Reaper had said did make sense. He supposed the clans would sleep better at night under the protection of the king. He was the biggest one there and he had to admit he was impressive in the air. Well, so be it.

"Alright, Reaper, let's go, but understand, you now have a job. You will be my Master at Arms."

Reaper started laughing again. "Yes, your Highness" he said with an overly exaggerated bow.

Oberon picked him up and threw him out of the mouth of the cave and laughed as he started flapping wildly. He took off shortly afterwards and they headed for the lake.

* * *

So Oberon accepted graciously and said, "The king would only be as good as its kingdom. There will be a council set up and all the clans are to be represented. It will be the decisions of all of you as to how this Realm is to be run. You will all need to choose a leader of your clan if there isn't one in place already. These will be our first council members. "

Heads nodded, groggy with ale. There were shouts of "Hail King Oberon" and "Long live the king." There were songs and merriment and then, one by one, the clan representatives, the same ones that were present at the meeting in the old world, came up and pledged their loyalty to the king. They would all abide by his decisions. Then stories of his bravery were told, much to his embarrassment. Myarra recounted his heroic rescue of her from the jaws of death, the dwarfs recounted his rescue of their enslaved peoples, how he snatched them as they were driven to work in the caves as slaves. Reaper told how he had blasted a fire line across the enemy's path, allowing them to get their young to safety. The elves told of his numerous trips bringing them the injured and the elves that were trying to save them in the fields. A few of the tales were of actions he had not remembered doing and he thought they might be the tales born of the ale.

He sat back and watched them all, thankful he lived now in a world with such marvelous creatures. It pleased him they were all so happy now; it was a big difference from just a few days ago when faces were long, anxious, and terrified.

The gathering quieted all of a sudden as Illustra got to her feet. She was steadier now than she was earlier and she made her way up to the king with dignity. Even at this tender age, she was a presence to be reckoned with. Everyone quieted and watched her with awe. She toddled up to the king and he bent his head down to greet her. She touched noses with him, then bent her head low to place her horn on him. There was an audible gasp as a golden glow encompassed Oberon. It lasted only for a moment, and then Illustra opened her eyes and backed up.

She said in her clear tiny voice, her head held high, "In honor of my king that I will always serve; a gift of wisdom with a touch of arrogance that this humble king will need."

There was a tittering of laughter at that, and she went on, "You will be a mighty king of the Realm and you will never need worry about treason. All your subjects will be true and loyal to you. Hail, Mighty King Oberon, from your unicorns."

A shout went up in celebration, joined in chorus by the masses.

Oberon bowed to Illustra and said, "Thank you, my Queen of the unicorns. The first born of the Realm and the queen that was prophesized to come. Is this not the best omen? It is a gift I will always treasure and never forget. A finer gift a king could not receive."

The dwarves pledged a medallion of gold not only for the king, but for everyone in the Realm who wished to wear one. A deadly air force was promised by the griffins. The elves pledged their healing services and songs for the Realm. The trolls pledged a castle of the finest stone, fit for a dragon king, and on and on it went. The more they drank, the more they pledged and Oberon thought if he could have chosen any kingdom anywhere, it would be this one right here. He thanked them all gratefully for every pledge.

He sat back and thought of the gift of the unicorns. To never worry about treason was enough of a gift. No king under the sun could boast a better gift than that. It alone was worth all the treasures you could hoard. Imagine a kingdom that was one hundred percent loyal, one hundred percent of the time. Yet a gift from a unicorn was true. Everyone knew that, and the gift from Queen Illustra was golden. He wondered what he would be like if he was more arrogant? He had to chuckle at that. How did one so small know so much about him already? He had never had an arrogant thought in his life, but he would have them now. It probably would come in handy.

After everyone had partied themselves out, King Oberon used his magic to clear up the pasture and restore it to its natural state, much to the delight of the elves who were pretty tired by now. King Orion came up and clapped him on the chest.

"One rule we seem to need is to limit parties to every other day." He laughed heartily at his own joke. "Isn't it wonderful that we have such valid reasons to celebrate? Usually the elves don't even need a reason, but I think even my subjects are weary now. When you can tire out an elf, well, then you've accomplished something."

Oberon laughed. "It is your people who have worked so hard trying to save everyone. It should be for their dedication that a party should be thrown."

King Orion thought for a moment, then smiled. "Maybe the day after tomorrow. Goodnight, my king, and my friend."

Oberon then flew back to his cave and stared out at the stars in the sky. So now, he was to be a king. His father would be so pleased, and of course, would be invited to attend the formal coronation that would be held when the castle was built. The trolls had been designing it all night, heads bent over parchment on a long table. They roared with laughter from time to time. They loved to build and this would be their biggest task. They had built the church in the old village for the very people who hunted them down and who had filled them with arrows. Well, that would never happen here in the Realm. It was freedom that had put joy in all of their hearts and now being king, Oberon would make sure it remained that way. That would be rule number one. Respect for all the clans, no matter what they believed in or what they did for a living. Everyone's rights would be protected.

He yawned widely. The ale had caught up with him as well, but he did think he felt a bit wiser and just a touch of arrogance was there, as well. Illustra was a bright star in his Realm. He wondered how she would be when she was older? Her beauty already took one's breath away, and so wise and knowing. All his clan representatives were top notch and he thought being a king with all those brilliant creatures would not be a hard job at all. How many blessings could he have? A safe land for his subjects, a healing lake from the Gods, and a legendary Queen of the unicorns, born right here on the very night they had taken up residency. The gifts of solidarity, wisdom, and arrogance. What more could a king ask for? He closed his huge golden eyes and thought, *I could pray for the strength and the fortitude to do the best job that I can, to rule fairly with everyone.* He still felt too humble to take the position. Who was he, anyway, to be made a king? Certainly, he was not the oldest or the wisest dragon, and who said a dragon should rule, anyway? But there it stood; he had already accepted and the decision was unanimous. There was no turning back now. It was true he had always cared a great deal for everyone. Out of all the dragons, he was the most social. But these magicals were all his friends. How hard could organizing these clans be? They had all been so thankful to move here that he really didn't see any problems at all. No one had complained about a thing, he could remember.

He opened his eyes and stared up at the stars again. What about the Dark magicals? He would have to work on a gate system to prevent them from entering and causing problems. According to Mordread, they hadn't wanted to join their Realm, anyway. Let them try to build a Dark Realm of their own. He could imagine the devilment going on now that there were no Light magicals to temper them as they had before. It would be like a plague settling over the world of the humans and by God, they deserved it. They were the ones who had driven them out. But maybe not all of them deserved the evil descending upon them, not Elijah nor Glynnis, nor the handful of other humans he knew. He was sure there were even more who were decent folk, but it was too late now. They had reaped what they had sown and they'd have to find a way to deal with it themselves. It would be dark times indeed for them if

Mordread had his way. It was all a game to Mordread, and the more deadly the game, the better he liked it.

Oberon sighed in resignation. It was no longer his concern, as it had been before. He had a Realm to rule and that would be his focus now. He felt a twinge of guilt at the thought. As a magical, he had always lent support to the greater good, be it human or otherwise. If no one wanted to go back to help now, well, no one could blame them for that. It had become much too dangerous. But if the cry went up for help, he would have to relent and help, himself, and he was sure he would not be alone. At least they had a choice in the matter now. As long as the magicals stayed in the Realm he could protect them. If they wanted to go back into the real world to help, he would give them as much support as he could but they would be essentially on their own. He knew his magicals had interacted with humans before escaping to the Realm and he was sure a lot of them still had friends there that they would want to visit on occasion. He saw nothing wrong with that as long as they knew they were taking a risk by leaving. All these matters would have to be taken up in council. One good thing about being a good king was that you really shouldn't make all the decisions. He would let them decide for themselves. If they couldn't reach a decision, then he would decide, weighing all the facts. He just prayed he was up to the job. Little Illustra said he was and he guessed that was good enough for him.

The trolls began right away, the very next day, hauling huge stones to begin building the castle. It would be huge. A dragon king would need very large rooms. The ground shook as they moved the groundwork into place. They had stayed up all night making diagrams and figuring out all the construction. All the dwarves helped as well, digging out large rooms underneath the ground floor area. There would be dungeons there. They also lent their expertise on the kind of rocks that would be suitable for a grand castle. The fancy gem work on the inside murals would be of their making. The elves brought large timbers to brace the walls under construction and to outline the floor plan of the castle itself.

Oberon came and watched, and flew up to place rocks on top of each other. The elves talked of the marvelous courtyards they would make bloom all year round with the rarest of flowers and plants. The griffins requested a large fountain in the middle and it was adopted into the original plans. It was coming right along. The fairies volunteered to inspect the rocks and crevices for hair-line splits that would make the structure unsound. The castle stone would be polished by the dwarves into a glass-like shine. It would be something that would reflect the Realm's pride in their new world with their chosen king. As time went on, the castle rose on the cliff, as did their spirits.

* * *

The Griffin Forest was alive with activity. The new noble had arrived with his court to take up residence in the previously de-serted castle. Lord McTavish, serving under his cousin, the king, surveyed his new home.

"It'll be a bit drafty, but once the tapestries are in place and we get the fires going, it will be as grand as it once was. Get the Guild in here and get it all prepared."

He raised his hand to shield his eyes as he looked up into the sun to see the tall towers. It would do just fine, he thought. He liked the fact it was on a bluff and guarded on one side by the sea. He stopped walking to pat the head of the blonde boy at his side.

"Well, Greccon, do you think we'll be happy here?"

The boy grinned and nodded his agreement. "Aye, my Lord, it is a mighty castle. May I have leave to explore the woods?"

The noble nodded and, distracted, rushed up to a group of his knights who were riding up.

"There are stables inside for the horses, men, just ride over the drawbridge and go to the right. Have the rest of my men made it through the mountains with the goods?"

The burly knight with the red beard grinned. "Not a bit of trouble, my Lord. A few curious lookers, is all. It seems peaceful enough around these parts. The pennants and standards will be up by nightfall."

Greccon became quieter as he walked through the forest. It was the kind of a forest you just felt you should pay homage to. The oaks were tremendous, the largest he had ever seen in his eight years of being alive. His father, Killwyn, was the court magician and he wanted to have a good look around before he arrived. Once there,

Greccon knew he could count on hours of lessons. He'd be a great magician too, or at least that was what his father had vowed. As far back as anyone could remember, his family had the real magic, or so it was called. Greccon didn't know the details of it all, just what he overheard in the adults' conversations.

He was a quiet boy, with a handsome face. Large, curious blue eyes noted everything he saw. He wasn't given to the pranks and mischief of boys his age. He was solemn, respectful and resourceful. Although he had every right to pull rank on the serving boys, being an official court magician along with his father, he found the privileges of the upper crust of their society were not as attractive as one might think. He still liked to play games and considered himself just one of the many children of the estate. His father was a kindly, although stern, man and gave his son leave to be a child and associate with whomever he wished.

"Greccon, you can't have enough friends, no matter their station in life. You never know whose hand you may need to grasp to save your life someday."

He had told Greccon that on a sunny day in a huge field, when he'd been watching the farmer's children chase around the new lambs. They were laughing and Greccon had wished to join them. Children of the court were picnicking on the grass and had turned a haughty eye away from the other children. They were much too proud to go and play with dirty farm children. Killwyn had a twinkle in his eye that day, as he knew his son yearned to run and play.

"I'm sure the laundress will be able to get the dirt and muck out of those clothes should you get soiled."

Greccon had looked up and smiled at him for a moment and then he ran down the hill to play. The other court children pointed and sniffed with disdain at his behavior and Killwyn thought it such a shame that they were so closed-minded. His son needed to experience as much as he could to be a good magician, and magic was everywhere for him to learn. The magic of laughter and sunshine were a reward all on their own, and it was a shame these other children would remain with their airs, in the shade doing and saying the correct things that their station demanded. Greccon would not be like that, he thought, as he gestured a greeting to them as he walked by. Knowing he was the court magician, and his son was in training, they would say nothing to Greccon about his choice of playmates. In truth, they were frightened of them both.

Greccon walked on, splashing in the wide but shallow stream. He stopped and stooped to watch a few fish and snails. He thought he'd heard a humming sound and he followed it to a stone cottage that had a young woman at a spinning wheel out front. He made his way through the trees and out into the clearing.

"Good morning, my Lady."

She looked up from her spinning and smiled at him. "Good morning, young man, and whom might you be?"

Greccon bowed and said, "I am known as Greccon the Fair of the household of McTavish, The Lord of the Griffin castle. I am a magician."

She stood up and pressed her hands to the small of her back, stretching.

"So, The new lord has moved into the castle, has he? Well, Greccon the Fair, court magician, welcome to my home. I am Glynnis Thatcher. Won't you have some fresh honey comb?" She nodded to a jar on her steps.

Greccon licked his lips. He hadn't had any honey comb in a long time. "Thank you, my lady. I knew I would find something good in these woods."

He smiled shyly at her and she grinned back, sat down, and continued to spin. Greccon sat on the stoop, savoring the sticky sweet treat.

Glynnis inquired, "So then, is your lord a gentle man, or will he be waging a war?"

Greccon licked his fingers deftly. "Oh no, we will be protecting this land from the barbarians. He is a good lord. You need have no fear for yourself or your child-to-be."

She looked sharply at him. She had suspicions of her own but was dumbfounded to hear this child talk of such things.

"And how would you know about a child that I don't have?"

He looked at her matter-of-factly. "I have the gift of foresight. I'm sorry if I've offended you. Sometimes I talk about what I see without being smart enough to think about other people's reactions. My father has told me time and again not to spout off like that. I am sorry, Mistress Thatcher. I do see a child, though."

He looked up at her apologetically. "It's a girl, and she will be a great friend of mine, and a mage in her time."

Glynnis saw that the boy was sincere and laughed in spite of her surprise. "Is that so? What should I name this great friend of yours?" She was joking, naturally, but the boy was as sincere as he could be.

"You'll call her Ilona and she will be of an everlasting spirit. I'm afraid I've said too much already. Forgive me, Mistress Thatcher, but I have to go and see if my father, Killwyn, has arrived yet. He would be dismayed if I was not there to greet him. Thank you for the treat."

With that, the young boy, still gleaning his fingers, ran back into the woods, leaving Glynnis staring into space at his declaration. *So I am with child*, she thought, *and I will name her Ilona?* The boy said she would be of an everlasting spirit and a mage. She wondered if this was just a young boy's fancy or if he really did see the future. She put a hand to her stomach, in wonder, and looked through the trees to where he had run. She'd heard of a mighty magician, Killwyn. This must be his son and if that was the case, the child may have great powers.

She went back to thoughts of a child. Of course it would be a girl. All the Thatcher women had girls. It was Elijah's child and he would give her a terrible time about marrying him, but she knew she wouldn't. She would, however, prepare for a child. She would mix up a beneficial herb tonic to take to keep both her and the child strong.

Mary came out of the house and saw how strangely Glynnis looked. "I thought I heard voices. Are you all right?"

Mary had stayed on with her since the day Glynnis had rescued her from the king's guards. Mary hadn't wanted to go home until her face had cleared of the bruises and her eyesight had returned to her right eye. She still could not see out of it; no matter what Glynnis had tried on it, the vision would not clear. Glynnis had been happy for the company and she and Mary had became good friends. Glynnis turned to look at her and smiled.

"Yes, you did hear voices. I just met a young man of perhaps ten years old who said he was a court magician in the Griffin castle.

They are moving in there, today, or so it seems. Anyway, his name was Greccon and he's adorable. He also told me I am with child."

Mary laughed at her. "Ten years old is awfully young to be a court magician, isn't it? Now how would he know a thing like that? That's a strange comment for a young boy to make."

Glynnis shrugged. "Well, he says he can predict the future. He's right, you know. I've felt as if it were possible for a few months now. He said it would be a girl named Ilona."

Mary bent to pick up the orange tabby cat that was brushing up against her legs. The cat purred in her arms, bumping his head against her chin as she kissed his head.

"Well, then, I guess along with the lessons on herbs that you've been teaching me, you'd better include some mid-wife instructions. I'll not leave you now until after the child is born." Glynnis smiled at her.

"I was hoping you would stay. It's been such a comfort to have someone to talk to. We'll send word to your family so they won't worry. I appreciate you staying with me, especially now. We'd better tidy up a bit. With the new noble moving in now, we're bound to have company. I believe even Father Murphy will be here." She winked at Mary.

Father Murphy had been there a few times since Mary had fled from his church. He came once to get his cloak and once to return the scrolls Glynnis had lent him. Glynnis knew Mary was in love with Father Murphy, even if he was a priest, and she also knew Father Murphy had tortured thoughts of his own. She could tell by the way he looked at Mary and how his face reddened when he said the wrong things. He behaved like a school boy around her and Glynnis had felt sorry for him and his vows.

CHAPTER SIX

Father Murphy knelt on the cool stone in the chapel, his head bent in prayer. After he had finished all his prayers by rote, he paused to examine his conscience and to clear his head of troubling thoughts, and he'd been sorely troubled as of late. It seemed as if he had been the target of all Father Johns' criticisms and would have to bear his accusations, and although he hated to admit it, his anger. Father Johns had been given to outbursts of a violent nature and everyone treaded lightly around him. Something was horribly wrong with Father Johns and he was asking God just what it was that he could do about it. It was so unnecessary for Father Johns to pursue this fantasy of his, as all of his charges were unfounded and frankly hard for anyone who knew Father Murphy to believe; yet, he persisted relentlessly to the point that Father Murphy needed to defend himself on a daily basis.

He raised his head to adore the statue of his Savior and put the matter to him. The face of the statue was serene and full of compassion. His arms spread wide to encompass all who entered the chapel. Around his feet were bunches of flowers that the villagers brought in, and it was a vision Father Murphy took into his soul for comfort. He waited in silence and listened to his heart for an answer, but it was slow in coming. Father Johns knelt a few rows away, lost in prayers of his own, and Father Murphy glanced out of the corner of his eye at him, feeling nothing but sadness. They were men of the Lord, and shouldn't be fighting the battle against each other, but should be united for the grace of God. He noticed the chapel seemed so much darker where Father Johns prayed. Funny, he had never noticed a dark place in the chapel before and he wondered why it was so, now.

It was a bright sunny morning and he could see the sunlight streaming in. He always loved this chapel for that reason. It was positioned to catch not only the glory of the rising sun, but lit in the setting of the sun as well. A few of the priests made scuffling sounds as they left to continue the morning routine and Father Murphy quickly bowed his head again so he would not appear to be staring at Father Johns. He really wasn't staring at the good Father, but at the darkness that seemed to surround him in a spot that was usually so bright. It was almost as if a cloud had covered the sun, yet he could see it streaming in. Just a trick of the light or perhaps a dimness because all the candles were lit in that area. He was sure it had nothing to do with Father Johns himself. At least he hoped it didn't. His eyes closed tightly, still waiting for an answer from his Lord, he heard Father Johns get up and slowly walk out of the chapel after he paused to stare at Father Murphy. He didn't move, although he knew Father Johns was standing to his left. He could feel his eyes burning into him, yet he remained still, not wanting to confront Father Johns with a look that may be misconstrued as a lack of concentration or some admission of guilt on Father Murphy's part. It seemed as if even breathing wrong caused an outburst and a point of the finger at him. He heard footsteps as he left and with a sigh of relief, he opened his eyes to find Father Johns gone. So was the shadowy darkness that had surrounded him. The corner he was in was brightly lit again with the morning sun. The whole place seemed twice as bright as it was before. Does the man harbor such dark feelings that it hangs on him like a shroud? Father Murphy shook his head in disbelief. He had to concentrate on finishing his devotions and moving on with the day.

He was to go out to Griffin Forest and bless the re-opening of the castle's chapel. It would be a wonderful day outside, and a good ride for Jenny. It would do him good to get out from under the blanket of suspicion that Father Johns loved to weave around him like an insect in a web. A day of fresh air and sunshine would serve him well and he looked forward to it. The celebration of a new

Lord in the area would be a wonderful distraction for him from his haunting thoughts of Father Johns. Of course, depending on which route he took, he could stop and see Glynnis and lovely Mary.

His thoughts collided again at the thought of Mary. He knew he was allowing himself favors of the imagination where she was concerned, and it was a sin of course, that would have to be confessed and forgiven. He should not let his mind wander in that direction and try as he might, it still kept slipping away from him and wandering about in areas that it did not belong in, like a disobedient unsupervised child. He admitted it freely and there was no sense in denying it. God knew his heart and everything in it. It was a constant battle to keep suppressed. As much as he could love the girl in the Christian way, he knew tendrils of his feelings were seeping out into areas that should remain pure. He would pray on it.

He stood now and brushed the small stones from his robes. The chapel was empty now except for him and he took in the view of his Lord in all his splendor, lit and shining from the morning sun. He absently let God know he would be on the road with Jenny soon and would be thankful for any suggestions on what to do with Father Johns. He knelt, crossed himself, and left.

He went to the kitchen and asked for a pack of bread, cheese, and some dried meat to take with him. He might be a few days in traveling. He filled a few skins with water and went out to check if Jenny had been made ready to travel yet. She was stamping impatiently when he arrived.

"Steady now, Jenny, don't waste all that energy. It'll be a good ride for you."

She raised her muzzle and made his hair look even more unruly than it usually looked. He said a few words to the stable boys and took Jenny out of the stable and loaded her packs, checking the straps. It seemed as if the old mule was as anxious to leave as he was. He did not take the morning meal with his fellow priests, but opted to stop and eat somewhere along the road in the splendor of the great outdoors, and avoid the scrutiny of Father Johns.

It was a few miles along before Father Murphy felt the darkness lift from his soul. The further away from the church, the lighter his heart became. Just knowing he could live, pray, and yes, even sing praises to the Lord without someone watching his every move had given him a sense of freedom he craved. Jenny's hooves picked up a pace to synchronize with Father Murphy's song. They would remind everyone they passed of a song and dance team, and they would smile and wave at the good Father and he would wave and bless them as he rode by. More miles went by and Father Murphy came upon the cross roads. He said a prayer which was the custom to do here and scratched his head, thinking. He lowered his hood now as the sun was high up in the sky. He should turn Jenny to the north, but the seldom traveled road to the west called to him. The further along you traveled on the western road, the more it diminished until you were just on a small overgrown trail. It led into the foothills and then on to the mountains. Most travelers avoided this way as it was rumored that the further you climbed up into the mountains, the more likely you were to run into magical creatures such as griffins and dragons. Father Murphy had never seen any of these. He did know Elijah, though, and he hadn't visited him in years.

Jenny snorted at the delay, but Father Murphy dismounted and stood for a long time just pondering his options and watching the tall weeds blow in the breeze. He drew down the skin of water and gave Jenny a drink. He could borrow more scrolls from Elijah and talk of the demons that he was certain plagued Father Johns without the man scorning his imagination. Elijah knew of such things and would discuss them freely with him. Being a scholar, he never feared the contempt of discussing subjects that were so sensitive a nature as to be banned from the church. It would delay him a day or so from the Griffin castle but he was in no hurry. There had been no date set up for the blessings.

His mind made up, he stowed the rest of the water and climbed back on the mule. He kicked her forward and crossed the road to take the western route to Elijah's home. He would speak with the man and perhaps get some answers. He asked the Lord to enlighten him on the road if he could, and he knew in his heart this was the way to find his answer. God worked in mysterious ways.

Jenny turned her head and rolled an eye up to meet his as if she were warning him he was going the wrong way. She knew the way to Baron's home and this wasn't it. He patted her neck.

"Just a short stop over to see Elijah, my pretty, and then we'll head over to the castle and on to Baron's. Alright?"

She snorted her displeasure but obediently plodded forward up the more rocky path into the mountains. A murder of crows cawed and scolded them as they passed under some large scrub trees. Father Murphy looked up at them and then scanned the sky for a griffin or dragon. Didn't Glynnis say that all the magical creatures were gone now? All that was left were the demons, and Father Murphy knew he believed in them. He nudged Jenny into a faster walk. He wanted to reach Elijah's home before the sun set. Jenny bobbed her head at the crows and they moved along in the branches, following them for awhile before losing interest and scattering. Jenny's footing was good as they rose higher into the mountains. The air smelled clearer and colder the further they climbed and Father Murphy pulled his hood back on. It was quiet in the mountains, save for a birdsong or two, and Father Murphy took in the beautiful landscape and was glad he had chosen this way to go.

It was late in the afternoon when he spotted the river and saw he was off course just a little and moved Jenny to walk alongside the water. She couldn't resist a drink and Father Murphy jumped off to fill his water skin again and to sit and eat some of the bread and cheese. He leaned up against the tree and let Jenny cool her feet and rest. It wouldn't be far now and she deserved a rest; he knew how she loved streams. He closed his eyes just for a moment. He hadn't noticed how tired he had been lately. He thought having so much on his mind seemed to drain his strength.

As the sun started to lower in the sky, Jenny poked at him with her nose. He awoke with a start, amazed that he'd fallen asleep at all. He got up and brushed off his robe. He hastily secured Jenny's tack and baggage and hopped back on.

"Now we'll have to pick up the pace there, old girl. Why did you leave me alone so long to fall asleep? Ah, but you're such a good lass not to wander off and leave me stranded here, aren't you?"

Jenny snorted at him and he laughed as she picked up her feet to trot, following along the stream bed. Father Murphy knew Elijah lived along this stream. In between the stream and the tall mountains that were rising up to his left, sat Elijah's stone cottage. A mighty dragon helped him to build it, or so the story went. He was sure he would come upon it soon.

He heard a flutter of large wings and, startled, looked to the sky again. It was a large pheasant taking wing, flushed out by Jenny's hooves. He chuckled at his wayward imagination. He was ashamed of his girlish fear. All these stories of demons and monsters, and well, he had just spooked himself without having realized it. Surely God, who had directed him in this endeavor, would shield him from harm. He had nothing to fear, but he whistled anyway, watching Jenny's ears twitch every time he hit a sour note.

Elijah met him out front. "Well, bless my soul, if it isn't Father Murphy. How long has it been, Father? Do come in, my friend."

Elijah led Jenny around back into his little barn. He had a donkey named Bonny and he put Jenny in with her and threw down a few pitchforks of hay for them both. Father Murphy took off Jenny's tack and bags and patted her rump as he followed Elijah out and into the house.

"I'm on my way to the Griffin Castle to bless their chapel. I thought to visit with your lady and Mary, but when I came upon the crossroads, God had other plans for me, or so it seemed."

Elijah motioned for Father to sit and poured them each an ale. He put out some bread and cheese and sat looking at his old friend, smiling. "Well, I wish your God would have told me of your coming. I would have caught us some nice fish for dinner."

Father Murphy opened his pack and put out the dried meat and cheese to add to Elijah's. "No, you are too kind as it is. I can't tell you how good it is to visit with you. I've just finished reading some of your scrolls on magic Glynnis had let me borrow. Had I known I was going to visit, I would have returned them myself."

Elijah raised his eyebrows at Father Murphy. "The scrolls on magic, you say? I didn't think the priesthood favored scrolls on magic. I knew Glynnis loves the subject, but it comes as a surprise to me that you would be interested in such matters."

Father Murphy looked a bit embarrassed. "I'm a teacher, Elijah. I have to keep an open mind even if it doesn't coincide with my faith. Knowledge of any kind is a good thing. Don't you agree?"

Elijah nodded in agreement.

"They weren't so much on magic, spells and curses and the like, as they were on the magical creatures. Glynnis has told me they've all gone away now. Would you know anything about that? I have to confess, I kept an eye towards the sky the whole time I entered the mountain area." He laughed a little at that and took a long drink of his draft.

Elijah sat back and took a drink of his own ale in response. "She tells you the truth. The magicals are gone. They've created a world of their own away from the humans who persecuted them. But I do see your point, Father, and you're right. You're welcome to any of my scrolls. Knowledge is nothing to hide. Now, I admit that I've written on many a subject, and the facts are only as good as the teller. Keep that in mind. I can't verify all the information and I have to admit a lot gets lost in the translations from one language to another. Sometimes just one word can make a world of difference and as careful as I am, some of the true meaning can be lost. It's a painful and laborious process. One too many sips of ale may have a profound effect as well." They both laughed easily at that.

Father Murphy chewed on a small piece of bread with cheese. "I understand. Yet, it is all we've got, isn't it? Tales told from one to another and then passed along. Glynnis is concerned the demons would overcome the population, and if the truth were known, I would tell you I'm concerned about one in my own order. I'm telling you, Elijah, in chapel this morning it looked as if this priest was wrapped in darkness. His temper and demeanor have been strangely menacing, and unfortunately it's directed at me for some reason. The fact that I'd visited your lady months ago for a cure for my back complaint started the whole thing."

He got up and began to pace, his arms were animated as he talked. "Well, I have prayed for a cure for the pain, Elijah, and who said God didn't direct me to Mistress Thatcher for the relief I needed? Now it's every move I make, every glance of my eyes. Each word I speak seems to be blasphemous all of a sudden. I hear he's going to the Bishop about it all. I tell you, I've never seen so much anger in this man before. Then I saw the strange darkness that surrounds and seems to follow him. Can it be true, Elijah? Can there be demons driving this man?"

Elijah sat up and stroked his chin. He supposed it was possible for a priest to contract a demon, especially if the priest wasn't secure in his faith. He could see how Father Murphy would be upset. Understanding that this was probably the crux of the matter for why Father Murphy had visited at all, he considered the problem, not wanting to be shallow or non-committal on the subject.

"Have you known this priest long, Father? Is he solid in his faith, or is he struggling with it?"

Father Murphy sat back down and shrugged. He took another drink and tried hard to give a truthful answer. "Who is to say who is solid in the faith? One day, I know my faith is so strong I feel it can never be shaken, then situations change and I wonder at God's intentions. The mind is a fickle thing, Elijah; it runs along the lines to suit itself. What is the truth one day may fall into question the next. I hope to say truthfully that my religion is secure. I always believed this questionable priest was true, but how can you live in the love of God and behave as he's doing? He thinks it is me who is the devil's pawn. He says I consort with pagan witches, poison my mind with blasphemous scrolls, and I am undertaking to bring down the church. All this is due to a simple powder for my tea to relieve the pain in my back." He looked down at the table darkly and shook his head. "I suppose after he's done with me, I'll be ex-communicated or worse, hung for a witch. They've hung several in the village already, for nonsense, if you ask me. I don't know what's motivating people lately, and yet they say this is all done in the name of God. It's wrong, Elijah. It's done out of envy or stupidity, but not in the favor of my God. I believe it's demons and they're so cunning they can make people believe they are avenging their religion when all they are doing is killing people who don't happen to act like they want them to, or do what they say, or believe in the same things they think they should believe in. Worse than that, they make up some offense, kill the person, and buy their lands. You could become very wealthy using this manner of execution. They use the fear in people's hearts to do it with, as well. I don't fear for myself as much as I fear for what they are doing to this priest. Now, I never warmed up to this man, it's true, but I never had anything against him either. He's a stern priest who would rather preach the wrath of God while I would rather preach God's love. We've always had different approaches to our priesthoods, but we could always agree on some common ground before, and now, well, now it seems as if even my existence is an abomination to him and his vengeful God."

Elijah watched Father Murphy very carefully. Sometimes people said more with their body than their words could ever reveal. But Elijah thought he was telling the truth, and was very disturbed over the whole situation. Murphy felt no disdain for this other priest, no wish for revenge; he was only puzzled as to why he had been singled out and punished so brutally by a fellow priest for consorting with a Druid. Well, that was nothing new or unusual either. It was prejudice, pure and simple, but the shadows he was seeing around this fellow priest concerned Elijah. That wasn't typical; and that, with the temperament change, could indicate a possession of some sort. He got up and refilled the tankards.

"I thought your order has ways of dealing with demons. It must be as obvious to everyone else as it is to you."

Father Murphy tipped his head to one side. "It's obvious I've upset this priest in some way, yes. The other priests seem to think he's just being himself. He's always been conservative and intolerant of other religions, so it's normal behavior for him except for the frequent outbursts directed at me or lashing out at one of the orphans. A few have mentioned their concern, yes, but I don't know if any have noticed the darkness that surrounds him."

Elijah ate some of the food in front of him. Swallowing, he said, "Do you fear for your life?"

Father Murphy pushed back his chair a bit and crossed his leg. A hand ran through his hair as he thought. "No. Not yet, at least. I don't like his manner towards me, but why would he want to kill me?"

Elijah cleared his throat. "Probably because you believe in magic. It has always been so, Father. All these centuries, magic has tempered the demons. Magic is a driving force to be reckoned with. Yes, they existed together, one in balance with the other, and now with the scales tipped, the demons will run rampant, destroying all memory of magic and the people who keep it alive in their beliefs. Without its influence, we are in for a dark time ahead. You are in very real danger, a man of your position. On one hand, you are devout in your faith and you still believe that magic is God's way of controlling the demons. On the other hand, demons will force you to choose. If they can make magic and those of you who believe in it more dangerous than the demons themselves, well then, they win." He threw up his hands for emphasis.

Father Murphy was having a hard time absorbing all this but he realized the outcome. "Then we all lose." He studied the backs of his hands, thinking, and trying to make sense out of it all. "My religion doesn't mention powers like that."

Elijah nodded. "I know, and that's why it's working. That's why the magicals were hunted down. If people would realize just what power is, just ability, nothing more."

Seeing the confused look on Father Murphy's face, he explained. "It's like a bird or a fish; a bird can fly while you cannot, just as a fish can breathe underwater while again, you can't. Now, some would say that was just what they were, but no one stops to see how miraculous that really is. The bird has the power to fly. Magicals can do different things, too. It's not so different. Dragons can transcend time, heal, mind speak and a bevy of other wondrous things. It's what they are. Besides, they can fly too."

He smiled a little at that and went on. "Unicorns are marvelous healers and give gifts to those who they deem worthy. Griffins can camouflage themselves so that they are just about invisible. Can you see what I'm saying? These are not demonic qualities. Magic has never, nor will ever be evil; it's just a trait. We were lucky to have them with us, as we are lucky to have fresh air and clean water, but I bet in the future we will abuse that privilege as well, to the point that we will kill ourselves. Greed, stupidity, envy, intolerance, well, they are all demonic. The magicals gave us light and love, beauty and hope. The demons will give us nothing but doubt, hate, darkness, and death. It'll be a world out of balance and it will spin out of control."

Father Murphy folded his hands as if in prayer. "What can we do, Elijah?"

Elijah drank. He set down the tankard. "I don't know, and that's the truth. Pray to your God and I'll pray to mine. We have nothing to defend ourselves with. Well, almost nothing," he added under his breath. It almost came out as a whisper, but Father Murphy caught the phrase and jumped on it like a cat on a mouse.

"What's that you say, Elijah? What have we got to defend against demons?"

Elijah shook his head. "I misspoke. Ah, nothing, really. The stuff of legends, is all. Nothing." He got up and brought out a blanket stuffed with hay and put it before the fire.

"You will stay the night, Father? I can't let you get lost in these mountains at night, and I daresay Jenny is sound asleep with Bonny by now. If I know that mule, and I do, she'll kick the religion out of you should you try to rouse her now." He grinned at that, but Father Murphy would not let the other subject go.

"I'm grateful, Elijah, to spend the night, as is Jenny, I'm sure. But what of this legend you have? Now, you know you can't say a thing like that and drop it as quick. If it is nothing, then tell me the legend and let me decide for myself."

Elijah put another wool blanket on top of the stuffed one on the floor. He took his seat again and sighed heavily. He knew he had said too much, but this Father wasn't stupid, not by a long shot, and he was Elijah's friend.

"Alright, Father, but you must treat this like the confessional."

The sun had set and Elijah lit the candles in the house with a splinter of wood from the fireplace, which he had stoked and placed several more logs on. The fire crackled and they could hear the sounds of the night. It reminded Father Murphy of old ghost stories the adults would tell the children around the fire and watch their eyes grow large. He waited patiently as Elijah finished his tasks. He refilled the tankards and placed more cheese and a few apples on the table. He refilled the bread and brought out some mountain honey. He sat back down and eating an apple stared into the fire as if it were the window to the world. Father Murphy dipped the bread into the sweet honey and savored the taste. He wasn't sure what Elijah would tell him, but Lord knew he was a patient man and with a jar of honey in front of him, well, he could wait forever. An owl hooted its bone-chilling call from up on the top of a mountain pine. It called eight times before Elijah started his story.

"It was back when the world was new. Good and evil balanced each other out, as the earth, air, water, and fire complimented and nourished each other. So did the magicals and the demons. Now, this is transcribed from dozens of accounts in all different languages, you understand, and I'm not claiming it's the God's honest facts, either. It's just what I know to be written, and in so many languages it has to make you wonder."

Father Murphy nodded eagerly, his hands now folded as one of his students might have done at one of his own lectures.

"Everything was fine until man came along. Now, be it your origins or ours, or anyone else's, it really doesn't matter to the legend. With the coming of man, the magicals and demons had something to wager on, something to compete with, and basically, something to do with their powers. So the battle began. At first it was harmless. The humans were so easily influenced and your God and ours, I guess, found the whole thing amusing. No one was being hurt and it gave everyone something to do, kept them busy, and gave them reasons to learn about each other and how to live in some kind of harmony. The humans grew in intelligence and began to realize they were being manipulated. They found that they didn't like it at all. They turned away from the Gods, the magicals, and the demons, but could not survive on their own, not being in balance with the universe. The humans needed the positive effects of the magicals, the sobering effects of the demons and the Gods to bless them with crops, weather, game, shelters and so forth. Then they learned to manipulate the magicals and demons to play against each other and get what they needed. When the Gods were insulted, they would punish them along with the magicals and demons alike. They would set up altars to their favorites and play the Gods against each other, as well. Not too different from what happens in our day, no?"

Father Murphy was listening to him intently, on the edge of the chair, the candle flame reflecting in his eyes and making light dance across his face. His head was propped up on his fists, now.

Elijah nodded and continued, "The demons, being what they are, found ways of impersonating the magicals and made the humans believe the magicals were the cause of a lot of their strife. The changeling demons could turn into anything they imagined, much like the dragons could and after awhile, no one trusted anyone. The humans who had the darker natures sided with the demons and the others went with the magicals. Under the demon influence, people began to kill each other, infuriating the Gods. In answer to that, the good people struck back and so on it went. One priest who had sided with the magicals had his whole family killed by demons and they intended on killing him as well. He was a powerful priest with a lot of influence and was converting the demonic people to repent and join his group. Since he was so unsure of who was whom, with the changelings, one evening he tried to kill a dragon who he thought for sure was a changeling. Once he was convinced that it was a magical he had almost killed, the dragon took him under his wing. They forged a dagger that could tell the difference between the magicals and the demons using magic. This priest worked long and hard with the magicals to charge the dagger, made of steel and obsidian, the sharpest material known to man, to be able to tell a demon in disguise. It took all of the magicals and dragon fire to seal in the spells. It had a cross of Obsidian as its hilt."

Father Murphy sat up in surprise. "Excuse me, Elijah, did you say a cross? Do you mean like the Christian cross or just a crossed piece of obsidian?"

Elijah showed him with his hands. "It was a cross that looks just like your Christian cross, out of black shiny obsidian. The elves made a wooden box for it to be kept in and carved a cross into the top of it. It is said that all demons would recognize this dagger and in turn, the dagger recognized who the real demons were. The dagger could never be used to kill a person or a magical. It would only kill demons, and kill them so deftly that no matter what they did, they couldn't escape the blade. It is said that the dagger actually sings when it sees a demon and will turn away from anything else. From what was written many years later, it was used to put the demons back under the control of the magicals, allowing the world to thrive once more. knowing the dagger existed made the demons respect the humans. It was passed down from one priest to another. It never tarnishes or rusts and the wavy blade never grows dull, but stays as sharp as the obsidian it's coated with. Only dragon fire could have done that as obsidian is a volcanic glass of sorts. Extremely rare, hard and sharp."

Father Murphy sat back and folded his arms. It grew quiet in the little cottage and when the owl hooted again, the good Father jumped, causing both men to laugh.

"Imagine that. A dagger that knows its enemy. What a marvelous legend, and if only it were true."

Elijah raised his head at that. "What makes you think that it isn't?"

Father Murphy waved a hand. "Oh, well, you know, forged by dragons and a singing blade that knows who is a demon? It would be a wondrous dagger, to be sure. I guess I think it too good to be true."

Elijah nodded, smiling now. He knew by watching the priest's face he had hung on every word of the story. "It is true, you know. This much I can verify."

Father Murphy laughed. "Aye? And how can you verify a story so old and strange, other than the writings you have, of course. But as you say, a writing is only as good as the person transcribing it and the information they've been given. Why, who knows? It might be a tale born out of a tankard or two of ale."

Elijah got up and rummaged around in his desk. "True enough. I did say that, but..." He slammed a wooden box down on the table in front of Father Murphy. "When you have the actual artifact, the story bears believing, does it not?"

Father Murphy had backed up his chair and stared in awe at the wooden box with the cross deeply engraved on the top. It was carved in the image of the Christian cross and its lid was carved to fit snuggly into its bottom. He looked from the box to Elijah and back again, speechless.

Elijah laughed. "Go ahead, have a look at it. It won't bite you, that is, unless you are a demon."

Father Murphy's hands shook as he touched the box. It felt warm as if it were giving off heat of its own. He looked at Elijah again. Elijah sat back down and put his hand on the box too.

"Yes, I know. It radiates heat all the time, even in winter. Sometimes I even slept with it." He chuckled at that. "I don't know why. It was never said why it generated heat, unless it's the heat of the dragon fire that remains for all time. After all, dragon fire is the hottest fire known on Earth."

Father Murphy carefully opened the box and gasped at the beautiful dagger. It shone as if it was newly made, and it was every bit the Demon Dagger that Elijah had described.

"It shines with the light of God," he said, before he could catch himself. He knew Elijah was a Druid and didn't mean to offend him, but it did have a glow about it. He raised it up by the hilt, feeling as if it gave him power by just holding it. It was expertly made

and perfectly balanced. To actually hold it in his hands was a wonder to him. The blade was as sharp as if it was just honed, and he
was cautious as he looked at it. He put it back gently in the box.

"To see such a thing with your own eyes, Elijah. How did you
come upon it?"

Elijah frowned. "It was a long time ago. I was leading Bonny
back from the marketplace in the village. I came upon an old priest
on a pilgrimage up in the mountains. He was dying and bade me to
take the box and to care for it until a priest came for it. Since it was
his dying wish, I did as he asked. I stayed with him until he entered
his kingdom of the spirits and I buried him up in the mountains. I
guess you must be the priest this was meant for, since you asked for
it." He pushed the box over to Father Murphy., who just stared at
it.

"But I didn't ask for it, Elijah. I didn't even know it existed. I
couldn't take this."

Elijah patted the priest's hand. "I can think of no other priest
that's more worthy of a blade like this, and you did ask about it,
even if you didn't know what it was you were asking for. You came
to me about a demon problem, did you not? Here is your answer.
Carry it well and it will serve you. I feel in my heart that it should
go to you. When you take it, then I have fulfilled my promise to
that dying priest, and you are the only priest that talks to me, you
know. Who else could it be meant for? Now, you've had a long
journey today and you have another to go on tomorrow. Why
don't you stretch out and rest and I will do the same."

Elijah packed up the rest of the food and stored it, then seeing
Farther Murphy stretch out on the blankets in front of the fire,
climbed into his own bed and before long, both men were fast
asleep. The box with the Demon Dagger remained on the table,
giving out its own heat as if it were alive.

When Father Murphy awoke the next morning, he saw Elijah
fitting the Demon Dagger into a sheath. It had not been made for
the dagger, but it did fit in there well. Elijah had put scrolls in the
box that it had come in for Father Murphy to take with him.

"They are copies that I've made of some local lore I thought you
might enjoy reading. The dagger you should wear in case you come
upon bandits in the woods. It would be no great loss to have the

scrolls stolen or the box, even if it was made by elves, but to lose the dagger I feel in your words, would be a sin."

Father Murphy washed at the stream and when he got back to the cottage he strapped the dagger under his robes at his waist. He could feel the warmth immediately. It felt as if he had always worn it, even though he had never carried a weapon in his life. He wondered what Father Johns would say if he knew. A witch blade, to be sure, but he wouldn't trade it for the world. Besides, what witch blade would sport a Christian cross? No, Elijah had been right all along. It was meant for him to have. First, the change of direction for him, and now this. God had brought him there and now had given him a weapon to use in case of demons. It would only kill demons, so he couldn't use it for anything else except as Elijah had, a bed warmer.

They loaded the packs back onto Jenny and Bonny complained that her stablemate had to leave. Father Murphy embraced Elijah and thanked him. He took a letter for Glynnis that Elijah had written that morning. He blessed the Druid as he left and watched Elijah smile and laugh at that. It was a force of habit, and as Elijah said, blessings from any God were always welcome.

CHAPTER SEVEN

Father Johns stood outside the door to the Bishop's office, pacing furiously. He was a man on a mission. There were some things that could not go unpunished, and not having the authority himself to put things right, he would have to seek help from the Bishop. He had about all of the backsliding he could take from Father Murphy and now something needed to be done about it immediately, before he managed to corrupt the entire order. Someone would have to take charge and he put himself into that position, seeing that no one else had the fortitude to step up and demand that this malignancy be cut from the fold. Members of the clergy averted their eyes as they passed Father Johns. The man had so much anger that it permeated the very air surrounding him. There was a chair for him to sit and wait on his Holiness, but he found that he didn't have the patience to sit for one moment. Surely the Bishop would see things his way and save them all from the plague of the good Father Murphy.

The door cracked open and Father Santini, the Bishop's personal attendant stepped out and closed the door quietly behind him. Father Johns looked at him expectantly. Father Santini cleared his throat.

"I'm afraid a small matter has come before the Bishop. It will be only a short delay, Father Johns. Perhaps you might take some refreshment in our dining area? I will come and get you when the Bishop is free to see you."

Father Johns huffed with impatience. "I'm afraid I am on a mission of some urgency, Father Santini. This matter is of grave importance to our order. If you could convey that information to his Holiness, perhaps..." His voice trailed off as he saw the complacent look Father Santini gave him.

Father Santini could see the exasperation on Father Johns' face. Every priest had a matter of grave importance to take up with the Bishop and this priest was no different, although he did look quite disturbed and he did give Father Santini a foreboding feeling. There was something dark and unnatural about Father Johns today. He had never noticed it before, although he had known the good Father to be a man of conviction and of strong will.

"I understand, Father Johns. I assure you, your problem will be dealt with as soon as it is possible. As you know, the Bishop is a very busy man. Wouldn't you like to take a seat and rest? Or perhaps I could take you to our chapel and you could clear your mind and pray while you wait?"

Father Johns took the seat by the door and then got back up and continued his pacing. Father Santini, seeing that it was of no use trying to make Father Johns comfortable, walked past him and went back to his errands. He nodded to Father Johns before he left.

The sun had risen high in the sky before Father Johns had been ushered into the Bishops office. Bishop Kelly was a rotund man with a rubicund face and a passion for sweets. He had brushed off the crumbs of a cake he had just enjoyed and, swallowing, indicated to Father Johns to sit. He wore a robe of fine white cloth with fine embroidery, and a cap to match. His gold cross hung about his neck.

"It is good to see you, Father Johns. Father Santini tells me you are here on a matter of some urgency. Please sit and tell me what this is all about."

Father Johns sat and the blood rushed to his face as he explained what he considered a catastrophe to the Bishop. He shook with nerves and had worked himself up into a state the longer he had to wait. The Bishop had taken all this in as he watched the man and wondered what could have affected the man to cause this condition.

"It's Father Murphy. I understand he is well known to you, your Holiness, but he must be excommunicated as soon as you can possibly manage it." He nodded once to emphasize his point.

The Bishop raised his eyebrows in question. He indeed knew Father Murphy very well and was very fond of the priest. He found him to be of delightful character and could not imagine what Father Johns was talking about. He had come in and thrown down a gauntlet without any reasons at all. He sat there for a moment, waiting for Father Johns to continue with some explanation, but he didn't. The two priests just stared at each other. The Bishop sat back and folded his arms, studying Father Johns carefully. There was a strange cast about him, and Bishop Kelly wondered if he had caused it himself, as he was certainly upset.

"I see. You think I should excommunicate Father Murphy with all speed. Is that right?"

Father Johns nodded emphatically.

Bishop Kelly gave him a wry smile. "I am not in the habit of excommunicating my priests on the word of just one priest. Exactly what grievous sins has Father Murphy committed to deserve this banishment? I would need reasons and proof that he has neglected his duties, or committed some crime, Father Johns. Surely you understand that."

Father Johns sputtered. "Yes, your Holiness, ah, of course. It's that I've been so concerned, you understand. It's an abomination, is what it is. Father Murphy continues to associate with the pagan witch of the woods and you know no good will come of that, I can promise you. And, he's been reading satanic scrolls. I saw them myself on his desk, from the other pagan recluse. I shudder to think what he has been teaching and he should be removed from the classes with all speed. Then, there was a time when the king's guards were searching the church for a run-away witch they were going to hang, and while she never was found, I thought I heard laughter from his room. Well, he denied that, of course, but still the fact remains that I did indeed hear it. He's often missing from meals and late to his devotions. He takes the potions this witch conjures up, too. I've seen him put it in his tea. He's off right now to Griffin's castle, and I would bet a week's worth of offerings that he's consorting with that devil's concubine instead." He gave the Bishop a wild look and Bishop Kelly became concerned.

"Let me see if I can make any sense out of all this for you. I know of the woman of which you speak. She is a Druid, one of the oldest families around these parts, as a matter of fact. I cannot dispute that she is pagan, but she's also the best healer we have in these parts. She's well known and trusted by many in the village. I do know Father Murphy suffered an arrow wound in the back when he was younger and was trying to get the village children into the church to protect them from a Saxon attack, many years ago. He still suffers today from that injury and I do not find it unusual that he seeks out a healer for medicine, which I'm sure was what he was taking in his tea. She has visited here on occasion and she's a lovely, respectful woman with a gift for her trade. I believe she cured me once of a spotted fever and I am thankful for that. Now, as far as these scrolls, I know of a scholar up in the mountains who is very educated. I have called upon him, as well, to translate documents when the need arises. Father Murphy is an avid teacher and he loves to read. He's a bit of a scholar himself. I don't know the context of the scrolls, so unless you happen to have them with you, who is to say they are of a demonic nature? I think, Father Johns, you are taking things in the wrong context. I know Father Murphy and he is lighthearted, not your average solemn priest, but I find it hard to believe he has committed sins against the church. Unless you have undisputed evidence that there have been sins committed against the church, I would advise you to pray on the matter and find it in your heart to forgive what you consider to be his sins. I will not excommunicate one of my finest priests. I will talk with him when he returns. I will not have him removed from his classes. I think you should return to your order and concentrate your efforts to the love of God and not waste time finding fault with your fellow priests. God knows every man's heart, Father Johns, and it is all in His hands. I will pray that he grants you peace in your heart and allows you to see Father Murphy in his true light."

Father Santini, who had been writing behind a desk in the corner, jumped up to show Father Johns the door. Seeing the Father out, he turned to smile at the Bishop.

"I believe that was your last visitor, your Holiness, would you like to retire to your chambers for awhile?"

Bishop Kelly sat, unmoving, in his chair. Distractedly he said, "What did you make out of all that, Father Santini? I have never seen Father Johns in a state like that. Do we have a rogue priest on our hands?"

Father Santini came over and sat across from the Bishop. "I agree. I know both of the Fathers. It is true that Father Murphy is a bit unorthodox, but he teaches the children and they love him. I guess because his heart is as light and as full of mischief as theirs is, but I don't believe a word that Father Johns is saying. I mean, I do believe that he believes it, but I can't imagine why. I do know he's like a kettle about to boil over, if that is what you mean. I would be more concerned about him than I would Father Murphy." The Bishop nodded sadly in agreement.

Father Johns walked the few blocks around the church, heading back to the rectory. He didn't realize he had even walked the distance as his blood was pounding in his ears and he felt as if he were going to explode. Both of his hands were clenched in fists. The only conclusion he could come up with was that the Bishop had been bewitched. Hadn't he said the witch had healed him, as well? The doubtlet's poison now ran through every cell in his body. He knew he was right. He was thinking clearly and his feet fell heavily on the dirt road. He would have to handle things, himself.

He stormed under the archway into the corridor. Father Murphy's room was the first one on the right, and he pushed open the door and stomped inside, closing the door behind him. It was a simple, humble room with a cot and a desk. A wooden cross hung on the wall. A small chest sat in the corner and he opened it. Rifling through it, he found only the folded robes of the priest. He slammed the lid shut and sat down at Father Murphy's desk. He examined every scrap of parchment and every book but found nothing that was out of the ordinary. There were prayers and some school records on the children in his class. There were quills and a pot of ink. He sat back, disgusted that there was nothing he could use to prove Murphy's guilt. The room was tidier than his own. A half melted candle stood on a stone base next to a carved statue of Our Lady. He stared at it menacingly, scrutinizing it for any deviation from the similar statue in his room, but there was none. They had been gifts to the priests from one of the villagers, a carver named Bartholomew. He implored the walls to talk, to tell him what perversions had taken place in this very room, but the walls were silent, cold and unrevealing. He picked at the droplets of wax that were frozen on the candle and closed his eyes. He could hear them laughing. A woman's laugh, lilting and sensual. He could see the candle lit and the woman in Father Murphy's arms, kissing him and removing his cross. Their shadows wavering in the candlelight as his vows were broken. Father Johns squeezed his eyes tighter as he sat there, a silent witness to the weakness of the flesh.

As the door was pushed open, he jumped up. Suddenly, he was back in the vacant simple room with the sunlight streaming through the two slit windows. A very perplexed Michael stood there with an armful of clean robes for Father Murphy.

"I'm sorry, Father Johns, I didn't realize that anyone was in here. Father Murphy is off to Griffin Castle and well, I thought I'd bring in his robes from the laundry and put them on his bed."

Father Johns wiped beads of sweat from his face and made for the door. "That's fine, Michael. Carry on. You startled me, that's all. I was bringing in some parchments for Father Murphy and sat down for a moment to rest."

Michael placed the robes on Father Murphy's cot and turned to look at Father Johns. His face was beet red and he was sweating, even though the room was cool. "Are you feeling well, Father Johns? Is there anything that I can do for you?"

Father Johns looked indignantly at the young man. How dare he assume that there was something wrong with him? "Of course I'm well. Don't you think you should be on your way to class? I imagine the good Father Murphy has left you in charge again while he gallivants across the territories?"

Michael went to the door, opened it and went through. "Yes, Father." He did not want to be on the receiving end of Father John's wrath. Everyone had noticed that he'd been acting very peculiar lately and it was best to avoid him completely. He wondered what he'd been doing in Father Murphy's cubicle to begin with. Everyone was aware that there was a riff between the two priests, and he hadn't seen the parchments that Father Johns had said he had brought in.

* * *

Greccon jumped back out of the way of the large horses bringing in Lord McTavish's furnishings into the castle. It was noisy and
boisterous with everyone talking and shouting. The dust flew and
the horses snorted as they sidestepped to avoid running into him.
Meg, the lord's elderly cook, grabbed him by the back of his tunic.

"Aye, Greccon, it's a busy day, isn't it? Why don't you find
something to explore out of the way of these horses. Your father
will have my hide if you get trampled now. I'm afraid he's going
to be delayed a day or so. Aye, that's what I heard." She nodded at
Greccon's crestfallen look. She went on, "It seems the weather has
turned foul to the north of here and it'll be another day until he
gets back. Run on now, there's a good lad, and come see me later.
If they get my pots and pans in, I'll cook you up something good
for supper, I will." She gave him a playful slap on the bottom and
he ran off.

He decided to check out the towers. They were the only parts
of the castle that weren't choked with people trying to move in
furnishings. He chose the east tower and began the long climb up to
the top. He thought he might have a good view of the land from up
there. He was disappointed that his father would be late in arriving.
That meant another day of putting up with Meg fussing over him.
She had been left in charge until Killwyn returned, and that ensured
tolerating more baths than he would like and an earlier bedtime
than he was used to. His father had gone to see his Uncle Mirwyn,
another wizard of great renown, and he had begged his father to
take him but time would not allow that, his father had told him.
He had wanted to be back in time for the move, but it didn't look
likely now. By tomorrow, everyone would be settling in already.

The tower stood tall and silent, towards the back of the castle
grounds. Entering the dark archway, he could see the steps went
up in a winding manner. He had started out taking two steps at a
time and found that he was getting pretty tired, so he slowed his
pace, careful of all the debris that had blown in through the cut
out windows in the tower walls. There must be years of leaves and
dirt, he thought. It was a long climb and a lot of the sections were
dark. The higher he climbed, the more his footsteps echoed in the
hollow structure. He imagined prisoners being led up here and kept
until they died. He worried a little about ghosts, and that slowed

him down just a bit more. He groaned when he finally reached the top and he came upon a heavy wooden door with a huge lock. He couldn't believe he had traveled this far up the tower to find the top secured against visitors. He reached out and jiggled the lock and it crumbled in his hand. He grunted as he lifted the solid wood bar and put it to the side. The door creaked open on rusty hinges, making a deafening squealing noise and he pushed it wider.

It was an empty room with small slit windows. They were large enough to let the air in, but too small, even for him, to climb through. He had to pull himself up to look out of them. It was like being on top of the world. The breeze was cool and birds flew by right next to the tower. The ocean was on this side and he looked out over the choppy waves. He ran to the other side and these windows showed the woods and fields in the distance. He could not see Mistress Thatcher's house, even though he was sure he was looking in the right direction. He tried to pull himself up higher, but his hands gave away on the debris on the window sill and he fell back, catching himself with his hands, but landing hard on his bottom. He sat there for a moment, looking around, and he felt a strange sensation, almost dizziness, and he rubbed his face. *I just bounced too hard*, he thought, and sat and waited for it to pass. His vision was a little blurry, but only when he looked to the ocean window. It cleared back up when he looked away. It was like a mist, or no, it was like heat on a black rock, he thought. Like a mirage that his father had told him they had in the desert. Heat waves from the sun, he called them. But it wasn't hot in there and the sun wasn't beating down in that section of the room at all.

He turned around, still on his bottom, and just stared at it. Maybe it was a real ghost. He studied it carefully. Everything was logical, or so his father had told him. It really didn't look like what he thought a ghost should look like. For one thing, it was shimmery, and it looked like a wall of tiny colors coming up from the floor. He was sure ghosts would float and have some human form. It made no noise, no groans or moans that ghosts were supposed to make and it didn't move around, either. It reminded him of a curtain or tapestry just hung in space.

He stood up and rubbed his behind and brushed off the dirt and leaves from his tunic. He took one tentative step towards it and stopped to see what it would do. It did nothing. He took another step, watching it carefully. He put out a hand to see if he could touch it and his hand seemed to go through it and vanish. Pulling it quickly back, he ran all the information through his mind. It was a portal, he thought, a gate to another place. Did he dare go through? His father had spoken of these; they were gateways to another place made by magicals. He stood there for a long moment, wondering where it led and if he did enter through it, where he would be and would he be able to return? He tried to use his foresight, but it never seemed to work on him. It always worked when other people were concerned, but never when it was just his future he was wondering about. He took several deep breaths.

The smart thing to do was to go back down and forget about all of this, his conscience told him. But what if someone else goes through it by mistake, not knowing it was there? The job of the court wizard was to handle all magical problems that came up. Well, his father wouldn't be back for a day or so, which made him in charge. It was his duty to check this thing out and make sure it was safe. What if it was the lord that passed through it and couldn't get back? That would mean trouble for all of them. Well, there was just no help for it. He took another breath and closed his eyes as he walked through the gate.

His eyes opened wide when he crossed over. He was standing in a green field of beautiful wildflowers. He turned around quickly to make sure the gate was still there. It was. He sighed in relief and studied the surroundings so he would know how to get back. He put another hand through just to make sure, and yes, the tower was still there. Satisfied, he took a few steps through the fresh smelling field. He looked up to the sky, dotted with fluffy white clouds and spotted a form heading right towards him. He froze where he stood, when a large griffin landed in front of him. He had never seen a real griffin, although he had heard about them, and his mouth dropped open. The griffin gave him a menacing look and drew even closer.

"Who are you and what are you doing here? Speak up, boy, before you lose your head."

Greccon managed a bow. "I am known as Greccon the Fair. I guess I passed through your gate. On the other side of it is our east tower. I was up there and I saw a shimmering light, so I walked through it."

He gulped audibly as a dragon was landing behind the griffin. He lost all the color in his face and he felt like he was going to pass out. He sat down abruptly and covered his eyes, as a cloud of dust accompanied the dragon's landing. He peeked through his hands, shaking now. The dragon walked up next to the griffin.

"What is the meaning of this, Reaper? How did he get through the gate?"

Reaper looked at the quivering boy and turned back to Oberon and shrugged. "I don't know. He said his name is Greccon and he just walked through the gate from the other side, or so he says. I thought we had enough spells on it to prevent this very thing, but it looks as if he got through. He's only a boy."

Oberon snorted. "I can see that. You. Boy. You say you just walked through?"

Greccon got to his feet, still wide-eyed and frightened. "Yes, Sir, er, Ma'am, er Mighty Dragon. Where am I?"

Oberon lowered his head to get a better look at the child and flicked out his tongue, just for effect. The boy backed up a bit.

"I am King Oberon, my dear Greccon. You have arrived in the Magical Realm, although I don't know how, but I intend to find out." He stared at the boy for a moment and then chuckled a bit, making Reaper look at him questioningly. Oberon sat back and rubbed his chin.

"Well, of course he passed through, Reaper. He's a magical. Can't you feel it? Greccon, do you have any magicians in your family?"

Greccon nodded avidly because it looked as if he were not to be consumed by these creatures after all. "Yes, my Lord, my father is the wizard of Griffin Castle. My uncle, Mirwyn, is also a magician. I am one, too, although I'm still in training and have a lot to learn, as you can see."

Oberon laughed now, and not sure what to do with the boy, decided he had better have a talk with him and convince him not to use the gate again, even though he could.

"Come on then, young wizard. Climb aboard and I will take you to my castle. It's alright, Reaper, I'll handle this."

Reaper nodded and flew off, leaving the dragon and the boy

behind. Greccon could hardly walk as his legs were shaking out of control.

He said sadly, "Am I to be your prisoner, my Lord?"

Oberon laughed louder. "My prisoner? I hardly think so. What I'm hoping for is that we could become good friends. I want to talk with you and then I'll bring you back to the gate to return to your home. The only reason you passed through the gate was your magic. If you didn't have any magic, you could have never seen or crossed through the gate. I admit I never thought I'd have to worry about humans getting through, but you are a welcome part of my Realm, young Greccon, so we might as well get to know one another. I've just completely forgotten about the wizards. If you have magic, and I know you do, well then, you are a subject of my Realm, too."

Oberon lowered himself and Greccon climbed on. Oberon told him how to hold on and to mind the wings, and the next thing Greccon knew was that he was flying through the air. He couldn't believe it. Had he fallen hard from the window and hit his head? He didn't think so, but he couldn't believe that all this was happening, either. The wind swept his hair back and he saw the castle in the distance, and in the fields he saw a herd of unicorns. He turned his head to see them better, and there were griffins and Pegasus. He held onto the shiny scales and watched the huge wings rise and fall. He was riding the King Dragon of the Magical Realm. He couldn't believe it. Tightening his grip as they landed, he saw the same griffin that had threatened to cut off his head bent over, facing a baby unicorn.

He dismounted as quickly as he could and ran at the griffin, throwing himself upon him and shouting, "No. You can't kill a unicorn."

Reaper grabbed the back of his tunic in his beak and shook him a number of times before dropping him roughly on the ground.

"Young fool. Griffins don't eat unicorns. Now, pick yourself up and turn around and pay the proper respect to Illustra, Queen of the Unicorns." He gestured at the small filly standing there, looking a little startled.

Greccon stood up and turned around quickly. "Queen? But, but, you're just a.. ah,.." He saw her staring at him with amused eyes, eyes that were amazingly clear and intelligent.

"I beg your pardon, I am Greccon, at your service, my Queen."

Oberon nodded with approval and Reaper turned his head to keep from laughing at the bewildered expression on Greccon's face. Illustra gave him a nod.

"Thank you, Greccon, and I am pleased to have you at my service. One so young, noble, and brave enough to take on a griffin to rescue me, will not be forgotten."

Reaper snorted. "One foolish enough to try and take on a griffin should not be alive long enough to be remembered. You have a lot to learn, young wizard, but I forgive you for your intentions were honorable, even if they were stupid. I was merely having a conversation with the young queen when you so rudely interrupted us."

Greccon reddened. He did feel stupid. How many times had his father told him to observe the situation before reacting?

"I'm so sorry. You're right, I am stupid and I have a lot to learn." He dropped his head in embarrassment.

Oberon nodded. "Reaper, could you be so kind as to show this young wizard, Greccon, where he can freshen up and get him something to eat? If I remember my lessons, boys of this age are perpetually hungry. Then bring him to me in my chambers when he's through."

He turned to Illustra. "Well, my dear, it looks as if you've acquired a knight in shining armor already, even if he's a bit on the short side right now."

Illustra bobbed her head. "Yes, my Lord, but I hope he will grow up with me. His heart is so very pure." She said as they watched them enter the castle, "I like him, my King. Can we keep him?"

Oberon shook his head. "No, I'm afraid not. He just stumbled in here and he will be missed in his world. He is a magical, though, and since I have plans for him, I'm sure you will see him again. Now, if you will grant me leave, my Lady, I must go to my chambers."

Illustra tossed her head and pranced away. Oberon looked after her, watching all those shining white curls bouncing as she pranced. She was such a vision. Even the boy, once he took a careful look at her, knew her to be the queen, even if she was still a foal. There wasn't anything juvenile about her eyes and the wisdom there.

A short while later, Reaper entered the royal chamber with Greccon running to keep up with him. With one claw, he dragged a chair out from the wall. Then, gripping the boy's collar with his beak, gently this time, sat him down in front of Oberon.

"The boy wizard, Greccon, as you requested, my Lord."

Oberon nodded to him and Reaper left, closing the chamber door behind him. Greccon breathed a sigh of relief when the griffin was gone. Oberon tried not to laugh at him. He could see the boy was having a terrifying day.

"You don't have to be afraid, Greccon. No one will hurt you here unless I tell them to. You're quite safe, really. Now, you have had enough to eat and drink, and you have attended to yourself, I presume? Are you quite comfortable now?"

Seeing the boy bobbing his head like a duck, he went on. "I have a need for a guardian of the gate in your world, Greccon, and since you already know about it, I think you would work out well. I have Reaper on this side, and I'm sure you'll admit that he does a good job. Yes? Now, all I would need for you to do is to keep it a secret. Just between you and us. I would need to know if the tower is to be used to contain prisoners. I know children seem to know everything that's going on, not so much from intelligence, but from being in the right places and being unobserved. No one pays attention to children very much, but they should, don't you think? Right. Now, I'm going to teach you a magic sign that will let you transfer your thoughts directly into mine. That way you can call me and talk to me, and I can talk back. We'll be able to talk back and forth using just thoughts, not words. Has your father taught you that yet? No? Well then, I will. Now, you only call to me when you have something very important to tell me or if you are in mortal danger. I don't have a lot of time for idle conversation, you understand. What has your father taught you already?"

Greccon swallowed. "Well, my Lord, he has taught me to make fire and to put up a protection barrier so I won't get arrows through me in a raid. He really isn't around much. I can tell the future, on my own. He never taught me that, I can just do it naturally, but I can't seem to be able to tell my own future. I guess I'm not much of a wizard yet, but I'll be happy to help you protect the gate. Can I ever come back?"

Oberon put up one claw. "Only if I summon you, or if you have a desperate need to come back. Then you can ask me with your mind like I'll teach you. Do you understand?"

Greccon nodded. "Yes, my Lord. Do the magicals come into my world?"

Oberon nodded. "Yes, from time to time, they do. That's why I need to know if there is anyone in the tower at any given time. You seemed to have come through backwards. When we use it, we end up out over the ocean and no one will see us. The gate extends to the ground so the unicorns can use it too, but they end up on a sandy beach on the back side of the tower and then they go straight into the woods. They like to visit from time to time. They get lonely for the humans, although it was the humans that drove them away. Almost all of the magical creatures of the Light Magics are here now. Oh, you have a few elementals and fairies, a few wood sprites to keep everything growing, but they do it for the Earth, not the humans."

The boy sat there, his eyes riveted on the king. Some small part of his mind was telling him he was dreaming, or passed out on the tower's flagstone floor, but it felt so real. Sure, he could keep it a secret because no one would believe him anyway. He knew the townspeople had claimed to see these creatures, even sold claws and horns, but he didn't really believe them, until right now. He watched carefully as Oberon instructed which sign to make to talk with him and they practiced it a few times so they both knew what it would sound like in their head. Satisfied, Oberon showed him one more sign and then watched him mimic it back at him. It was a sign to call the fairies. He could do this if he was ever alone in the woods and wanted a bit of company. They were charming creatures, full of fun, and they loved to talk and ask questions, especially of children.

Greccon smiled at this. He had a few friends, but he always felt odd around the other children. He would enjoy visiting with the fairies. He wished with all his might that this was real; he wanted it so badly to really be happening. He was so afraid he was dreaming and he would wake up and watch it all fade away and then not be able to remember it afterwards. He practiced the hand signs again so, even if he was dreaming, he could at least try them and see if they worked anyway. Oberon felt some compassion for the boy.

"You can believe in all this, Greccon, it is really happening; you are not dreaming. Now, I will have Reaper take you back to the gate. It was a pleasure to meet you, Greccon."

Greccon bowed low. "I am ever at your service, King Oberon."

Oberon sat back up and mind-called Reaper. "And so you shall be, Wizard Greccon. I'm counting on it."

Reaper led him back out into the courtyard, where he saw some elves sitting around the fountain. He had seen them in the dining area as well. One little girl with emerald green eyes blew him a kiss, then giggled as he blushed. Reaper ordered him to get on and hold on to the fur, not the feathers. First a ride on a dragon, then a ride back on a griffin. Oh, he had to be dreaming. The griffin's flight seemed smoother and faster than the dragon's and he told Reaper so. Reaper told him never to tell that to Oberon; he was a little sensitive about that. He landed at the gate and gave Greccon a nod.

"It was nice to meet you, young wizard. I'm sorry if I frightened you. It's my job, you understand. No hard feelings?"

Greccon shook his head and held out his hand. He wasn't sure if you should shake a griffin's foot or not, but he thought he'd make the gesture. The griffin grabbed it faster than he thought he would and shook it. Greccon smiled, took a deep breath, and walked through the translucent curtain back into the real world of his own.

Reaper remained on his side of the portal and waited, humming to himself. He saw the small hand pass back through the gate again and he reached out and touched it with his claw. It pulled back quickly. Reaper laughed to himself and signaled to Oberon that it was nothing, just the boy trying the gate again like he knew he would. That's a boy for you. He shook his head and took off.

Well, he was back in the tower again, and he was wide awake. The shimmery light was still there and he reached out his hand to touch it again. His hand went through it, vanishing from his sight, and then he felt something sharp touch him and he pulled back. It was real alright, just as real as the griffin that touched him. He stared at the portal to see if he could see through it, but he couldn't. He glanced back out of the window and saw the sun was dipping lower in the sky. He made his way back down the stairs that wound around the tower until he was back outside in the fresh air. He looked longingly at the forest. He really wanted to try out the hand signals for the fairies, but he guessed he'd better get back and let Meg know where he had been. He wasn't sure how long he had been gone, but it had been awhile.

He ran across the grass, dodging people and horses until he came upon the main entrance. He found the kitchen by following his nose. There was bread baking. Meg was busy stirring a pot over the fire. He remained still until she noticed him.

"Ah, there you are. Where have you been, Greccon? I looked for you a bit, but I've got to get this food going in here. Say, cut up those potatoes over there, will you? I know I'm supposed to have some help in here, but they haven't shown up yet. No. Wash those grubby hands first in that bucket of water there. Aye, and then the onions and the turnips, as well. There's a good lad."

Greccon took a sharp knife and began cutting the vegetables and putting them in a pottery bowl. Meg would talk forever without really expecting an answer, so he knew he wouldn't have to tell her anything at all. He followed her directions to the letter, pouring the full bowl of vegetables into the large iron pot hanging over the fire and then stirred it a bit. Then he began to cut chunks of venison and put them in the pot as well. When Darcy and Ann finally showed up, he ducked out to watch the workers put all the furniture in the castle. He found a wooden chair placed by one of the walls and he sat down to watch, keeping out of the way. He found he couldn't keep his mind on the activity; his mind was flying high over the Realm, on the back of a huge black and gold dragon.

"You, boy. Are you just going to sit there and watch everyone else work? Get out to the stables and help with all the horses. No time for daydreaming today, Greccon."

Greccon jumped up and ran out to the stables. The stableman handed him some buckets and pointed to the well in the center of the courtyard. "When you get those filled, there will be two more in their place. You keep the water coming. We've got a lot of thirsty horses here."

By the time Greccon was through and had eaten a bit of supper, he found what was to be his father's room and sprawled out on the small bed. He wouldn't have to worry about dreaming tonight; he was much too tired to dream at all.

CHAPTER EIGHT

The pathway was winding downwards as it was supposed to, but Father Murphy was still a little doubtful about the trail, finding a bridge, and then leading back to the main road to the Castle Griffin. Elijah had told him that this would be a shorter route then backtracking the way he had come. He saw no sign of a bridge, although he did hear the river running off in the distance through a tangle of trees. Jenny plodded along, not caring, trusting the good Father to lead her in the right direction, like so many of his church members. Little did they know Father Murphy was just as unsure as they were, most of the time, but his faith was strong and no matter what the outcome, he knew the Lord would watch and guide him in the right direction, as he had done yesterday. Through the trees, now, he saw a wooden bridge over the river. It looked a little worn and wobbly, but Elijah had told him that it was sturdier than it looked. Unfortunately, Elijah hadn't talked to Jenny about it and the mule took one look at it and stopped. Calling to her gently, he kicked her to go forward. She stood as still as a statue and finally, Father Murphy dismounted and tried to lead her by the reins. Jenny balked, planted her feet and began to back up.

"Now come on there, Jenny girl, it's safe enough. Come with me. Jenny, we have to get across to the other side, now."

The mule shook her head and remained backing up to the point she actually sat down. Father Murthy dropped the reins in exasperation and sent up a silent prayer for guidance on this situation.

He stood there with his hands on his hips.

"Ho. Good Father." The sound came from above him and he jumped.

Scanning the trees, he spied a waif of a boy climbing down. He wondered what a boy that young was doing so far from everywhere. He watched as the boy jumped from the bottom limb of a huge water oak to the ground. He was about ten years old or so, with a strikingly handsome face, chestnut hair, and laughing emerald eyes.

"Well, hello there. I seem to have a hesitant mule on my hands. I'm Father Murphy. Who might you be?"

The young lad walked over and skirted around to the front of the mule, planting a big kiss on Jenny's nose and gently brushing her forelock out of her eyes. He looked up as he scratched behind her ears. "I'm Erastis. She's such a lovely mule, isn't she? I was resting in the trees above when I heard you trying to convince her to follow you. Well, she's scared half to death of bridges, aren't you, Jenny?"

The mule relaxed at the boy's touch and nickered at him. He continued to talk softly to her in a language that Father Murphy wasn't familiar with. He watched the boy in amazement as Jenny got back to her feet. Still murmuring to her, he took the reins and winking one large green eye at Father Murphy, began leading the mule across the bridge. Jenny followed the boy calmly as if she had intended to walk across anyway, moving in a steady walk behind Erastis. Father Murphy was wondering how many miracles he was to have in one week, and he followed behind them, still wondering how the boy had managed it.

Once on the other side, Jenny was licking the laughing boy's face. Father Murphy stood there in wonder, his hands on his hips. Jenny was a good mule, but she was always shy of strangers and yet here she was, so in love with this young man. He didn't remember telling the boy that her name was Jenny either. How did he know?

"Erastis, is it? My fine young man, how did you ever manage to do that?"

The boy wiped his face on his tunic, and patting Jenny, walked to stand in front of the priest. "You can call me Razz. Everyone does. I didn't really do anything. She was frightened of the bridge, so I just ah, suggested to her that it wasn't a bridge at all. It was a field of her favorite flowers, which are violets by the way, and once she saw that picture in her mind, she was fine." He smiled widely and shrugged as if it were the most natural thing in the world to do with a balking mule.

Father Murphy gasped. "That's unbelievable. Are you a magician?"

Razz laughed as if it was the funniest joke he had ever heard. "No, I'm an elf."

Father Murphy just stared at the boy for a moment. He had heard that elves were among the population, but he never knew of any. "You're an elf, Razz? I thought all the magicals had gone. I'm very thankful to you. I would have never gotten Jenny over that bridge, as you saw. You're not trapped here, are you? Oh my, they haven't left you behind by mistake? You can come with me if you are. I won't let anything happen to you."

Razz looked as if he were going to cry. He hugged the priest. "That is so very kind of you, Father Murphy. I'm fine, really. I'm helping my brother, Tannis. He's off there in the distance. We noticed when we came here that a lot of the trees were diseased and we come back from time to time to check on them. I'm perfectly safe, but thank you."

Father Murphy nodded and went for a pouch on his belt. "A coin for your troubles, then?"

Razz shook his head. "I have no use for coins, Father. I'm glad I could help and I'm glad I could meet you and dear Jenny. Take good care of her, won't you?"

There was a whistle that sounded like a falcon's cry. "That's my brother, Tannis. I have to go."

Father Murphy patted the boy's back. "Then go with God, my son."

Razz gave him a smile and scaled the oak by them so fast that Father Murphy didn't even see him go. He stood looking at the starry-eyed mule. "Well now, Jenny. I'll have to remember to pick violets for you."

He climbed on her back and followed the trail to the road. There was a chaos of activity. Clouds of dust rose as horses ran past, to and from the castle. Keeping Jenny as far to the edge of the road as he could, he waved in greeting to the horsemen and knights bustling back and forth. One burley knight rode up next to him.

"You must be Father Murphy, coming to bless the chapel. Is that right?" The priest nodded. The huge man went on, "We've been expecting you. I'll ride on ahead and tell Lord McTavish of your arrival."

He kicked his charger and left them in a cloud of dust. Jenny, who had been a little intimidated by the huge war horse picked up her pace to a trot and snorted at the dust in the air. He could see the castle now, looming a short distance away. Where once it was so vacant and brooding, it was now alive with a flood of people coming and going. Carts of everything from vegetables to barrels of ale headed towards the castle. It looked so much more alive now, and thriving. He thought there was nothing sadder than an empty castle. Hopefully they were in a time of peace now and there wouldn't be the upheavals and warring factions conquering the lands again. That's why Lord McTavish had been given Griffin's Gate Castle - to protect the borders to the north, and to defend the coast against the Viking pirates who were even more ruthless and murderous than their barbarian counterparts. Lord McTavish was known as a wise lord, preferring to defend instead of attacking. He had no love for war, but would be a worthy foe in protecting his lands. He never caused the troubles, but he wouldn't back down from an attack either.

Jenny froze at the drawbridge and Father Murphy would have given his cross to have Razz back for only one moment. He got off and whispered, "It's nothing but a bonny field of violets, Jenny. Remember the field of violets? Come on, girl."

Jenny was not convinced, as the good Father did not have the same powers of persuasion as a princely elf. She rolled a suspicious eye at him and stood steadfast. Seeing the father's predicament, the knight that had met him on the road crossed the bridge. He cantered around Jenny and had his horse nudge her from behind. Jenny had watched the horse circle her but did not expect the little boost she received. She brayed and bolted forward and was on the other side of the drawbridge among a crowd of people who were laughing at her and Father Murphy. Father Murphy waved his thanks to the knight and led the insulted Jenny through the castle streets to the stable. A young page met him and removing the packs, handed them to the priest. He led the mule off to board, promising her a nice hot mash for having to swallow her pride on the bridge. Father Murphy walked to the castle, telling the guard that he was expected. It was a needless gesture as Lord McTavish bounded out of the door.

"Father Murphy. My knight told me you were just about to arrive, and here you are. Come in. Everything has been topsy-turvy here for the past few days, as you might well imagine. I've got some of the boys sweeping and tidying up the chapel. I'll take you there. I'm afraid it needs some repair, and I've ordered more stained glass for the windows. The damn barbarians- ah, excuse my language. Well, the blasted apes have broken every window in it, but with your blessings and my repairs, it should be ready to use soon. I know I'd need to speak with the Bishop, but would you consider being the priest of Griffin's Gate? It's a long way for any of my subjects to go to worship at your church. A lot of these people will be settling the areas around here and there will be need of a priest. Out of your entire order, I would choose you, Father. You have a kind and forgiving way about you and you preach the love of God and not his wrath. We'll be having marriages to perform and children to christen, and hopefully dead to be buried only from old age, but times are changeable. I would feel better to have a priest in residence here. Of course, your needs would be provided for."

Lord McTavish gestured broadly as they walked along the sunny street to the chapel. Father Murphy smiled. This would be wonderful, and he told the lord so. It might be just the solace he needed to be away from Father Johns.

"I suppose young Michael can handle my classes well enough. I certainly can handle all your religious needs here, and I can teach your children to read and write, if need be," Father Murphy offered.

Lord McTavish opened his arms wide. "This is well, then. I have a need for a scholar to teach the children. All of them, though, Father, the girls as well as the boys. I think they should all be able to read and write so no man will have the advantage over them. I know it isn't really acceptable to teach the girls, but it is something

I feel very strongly about and I will not yield on that matter. I shall write the Bishop directly and send it with my fastest messenger. Can you stay a few days, Father? There are many matters I wish to discuss with you."

Father Murphy nodded. "Actually, I have a friend that lives on your land, out in the wooded area. Perhaps you know a Mistress Glynnis Thatcher? No? Well, you have another blessing to be thankful for and you didn't even know it. Mistress Thatcher comes from a long line of healers. I see her, myself, for this misery in my back. True enough, she's a Druid, but she is a healer of well renown. I'm sure my Lord will be pleased to let her stay in her home. A member of her family has lived there for over eight hundred years or so."

Lord McTavish rubbed his curly beard. "That is strange. None of my scouts have reported a home in the woods, but if you say she is there and she is a friend of yours and the Church, then she can remain. It's true; a healer nearby would be a blessing. I have a court mage that is gifted in healing as well, but there are times too horrible too mention where more than one healer would be needed. Perhaps you can bring her to my court, and if I have her allegiance, well then, she will have my protection for her services."

Father Murphy said he would bring her by as soon as he could. Lord McTavish gestured to the church and was caught up in a skirmish between one of his pages and a merchant who had cuffed the boy. The lord was well known for his fairness with children and, telling Father Murphy that they would meet up again later, he strode over, red-faced, to hear the reason for the mistreatment of one of his best pages.

Father Murphy gave a little bow and went towards the church archways. He stopped and winced at the condition of the chapel. It had been ravaged. As he walked through the doors, he saw two boys busy sweeping. They stopped to stare at him.

"Hello, lads. I'm Father Murphy. I've come to bless this chapel. Come here, please."

The two boys walked over, brooms still in their hands. Father Murphy reached in his pouch and gave each of them a coin. "This is for doing such a good job. I can see my two new altar boys, right here in front of me. Now, I would like to finish the cleaning. It helps me to feel closer to my God, so off with you both."

One boy ran out of the door, but the tall blonde child remained, studying the priest carefully. "It's nice to meet you, Father. I am Greccon, the court mage's son. I have the gift of foresight. Would you like to know what is to pass?"

Father Murphy took a seat on the long row of stones fashioned into short rows for people to sit on. He motioned for Greccon to sit down.

"Well now, Greccon, that would be quite a gift. Why don't you tell me what you see for my future?"

Greccon was pleased that this man did not scoff at him the way so many others did. He sat down and brushed off his hands and clothes. He had a distant look in his large blue eyes as if he were watching something that only he could see. Father Murphy was mesmerized by the sincerity on the young boy's face.

Greccon began, "You are coming to stay here with us, and everyone will be happy for a long time."

Father Murphy smiled. "Well, that is good news, Greccon. I will look forward to it."

Greccon's face clouded. "Then, the trouble will start. It will be years from now, but you will save a great many people with your dagger, and you will be helped by the magicals." He squeezed his eyes tight for a moment, then rubbed his head. "That's all I see for now."

Father Murphy felt a little unsettled. This boy must truly have the gift, he thought, to know of the dagger. He wondered where the trouble would start from, but he could see the boy had told him all he could. He put out a hand and brushed the boy's hair back.

"'Tis enough, Greccon. I'm glad that you told me this. If you see anything else, I would like to know that, too."

Greccon nodded. "I see only that you will save a man that troubles you, and that is in the near future, not years from now. He won't understand and will cause trouble for you, but you will be sent here instead of being punished. I don't know if that means anything to you or not; it's just something I see. I don't always understand everything."

Father Murphy frowned. "I don't understand everything either. Sometimes the reasons become clear later on and sometimes they never do."

Greccon smiled at the priest and got up to leave. As he was about to walk out the door, he turned and caught Father Murphy's eye. "She loves you too, Father. That blonde woman. I don't know what you are going to do about that."

And with that, he left, leaving Father Murphy sitting on the row with his mouth hanging open. He sat for a long time trying to sort out all the information the boy had told him. This child would grow to be quite a mage if his predictions grew as he did. Already he knew about the dagger, Father Johns and Mary, and all from just being with him for a scant few minutes. So, he would do something to help Father Johns, only he didn't have a clue as to what it was he was supposed to do to save him, and then get banished to Griffin's Gate, which would not be a punishment at all. But in the eyes of the order, he would be sent away by the Bishop. It really was a reward in disguise, and both he and the Bishop would know that. He would have his own church and parishioners. He would have a flock of his own. This was such a strange part of the world. Elves in the forest, his friend Glynnis not that far away, and now his new friend Greccon, the young wizard.

He took a deep breath and stood up. He took the broom in his hands and swept. Just the familiar task made him feel better. He would come to know every inch of this church. It was true; hardly a window remained unbroken and it really was a shame. The church felt right to him somehow, like the dagger did. It seemed that they all belonged together in this big puzzle. All the pieces were meshing together to form an interesting tapestry. It was cool inside and Father Murphy finished his sweeping and knelt to pray at the altar. The large crucifix remained, although it, too had suffered damage. He closed his eyes and was given a vision of the church in its restored state and he could see the families inside coming to worship. A large shadow came over him and he started. It was Lord McTavish, standing in the doorway.

"I'm sorry, Father, I didn't know you were praying. I didn't mean to interrupt."

Father Murphy stood up and walked towards him. "Nonsense. When do you ever find a priest when he is not praying? It's a beautiful church, my Lord. A few repairs and it will shine like the sun. I've already met a young mage here, and he's quite intuitive, really. He said I would be the priest here and that everyone would be happy here for a long time."

Lord McTavish threw his head back and laughed. "Ah, yes, that would be Greccon. His father is my court mage. The boy is showing signs of great abilities, like his father, Killwyn. You'll meet him later tonight, I hope, if he returns in time. There is foul weather to the north and he has been delayed in returning. He's not a Christian, Father, but he is unmatched in devotion and has amazing powers. I was hoping to convert them, the boy and his father, eventually.

Father Murphy nodded. "The Lord has room for all kinds in this world, Lord McTavish. We can hope they embrace our religion, but whatever their beliefs are, they are our kinsmen and will be respected as such."

Lord McTavish grinned and slapped the priest on the back, almost knocking him over. "I knew that wouldn't be a problem for you, Father Murphy, and that is well, for I have all kinds in my service and all of them are dear to me. I'll not try to make them all believe the same things, it just doesn't work. As long as they all believe in the kingdom and they are all loyal, it is enough for me. A good priest realizes this, as you do. That is why I will be very persuasive to the Bishop in my letter. Not that you will need it. If young Greccon has seen it in the future, I am confident that it will come to pass. I have never known the boy to be wrong. Even at five years of age, he predicted an attack in the absence of his father. He was away as he is now, and the young waif was spouting that there was a band of attackers approaching from the south. He was so livid and none of us could comfort the boy. Well, I didn't really believe him, so I sent out a scout, and sure enough, there was a band of attackers camped just to our south. Of course, I dispatched a regiment to take them prisoners, and I can tell you, they were surprised. I always take Greccon seriously, as should you. He's young, but he's not given to fancy. He is a serious child and tells the truth and he sees things in the future."

Father Murphy agreed. "I will always keep that in mind. Now, I will bless this holy place and I will hold mass in the morning for your people. They can come early if they need to confess and I will be having communion. I've brought everything with me. It will be a glorious day tomorrow."

Lord McTavish smiled. "I'll have it posted immediately and have my pages pass the word. When you are through in here, come find me in the castle and I will show you to your quarters."

The husky man walked out and Father Murphy rummaged in his bags for his holy water. As he went around the room he felt the dagger hum and he thought he could see dark forms leaving as quickly as they could through the broken windows. He covered every space and then knelt to pray again. He felt as if he were home. He had cast out the shadowy demons here; the dagger seemed to give him the vision of where they hid in the darkness. This church was sanctified now and he swore he would keep it that way. A pure holy place for people to come to worship. He wondered if the dagger could give him the same power in the church back home. Would it give him the power to save Father Johns? He would keep it secret, and asked God to bless him even if he kept the dagger a secret from the Bishop. He felt the dagger was between himself and God and no one else need know. It felt right to him that way. It must be the way it should be or he would feel guilty about hiding it, and he didn't. Surely a priest carrying a weapon was outrageous. He had never heard of one doing so. A staff, perhaps, to fend off trouble on the road, but never a dagger. But this was not an ordinary dagger. It would not kill anything but demons and was originally made and carried by priests in the past and all he was doing was ensuring that the magical aid to goodness would carry on its deeds. Here was a case of religion and magic working together in peace. One could not be so blind-sighted as to ignore an icon that could benefit all of humanity. It was a sacred trust, and he would keep it and use it well. It amazed him that he did not even have to draw it to reap its benefits. It would hum so softly so that only he could hear it and it would generate more warmth to his senses to let him know the demons were present. They knew it was there and they ran from it. If only there were more daggers for every priest to carry. It would make the job so much easier to cast out demons and return the world back into God's gracious love and light.

Father Murphy sat back and worshiped the damaged cross. And who was he that he should be entrusted with this miracle? *I'm nothing special*, he thought. *I'm not even as devout as a lot of my brethren. I sin more than most, not intentionally of course, but I do, nonetheless.*

*I have not lived a life worthy of such a trust and surely there must be
more deserving of its wonder.*

He went over his life slowly in his mind and no deed or any special occasion stood out that would make him different or more worthy than anyone else. If anything, he thought, as he begrudgingly
thought of all the instances of backsliding that he could remember,
he was a bit of a disgrace. He felt his face flush in embarrassment.
He had always repented in earnest and had always reached an acceptable state of grace in his own mind, but nothing he could think
of would have been the key factor in bequeathing this dagger to
him. Was he really supposed to be the custodian of such a weapon?
Maybe it had been meant to find a different priest, one that would
come purposefully to Elijah for it sometime in the future and he
had mistakenly given it to him. Wouldn't that be awful? It would
disrupt the whole balance of the way things should go. But no, God
did not make mistakes and if it was His will that he carry it, then
it was the way things were supposed to go and there was nothing
left to doubt. It hadn't been his decision to have it. Things had just
worked out that way and he had to believe it was the right of it. He
did not need to know the reasons and it would do him no good to
know them. Hadn't he just spoken to Greccon that a lot of things
were confusing and sometimes you'll never know or understand
the ways of things? But he would like to know why, and wondered
if that was a sin all on its own. It wasn't that he was questioning
God's will - no, never that, but he just wanted to know if and why
he was the right person to carry the dagger. He cleared his mind of
all thought as he always did, in case the good Lord wanted to reply
in his thoughts. Stand still and behold the power of the Lord, thy
God.

He remained that way for awhile and a thought did come to
him as it always did. Hadn't Greccon just told him that he would
save a lot of people with that dagger? Perhaps the boy thought of
it as a weapon and that he would use it as one, but nothing could
be further from his mind. It would save a lot of people; indeed it
would, by keeping the demons from stalking and possessing them.
A tear rolled down his face in rapture. That was the answer, after
all. Without the magicals to intercede on the humans' behalf, they
were left exposed to the demons' pleasures. So, he was a priest and

a knight of sorts for the magicals, to do what they could or would not do in these troubled times, and his dagger would be the Excalibur, of sorts, to protect the humans, himself included. He bowed his head again and gave thanks as he always did for God giving him the answers he needed. God had created the magicals to help look after things here, just as he had created everything else, each to its own purpose, and the church's attitude toward creatures of magic had been disturbing, at best, of late.

They were rolling up the magicals and demons into one category, just as they had always done. Anything that was different was wrong. He had always had a problem with that and had always thought that God had never meant to have it that way. Why would he make everyone different if they were all supposed to believe in him in the exact same way? Other people had different names and different ways of worshiping Him, and if you got right down to it, it was all the same and it was all right. He had one set of rituals and other people had their own ways of doing things. Who was to say their way was the right way to worship? He could debate all this in his mind for days on end, and he had.

He shook his head to clear it and got up to make his way back to the castle. His stomach was rumbling, and he thought he might just find his way to the kitchens and see if he could talk the cook out of a slice of bread. He would stay for a few days, rejuvenate his soul, visit Glynnis and Mary, and then head back home. He doubted if the Bishop would make a decision on his transfer that fast and he would have to return home to face the persecution of Father Johns once more. Meanwhile, he had a sermon to write for tomorrow's service, and he thought a proper subject would be God's love and tolerance. Nodding inwardly, he squinted at the bright sunshine and watched as he crossed over the maid path. Everyone was so excited and moving very fast, getting things in order. He glanced skyward to see archers already posted on the cat-walks. Lord McTavish was a cautious lord. It was like him to have secured the watches even though he had yet to settle in. He would be a good lord to serve under.

* * *

King Oberon sat in his court, listening to the comments and minor problems of his constituents. All of the magicals were well represented and by the sounds of their praises, things were going very well indeed for the Realm. It pleased him to think for once, these different factions of the magical community were in harmony with one another. Of course there were problems; it seemed there were always ways of improving things, and he found that if he just sat back, they were very anxious and willing to help each other out. He had very little to say, but sat there very satisfied that as he suspected all along, they really didn't need a king. They just needed an excuse to act properly and treat each other with dignity and respect, and they were.

They were all going to have a celebration, one community at a time at the end of each week, to which everyone was invited so they could see how each village had grown and thrived. Populations were still down, but the elves were convinced there was no better way to boost reproduction than to have a party. It would take awhile to repopulate their numbers to where they had once been before the slaughters had occurred, but then they had nothing but time. At least they were all safe here and temperaments had improved with security.

The dwarves had resumed trade with the humans, visiting infrequently, but they had established a trade routine that seemed to satisfy them. The elves had returned, traveling back and forth to soothe the land and keep the trees and vegetation thriving for the earthly animals and birds. The fairies came and went as they pleased. Only the unicorns had not returned. It was still too soon for them, it was said. More time had to pass before they could be seen again and not hunted. A few of the griffins had visited to hunt, even though they had their own herds of deer and smaller mammals in their own woods here. If the truth were told, as happy as they seemed to be, they felt guilty about leaving the humans behind to deal with the demons on their own.

"They are getting exactly what they deserve after the way they've acted." Brodrick, head of the dwarves, shouted. He rubbed a hand over his eyes, remembering his people being enslaved and tortured. The dwarves had no love of humans, but they did trade for the fine metal tools they needed to procure their gemstones from the caves.

King Orion looked away from him. His people had not been as persecuted as the others had, being of a warmer demeanor and having healing qualities. The humans seemed to appreciate them more than the other magicals, but his people had worked to exhaustion trying to heal the other magicals that atrocities had been committed on. He remembered the poor unicorns and griffins. They had been treated as trophy animals and not the fantastic beings that they were, and he could sympathize with the dwarf's anger. Even though his elves returned, they were cautioned not to interact with the humans, as a precautionary measure.

The trolls were silent. They had lost a few members as well, but were not ones to dwell on the past. They had been the busiest of all with their remarkable building prowess. They were asked to help at almost every village and did so gladly. They had never even thought of returning to the human world. They were content right there in the Realm. It seemed as if everyone was living in the manner they were accustomed to living in, and they were all getting along very well, in fact, better than they had been in the human world. It stood to reason that hearts were lighter when they did not have to worry for their children or their lives.

The fairy representative painted quite a dark picture when she reported. Most of the fairy people had stayed behind, being connected with the Mother Earth.

"The demons are prowling on the humans. A lot of them are going mad or behaving in a manner that is demonic. The church has been hanging these people on a regular basis. The land suffers when the demons pass. We have had to ask King Orion for elves to help us restore the plant life, which he has graciously sent." She flashed King Orion a brilliant smile, which he returned and winked at her. She went on, "The water turns foul as well, and the demons rejoice. It is very hard to watch this and a lot of us are considering coming to the Realm. I just wish there was something we could do to suppress their outlandish behavior."

King Orion spoke. "When they contaminate their land and water, it is only a matter of time before the humans die, but then the demons will take over as they have before. It took the magicals and the humans working together to diminish the demonic activity in the past. It won't happen now, with all of us gone."

Brodrick snorted. "Well then, good riddance, I say. Let the demons take over. Then they have their Realm and we have ours. What is the difference?"

The griffins spoke up, "The difference is the wildlife there, Brodrick. Humans are not the only species there, even though they act like it. What's to become of the wildlife? Surely you don't think they all deserve to die, as well? The demons aren't good for anyone but themselves. What good will all your mining and jewelry making be when you have no one to trade with, no reason to leave the Realm at all."

Brodrick scowled at him and King Oberon could see things heading south rather quickly. He cleared his throat. Everyone stopped arguing amongst themselves and turned respectfully to look at him.

He nodded in appreciation and spoke. "If we could have remained in the human world, we would still be there. I still have a great deal of respect for the wildlife there and the trees and plant life, and the humans that are of sound thinking. I do believe they will find a way to combat the demons and they will realize what the pollution will do to their futures. It isn't for us to cater to their needs, especially considering the treatment of a lot of our members."

Brodrick nodded in agreement as Oberon continued.

"I was reminded just the other day of a group of magicals that we've forgotten and have left behind."

The magicals turned and looked at each other and turned back to Oberon, confused. King Oberon held up a claw.

"Yes, my dear friends, we have left some very valuable members behind and it might be through them we can help the humans without having to put any of us at risk." He had captured their attention now.

"We have quite a few wizards. One very young one actually found his way through the gate to the Realm just the other day, taking us quite by surprise. How old was he, Reaper?" He wrinkled his forehead and tried to remember.

Reaper held up a claw. "I believe he said he was eight years old."

Queen Illustra nodded in agreement. The crowd gasped. They

had never heard of an eight year-old wizard. The wizards they had been in contact with were grey-haired and elderly. Oberon nodded.

"Yes, he was eight years old and very intelligent. His father and uncle are wizards as well, and there are a lot more of them out there that I have no knowledge thereof. I believe we should lend the fairies and elves a hand in preserving the land, but as far as the humans are concerned, let their wizards try and help. We can help them to help the humans if need be. After all, they are our subjects just as much as any of us sitting here."

Once again, Oberon had cut through the arguments to the heart of the problem and had offered a very reasonable solution that seemed to satisfy everyone and they nodded in compliance. Oberon tapped the table with one claw. The chatter stopped and they turned their attentions back to him.

"We are not totally helpless to solve some of their problems. If the demons send a plague, then we send a cure. If they cause a famine, then we make the land produce. If they send foul weather, we calm it. We need to form a commission to work on these problems and I would like to ask the Fairy representative to head up this commission. They are more aware of what is befalling these humans. Also, I would ask that elven members consider serving as well, since they seem to go about the human world unnoticed, looking much like them. We do not have to sit back and watch former friends suffer for the sins of a few misguided humans; we can be very helpful."

The fairies agreed and called for a commission meeting following the court session in the court chambers and Oberon gladly gave his consent. He also announced that any magical might participate in this endeavor to thwart the demons. After all, it was once what they were doing to begin with, and Oberon thought a game of chess with the demons would keep these magicals sharp and interested in the world around them.

CHAPTER NINE

Father Murphy sat at his fine oak writing desk and lit the candles. He opened a container of ink and then sat down, a quill pen in his hand. A cool breeze marking the beginning of fall blew in through the window, making the candlelight flutter. He wrote:

> **It has been fifteen years to this date that I have come to be the priest of Griffin's Gate Castle. So much has transpired in that time that I fear if I do not write it all down while I still remember; it will be lost for all time. My God, being my only confessor, shares the incidents with Father Johns, and I am too cowardly to tell another living soul for fear that I will have to endure the same fate as Father Johns. Lord McTavish had offered me this post and had written to the Bishop. Of course, the Bishop in his infinite wisdom, consented to allow me to serve Griffin's Gate, as the Pope had wanted to expand the religion in a northern direction anyway. Certain events had transpired to make this almost immediate. It dealt with Father Johns who had been acting so out of character as to raise the Bishop's concerns for his mental state. By the time I had returned, several days later, there wasn't a priest in the order who was not terrified of Father Johns.**

I had settled back into my cubicle after checking with young Michael, who is now a priest and a very respectable one in his own right, about how my classes and students had fared in my absence. It was long after midnight mass when Father Johns entered my cubicle, a large kitchen knife in his hands. By the grace of God, I had not been asleep yet as my body was readjusting to the stiff cot below me. At Griffin's Gate, I had been given a glorious feather bed and was enjoying the worldly delights of a very warm and soft bed. My back was once again complaining and I had thought to get back up and make a cup of tea, adding some of Mistress Thatcher's medicine. It never cured the ailment, but it did make it bearable enough to sleep. I had just sat up when Father Johns came into my cubicle and I tried to recognize just what it was that he was carrying. Identifying the object to be a rather large knife, I sat up and addressed the Father.

"Father Johns, what are you doing with that knife and why are you in my room?"

He had a strange look on his face, as if he had never heard me at all and he raised the knife in the air. A beam of moonlight glinted off of the sharp blade. I could see the demons through his eyes cackling and urging him on. He seemed to be covered with them, as a man is covered in bees when trying to steal honey. I jumped to my feet and grabbed the hilt of my dagger, which I had never removed before from the sheath tied to my side. I drew it briskly and pointed it at the Father and watched as he screamed. A shrill mournful sound escaped his mouth along with the demons who were flying out of every orifice of his face. I had never seen a more horrifying and gruesome sight as the demons left his body with screams of anguish, blacking out his features as they rose to escape through my window. They came out in a flood, spinning him around. Father Johns collapsed then, falling unconscious on the floor, the kitchen knife still in his hand. I sheathed the dagger then, placing it in the leather sheath under my robe and knelt to tend to Father Johns when a score of fellow priests stormed my room. I looked up at them.

"He tried to stab me, but by the grace of God, he passed out first."

They looked at each other and one ran for the Bishop and his guards. Of course, when Father Johns had regained his senses, he told everyone that I had tried to kill him, but I had a bevy of witnesses that saw that I had no weapon, and that only Father Johns had a knife in his hands. They took Father Johns off the next day to a cloister somewhere outside of Rome for treatment and we never saw him again. I know the demons had been vanquished and for that I am thankful. Once he regains his senses he should be hale again. Even though I know the demons ran from the demon dagger, I had no time to explain to Father Johns that I had no intentions of killing him and for that I am sorry and wish I had it to do again. He was sane enough to know I had held a dagger at his throat, but he had no idea I would have never used it for the purpose for which I stood accused. No one ever checked to see if I had a weapon. They all believed Father Johns was suffering from a delusion and since it was he who held the knife and not me, he was sent away. I wonder if it ever plays in his memory, or if it troubles him in the dark of night, as it does me. I considered making a trip to Rome, but I would not be allowed to visit him and was told to take the position at Griffin's Gate as soon as I could manage the trip. The sight of the demons leaving Father Johns still haunts me to this day even after all this time has passed. I did not know so many demons could inhabit a body, and in the still of the night it will fall over my mind and I see it again as if it were happening right in front of me. Some things you do not forget. I have never heard how Father Johns fared, but I still pray for him every day. I wonder if he thinks I am still an insane priest carrying a dagger and a danger to everyone I'm around. I hope not. I hope his mind has been kind to him and that he has no memory of his past since he had harbored his first demon. Young Greccon had prophesized I would help the man, so I pray that ridding him of those demons did indeed save him. Even as I sit here writing, the dagger is securely strapped to my side and comforts me, allowing me to know there are no demons where I am.

And so, I cleaned out my cell, packing all of my personal belongings, which were few, and loaded them back on Jenny. She looked at me as if she did not believe we were leaving again so soon. I exchanged blessings with my fellow priests and they watched me as I trotted Jenny down the road. I looked back only once and waved. As I recall the trip, I remember coming onto the crossroads. I visited Elijah and carried a letter to Glynnis for him. It had said he was going to travel east to the orient and would beg her to marry him again when he returned. After fifteen years, he has not returned, and we are all concerned.

Glynnis gave birth to his daughter, who I christened Ilona. I think she let me christen her to soothe my own soul, as she has been and will always be a Druid. The baby was healthy and had grey, happy eyes and curly brown hair, much like Elijah's. The young woman is fifteen now, and is as proficient as her mother in the healing arts. After five years, Glynnis and Mary made the trip to Elijah's cottage and packed up all his scrolls and books, lest bandits destroy them. Ilona has read every one, being the best student I have ever taught, bar none. Lord Mc-

Tavish was wise to insist the girls were to be taught the same as the boys, for Ilona has far surpassed my expectations for her and I implore her mother to send her to France to study in Paris and continue her education.

Greccon is now twenty-three and is the court mage since his father had never returned from the north. Even at the tender age of ten, he had stood by Lord McTavish's side, advising him. I noticed Ilona has caught his eye and although it is rumored that Thatcher women never marry, I hope to be sealing their wedding vows soon. Greccon has confided to me that Ilona has a strange magic of her own. Now, I am just unsure if he means it literally or if it's just that she's put a spell on his heart. They have been friends since she was old enough to talk, but his renewed interest in her now that she has come of age has my hopes for a lifetime of happiness for them. They suit each other well, and although I do not attend their Druid festivals, I know both Greccon and Ilona have and it is rumored they are smitten with each other.

Mary never did return to her home as she had planned, but her relatives did come here to attend her marriage to Lord McTavish. I introduced them and any love Mary had for me, other than the Christian kind, was now for Lord McTavish. They never stopped looking at each other, and if you believe in a destined love, it was the case here. I performed the ceremony, myself, and it was a glorious one with much revelry. I rang the church bells loud and clear for the county to hear. I guess it was destiny that led her to my attention and saved her from being hung as a witch. She was now the Lady of Griffin's Gate, and although the nobility snubbed her at first, not having a title of her own, they soon accepted her into polite society, for she was kind and charming and won their hearts as she had

once won mine. I did not find it hard to believe that everyone in the kingdom loved her. God works in mysterious ways and has always presented solutions to my problems. I am so very comfortable here. Every need I have is taken care of and I'm afraid I do enjoy the luxuries that were non-existent in the former church I was in. I have my own quarters, lavishly furnished, and I've put on a few pounds due to the wonderful cook here. I feel as if I am being rewarded every day that I am here. My God has truly smiled upon me and I am so very thankful.

A shout from outside made him drop his quill and run to the door.

"To arms. To arms. Look to the sea." There was a clatter of men running.

"Women and children to the church."

Father Murphy broke into a run and slammed open the church doors and a flood of women and children came pouring in. There were women carrying babies and dragging sleepy children. The older children ran with wide eyes. A horn was sounding now, and a thundering of hoofbeats could be heard. One knight stationed himself outside of the church door, his horse circling.

"What is it, Sir Collin?" Father Murphy asked the knight as he stood to the side, helping women through the door.

The knight looked down from his huge mount. "Ships on the sea, looks like they are heading into the shore. Hasten the women and children inside and secure the door, Father. No one will get past my sword, no one ever has."

Father Murphy swallowed hard and motioned the children to hurry inside. Vikings, no doubt, he thought, and they spared no one. They had no respect for the church and would burn them out if they could, killing women and children as if they were rabbits. The children were crying and mothers were comforting them the best they could. Seeing no more on their way in, Father Murphy sealed the doors with the heavy wooden bar that he'd never had to use before. He spread his arms wide to embrace the crowd of frightened parishioners.

"All right now, we have Sir Collin guarding the door and there's no other way in. Let's join in a prayer for strength and salvation during this emergency."

He led them in prayer, his eyes and ears to the windows. They were high enough to prevent anyone from climbing through from the ground. It was strangely silent, although he could hear Sir Collin's horse stamping and snorting in anticipation of a charge. He could hear the men shouting back and forth and wondered what was going on. His mission was to comfort the families and keep them from panicking. He took a deep breath.

"Now, let's do the rosary." Obediently they murmured the prayers along with him and it seemed to quiet the children to hear their mothers repeating the prayers that were so familiar to them. It was hard for anyone to be thinking of a battle while having to repeat prayers. The point was that the women and children were safe for now and out of the way of the men who may have to fight, and out of the way of arrows. He unconsciously put a hand to his back where he had been struck by an arrow, long ago. The repetitive drone of the prayers went on in unison. The voices shook a bit in fear; it did seem to comfort them, if only a little.

Lord McTavish climbed up to the parapet. "What pennants are they flying?"

The lookout squinted. "One looks to be from Spain, the other I do not recognize, it's a bird of some sort."

McTavish growled. "We have no quarrel with Spain. The other must be a bloody Viking ship chasing her." He turned and shouted, "Secure the shoreline. Keep an eye to the boats. Archers and long bows up on the walk." To the lookout he said, "Can you see any oarsmen in boats approaching from the ships?"

He studied the sea in the moonlight. "Nay. It doesn't look as if it is an attack on us, my Lord, just a chase." Both men shielded their eyes and jumped as both ships suddenly exploded into flames with a deafening roar.

"Good God." There was a flurry of shouts from his men as they watched the ships explode into an inferno, turning the sky and water into a bright orange glow. Both ships were engulfed in a bright blue and orange fireball that could be heard crackling even from where they stood. Clouds of smoke were blowing in and it would be hard to find anyone in that haze.

McTavish shouted, "Oarsmen, get the long boats out there and search for survivors. Get the knights down to the shore. Let the women and children go back to the castle. There will be no attack tonight, I promise you. I don't think many could live through that explosion. You, set up an infirmary. Get Greccon and send him to the Thatchers. We'll need both of the Thatcher women tonight. Tell them to bring medicine for burns."

He climbed down and ran into Mary. She was dressed for battle. She would never run to the church with the other women, but had always stood by her husband's side, ready for battle, a sword strapped to her side like a man. She said she had six brothers and could fight as well as any man, and as a lark, Lord McTavish had sparred her and was quite impressed with her ability. He let her remain with him. He caught her eye.

"My Lady, there will be injured rowed ashore. Can you help set up an infirmary? If any of them are Vikings and cause trouble, kill them. We will help the peaceful, only. "

She nodded and ran in the opposite direction, asking no questions. He allowed himself a few seconds of admiration for his wife. He adored her and her ability to anticipate his every wish. He pointed at two men, "You there, get litters down to the shore, as many as we have. We have injured on the way."

He looked up and saw Greccon tearing out of the castle entrance, headed for the woods on a very fast horse. All that was left to do was wait. He saw Father Murphy and motioned him over. "Father, one of the ships was from Spain. They may need a priest in the infirmary to administer last rites." Father nodded and ran to where the infirmary was being assembled in the front hall.

The lookout shouted, "We have two of our long boats arriving back, it looks to be several injured. They are not yet to the breakers."

McTavish hoped Greccon would hurry. He would need healers. He would have to assemble a salvage crew to burn any dead bodies washing up along with any unusable wood or goods. He couldn't imagine what they could have had on those ships that would make them burn so fast and hot. He doubted if many would survive, but he would do his best to help them. He climbed back up onto the

parapet to watch. You could barely see the ships for the smoke
billowing in. He could not make out any of his longboats and wondered if there were any boats launched from the ships. There hadn't
been enough time for them to launch the boats before it blew up.
One minute they were chasing the Spanish ship and then there were
flames. The ships had collided for sure, but what could have caused
the explosion? He hoped enough of the people would survive to
help him understand exactly what had happened.

There was a huge sucking sound and the Spanish ship foundered.
They watched as the stern vanished into the deep, followed by the
bow in a vertical dive. Then it was gone. The other ship was about
to do the same thing. The smoke had thickened and he covered his
mouth and nose with his sleeve and saw his men were following
suit.

The lookout pointed. "Two more survivors being rowed in."
That made five so far, he thought, that they knew for sure. Not
very many, considering the size of the ships and the possible number of the crew. He shook his head. He hated the waste of lives. The
sea had demanded too many lives today, but he would try to save
the few that the sea had given up.

He saw Greccon arriving with Glynnis and Ilona. They threw
their reins to pages, who hurriedly took their horses to the stables.
They carried their packs and ran for the infirmary where a few
of the injured had already been brought in. Glynnis was shouting
for water to wash the sea water and blood off of the people. There
was the sounds of water splashing and the people moaning. Glynnis
treated the injuries that she could detect as more were brought in.

"Greccon, you get that one over there, would you?" She threw
him a small clay pot of salve. "Wash them with the clear water and
apply this to the injuries until I can get over there. Cover the burns
with the salve. If they are losing a lot of blood, get me right away."

Ilona was already working on another one of the injured. Greccon caught the clay pot and, taking a pail of water from one of the
helpers, he began to wash the body of a young woman. Her clothes
were black with burns and he couldn't tell if she was injured. He
tore away the shreds of clothing and poured the cool water on her.
Seeing bleeding and blistering wounds on her legs, he began to apply the salve. She woke then, having been unconscious.

"Get away from me, you pig." she screamed and Glynnis ran over.

She motioned Greccon over to the patient she had been working on instead. The girl was frantic now and began to scream and thrash about in hysterics. Glynnis poured a vial of some liquid in her open mouth and she sputtered.

"Peace. You are safe now. You are at Griffin's Gate castle under the protection of Lord McTavish, on the Isle of Brittany. You are burned and we have to treat these wounds or they will become infected. My name is Glynnis." The girl's blue eyes were full of tears but she quieted and listened to her. Glynnis smiled. "It doesn't look so bad, my dear, you'll be fine. Now, I have others who are in worse condition. I'll send you back Greccon. Try not to insult him again. He's our very talented court mage. He may turn you into a toad if you cause him any trouble. He'll get your name and any other information you can give us on this attack. We can send runners to contact your people. Alright, now? I've given you medicine to calm you. It might make you sleepy. I promise you, you will be safe enough if you decide to sleep. I'll be here all night. Call me or my daughter Ilona if you need anything."

The girl nodded and reached for Glynnis' hand. "I'm sorry. I'm so scared. I did not mean to be rude. Thank you."

Glynnis smiled at her. "Quite alright, we understand."

Glynnis left her quickly to attend to a man that was badly burned. Greccon went back over to the girl and knelt by her side and placed a soft white cloth over her. She gripped it in her hands and stared at him.

He smiled sympathetically at her. "I won't hurt you, my lady. Can I get you some water to drink? Would you like to tell me your name?"

She blinked a few times and took a shaky breath. "My name is Felicia from the House of Carro in Spain. My whole family was on that ship." She tried to look around her to see if she could find any of her family members.

Greccon looked up as well. "It would be impossible to tell right now, Felicia. No one else is awake enough to tell us who they are, and the men are searching the waters now for any more survivors. Why don't you rest, and perhaps by morning we will know more.

You are very lucky to survive that explosion. Glynnis said you'll be just fine."

He held her hand and she did not pull away. He helped her drink some water and asked her if he could get her anything else. She shook her head and her eyes closed. She had fallen fast asleep. He gently let go of her hand and laid it beside her. She was so frightened and he wished he could do something to make her more comfortable, but more injured were coming in and he glanced at her beautiful face once more, then hurried to help with the rest of the casualties.

They worked well into the next morning. A few had died of their injuries and Greccon could not find any of the girl's family among their patients. When they had attended to all of them, they sat together and a page brought them food and drinks. They were exhausted, but Glynnis would not leave until she had done everything she could. She wanted to check the injured once more to make sure the wounds were clean and so, after eating, she began the long process of rechecking every injury. Ilona helped her, knowing what to look for.

Greccon sat there, wishing he had more training. He could tell the rest of them would live by his foresight, but that was all he could tell Glynnis. Several times he started the fire in the fireplace to burn warmer. He had done all he could and he left to go outside and get some fresh air. Felicia's eyes haunted him. He wondered how old she was. He wondered what she would do now that her family was gone. He knew how she felt. His father had never returned from his trip and there were nights that he would lay awake and listen for his footsteps. They never came and with each year that passed by, his hopes grew dimmer of having his father back. *If he were still alive he would contact me somehow,* he thought, but he never had. She would be as alone as he was.

He yawned and watched the first hints of sunrise lighten the sky to a dark grey. It seemed as if the smoke from the ships still hung in the air. He pulled his cloak around him tighter. It was always the coldest just before sunrise. He leaned up against the stone wall of the hall, knowing he should go back inside and help Glynnis and Ilona. They had worked harder than he had, knowing so much more about healing than he did. If anyone deserved a break in the fresh air, it was the two of them, but he knew they would not leave until they were sure everyone was treated. The smell of the hall had become intolerable. It was from the smoke, burnt clothing and hair. The smell of blood was heavy and he didn't know how they could stand it. Ah, he was just weak. They were the toughest women he had ever known. They and Lady Mary just put him to shame with the way they worked. *If only I had their constitution*, he thought, *how much better I would be as a mage.*

Closing his eyes, he reached out to the future to see if he could see any other attacks on the horizon. He saw none. This had been an attack on the Spanish vessel and not on the castle. That eased his mind as it would give the people a chance to heal and their warriors a chance to stand down. A tap on his shoulder brought him quickly back to the here and now.

"You were so far away, Greccon. Were you seeing into the future? Will we be alright for now?" Ilona's soft voice asked.

Greccon smiled at her and pushed back the brown curls that had escaped from her braid. "Yes. The attack was not for us. How are you faring, and your mother? It has been such a long night."

Ilona nodded sadly. "I'm alright and Mother just keeps going. You know how she is. She has always found the strength she needs to heal. She is just finishing up now. Everyone seems to be responding well. We'll take turns sleeping. She insists that I sleep first. I'm heading over to the castle to find somewhere to sleep."

Greccon hailed a page and instructed him to show Mistress Thatcher to his room.

"You can sleep there, Ilona. I'll stay and help your mother. I'm too anxious to sleep right now. Go and get some rest. You worked so hard last night."

He kissed her forehead, turned, and went back into the hall. He told Glynnis where Ilona had gone and carried the bucket of water that Glynnis had been hauling around. She allowed herself a chuckle.

"Well, Greccon, a lady asleep in your room will certainly get the court ladies' tongues wagging."

Greccon froze. He hadn't thought of that; he had just thought it was a bed ready for her to sleep in. He smacked his forehead in dismay. "Good Gods. Honestly, Glynnis, I just didn't think of that.

I guess I'm just not thinking at all."

She smiled at him and patted his arm. "Ah, it will do your reputation a world of good to generate a little gossip, and you know Ilona, she wouldn't care a bit anyway. She is very tired and it was generous of you to give up your bed and help me. Now, don't give it another thought. I have two more people to check, and then I must ride home and get more medicine. I'm afraid I didn't bring all that I needed, and there is some pain medicine I have that will help numb the pain of the burns. We were in such a hurry to get here. I also want to keep a lot of them asleep for awhile until the worst of the wounds have a chance to heal a bit. Father Murphy will be here shortly to help you. Just give them water for now. They should be alright until I get back. Don't administer any medicine, but you can put cool compresses on them if they complain."

Greccon nodded. He took Glynnis' hand in both of his and closed his eyes in concentration. He willed power to transfer from himself to the healer. She sighed and thanked him for the boost. King Oberon had taught him how to transfer his power into strength to people in need, and by the looks of Glynnis, she had really needed it. It left him a little low in strength, but she was the one doing all the work, and she would be needed again when these people woke up in pain. Greccon had seen Ilona transfer some of her power to her earlier. Even though Glynnis insisted she wasn't magical, he knew it couldn't be further from the truth.

She had power, alright, and plenty of it. Ilona had it, too. He guessed that it was her way of protecting herself and Ilona from all the villagers that would point fingers at them and call them witches. What witch would work as long and compassionately as Glynnis and Ilona had in healing these misfortunate strangers? They had worked tirelessly and were always kind and gentle, soothing even the most irate patients. He felt a flush of anger at anyone who would dare fault them for doing what they were put on this earth to do. He noticed she healed with her hands as well, closing wounds with just a touch of her hands, using no sutures or fire to cauterize them. She was using magic alright, no matter if she would not admit it. He knew because it was a field he could actually see. Ilona wouldn't talk about it either, even when they were alone and he would ask her. It was a family secret of some sort, and they guarded it well.

He had been best friends with Ilona since he could remember, and it hurt just a little that she wouldn't confide in him, but he shrugged it off. They must realize that he would know these things, but they would never talk about it. Sometimes he wished they would. They could talk about it and learn from each other. It was a lonely life for him.

Some, like Father Murphy, made much of his friendship with Ilona and expected him to marry her. In truth, he had asked her just a few months ago in private, and she had refused. She was more like a sister to him, and they both found it awkward to place themselves in the position of a couple. When he was twelve, he had taught her how to ride a horse and then would take her riding after that. He was eight years her senior and would always be put in charge of minding her when Glynnis was called back into the village to heal. She would bring her to Mary who would then look to Greccon to keep the child entertained as she attended court with the Lord. He taught her how to hunt and fight with a sword, and was surprised when she could out-shoot him with a bow. She always confided in him and looked to him for the answers to all her questions.

Ilona had changed these past few years and it was having quite an effect on him. He was noticing a lot of things about her that he hadn't thought of before. When did she grow up to be so beautiful? He did love her and she felt the same towards him, but she said that Thatcher women never married and they could be just as happy without the formalities, but he found that hard to take. He wanted things to be proper between them. He had been raised by Lord McTavish and his Lady as a son, and he would do nothing to bring shame to their good names.

He watched as Glynnis left the hall to ride back home. He heard her horse being brought around by a page and saw the glow of early morning through the door as she closed it behind her. He turned then and put all thoughts of Ilona out of his mind. He gathered the piles of torn and burnt clothing up to be discarded. Glynnis had taught him that everything needed to be kept as clean as possible around the sick. He threw them outside in a sack to be taken and burnt. Father Murphy was hurrying across the courtyard, yanking his robe as if he had just thrown it on.

"Greccon. I had thought to rise earlier. I wanted to be here before sunrise, but here I am, late again. I've asked the cook to send over some broth and bread when she could, to give to the sick. We have to keep their strength up."

Greccon nodded and told Father Murphy he would fetch more buckets of water from the well. He dumped out all the dirty water. When he arrived back with the fresh water, Father Murphy pointed and told him there was a woman asking for him. It was Felicia. He hurried over. She was sitting up now and looked a lot better than she had last night. "You're looking much better, Felicia. Would you like to get up and walk?"

She nodded at him and he helped her to her feet. It seemed the worst of her injuries were the few burns she had suffered on her legs. She winced as she put her weight on them, but she could walk and he led her to the door to get her some fresh air. Father Murphy thought the same thing, that they would fare better to air out the hall and he had opened the shutters on the windows to let the fall breeze in.

"Are you hungry, Felicia? I can take you to the dining hall for something to break your fast."

She nodded again and he walked her over to the castle, an arm about her waist for support. He motioned for a page to take her to get something to eat and find her a room of her own in the castle. He told her to come back when she was through to check in with Glynnis for the burns. The page led her away and he watched her leave. He wondered what he could do for her now that she was all alone. He could only hope they had some of her kinsmen in the hall that would look after her once they healed.

He went to find the watch. He was standing up on the cat walk, shouting at someone below the castle wall. Seeing Greccon, he held a palm up to motion him to wait for a moment while he continued to shout at the men below. When he was through, he turned to Greccon.

"Hellava mess we have washing ashore. But we can be thankful the attack wasn't meant for us. I know what you are going to ask, and there are no more left alive. What you have in the hall is the sum of it, I'm afraid. I've been watching the sea scavengers feast all night and again this morning on what was left. The tide has gone out, but when it comes back in, we'll be loaded with debris. I've got men burning up whatever washes ashore that isn't usable. It looks as if the Spanish galleon was carrying barrels of oil. There is a slick miles long out there. No wonder she burned. I've got the men looking for sound barrels. We could use the oil. Maybe some good will come out of all this."

Greccon frowned as he listened to the wild cry of the gulls. So many people were dead, and for what? A few barrels of oil? He shook his head and waved thanks to the watch and headed back to the hall. He helped Father Murphy feed the ones who could eat, giving them bread soaked in broth if they could manage it. Glynnis came back and he rushed over to carry all the packs she had brought. She had changed her clothes and somehow, looked refreshed. He didn't know how she did it, the woman had been up all night and should be ready to drop, but she made her way through, checking on everyone again. She caught his eye and he went to her.

"Well, Greccon, we seem to be missing a young lady. She wouldn't also be in your bed, is she?" She tried to keep the amusement out of her voice and Greccon made a face at that.

"No. She was better this morning and I took her to the castle to eat and asked a page to get her a room there. I told her to come back so you could check on her injuries, but she seemed well enough to leave. I'll clean this spot where she was, but I checked with the watch and no more will be coming in. Only these few survived."

Glynnis nodded. There was only one man she was really concerned with and she was glad Felicia was well enough to leave. Greccon must be tired, she thought; usually, he would have been in a better humor and would have responded to her sarcasm.

Weeks later, Greccon would be depressed to learn the survivors were members of the crew and not any of Felicia's clan. Four had been crew members up on the deck and had jumped to escape the fire when all hopes of saving the ship were gone. It turned out that another crewmember, who had not survived, had thrown Felicia over the rail. She had been on deck, sick again from the heavy surf. When her dress had caught fire, he just grabbed her and threw her overboard. It was a miracle she survived. Luckily she knew how to swim, and she was swimming away from the ship towards the torch lights she had seen in the distance. The other two men were from the Viking ship and would not talk or cooperate with them at all. When they were sturdy enough to move, Lord McTavish sent them to the king to stand trial for piracy, while the Spanish crew members left for the ports to be hired on with another ship. Only Felicia was left.

She had become attached to Greccon and he didn't seem to mind. As a matter of fact, he found he was very intrigued with her. She had no attachment with the house of Carro, as it turned out, but her people were gypsies and had contracted on the ship as servants for passage to the islands south in the Caribbean. She was twenty years old and her father had hopes of selling her to the rich families on the island as a servant. She did not really want that sort of life, but would obey her father's wishes for the good of the family. Now they were all gone.

Greccon was fascinated with her as she confessed she knew gypsy magic as well. He would take her for long walks in the forest and they would sit and talk of the things that only Oberon had talked to him about. She had waves of black curly hair and deep blue eyes that Greccon found enchanting. He began spending more and more time with her until he felt he could not live without her. He asked Father Murphy to marry them. Although a few of the court ladies' hearts were broken, and even though Ilona was happy for him, he found that everyone agreed it was high time he married. He was told he should have married years ago. He felt guilty about Ilona, having asked her first, but she told him that she would not marry at all, and he was doing the right thing in taking Felicia as his bride.

This gave the court something to celebrate and Felicia was surrounded by the ladies, who were fussing over every detail. Clothing and a beautiful wedding gown were being made for her. Greccon, being the court mage, was to remain living in the castle and a new room was being prepared for them, more suitable to a couple instead of a bachelor. He smiled at how excited she was and how strange events seemed to surround him. Who would have thought his bride would be delivered from the sea? He always thought he would wear Ilona down and convince her to marry, but even though it was a shadow on his happiness, he felt that marrying Felicia was his destiny.

CHAPTER TEN

King Oberon leaned up against the wall of the Counter Building, intently listening to River, one of his male fairy representatives. The Counter Building had been constructed by the trolls to house its many members whose jobs were to counteract the demonic influence in the mortal world. It had always been the magicals' life work to balance the good with the evil, and now being able to run missions back and forth was tedious but necessary. It had been easier to work while living in the mortal world, but it became too dangerous. A headquarters was needed and now that it had been constructed and operations were going on at regular intervals, Oberon found he spent a lot of time listening and advising the organization. It surprised him they were having the most trouble from the organized religions in the area. Battling demons was one thing, but what was there to do about humans who were acting of their own accord, believing the hysteria, and believing they were doing the right thing?

"My King, there are no demons to vanquish here. We can do very little to save these people from themselves. It's a change of attitude that they need. It seems every day that innocents are being executed for witchcraft for sins no greater than sporting a wart where it can be seen. I've never seen the like of it. It gets darker and uglier every day."

River cast his eyes down in dismay and sighed. Shaking his head he continued, "We've tried everything. We even asked the muse to give them more music and art. You know how powerful that can be and yet, it isn't art or music to glorify their God, it's considered blasphemous. A few were hung for that, I can tell you. The elves are doing everything they can to lighten their hearts but it seems it's a sin now to be happy. The dwarves are faring no better. Their beautiful jewelry can only be worn by royalty or it is considered vanity and then punished."

They both turned to listen to a water nymph that had been privy to their conversation. Ripple was one of the elders of the water nymphs and very wise. "I don't think it has anything to do with attitude. I believe it's a disease. Their sanitary habits are deplorable. They eat spoiled meat and molded breads. It's healers that we need. They live in filth. I predict a disease will take care of all your problems. Many will die. We can hardly keep up with the garbage poured into the streams and lakes. They are bringing this all on themselves. They do nothing but pray. Although I'm sure it has its value, it is the lazy way of taking care of things. Isn't it so much easier to sit and pray than it is to get off your backsides and help to change things?"

Oberon looked from Ripple back to River. "She has a very valid point. Sometimes history will just run its course. The wise will learn from it and the ignorant never will and they won't live long enough for us to worry about them. Back when they actually believed in us, it was easier and we would have more cooperation. I believe if we can handle the demons, they should at least be able to care for themselves and the land that gives them life."

They were nodding in agreement when Oberon caught sight of the young griffin, Argon, who seemed to be very disgruntled and purposefully making his way to the gates of the other world. Oberon excused himself and stood directly in the griffin fledgling's path. The small black and silver griffin looked at him nervously and dropped into a bow. "My King."

Oberon was trying to determine what had the griffin in such a state and decided to simply ask. "What's wrong, Argon? Surely you are not intending to go into the real world without an escort. You know you are much too young for that. I am not willing to risk your life. I'll need you for my guard."

Argon made a face. "I did. It seems as if my home is no longer here, my king. My mother has sent me away."

Oberon sat up in disbelief. "Why would she do such a thing?"

Argon sat down in a huff. "Because I am no longer welcome, what with my new brother, Shylock, to look after."

Argon lowered his eyes and dug one claw into the ground. Oberon could see the griffin was having all he could do to look brave and nonchalant. He could see the griffin was frightened and miserable. His mother had taken another mate after the death of Reaper. It still stabbed his heart every time he thought about Reaper's death at the hands of the humans. They had caught him in a net and killed him before Oberon could come to his rescue. Reaper's death had a profound effect on Oberon. Not only was Reaper his best friend, but the best guardsman he ever had. Argon was Reaper's son, and not an easy griffin to love. He was ferocious and morose since his father was killed. They had been as close as a father and son could be and at his young age it was hard for him to cope with the loss of his father. He resented his mother for taking another mate and hated the adorable Shylock, newly born, even more. Argon had barely learned to fly, and knowing how distressed he was over Reaper, he was shocked that his mother had sent him away. Oberon guessed he was old enough to hunt for himself. He would probably go hungry more often than not until he perfected his hunting skills, but it was his broken heart that Oberon worried about; that and the isolation for one so young. He tapped a claw in thought.

"Well, Argon, she's probably right." Argon looked up at him sharply, in shock. Oberon continued, "I hadn't realized how much you've grown. Yes, I believe it's time to get you into training. I think you should move into the training cliffs and I will see to it right away. If you have inherited your fathers amazing abilities, well then, I will want you right by my side in a few years or so. I believe there are some griffins training right now over the unicorn field. I think you should go and watch for awhile and see just what it is that they can do."

Argon had straightened a bit at the mention of his father and Oberon could see a spark of interest in the large sharp eyes. He nodded to Argon as the griffin ran towards the fields.

Argon hurried along with excitement. He thought, *Of course I could be the king's guard. He's right. I'm not a nestling and I can fly now, too. I am too old to be with my mother and I should be learning maneuvers.* He could see the griffins flying in the distance, and he quickened his pace until he was directly below them. A few of them had come in for a landing. They were twice, maybe even three times his size, but he was his father's son and it didn't really bother him. They stood, beaks gaped, breathing heavily.

Gunther, a drab olive colored griffin that Argon recognized as the trainer laughed as he walked over, his eyes clear and bright. "Well, if it isn't young Argon. Hey, come and see Ripper's boy, you guys. Have you come to watch what the fighters can do?"

Argon nodded. "Yes. I'm to become the king's guard. I guess I'd better start training as soon as you can teach me, Gunther."

Gunther guffawed at that and reached a claw out to grasp Argon's shoulder. "King's guard, you say? Aye, laddie, that's a good one. Now, you stand back a bit as we're going to do some verticals. Who knows? Maybe in a few more years, you might just be flying with us. Now run along, boy."

Argon's face fell as he sulked off to the tree line to get out of the way. He would not be accepted here, either. What a fool he was to think he could train with the fighters. There was no place here for him and he knew it.

He caught sight of two elves heading for the gate and ran to get through behind them. Once through the gate the elves headed for the trees and moving silently, he was right behind them and they never even noticed. He split off from them now and headed for the thickest part of the woods. Once he was deep inside the shadows he slowed his pace to a comfortable walk. His head bent low as he sorted out his thoughts. *I'm too young to fight and too old to stay at home. Where am I supposed to go now?*

He snatched at a mouse scurrying by but missed, adding to his misery. He was hungry, too. At least it was cool and quiet in the woods and he could blend in rather well. He looked up. The lowest branch was pretty high up and he didn't know if he could fly that high yet, at least not from a sitting position. Maybe if he could run and gather speed, he could climb that high once he was in the air. He looked around and saw there was very little room to run, the ground being covered with brambles and low growing scrub. He backed up into a thicket and put his head under his wing and slept.

He was hungry and tired and didn't know how to get back to the gate. He had only been here once before with his father, and that was before he could fly. He went into a dreamless, hopeless sleep.

Droplets of water splattered him awake. It was an afternoon rain and now his feathers and fur were soaked. He stretched and fluffed his feathers hoping to put a layer of air in between himself and the water. It was futile, as the rain increased to a downpour. He crouched under the trees and closed his eyes. His stomach rumbled and he thought he was as miserable as he could possibly get. It subsided around sunset and now the rain was gone but it became increasingly darker. He came out of the brush, fluffed, and stretched. He heard a stream in the distance and thought maybe he could catch some frogs or lizards.

He drew back in fright when he saw a torch light coming towards him and he jumped back into the brush and watched with wary eyes. It was a human alright, a pretty one, but a human nevertheless, and that meant danger. To his dismay, it looked as if she was going to stay right there and not pass by. She thrust the torch in the ground, removed her clothing and jumped into the stream. He kept as still as he could and waited for her to come back out, dress, and leave. She was in the process of doing precisely that when he sneezed. He could have died a million deaths as she looked in his direction, raising the torch so she could see.

"Who's there?"

He held perfectly still, or at least as still as you could when you were shaking like a leaf in the wind. She saw him then, and he thought to run but he found he could not move a muscle. She bent over, looking him right in the eyes and smiled.

"Well, if it isn't a little griffin. Why are you here? Come on now, I know you can talk. I won't hurt you. I'm a magical, as well. My mother knows King Oberon. It was my favorite story when I was younger. I'm Ilona Thatcher."

Argon swallowed and blinked his eyes, not knowing what to do. He was caught, that was for sure, and not being able to escape, he thought to fight, but she wasn't threatening him. She made no move to touch him and she knew about griffins.

Having nothing to lose, he ventured, "I'm Argon. I guess I live here, I don't know, I arrived here today."

She nodded and looked concerned. Knowing that it must be a very juvenile griffin, she thought he must be lost. She had never seen one, but her mother told her they were bigger than her horse and this one was barely the size of a dog. She needed to go back home but couldn't seem to leave the little magical. He looked so miserable.

"Well, Argon, I have to go back home now. Why don't you come with me? Are you hungry? I can get you some food and you could dry off by the fire. I promise you we won't hurt you and you're free to leave anytime you like, it's just that you look so wet and cold. It's not far."

Argon turned his head and looked at her sideways. He was hungry and there was no doubt about him being soaked to the skin. It could be a trap, but then what did it matter? He had no idea what he was going to do or where he was going to live. He straightened up. He hadn't realized that he had remained in a crouch until just then. He shook again.

"Alright, Ilona. I am hungry and I haven't been able to catch a thing. Then it rained, and I haven't found shelter either. I'm very dangerous though, so don't try to grab me." He gave her the most menacing look he could muster as pathetic as he looked.

Ilona tried not to laugh. She knew griffins were very respectable, or at least the full grown ones were and she did not want to insult her new little friend.

"I understand. No one will touch you, and in return I must ask your vow not to hurt any of us or the animals on our land. Is it a deal?"

He nodded earnestly and water dripped off of his beak. He followed her cautiously, ready to bolt and run if she should try to trap him, but she didn't. She paused once to check and see if he was following her and pointed ahead of her.

"See? Right through the trees there, is my home. Mother is at the castle right now, so it'll just be you and me. You're lucky. I just went fishing today and I have a string of fish drying. I've picked berries too. I bet you like berries, don't you?"

He had paused the same time she did. "Yes, I do."

She giggled and led the way into the house. He had never been inside a human shelter before. He gazed around in curiosity. He wasn't used to the frivolous trappings of humans, but still, it was warmer and drier, even if it had a lot of objects and colors. Ilona motioned him to sit on a folded blanket she had placed by the fire

"There now, doesn't that feel better? You'll dry out soon. I'm going to get you some fish and berries. Just stay right there and try to calm down. You're perfectly safe."

She left the room and Argon fluffed his feathers. It did feel good, but he wondered if he should be there at all, and having no one to ask, he just sat and waited. Ilona was going to bring him food, and that was what he really needed the most. He almost felt faint from hunger. He hadn't eaten all day. She came back shortly afterwards with a platter of fish and berries which she set before him with satisfaction.

"Go ahead and have some. I caught those fish myself this morning and the berries are sweet. Oh, I nearly forgot. What would you like to drink?"

He still sat there staring at her. "I drink water."

He looked down at the plate. He was used to eating freshly killed game, but these looked and smelled wonderful to him. He had never had smoked fish and he nibbled at one. Before long, the plate was clean and the pain in his belly went away. He drank some of the water she brought and stretched out on the blanket, feeling a lot more relaxed. She sat in a chair, busy sewing, but he saw her watching him out of the corner of her eye. He felt embarrassed that he had been so rude to her.

"Ilona? Thank you for the food and shelter. You are very kind to take me in. I hope you won't get into trouble for sharing your food."

She put down her sewing and sat on the floor beside him. He flinched and moved away just a little, but he looked a lot better than he had before. His feathers had dried and he fluffed them. His shiny black coat was fuzzy with the fur of a baby griffin. His wings were tipped with silver as were his nails. Ilona thought he was adorable and would love to hug him, but she knew better than to try to touch him. Griffins were not to be pets. They were an amazingly intelligent species all on their own and deserved a lot of respect. Even at this tender age, she knew Argon would be capable of removing one of her hands with that sharp beak, and the claws were just as deadly. They were supposed to have a nasty temperament, but this one was just scared and lost. She remembered Greccon had told her he rode on one when he was eight or so.

"You're very welcome, Argon. I hope we can be friends. Would you like some more to eat? There's plenty more, and I can go fishing again tomorrow. Now, since you have no shelter yet, why don't you just stay here with me, that is, just until you can find a place of your own? At least you wouldn't be hungry or wet again."

Argon didn't really feel comfortable inside the house. Griffins liked open spaces where they could take wing at a moment's notice, but it had begun to rain again and the thought of sleeping in a puddle disgusted him.

"Thank you, Ilona. If I could just rest here tonight, I will find shelter and food for myself in the morning. I guess I'd like to be your friend. We don't like humans, but you've helped me and I won't ever forget you."

She nodded. "Rest then, my friend. Maybe I can help you find a place of your own tomorrow. If not, you can certainly go fishing with me if you want to."

He gave her a nod, but with a full belly, his eyes were closing and he yawned. His head tucked under his wing and he was fast asleep, taking deep breaths.

Poor little thing, she thought. She wondered why he was really here. Certainly he was too young to be so far from his clan. She couldn't wait to see the expression on her mother's face when she saw him.

She didn't have to wait long. Glynnis first saw her daughter's finger go to her lips as she pointed to the furry feathery lump on the blanket in front of the fire. She looked in disbelief and motioned her daughter outside and backed through the door that she had just come in through.

"Ilona, is that a baby griffin? Where on earth did you find it?"

Ilona grinned. "Isn't he the cutest thing? He was in the shrubbery by the river, sitting there, miserable and soaked through to the skin. So I brought him home and gave him the fish I caught this morning with some berries and water. The poor little thing was starving and exhausted. What could I do? His name is Argon and he's pretty scared. He says he's here to stay, as soon as he finds shelter for himself." She shrugged her shoulders and Glynnis put her hands on her hips.

"But Ilona, he's too young to be away from his mother. She must be frantic by now. Can you still call Greccon in your thoughts?"

Ilona looked down at her feet. "Sure, I mean I guess so. I haven't called since he became engaged. Why should I call him?"

Glynnis peeked in through the door. Argon had fallen over on his side, still sleeping soundly. "Greccon can call King Oberon and let him know Argon is here. I don't mind that he's here or that you gave him a good meal, bless his little heart, but the magicals must be told that one of their own is here. He must have gotten lost or fell through the gate. Try to get Greccon to come right away."

She went back in then, leaving Ilona outside to concentrate. She paused to look at the little griffin. He was much too young to be there. A predator would have had him by now. He slept like a baby should, without a care in the world, but he wouldn't survive out there by himself. After the massacre of most of the griffins, she knew Oberon could not afford to lose even one, especially one as dear as the babe sleeping in front of her.

Ilona came back in. "He's on his way. He wasn't happy about it, but I told him it was urgent and that you wanted him to come right away. I couldn't very well tell him that I needed him. What would he tell Felicia?" She sounded a bit jealous for a moment, but she knew there would never be anything between Greccon and her.

Glynnis agreed. "I don't care what excuse you gave him as long as he comes and helps us to contact this little angel's parents. Argon didn't ask to go home?"

Ilona shook her head. "No. He's a feisty little thing, telling me how dangerous he is. I almost laughed, but I remembered you told me how proud and gallant the griffins were, so I tried not to look amused. He's a tough little boy with a mind of his own. He certainly wasn't whining or complaining. I had to talk him into coming with me or he'd still be out in the rain. If you ask me, I think he ran away from home."

Glynnis sat down and shook her head. "No. Oberon would have never allowed it. He must have fallen through the gate."

Ilona sat and picked up her sewing while her mother read. Neither one could concentrate as they were both infatuated with the young griffin. He fluffed, yawned, and flipped over without a thought to the world. He hadn't even noticed that Glynnis was there. His lion's tail switched back and forth as his feet twitched, obviously chasing something in his dreams. Ilona tried not to giggle, but Glynnis could tell that Ilona loved Argon and it would be hard for Ilona to let him go home. She could tell that Ilona wanted to keep him, and although it would be fine for awhile, griffins were natural born killers when they got older and grew to be the size of a full grown horse, some even larger. No, this baby had to go back home and she knew it would break Ilona's heart.

Glynnis whispered to Ilona, "Why don't you meet Greccon at the river? That way he won't wake or scare little Argon."

Ilona quietly got up and slipped out of the door and made her way through the woods to the river. It was a cool night and the rain had stopped but the woods smelled wet and green. She heard the horse's hooves splashing through the water and hailed Greccon. He stopped his horse and dismounted when the horse had reached her side of the bank.

"This better be important, Ilona. We had guests."

Ilona couldn't hide her excitement. "Of course it's important. Why would I bother you now if it wasn't? Certainly you don't think I just wanted to see you?"

He relented and kissed her cheek. All of the anger out of his voice now, he asked, "What is it?"

Ilona watched the horse bend to drink in the river. "I found a baby griffin today named Argon. He was wet, cold and hungry so I took him home. Mother said that you could contact King Oberon and tell him that Argon is at our home. She's afraid that they might be looking for him."

Greccon looked astounded. "A baby griffin? Why didn't you tell the fairies? They would have taken the message right to Oberon."

Ilona shrugged. "He said he was living here, now. I'm not that familiar with the griffins. I didn't realize he was much too young to be here or I would have. Then it rained and the fairies were gone anyway. You know they hate the rain. Well, it's too late now, so will you call him? Mother said they must be frantic by now."

Greccon scratched a mosquito bite on his arm absently. "Argon, you said? That wouldn't be Reaper's son, would it? I think it is. Why would he be here? Take me to him, Ilona." She nodded and he walked behind her, leading his horse.

Oberon had finished up the court for the day and went outside to fly the perimeter, as was his habit everyday. He saw a griffin fly by and signaled a greeting to him. Then it suddenly occurred to him Argon was still at loose ends. He immediately changed direction and flew towards the griffin cliffs. Landing where his fighters were dwelling, he motioned for the first griffin he saw.

"My Lord." The brilliant purple sentry said as he bowed.

Oberon looked around franticly for the young black griffin and did not see him. "Young Argon, Reaper's son. He is here, isn't he? I told him he could move into the fighter's quarters."

The sentry griffin looked dumbfounded. "Reaper's young fledgling? Ah, well, no, my Lord, he isn't here. Isn't he a little too young to be moved in here with the fighters?"

Oberon looked exasperated. "Of course he is, Tempest, but he was having trouble at home. His mother has pushed him out and frankly, I didn't know what to do with him. He was heading for the gate, so I sent him to observe the fighters and told him he could move in here. I know it's a bit irregular, but he could be made useful here for awhile. Are you sure you haven't seen any young griffins hanging about?"

Tempest nodded. "Yes, my Lord. Perhaps he went back home."

Oberon was considering that when he saw Gunther landing. "Gunny. Have you seen young Argon today?"

Gunther folded his wings and hurried over with a bow. "Aye, my Lord. He's a spunky little imp. He came out to watch the practice today. He tells me he's going to be your wingman and needed to practice. It was really funny. All the fighters got a big charge out of it. I told him to come back in a few years and sent him on his way."

Oberon groaned. "Have you seen him since?"

Gunther shook his head. "No, my Lord, is he missing?"

Oberon moved to the edge of the cliff. "Yes. Send out a few scouts, Gunny. I'll go and talk with his mother. I don't know where he's gone. If his mother insists he should leave the nest, I want you to make a place for him here. We owe that much to Reaper. I'm sure you can find something for him to do and you can start some preliminary defensive training with him."

Gunther said, "Yes, my Lord. I hadn't realized the situation. The scouts will be up in an instant and he is welcome here. No griffin goes by the wayside while I have a breath in my body." At that, Oberon took flight and Gunny was shouting for scouts.

The young griffin's head popped up in alarm, his eyes wide. He ran for the window, leaping over a table in the process and scattering its contents. In an instant, he was outside and running through the woods. Glynnis shouted after him, to no avail. She didn't know what had frightened the young griffin until she heard the horses' hooves and her daughter and Greccon talking. Argon was gone.

Greccon and Ilona heard the rustlings of a small object moving very fast through the underbrush. Greccon acted immediately, knowing it must be Argon making his escape. He froze the little griffin in his tracks, with an immobilizing spell.

"Argon. It's Greccon. Do you remember me? I won't hurt you. I knew your father."

Argon's eyes were wide and frightened and he found he could not move a thing, which only frightened him more. Greccon bent low to touch his feathery head.

"It's alright, Argon. I put a spell on you to keep you still long enough to talk to you. I didn't feel like chasing you all through these woods in the dark. Now, relax. All I want to do is find out why you are here. You remember me, don't you? Your father, Reaper, brought you here a while ago when you didn't even have your flight feathers. You sure have grown up." Ilona smiled as Argon seemed to calm down a bit. Then she heard the twang of a bow.

"Hunters." She screamed, as she covered the little griffin with her body. The arrow struck her in the back and she lurched forward, Argon still in her arms. He still could not move. He was terrified now and trapped under the weight of her body. Greccon spun around and instantly killed the two hunters running towards them with bolts of lightning from his hands. They fell in two lumps into the dead leaves. He looked in horror at Ilona, whose dress was dripping in blood. He closed his eyes tightly and called for Oberon.

"My King. Ilona has been shot protecting Argon. Help me."

Oberon heard the cry in flight to Argon's home. He turned

quickly and called for Illustra. He told Greccon to construct a portal where he was, and picking up on the magic signal, he accelerated his flight. Illustra was in full gallop to the exact spot. They reached Greccon's portal and entered into the mortal world. Illustra ran right to Ilona and placed her horn on her head, keeping her soul intact while Oberon transformed into human form and removed the arrow. Ilona was murmuring, and he could hear her asking if Argon was safe.

"Yes, dear Ilona, rest still now and let me heal the wounds."

Oberon worked diligently, locating the injuries and healing them one at a time until she was once again sound except for the loss of blood. Illustra backed away as Oberon lifted her off of the panicking griffin. He cowered, and free of Greccon's spell now, ran to Illustra who soothed him. Greccon stood there and reached for Ilona's hand. She had fainted and Oberon instructed him to carry her into the house.

Glynnis threw open the door at the commotion and watched in horror as Greccon carried in her daughter and laid her on the bed. Recognizing Oberon she bowed. "My King."

Oberon put his arms around her. "She's alright, Glynnis. She took an arrow but Illustra and I have healed her. She has lost quite a bit of blood and will be weak when she awakes."

Greccon faced Oberon. "It was the damn hunters again. Oberon, The lord of the castle has said he is giving me the forest as a wedding present. I would have it protected against the hunters. Will you help me to set up a protection spell to cover the whole forest?"

Oberon sat down heavily. "We will talk of those things once we have Ilona back on her feet." He scowled at Argon, who was hiding behind Illustra.

She was standing in Glynnis' home, monitoring Ilona's life force, which seemed to be strengthening now that the wounds were healed. She tossed her head and turned compassionate blue eyes towards Glynnis. "She would have lost her life today, but Greccon was very wise to summon us here as quickly as he did. She will recover. I would say at least three days of rest."

Glynnis nodded, wiping the tears from her eyes. Argon pushed to the front to look at Ilona. He watched her breathe. He turned towards Oberon.

"My Lord, I would stay with her until she is well." He lifted his beak defiantly. "It was my fault she was hurt and I will make her better."

Oberon stood up, ready to strangle the young impudent griffin for disobeying him in the first place, but Illustra winked at him, catching his eye.

She said, "Yes. I think it would be appropriate that he stays with Ilona for a few days, if Glynnis will allow him to."

Glynnis nodded.

Oberon spoke, "I hope you have learned that nothing good ever comes of disobeying your king, young griffin. See what trouble you have caused in your stubbornness? You will stay and help Glynnis heal her. Greccon," He shook the wizard's hand. "You have done well. I will send griffins to take care of those hunters. I believe the sharks will appreciate them. Illustra and I will leave now. I will be back in three days' time to collect my arrogant griffin. Meanwhile, I would work him into exhaustion to pay for his bad decisions." He winked at Glynnis who nodded in return.

She was overwhelmed with a dragon, a unicorn, a griffin and a wizard in her home, all at the same time. Greccon stayed for a little while, wondering how he was going to explain all this to Felicia. She would never believe all of this. His heart was still with Ilona, watching her sleep peacefully. Thank God he was in the right place at the right time for a change. He knew the arrow had killed her, and he knew the only ones who could save her would be King Oberon and the queen of the unicorns, and it had to be immediate or it would be too late. Ilona would live, and he was thankful. After Greccon left, Glynnis found herself face to face with a penitent baby griffin.

"Argon, why don't you pull that blanket over by her bed and you can watch for any changes that you think I should know about?"

He dutifully yanked on the blanket until he had it next to her bed. He sat on it with his front claws on the stuffed mattress. He sat there staring at her, watching every move she made. Glynnis hadn't meant that he should watch her that closely, but she dismissed it. The griffin had a lot on his mind and maybe he could work it out while on duty. Satisfied and exhausted, Glynnis went to her own bed.

Argon watched her leave then turned his attention to Ilona. He sniffed. It had been his fault she was hurt. He couldn't believe this human cared about him that much to give her life to save his. There was no love between humans and griffins, that is, until now. They had became friends just hours ago, and yet she loved him. He heard her ask Oberon if he was unhurt. There she had been, close to death and fading fast, and her only thoughts were of him. He swallowed. No one had cared about him that much except perhaps his father. Illustra cared about him, but Illustra cared about everyone and he was no exception. But this girl, Ilona, she was different somehow. He thought he saw her eyelids twitch. He slowly moved closer until his beak was almost touching her nose. He stared.

Ilona opened her eyes and blinked, seeing a very large pair of griffin eyes so very close to hers. "Argon?" She took a deep breath, "Are you alright?"

He had blinked back at her and jumped a little when her eyes opened. "Yes, Ilona, you saved me and were killed."

Ilona winced. "Am I dead, then?"

Argon shook his head quickly. "No. King Oberon and Queen Illustra brought you back. It was my fault. I should have saved you from the hunters, but I couldn't move with that spell Greccon put on me," he said bravely. He knew he could have never saved her from the hunters, but it sounded good and if he was bigger and stronger he could have; he was sure of it. He watched as she tried to sort out all the events that had taken place and he knew she was having a hard time with it.

"You'll be just fine, Ilona. You need to rest for a few days and I'm going to stay to help you. Illustra said I should, and do you want to know a secret?"

She blinked again and nodded.

He bent his head conspiratorially and lowered his voice. "I heard her give you a gift for saving me. I don't really understand it, but she said friends such as we are should never be apart. She gave you an immortal soul to stay with me as long as I live, and griffins live forever, if we're not killed. She said for the gift of my life, you were to have a gift of your own, so we could always be together. Isn't that great?"

Ilona thought it was, even though she really wasn't understanding what the griffin was saying. She was tired and thought she would think about it all later. She was having to struggle to keep her eyes open and finally she gave up. She patted the bed and moved over so Argon could jump up. "Come on, then, best friend. Let's both get some sleep, shall we?"

Argon jumped up and snuggled up to her, his head on her chest. She put one arm around him, being careful not to ruffle his wings and before long she was lulled asleep by his purring snores. Glynnis had gotten up to check on them and was comforted by the sight of the two of them asleep together. She smiled and shook her head. She was glad to see Ilona's color had returned and she couldn't be more comfortable then she was, snuggled up to a warm fuzzy griffin. Neither one of them woke up to see her grinning, but Glynnis knew a life-long friendship between the two of them had begun. You couldn't do better than having a griffin for a friend. She knew as the years went by, she would see a lot of Argon. They both had a lot in common. Neither one of them had their father, they were both very intelligent, and it seemed they were both lonely. She knew Ilona was missing her friendship with Greccon and it seemed Argon didn't have any friends either. They suited each other well. It was ironic that fate should bring these two together, as unlikely a pair as you could imagine, yet so very right for each other.

As the three days went by, the two of them learned a lot from each other. Ilona taught him how to mind-speak back and forth with her so he could always talk to her and vice-versa. He learned that quickly. He wanted to teach her how to fly, but she seemed to be missing the necessary equipment. Glynnis had to laugh at him wanting her to fly.

She offered, "You know, Argon, when you get large enough to hold her weight, she could fly with you then."

That seemed to satisfy him. Ilona gained back her strength slowly, a lot slower than Glynnis had hoped for. She was unable to attend Greccon's wedding, but Glynnis went and told her it was a lovely wedding and Greccon had asked for her and seemed concerned that she was not well enough to attend. It's probably all for the better, thought Glynnis, who knew Ilona had loved Greccon and refused to marry him. Thatcher women never married, or so the tale went. It was said that if they married, they would no longer be able to heal. Glynnis was sure it was an old wives' tale and told Ilona so, but she hadn't married either and Ilona saw that. Of course, Elijah had never returned, but she wondered if she would have married him if he had asked her again. She really didn't know. Thatcher women liked their freedom. They were free to heal and travel to where they needed to be. It would be hard to do with a husband and family.

Argon was sad to leave Ilona, but he promised to talk with her every night and she agreed. He would not ask King Oberon for more time there, as he feared he was in enough trouble already. The king was pleased to see Ilona up and about and he thanked her for saving the life of his griffin, to which she reciprocated by thanking him for saving her own life. He saw how the friendship had blossomed between Ilona and Argon and he agreed to have an elf or a dwarf supervise his trips back to visit her. It would not be every week, as he told Ilona, "This griffin has a lot of work to do. He has a room in the fighter's wing at the Realm and he has to begin his training immediately."

It had sounded important and Argon stood tall, although he felt like crying when he had to leave.

CHAPTER ELEVEN

"What shall we call him?" Felicia asked Greccon as Glynnis placed his newborn son in his arms.

Greccon wiped a tear from his eye as he looked into the face of the crying swaddled child. He leaned over to kiss Felicia and said, "We shall call him Ursan, for the constellation, Ursa Major. Those were the stars I saw in your eyes when you bewitched me."

Felicia laughed, exhausted but elated. She took the struggling baby back and put him to her breast. Comforted, he nursed.

Glynnis hugged Greccon and then Felicia. "A fine healthy little Ursan, too, I'm happy to say. He's perfect."

Greccon thanked her as he sat next to his new family. Glynnis picked up her things and put them in her bag. "It won't be long before Mary delivers her child, as well. It's such a happy time, isn't it? Well, I'll leave the three of you alone. I need to get back anyway. Ilona will be frantic for the news."

Greccon watched her leave and turned his smile back to his wife. "He's a handsome boy, Felicia, and I can tell he has magic already."

Felicia laughed. "Greccon, really, he's but an hour old, How would you know such a thing?"

Greccon nodded. "I can tell, Felicia, really I can. He'll be a powerful wizard when he grows up. So powerful, he will transcend time and space."

She looked down at the boy, his little hands bunched into fists, and caressed his head. "It sounds like a proud father, to me, who would like his son to be just like him."

Glynnis stopped to talk to Father Murphy as she loaded her bags onto Baron. "A fine healthy boy, Father. They are calling him Ursan, for the stars."

Father Murphy clapped his hands together in joy and lifted his eyes skyward in a prayer of thanks. "God bless them. Have you seen Mary? Is she well? It shouldn't be long before we have an heir to the kingdom, here. An heir and a new mage. I wonder if little Ursan will have mage powers like his father?"

Glynnis tightened the straps on Baron, who stomped in the dirt. "I think so, and Mary seems to be doing fine. I just left her some tea to relax her. She's as anxious for this baby as everyone else is, but you know, Father, the baby will come when it's ready and not before. Thankfully, I'm not far away." She smiled as she mounted the horse.

Waving good bye to the Father, she trotted Baron through the woods. Small snowflakes had started to fall and Glynnis looked through the trees to see the sky. It was a sunny day when she arrived at the castle, but it turned grey and cold. She gathered her cloak around her to keep out the biting wind. She kicked Baron into a canter and he obliged willingly, anxious to get back to his warm stable.

By the time they reached her cottage, the flakes were larger and very wet. It was snowing heavily now, blanketing the landscape into a brilliant white wonderland. It would be the sticking kind of snow, and Glynnis brought down a heavy blanket for Baron from the rafters. Rosey, Ilona's rose grey mare, nickered a greeting and a reminder that she needed a blanket as well.

"We'll get out the really warm blanket for you tonight, Baron, and one for you too, Rosey. "

He snorted in reply. She brushed him down and filled his water pail. "I'll stoke up the fire tonight, boy. That should keep you nice and warm, and I'll heat you both up a warm mash for dinner." She slapped his rump twice, scratched Rosey's ear after covering her with another warm blanket, and left to go into the house.

Ilona was there, sorting out dried seeds for her. She looked up as her mother walked in and smiled.

"Was it a girl or a boy?"

Glynnis hung up her cloak and stamped the snow from her feet. "A fine healthy boy that they named Ursan."

Ilona smiled. "When can I go see him? I love babies."

Glynnis laughed. "I'd give it a few days. Let Felicia get back on her feet. Don't you worry, I'm sure they'll be placing him in your care often enough. Everyone likes to leave their children with healers instead of just ordinary people. As if we have any magic power over their children. I guess they think if the child gets ill, they don't have to worry. Either way, I'm sure you'll have your fill, what with Greccon's son and Mary's baby when it arrives." She added another log to the fire and then bent down to warm her hands. "What do you hear of Argon?"

Ilona came around the table and sat by the fire on a thick braided rug. "He's been busy in training. He's grown a whole lot larger and stronger than he was a few years ago. He took a bad landing and broke a few feathers. Anyway, he doesn't want to visit until he looks presentable again. You know how vain he is." She giggled. "I haven't seen him in months. I miss him. He said, in another year, his brother, Shylock, is to join him in the training."

Glynnis stood up and went into the kitchen to put a stew on for dinner. "I know you miss him. I guess you'll see less of him, the more he trains. I'm glad he's doing well, though."

Ilona took the cooking pot from her mother and hung it on a hook over the fire to heat. As they sat down to eat Ilona said, "When he's fully trained, he's going to be in charge of protecting the gate and our forest. The protection spell that Greccon and King Oberon have set in place will alert him and us at the same time. It's woven like a spider's web, Greccon told me, and it's very sensitive so that no evil or harm can pass it. I'm glad we don't have to worry about hunters anymore. Right now, Tempest is on duty, but Argon insisted it will be his job when he's ready. Then, we'll see him a lot more."

Glynnis nodded. "It's a comfort to know we are to be protected. We're very lucky that you have such a powerful friend."

Ilona pushed the vegetables around on her plate and opted for a chunk of venison. After swallowing, she said, "I heard King Oberon had a son as well. Harmonia hatched her egg not more than a month ago. His name is Titanion and he's supposed to go and live with his grandfather on a continent south of here. It's customary for the grandfather to train the grandchildren for a hundred years or so. That sounds like such a long time, doesn't it?"

Glynnis drank some wine, leaned back in her chair, and allowed herself to relax a little "No, not really. For a dragon, it's a short span of time, considering they live forever ."

Ilona nodded. She hadn't thought of that. "He's a silvery blue color, according to Argon. So, now King Oberon has an heir. Isn't it strange that all these babies are being born in the winter time? I thought most babies were born in the spring."

Glynnis had cleaned up the dishes and was now sprawled out by the fire, her eyes closed. "They come when they are ready to be born. It really doesn't matter what time of year it is. Usually, it's when I'm good and comfortable and don't feel like delivering them.

* * *

"Harmonia, for the last time, I'm telling you he goes to my father's cave to train. Don't be so pig-headed, and for Gods' sake, don't make me command you."

Harmonia turned her back on Oberon, clutching her son to her chest. "No. I'll not let him go. He's my son, too, and I want to keep him for awhile, if you don't mind. You were not the one who had to sit on that egg for years. Now, go away Oberon and don't bother us."

Oberon roared with impatience and blew out a tremendous plume of fire. "You cannot talk to me like that, Harmonia. Not and keep your head. I am the king now, and as your king, I must de-mand respect from everyone, including you, or you can damn well go back and live outside the Realm. I understand he's still little and he can stay until he is of an age to leave, but he must go to Elgin. It has always been that way and it will stay that way. Who better to teach him than the elder? Didn't your grandfather teach you? He is my son and heir and I say he goes to Elgin and I don't want to hear another word against it."

Harmonia looked insulted and angry now as Oberon turned his back on her this time and took off to fly off some of his anger.

She was impossible. Somehow he had always known she would be. Why had he chosen her to mate with? It had been his father's idea and he may just need his father to come and get Titanion when the time was right for him to go and train. She was bad enough when she was hatching the egg. Get me this, get me that. Of course he would; it was his duty to keep her fed and comfortable while she incubated the egg, but his son was here now, and very shortly, her job would be done. *I'll give her another month or so, and then he has to be trained.* He couldn't wait to be out from under her challenging ways. Once Titanion was with Elgin, he could forget all about her.

He realized he had circled the Realm twice already, and still, he did not feel better. He would never choose a mate again. One heir was sufficient. He would rather go into battle than have to deal with any more women. Titanion was a treasure, though, he thought, and he softened a little. He was a striking silver blue and showed remarkable intelligence already. *He had to take after me; his mother was just too crazy to produce a dragon of Titanion's caliber.*

He enjoyed talking to Titanion and watching him try to fly. He had a very large wingspan and Oberon thought he would grow to be of a record size. He was well pleased with the boy, if only he didn't have to be in contact with his mother. Harmonia was wearing on his last nerve now, and it was all he could do to contain himself.

Looking down, he saw Illustra grazing in the flowery field below. She bobbed her head when she saw him and he decided she would be the best one to talk to, to make him feel better. Illustra turned her head and closed her eyes as he landed a bit too fast, stirring up a cloud of dust.

"My dear Illustra, I do so need to speak with you on the subject of impossible women."

She tossed her mane and pranced a little. "I'm sure I don't know what you mean, my king. Women aren't impossible. It is the men who are insensitive and controlling that are the problem."

He looked at her with a disgusted look and sat down, defeated. He gave her a sideways glance. "I suppose there is an element of truth in that, my queen. It's Harmonia who is trying my patience. She vows that she will never let Titanion leave. She intends to keep him with her and you know he needs to go and train with Elgin if he's to be worth his salt as a leader someday."

Illustra munched a mouthful of bright green grass thoughtfully, and Oberon waited for an answer. Swallowing, she said, "You have nothing to worry about."

He looked at her with incredulity, and, laughing at his expression, she went on, "Everyone thinks mothers are so all encompassing. She will gladly send him to his grandfather as soon as he starts to be underfoot, bouncing around and into mischief. Right now, he's helpless and adorable, and you know how long she had to sit and wait for him to arrive. Give her time, Oberon. Let her enjoy the miracle of a new child without fear of having him taken away from her. It's a bonding time she is in right now. Everything will work out just as you want it to. Trust me and be kind to her. Titanion will reap the benefits of a happy mother instead of an angry one."

Oberon took a deep breath and let it out slowly. She was right, of course. Illustra was always right. Why hadn't he thought of that himself? He had tried to strong-arm Harmonia and he could see very clearly now how wrong he had been. As old as he was, it amazed him how stupid he could be at times, and he felt regret and embarrassment at the way he had snapped at Harmonia.

Illustra nodded at him, knowing exactly how he felt. At least he was king enough to acknowledge he had made a mistake, she thought, and then looked up as King Orion emerged from the woods with his young son, Razz. The child broke into a run to hug Illustra, and she rubbed his cheek with her velvety muzzle, in delight. He was such a loving child, everything an elf should be.

Orion hailed them and joined them in conversation, but his mood was dark and he brought only sad news. Understanding that the men were to talk of grave issues, Illustra flipped Razz on her back to give him a ride. Children should be spared from the frightening news, and King Orion did not often look so upset.

As she bounded away with the laughing child scrambling to hold on, King Orion said, "My scouts have reported zealots in the woods. They plan to seek out the healer and burn her for a witch."

Oberon narrowed his eyes. "Are we to go back to the old times, again?" He huffed with exasperation. "Well, they will never get past Tempest. All he's had to do was cry out or growl and it usually sent them all running away. He would contact me if he needed help, and I'll send Gunny. Why do they persist in these false accusations and their attacks? Have they no lives of their own to be concerned about?"

King Orion shook his head in dismay. "I believe they're frightened. The church blames everything, from foul weather to plagues, on witchcraft and demons. They feel that if they execute the witches, all will be well again. It is also an attempt to unite the people by eliminating the ones who will not conform to their new religion. Conform, or be hanged as a witch."

Oberon snorted with contempt. "Glynnis is no witch. What she is, a talented healer with a touch of magic, is what would possibly save them from all these illnesses that they, for the most part, bring on themselves with their filthy habits, not to mention spreading diseases by constantly being at war with each other. Why can't they see that?"

They turned to watch Illustra giving Razz a bouncy ride through the fields. Orion said, "What? And blame themselves? It is much easier to point the finger elsewhere, and right now, they seem to be pointing the blame on Glynnis. Oh, by the way, she has just delivered the Lord of Griffin's Gate castle a new heir. It's a girl. They've named her Alyssa and I hear she is very fair. She will make a wonderful playmate for Greccon's new son, Ursan."

Oberon trimmed a nail and nodded. "Well at least you have brought me some good news, but this news of Glynnis disturbs me. As you know, she has a young daughter, herself, named Ilona. Argon has become quite attached to the girl since she saved his life. I will have to keep this news from him. You know how he will react if he thinks Ilona is in any danger. He's grown quite a bit since then, but I don't think he's ready to test himself in a real battle yet. He needs to grow a bit more, although Gunny says he is at the top of his class. I expect good things from that griffin once he has the experience he needs."

King Orion agreed and sat down in the grass to watch his giggling son ride Illustra. He smiled at the joy and innocence of his handsome young son. Turning back to Oberon, he said, "I've noticed a change in Argon's attitude since he's known the girl. She seems to have softened him a little. Perhaps she has a place in his heart. He's had a hard time adjusting to the death of Reaper. Perhaps he's trying to impress this young lady as he would his father, were he still alive. Either way, it has done him a service."

Oberon laughed softly and said, "It's all about love with you elves, isn't it? I'm sure it's gratitude to the girl and nothing more. As for me, I've had more than my fill of women. I don't know how you elves manage it. It's all so complicated and hopeless. Don't you ever argue with Arianna? I know I could have strangled Harmonia today. It's a blessing that we're not pair-bonded."

King Orion looked amused. "What else is there, if not love? Arianna and I are love-bonded. We've had children, and every one is a treasure. We never argue. We have a lot of life to go through yet, more children to bring into the world. I couldn't imagine life without her. You dragons are much too stuffy and arrogant. Life is to be enjoyed, not fought over. Look at Erastis, there. Not a care in the world, besides hanging on so he doesn't fall. Life is like that, Oberon. You just hang on and enjoy it as much as you can."

With that, he left, walking back to the woods and leaving Oberon to watch Razz and Illustra play in the field of flowers. He wished life was really that simple.

* * *

Two years passed by without any remarkable incidents. Tempest had guarded the Griffin forest well, and there were a few troublesome villagers missing, further adding to the mystery of the woods. The villagers were becoming more and more disgruntled with the way their leaders were manipulating them , but in the Griffin Castle, life was good.

Lady Mary and Felicia sat in the courtyard, watching their toddlers play in the bright morning sun. Alyssa was growing faster than Ursan and stood a whole head taller than him already. Ursan tried to give her a big soppy kiss and she had pushed him down. His pride hurting more than his bottom, he sat and pouted while she tried to buy back his favor with a wooden toy.

It was spring, and the ladies were excited about going into the village that afternoon to buy some bolts of cloth for new festival dresses. They had been told a new shipment from Paris had arrived at the port and were anxious to see what other finery had been imported. Ilona, now twenty, was riding over to mind the children. Any of the court would have been happy to oblige, but Ilona had such a way with the children, and they loved her more than any of the court women.

"We will have to have some help to get dresses ready in time for the festival. I wonder why the ships were so late into port? They were due in a few months ago, and the weather has been fair" said Mary, her eyes on her daughter.

Felicia stood up and faced the woods. There was still no sign of Ilona. "Oh, I'm sure we'll manage. We'll have a sewing party until they're all done. I wonder where Ilona is? Usually, when we ask her to mind the children, she comes so early."

She picked up Ursan and wiped the dirt off of his face. He wriggled to get back down. Alyssa was sitting on the ground, placing blocks on top of each other, and he wanted to help her. His feet were already moving before he touched the ground. He sat next to Alyssa and they took turns placing blocks, one at a time, on top of each other to form a tower until they tumbled down. They were repeating the same game, bubbling over with laughter as the blocks fell, when Ilona rode up.

"I would have been here sooner, but I was waiting for Mother to return from the village. I was hoping to take Baron here, so I wouldn't have to tack up my horse. She was due back earlier, but I hear there is so much sickness in the village now that she must have been called to help others. I had to chase Rosey all over the woods. She didn't want to go for a ride." She laughed as she patted her horse's neck.

She dismounted and handed her reins over to a stable page as she was barraged by two very excited children. She kissed them both and admired their toys and clothes. They hung on her like ornaments and she laughed. Felicia and Mary left then to find their escorts to go into the village.

Lord McTavish, knowing the restlessness in the village, sent two of his knights, a carriage driver, and several pages to accompany the ladies into the bustling town. There was a constant cloud of dust in the air as horses and people hurriedly went about their business of advertising their wares. Felicia held up a length of rich purple cloth for Mary to admire. It was smooth and well woven. Mary nodded as she measured out enough for several dresses. A deep forest green length of fabric was held up to Felicia and Mary thought the color was just perfect for her, and the exuberant vendor lent his approval as well. Of course, he would have approved of anything the women were willing to buy from him, and it looked as if he was going to have a very profitable day. By the time they had finished with the cloth and trimmings, they were quite a few coins lighter and the sun was beginning to descend. The pages were running back and forth from the carriage, carrying the bundles of wares that the ladies had purchased.

A few blocks away, there seemed to be a disturbance and the voices sounded angry and loud. Shielding her eyes against the sun, Mary said, "I wonder what could be the matter?"

Felicia turned to look as Sir Collin opened his arms in a protective manner. Looking over his shoulder, he escorted the ladies back to the carriage. Frowning, he said, "I think it is time we departed, my Lady. There seems to be a bit of trouble and we'll want to avoid that."

Felicia curiously said, "What is happening, Sir Collin?"

He shook his head. "I'm not certain. I can send a page to find out, if you wish, but at any rate, we should depart, and the sooner the better, if you don't mind my saying so."

She nodded and he helped the women back into the carriage and nodded to the driver to go. Flanked by the two knights, the carriage was back on the road. The trouble forgotten, the ladies talked of the work that would be needed to turn all their treasures into beautiful gowns. Sir Collin sent a page to investigate the trouble, with instructions to ride straight to the castle as soon as he determined what the ruckus was all about. Sir Barret split from the arriving party to ride through the woods, which was his custom, to ensure the woods were safe for the carriage to pass. The lord wanted the women to have a pleasant shopping trip and it wouldn't do to be attacked from the woods this near to the castle.

Ilona was holding Ursan and had Alyssa by the hand while the pages unloaded the bundles and brought them in. The women splashed water from the well on their faces to remove the dust from the road and turned to Ilona and the children. Felicia reached out for

Ursan and kissed him warmly. Alyssa hugged Lady Mary's legs.

Ilona beamed. "They were good as gold for me, as usual. I see you had a good day at the market." She watched as the pages ran back and forth.

Mary grinned. "Yes, the new materials were wonderful. I bought a length of material the color of new sprouting leaves, a bright green, and you will be getting a new dress made out of it, and I don't want any protesting about it, either. You never let us pay you for all the favors you do for us. Your mother will be getting a red dress, too, just in time for the festival. You will stay for dinner and hear all about it, won't you?"

Ilona hesitated. "I'd really like to check and see if Mother is home from the village yet; I'm beginning to worry about her." Her face looked pained.

Sir Barret glanced up, overhearing Ilona. "Oh, aye, Mistress Thatcher is at home. I've just passed her cottage awhile ago and I saw the cobb grazing in front."

Lady Mary smiled broadly. "There, you see? She is home and you can stay a while longer. We're going to have to measure you for the new dress. You are going to love the beads and trimmings we found, and the vendor gave them to us for practically nothing. Of course, you will have to help us sew all these dresses together. There's so much to be done."

Ilona picked up Alyssa and followed Mary into the castle.

They were sitting at dinner, when Lord McTavish said they sounded like a flock of quail and he was taking his meal to his room. The ladies were absorbed in the length of sleeves and embroidery patterns. Ilona was as excited as they were. Times had been hard lately and a festival was exactly what everyone needed to boost their spirits. It was spring and the long winter of record snowfall and very little food was over and the people would rejoice. Ilona had not yet viewed the new trappings as they had not been unwrapped from the bundles. It could wait until they had eaten dinner. Mary and Felicia hadn't eaten since breakfast this morning and were ravenous. Pages were refilling their glasses with wine as they ate.

Suddenly, she noticed Mary had pushed back her chair and Ilona looked up from her conversation with Felicia to see Mary's face a bright red. Concerned she asked, "Mary, are you feeling alright?"

Mary put a hand to her face. "I just feel a little dizzy all of a sudden. It must be all the excitement, I'm sure."

Ilona stood up and walked over to her and placed a hand on her forehead. Ilona startled at how warm Mary felt. "Why, Mary, you're burning up. Let's get you to bed."

She summoned a page to get her bag from her horse's pack and sent Mary up to bed. Felicia followed and it wasn't long afterwards that Ilona had to put her to bed as well. Both of them had fevers. Ilona had pages tell their husbands that they were both ill, and to keep the children away. Ilona mixed up herbs and water and gave it to them, but the fever kept climbing at an alarming rate. She began to place cool wet towels on their faces.

Greccon arrived and looked at Felicia with concern. "Today must have been too much for them. That, or all the wine at dinner, perhaps?"

Ilona shook her head in puzzlement. She pulled Greccon out of hearing distance from the women. She had an anguished look on her face as she said, "Greccon, I'm not sure what it is. It all came on so fast. One minute they were fine and then they were burning with fever." She looked over at the women as Felicia moaned. They had both slipped into unconsciousness. Then she looked helplessly back at Greccon. "Send for Mother, and I'll do what I can, but hurry, Greccon. I've never seen a sickness progress this quickly."

Greccon bolted for the door and Ilona went back to examine the women again. She took a deep breath and ran everything she could remember through her mind again. She checked them for red blotches or hives but there were none. Taking Mary's hand in hers, she thought of all the causes for fever, but could come up with nothing resembling what was going on here. By chance, she felt a blister on Mary's finger and she quickly turned her hand over to find that the inside of her hand was riddled with them. She checked the other hand and it, too, sported an outbreak of blisters.

She went over to Felicia and saw that she also had the same symptom. Ilona's breath caught in her throat. It had been something they had handled. It was transferred by touching the substance they had both been in contact with. Something strong enough to burn first their hands, then their bodies. Her heart sank and she desperately wished her mother had been there. It had to be a poison of some sort. Someone had poisoned the women.

The cloth. It had to be the cloth that they had handled. She turned as Lord McTavish entered, red faced and upset. She ran to him, talking all at once and he had to shake her to calm her down and make her coherent.

"My Lord. It has to be the cloth. The fever, the blisters, the women have been poisoned. At least that's what I think. Look at their hands. It's the only explanation. Oh, please, don't let anyone handle those bundles of cloth. I wish Greccon would hurry. I don't know what kind of poison it is. It's like a fire, burning them from inside."

Lord McTavish looked in horror from his wife to Felicia. They seemed too still, now, and he ran to their sides. He wailed in despair. He looked at Ilona, tears springing up in his eyes. "You've done what you could, Ilona, but it's too late. They're gone. They're both dead."

Ilona sank to her knees and covered her eyes with her hands. She had failed and now the Lady and Greccon's wife were gone. She let her tears flow and desperately wished for her mother to come. What had she done wrong? Why would someone do that? Why would they poison the cloth? It had to be the material. Oh, Gods. The children. The poor children. Little Ursan and Alyssa would never know their mothers.

Lord McTavish yelled for a page to get the priest. He held his wife in his arms, rocking her as he would Alyssa. Ilona was finding it hard to breathe; her sorrow was so intense. Father Murphy ran through the door and put a hand on her back, staring at the two dead women and the Lord. McTavish got up then, and laid his wife back down.

"They've been poisoned, Father. Heads will roll for this. Give them the rites."

He stormed out of the room, screaming for his knights. He would have the cloth seller. No one was to touch the bundles. A page ran to the stable to saddle his horse.

Father Murphy put a vestment around his shoulders and began to give the women their final blessings. Sweet little Mary, the one woman he had loved and had fought so hard to hide his feelings for, so no one would discover his sins; and firey Felicia, the gypsy woman who had captured Greccon's heart. And now, they were both with God.

Ilona sat in the corner and found she could not stop crying, her head lowered. Where was her mother and Greccon? Couldn't they do something? A healer and a mage should be able to bring them both back. She thought of Mary and Felicia, laughing and full of excitement at dinner, and could not believe they were gone now. She felt so young and stupid. She was no healer. She still didn't know what kind of poison it was. She looked up when she realized Father Murphy was bending over her, talking.

"Ilona, it wasn't your fault; it was God's will. They are in the loving arms of the Holy Father now."

Ilona wiped her face on her sleeve, not comforted at all. "God's will? Is it God's will that happy, vibrant young mothers should die? Is your God that angry and harsh to take women that have done nothing to deserve death? No, Father, it's because I didn't know enough, I didn't act fast enough, didn't recognize the symptoms. It's my fault for not sending for Mother immediately. But it was so fast. I don't even think she could have ridden here quick enough, either. It just happened so fast." She covered her face and began to sob again.

Father Murphy pulled a chair over and sat next to her, his arm around her. "You must be strong, Ilona. Their children love you more than anyone else. They will look to you for comfort, now. They will be unable to understand what has happened and will need a compassionate heart to love them."

She didn't answer, but rocked back and forth. She loved those children, and she knew she would always be there for them, in atonement for what she could not do for their mothers.

Father Murphy was still by Ilona's side when Greccon came back. He went to Felicia, and breaking down, took her in his arms. Father Murphy went to him. "She's gone to God now, Greccon. There is nothing you can do." His voice shook with emotion as he tried to comfort the mage.

Ilona glanced around for her mother. "Greccon, where is Mother? Can't you bring them back? Can't you bring them both back, now? You're a mage, do something."

Father Murphy looked from Ilona to Greccon. Surely, she

couldn't be serious. Did Greccon have that kind of power? He said nothing, but he did know their souls were with the Lord and he didn't think the Lord would give them back.

Greccon shook his head and the tears flew. "It's too late. Maybe if I was here just before, but now it's too late. Her soul is gone now and there is nothing I can do to bring her back."

Father nodded in agreement, his mouth slightly open, relieved that what Greccon said was true. He never knew what to expect when he was around mages. Greccon kissed Felicia and gently returned her to the bed.

"I don't know where your mother is, Ilona. She's not at home. I put Baron back in the stable so he wouldn't wander off, but he's still tacked up. Some of his bags were torn off." He put up his hand to stop her from running away. "Before you run off, I've asked Sir Collin to go and look for her. Ilona, it's dangerous out there. Stay here with me until he finds her."

Ilona was torn between comforting Greccon and running to find her mother. Sir Collin was the best knight they had and would surely find her. All the other knights had gone with Lord McTavish to revenge the deaths of their kinsmen. Ilona just sat back down and cried; her emotions were raw now, and Greccon cried with her.

Father Murphy prayed and wrung his hands. What could have happened to Glynnis? Father Murphy knew her well, and it was not like her to not care for her horse. She loved Baron. She would not leave him tacked up and able to wander. He remembered a time Baron had slipped out of the stable and trampled her herb garden. She was madder than a wet hen at him and told Father Murphy that if she didn't keep track of Baron like a hawk, he would sneak into some kind of mischief. She would not leave him on his own. Something was very wrong.

CHAPTER TWELVE

Glynnis rocked back and forth with Baron's pace and it almost lulled her to sleep. She had been up all night with the Smith's children. The two boys had been racked with fever and delusional. She administered medicine and kept them cool with clear water and soaked rags. By morning, the high fevers had broken and she stayed to make sure they would not return, still giving them the medicine. Their spirits were better and they had shown signs of thirst and hunger and that was always good. She left two bottles of medicine with them, making sure Mistress Smith knew how and when to administer it, and although she would not accept any payment, the Smith's offer of new shoes for Baron when he had worn down the ones he was presently using, was gratefully accepted. Now she just wanted to go home and rest.

She had Elijah's book on magic and King Oberon with her. It comforted her to have his handwriting that was so familiar, with her in the early morning hours when she missed him the most. She wished he would come back. When she learned he was gone to the Orient to study, she expected him to be back in at least a few years, but here it was over twenty years ago, and she wondered what had befallen him.

She had a hard time keeping her eyes open as Baron plodded along the worn road. She wanted a nice warm bath and at least a few hours of sleep. She knew Ilona was to mind the children of the Lord and Greccon today, and she hoped she would get home in time to see her before she left. Mistress Smith had given her wonderful nut bread and she thought they might share it with a cup of tea before Ilona had to leave. Then she could take a nice bath and sleep. She wondered how she had landed herself in this healer position where a few hours of sleep would be a treat. She shook her head. Why hadn't she married Elijah and settled down like any other good wife? Well, she had all she needed, and that was a lot more than most people had these days. She was just tired, and when she was that way, things would annoy her a lot more than they would ordinarily.

Glyniss closed her eyes and listened to the early morning birdsong. She identified each one mentally, enjoying their calls and songs. She heard several that she did not recognize. She opened her eyes to see if she could identify the singer. She couldn't find the bird, and then she heard an answering trill that she had never heard before either. That was odd, she mused. *Oh, maybe I'm just too tired to even think correctly.* She was sure she knew every bird that lived in the area.

Baron's ears pricked up as if he were trying to help her listen. Glyniss was smiling, wondering how her beloved horse always knew what she was thinking. Her smile faded as he snorted, stopped, and stamped his feet. That was a sure sign of trouble. Alert now, she tightened the reins and looked around to see what was spooking him. The road was deathly quiet now, with no birds singing and even the hum of the insects had stopped. "What is it boy?" she whispered to the horse.

A moment later, they were on her. Two men ran from the woods and grabbed her, pulling her off of Baron. The horse shrieked and reared, trying to kick the intruders. Two more men yanked the bags off of his pack and he bolted and ran. The first group of men covered her head with a musty sack and bound her with ropes. She heard them laugh and shout, "We've got her now, by God. We've got the witch."

She tried to scream at them, but something heavy hit her in the head and that was the last thing she knew. After she collapsed, one of the men tied her onto his horse so she would be laying face down across the front of his saddle. They sped back to the village with their prize.

"What about the horse, William? I wanted the horse, too. He looked like a sturdy one that I could use. Why didn't you grab the reins?"

The man called William turned and grimaced at his comrade. "I didn't grab him because he was kicking and biting. If you want the blasted horse, you run him down. The way he took off, he's half-way to the castle by now. If you want to take on the Griffin's Gate guards, you go after him yourself. I got what we were after. We'll hang her now, by God."

The other man ran a hand over his chin whiskers. "William, you know she has the protection of Lord McTavish. We could be in for it for hanging her."

William turned his head and spat in the dirt. "McTavish be damned. He sits there in his castle demanding taxes while we starve. She hasn't put any curses on him, I'll grant you. No, she saves her curses for us. We damn near starved this winter, didn't we? No food, and fevers; nothing but trouble, and here is the cause for it. She prances that pony through town, stirring up woes for everyone and is protected by McTavish. Well, she'll be swinging from the end of my rope in the center of town, now. Let McTavish look on her then. She'll be dead long before he can do anything about it, and we'll be free from all the damn curses."

Sir Collin had a heavy heart as he entered the castle. Lord McTavish had not returned and he had to give the news to Greccon, who was already racked with grief over the loss of his wife. He stopped outside the room and motioned to Greccon who was still trying to cope with his grief and with Ilona, who was in quiet conversation with Father Murphy.

Greccon got up and closed the door behind him and looked at the knight anxiously. "Have you found her, Sir Collin?"

The knight nodded grimly. "Aye, Greccon, The townspeople hung her, this afternoon. That's what was going on when we were in town today and I whisked the ladies home. That was the disturbance. I was there, within distance to save her, and I didn't even know it was her being hanged. We have to tell Mistress Ilona. There is nothing to be done. They accosted her, hanged her, and then burned her for good measure." He choked a bit on the last sentence, but stood erect. "Would you like me to tell her, Greccon? You've been through enough and I . . ."

Greccon cut his words short with a gesture. "No, thank you, Sir Collin. They are my friends and I will tell her. Oh, my God, I can't believe all this is happening. What fools those villagers are. I bet the only reason she was in town was because she was caring for the sick there."

He shook his head and felt like crying all over again. Just when you thought you had no more tears left to cry, something horrible happened. "That's three today that we've lost at Griffin's Gate. It's unbelievable."

Sir Collin gave him a sympathetic pat on the shoulder and turned and left, not being able to bear seeing Greccon in such a state.

* * *

Ilona broke from the room at a run and hurried to the stable to get Rosey. Her mother was dead, as well as Mary and Felicia? She could take no more of death and despair. She had to go home. She just had to. What had they done? Why did they hurt her? Why would they kill her after all she's done for them? A million questions raced through her mind as she took the reins from the stable boy. She took off at full gallop, surprising Rosey, who was used to a calm steady walk, but she obliged Ilona and ran for her life towards home. When she reached the thickest part of the woods, she reined Rosey in as the horse was huffing from exertion. She stopped the horse and let her rest. Her mind was still whirling and she screamed for Argon through her tears.

When she arrived at the cottage, she put Rosey in the stable with Baron, who was still tacked up. She removed his tack and Rosey's. She fed and watered them, through her tears, and went around to the front of the house. She had no idea what she was doing or what she was thinking.

Argon was sitting on her doorstep and she threw herself onto him and cried until his feathers were wet. He held her, being careful not to scratch her. He had never seen her so upset. She told him what had happened and he hissed with contempt. The bastards. First, they killed his father and now Ilona's mother. He ushered her into the house and they sat together until she had cried herself to sleep. He made soothing little purring noises to her, as his mother had done when he was little and it seemed to sooth her. He laid her down by the fireplace and pulled a blanket over her. He would not leave her. He sat and mourned Glynnis in his own way.

He thought he heard a noise and his ear tufts pricked up. Yes, there was someone coming through the woods. He got down and stalked noiselessly to the front door, his eyes pinning and his claws flexing in anticipation. If they thought they were going to get Ilona too, they had a big surprise coming. A big, vicious surprise. He fatigue-crawled to the bushes alongside of the door and waited. Yes. A man was approaching her door. Argon sprung into action and had the man flattened against the ground.

Greccon screamed, "Argon. Have you gone mad? It's me, Greccon."

Argon made no moves but hissed, "No one will take her, Greccon, no one, not even you. You and your lousy race. Look what you've done to us. First my father, and now her mother. Is there no end to your brutality? I'll kill the first one that shows up here and everyone else after them. The only reason you are still alive is that I'm being charitable. Now go, and do not return here ever again."

He let Greccon up then, but his look was menacing as he kept the griffin fighting stance. Greccon had not realized how much larger Argon was now. He was in no mood for this.

"Argon, let me go to her. She loved me, once. I can help to calm her."

Argon snapped at him and he backed up quickly. The sound of the beak snapping shut echoed throughout the woods. "No! Go away! She will see no one!" Growling, he took a slash at Greccon and he had to jump out of the way. Argon was growling now, his tail swishing back and forth in agitation. This was not going anywhere, thought Greccon, so he bowed at Argon and turned and walked back through the woods. Well, Ilona would be taken care of, that was for sure, he thought. She and Argon had a special bond and he guessed Argon would not leave Ilona as long as she needed him. He went back to the castle to mourn Felicia.

Argon heard her call his name and he turned quickly. Fluffing his feathers, he ran to her and gently bumped his soft head against hers in a sign of affection. She reached for him and he sat by her as she leaned against his warm black fur.

"I heard you growling. What is it?"

He sighed. "It was nothing, Ilona. I'll make you a pact. If you promise never to leave Griffin's Gate properties, I promise you'll never have to worry about people again. I will protect you with my life."

She nodded. "I will never leave, Argon. I will never go into the village again. Let them die of the sicknesses that they get. I don't care. I'm all alone now, except for you, my best friend." She clung to him in desperation, the tears streaming down her face. He nodded and put a claw carefully around her. They sat there for a long time.

Argon stayed with Ilona for days, never leaving her side except to hunt and bring her fish from the stream. He followed her on the ground or watched over her from the air. She could hear the church bells toll the deaths of Mary and Felicia and a third time again for her mother. It was the saddest time she could remember, but Argon was there for her, and they grew even closer, leaning on each other for strength. She would keep to herself and make medicines for the castle, and that's all she would do. She would study all the books that her mother had left her, including the ones that were her father's. She knew magic secrets were contained in them and she would study them to the letter. Ilona knew she was a mage, but untrained. Her mother thought it was best they just stay healers. There were no female mages she knew of, and her mother was afraid they would be accused of being sorceresses if they knew all the magic, too. Ilona was not satisfied with that anymore. She would be a healer, yes, but she would have the magic and she would use it if she had to, and Argon agreed with her.

She put all her energies into it and as the years went by, she grew more powerful and Argon nodded with approval. She did have a visit from Illustra once. The beautiful white unicorn came to give the condolences of the Magic Realm to her and to explain the gift she had given her so many years ago.

"I thought it was time to explain my gift, my dear. I gave you the gift of an everlasting soul. You will grow older, yes, and perhaps infirm. Then you will call for me and we will transform you back to the state you are in now. You can change your name as you go to avoid suspicion. You can claim you are anyone that you want to be. The point is that you will be Argon's friend forever, just as he will be yours."

Ilona listened in amazement. She had remembered that Argon had told her Ilustra had given her a gift, but she never really understood it until now. So, she would live forever, or at least as long as Argon did, and that was fine with her. She loved Illustra and was always pleased to visit with her whenever she was in the Griffin forest. She wasn't alone after all, she thought. One mental shout and she would have Argon with her at any time and wherever she was.

Greccon made a second attempt to see Ilona. This time, Argon was in the trees and he shouted that he was bringing the children to Ilona. They missed her. Argon nodded and let him pass. Ilona cried happy tears as the children crawled all over her. She laughed and tweaked their cheeks and covered their faces in kisses, much to the children's delight. Greccon sat at the table, one eye out of the window for Argon. He had taken a risk, he knew, but he missed Ilona and the children loved her so. He knew Argon would not hurt or scare the children. Griffins were a very civilized species, well educated and usually well mannered, until someone made them angry. Ilona followed his gaze.

"Yes, that's Argon. He's been such a blessing to me, Greccon."

Greccon scoffed, then thought better of it. At the look she gave him, he thought he should explain. "I came to see you the night of the tragedies. Argon practically tore me up and he wouldn't let me see you at all. He's very protective of you, you know. I was almost afraid to come with the children."

Ilona looked shocked. "Greccon, I never knew. I will speak to Argon. Sometimes he's too protective. He would never hurt the children. You must know that; he didn't hurt you, did he?" Her eyes had grown large.

Greccon shook his head. "No, not that he didn't try. He snapped at me and threw a punch with those sharp talons of his, but I'm pretty quick. When I saw how worked up he was, I just left and went back to the castle. I knew he would take good care of you."

She handed Ursan and Alyssa to Greccon as she got them some cooled tea to drink. To the children, she gave sticky honeycomb and Greccon made a face at the sticky mess they were making with it, but Ilona laughed and he joined her, thinking it was good to laugh again. Ilona told him he could bring the children over anytime, but she was not leaving the cottage for reasons she did not have to explain. She cleaned up the children the best she could and Greccon waved thanks to Argon who nodded at him, but watched every move he made.

Lord McTavish had taken his revenge. The bolts of cloth had been destroyed and the merchant ran through after he confessed to poisoning the cloth. He was part of a pirate crew and they wanted to test the poison. They had no idea they would kill a Lord's wife in the process. The king, at McTavish's request, sent ships out to hunt and destroy the pirates. The lynch mob that had hanged Glynnis was now in the castle dungeon, chained to the wall. He had been sent messages to send his healer to town to help the sick and each one was refused. The healer would not go. That was the price they would pay for executing his best healer. Disease had begun to run rampant, but the families at Griffin's Gate fared very well. Ilona would and did look after every one of them, although it was hard for Argon to accept her having visitors. They had worked out a mental code and he was to let everyone approach. Greccon had changed the spell to let castle residents pass through their magical web without setting off alarms, but still, Argon was watchful. He did get plenty of exercise, as he loved to pick up poachers and dump them into the ocean. This started even more rumors about the forest. Most of these people had no idea what a griffin was or that they even existed. Most never saw what had attacked them; they just knew it was a long swim to shore. There was a saying going around that if you tried to hunt Griffin Forest, you better know how to swim. Argon became the topic of every highlander with a belly full of ale. He had been slain by more knights than he had ever seen. He had to laugh at that. He had a lot more than nine lives, and so did Ilona.

When the tavern patrons had exchanged all the local gossip and the conversation was sparse, the tales of the monster in the Griffin Forest would begin. No one really knew for sure what it was, but everyone had an opinion, one way or the other. Some said it was a lion, some said it was a winged demon. There were plenty of ghost stories to fill the night and disturb the sleep of the very vulnerable. Each one swore what they saw or said was the plain truth, and the more ale that kept the mouths moist, the larger the tales became, until hardly anyone would take one step into the forest. The tavern owner gasped and scoffed alternately to encourage the talking and the drinking. As long as there were tales to be told, the men would stay, and the more they talked, the more they drank. Argon was really very good for business. The tavern owner hoped that the monster, no matter what it actually was, would stay and produce at least one incident a week to boost his profits. Most of them liked scaring each other, but there was a group who listened carefully and planned and plotted to rid the woods of anything that kept food from the mouths of their children. The doubtlets swarmed these patrons, filling them with hatred and a feeling of being weak against what surely was a foe they could conquer easily. While the rest of the men were toasting each other, laughing and slapping backs, they sat huddled together in the corner making plans. They thought their troubles were over when they hung the witch that lived in the woods. Now it was known that a daughter remained and she was just as much of a witch as was her mother. It was also known that she wouldn't come into the village to help heal the sick there, as her mother did. She sat there in the woods with all the cures to their sickness and wouldn't budge. The folk at Griffin's Gate fared very well under her watchful witch's eyes and the people in the village died miserably. It wasn't so much the monster that they wanted, but the witch that cursed them for destroying her mother. It was revenge, pure and simple that compelled her to stay away. The problem was that if it was mentioned to go into the woods to get her, people would either laugh at you and walk away, or hurriedly find someone else saner to converse with. No one wanted to chance encountering the monster or the witch. Deidre, the tavern's serving wench got into the mix and the men roared with laughter and ordered another round.

"I'm telling you the truth. I saw a unicorn in them woods. They visit virgins, you know. She was as white as pearls, she was, with a golden horn and hooves. She was the most beautiful thing that I ever saw in my whole life, and I'll never forget her."

One of the men pinched her and said, "A virgin, eh? That must have been a long time ago, Deidre."

Insulted, she slapped the man and took her tray to the back as the laughter followed her.

On an outcropping of rocks between the tavern and the black smith's barn, sat Mordread, his head in his hands. Swarms of doubtlets circled him like annoying flies and he grumbled and swatted at them when they hovered too close. He was tired of the village and its miserable people. The magicals had been right to leave, he thought. The demons were running wild now and were having the best time tormenting the villagers and causing so much havoc that they were starting to become more noticeable and harder to cover up or blame others for. A few of the more reckless demons had been captured and destroyed, right along with the witches.

The witches, yes. He had to smile in satisfaction that they had hung the witch of the woods. He knew she was a friend of Oberon's and his only wish was that they could have hung the daughter, as well. His minions had managed to find where she lived, but none of them could get past the magical barrier she had barricaded herself in with. He also knew the gate to the Realm was contained on the Griffin Gate property and he still had no way of getting to it. Not that he wanted to visit, but it would be nice to prevent the magicals from coming and going back and forth, healing the land and curing the sicknesses he had worked so hard to perpetuate. It was the damn living conditions here. Just because you were evil didn't mean that you wanted to live in this wretched land. He longed for the comfortable life. Good food, soft beds, and enough power to command the evils into being sensible about their attacks. They were running around, willy-nilly, going from one person to another, and they were just so damn unorganized. If the magicals could create a world of their own, well then, so could they. They could come and go, as well; cause trouble here, and then escape back to comfort and the sweet indulgences of what life should be. He stood up and swatted a doublet to the ground, and it shrieked with pain and began to whimper.

"No. Blast your hides. Go find some human to haunt."

Mordread needed to organize and he would begin to spread the word. He knew several demons in the tavern and decided to go and have them round up as many demons as they could find. They would have a meeting as well. He looked down on the sniveling demon doubtlet he had just swatted to the ground. It looked back up at him with anger and fear in its eyes. He felt sorry for it; after all, it was one of his own and he was its master.

He sighed with impatience and said in a condescending voice, "Well, come on then. I'm going into the tavern, and you can find someone else to crawl all over, alright?"

Like a happy dog, glad to be back in its master's good graces, it leapt up and obediently followed Mordread into the tavern. They were his finest creations, those damn doubtlets, but they could be just so annoying and hovering. They weren't supposed to be bothering with him. Doublets were creatures of the dark, unnoticeable to the human eye, and were working wonders, driving the humans mad. They were self-sufficient, drawing their life forces from the victims, and exhaling doubts, suspicion, greed, and worries that turned into real paranoia for the unwary.

While he was walking, a grounder reached up and tripped him. When he looked back, it was gone. "Damn them." Even the grounders were getting out of hand. They were one of his ideas as well, causing countless accidents, but they were not allowed to plague him and they all knew it. Yes, things were getting way out of hand and he would have to do something to remedy it, and the sooner the better.

The demons met out in the graveyard, its huge pillars marking the places where the kings of old rested. More had come than he had hoped for and he looked at them all, lounging about, waiting for news as to why this emergency meeting had been called. A few fights had broken out and he stopped them with a bolt of lightning from his hand. He had no time to waste on territorial problems today.

"Settle down. Listen up. I've called this meeting. As most of you know, the magicals have fled to a Realm of their own."

There was a mix of cheers and jeers at that bit of news.

He went on, "I think most of you will agree that we haven't the best of accommodations here, and frankly, I'm tired of this place. Now, what I'm proposing, with your help, of course, is to create a Dark Realm., I'm sure I will hear you all say we'll be a mirror to the Magical Realm, but so what? They had the right idea, and I'm man enough to admit that and learn from it. We need a place of our own. We can make it, just as they have, in any manner we wish. We have enough magic to do whatever we like and improve the standard of living that we need."

He looked around at the skeptical faces. That was the problem with demons, the problem that the Magic Realm didn't have to bother with. There were no large organized groups such as the elves or griffins. No one in the Dark Realm would ever trust another demon. It was going to be hard to get them to agree.

One of his demons demanded, "So how are we supposed to create this Realm, huh? We got no dragons. You know they have the most power."

Mordread pointed at the demon and he ducked, just out of force of habit, but Mordread was just pointing, not delivering a magical blow. "We don't need a dragon. We have the Furies and the Sirens. Together, if they will grace us with their powers, they are enough to do the exact same thing the Magicals have done. We can have a separate world, just like they have. We can still come and go, still cause as much trouble, but we would be out of this mess we have here. We can still come back and cause a plague or a few wars, but meanwhile, we don't have to live among them. They're dirty, nasty people and I like things neat and a savory meal once in awhile, not this moldy bread and cold damp mats to sleep on. We deserve better than this."

There were nods of agreement at that. He thought he had them now. They looked interested. Lorelei, one of the Sirens, sauntered forward, pushing the lecherous demons out of her way. Mordread raised his eyebrows at the beautiful Siren.

She said, "Well, Mordread, it sounds so lovely, but you never said who was to lead us in this venture. You wouldn't want to be in charge now, would you? I just don't see you using the Sirens and the Furies to do your bidding, and then expect us to serve you as well. I, for one, don't think the Sirens would be interested. We have our own land already, and we do alright on our own."

Mordread nodded and put up his hands to placate her. "Yes, Lorelei, of course, I understand what you are saying. Me? Why would I want to be in charge?" An innocent grin played across his face as he seethed inside. He needed the Sirens or the whole thing was finished. He smiled. "I just want a decent meal. It would be nothing for the Sirens to help us, even if you didn't want to live there, considering the vast amount of power you all have. I would think you would do it as a favor to those of us who can't do the things that you are capable of. The unfortunate, you understand. Look around at all these demons that can't even dream of possessing the power of the Sirens. Don't they deserve a decent meal and a warm place to sleep, even if they are so pitiful? Where are my Furies?"

Three women looked at him and moved to the front. Their hair was a tangle of writhing snakes and their dark wings were clamped to their backs. Mordread spread his arms wide in a gesture of embrace.

"Ladies. It's been a long time since we've seen you. This is such a pleasure. Now here are three women to be respectful of. What say you lovelies to this idea? You've kept yourselves so secluded that most of these demons think you are all but a legend. Wouldn't it be so satisfying to show them that all they have been taught of you is real? I know you have the power to awe them, but they haven't a clue as to what you three ladies can really do. It would be fun to watch."

They talked together, the three Furies, and their wings fluttered a bit as if they were huge birds fighting over carrion. The snakes in their hair attacked each other when they were close enough and there was a great deal of hissing and spitting while they argued. Furies always argued, thought Mordread. He never knew a time when they were complacent. Every decision they made came after a huge argument and he folded his arms to wait. Some of the other demons tried to get in on the fight and they struck them with their wings, never losing momentum in the disagreements. It was going to be a job getting them to work with the alluring Sirens, but he felt it was worth the effort. It was a shame they didn't have an entity that had the power of a dragon. It would take several of his evils to accomplish what just one dragon could do. He wished they had an evil dragon, but the Furies were about as nasty as they got, and the real dragons were such do-gooders. He couldn't imagine having all that power and not using it for his own purposes. It was a distribution problem. Power should have been divided up equally. He had always felt like a brown sparrow compared to the magicals' peacock. It would take twice the power of his members to be able to create a Dark Realm, but the point was that it was doable, and all he had to do was convince them it was worth the effort. It would be more of a problem to get them to work together; it wasn't so much the power that was the problem, as it was the cooperation. Demons just don't work or play well with others. It was a problem that had always been. If they could organize and really pull together, the magicals wouldn't have a chance against them. But Mordread, as much as he would like it, knew this would never happen. It was the nature of the beast. No one could trust anyone and alliances were almost non-existent. That's where the magicals had them beat. Of course they had more power over people, as they were basically evil in nature, anyway, and so damn easy to persuade, but organization was what they needed and if he could just get over that barrier, he knew it could work to their advantage.

The Furies were still arguing and he sighed. One of them, Megaera, broke away from the pack and asked in a annoyed voice, "Mordread, what I want to know is why we weren't asked first, instead of them." She jabbed a finger at the Sirens. "Our power is more formidable than theirs is."

Lorelei huffed in disgust and turned her back toward them. Mordread would have to be careful now. This Fury was one of the worst and jealousy was one of the emotions that powered her. He'd have to please her to win the three of them. He thought fast.

"Meg, my sweet, I would have asked you both at the same time if I could have. I just can't decide which of you ladies is the fairest. I can't help myself, but it doesn't really matter; you all are held in the highest regard. I need both of the groups to work together and I know that, with your intelligence, you know that as a fact, as well as I do. Alecto, Tisiphome, you both know how I feel about the three of you. I love you all the same, and now I need your help. We all need your help on this one. Once we get the Dark Realm up and running, you can choose your own place to live, wherever it suits you all. A nice condo, maybe? You've seen those - you can see into the future."

They turned and began to discuss that bit of information while the lesser demons looked on. Beelzebub stepped forward. Being a major player in the Dark world, he was recognized immediately.

His black massive form showed signs of irritation and he thrust his bulk forward. "I think it's a done deal, here. I want a bakery for my part in the construction. I've always wanted a bakery and now I will have it. There is nothing more satisfying than a red hot oven. If they resist helping us, Mordread, I can make them do it, and they know it, too."

He glared at the Sirens and the Furies and Mordread didn't know what Beelzebub's power was over the ladies, but he would sure rather deal with him than a pack of cackling hens. Mordread gave him a thumbs-up sign. "Right you are. I can see it now, Bubba's Bakery, and the special will be devil's food cake. I'll be your first customer, too."

Beelzebub looked smug as Mordread continued, "You see? That's exactly what I'm talking about. We can have our own interests, there. Do what we like without the church stomping on us for what we are. It won't be long before our numbers dwindle. Look what they did to the magicals, and they were doing good things. What will happen to us when they figure out who's causing the problems they're having? Sure, we get them to point their fingers at each other now, but how long will that last?"

Now he had everyone's attention. They looked at each other with worried expressions. That was good, thought Mordread. If they get scared, maybe then it will be enough to make them pull together, even if it is just this one time.

"Now, you all understand. I know no one has any love for another here, but if we can just put that all aside for one afternoon, get this thing built and move it on over there, we all win, don't we?"

Even the Furies had stopped arguing and listened for a change. If they all had something to lose, then they all had something to gain, too. Beelzebub stepped forward, pushing his way through the crowd.

"I say that's enough discussion. We can stand here all day, waiting for these contrary women to make up their minds. I say we do it or I challenge them all, one at a time."

Beelzebub scanned the crowd with a menacing look, folding his arms across his massive chest and daring anyone to challenge him. Mordread resisted the urge to clap and jump for joy. No one would take on Bubba. The lesser demons shrank away from Beelzebub and tried to blend into the background. Making an ominous presence, Bubba said, "Mordread, set the thing up. I'm not good at that sort of thing. You'll be in charge of it, too. I got my bakery to run. Everyone agrees, right? If you don't, line up here and take the challenge."

He cracked his knuckles and everyone just stared at Mordread, not wanting to meet Bubba's gaze. He was one of the worst demons.

Mordread nodded and managed to look surprised. "Well, alright, whatever you say, Bubba. Sure, I can organize things. I'm going to need the Furies and the Sirens up here. Tomorrow, we make the move. I take it that everyone agrees?"

There were hesitant nods of consent and a few grumbles from the dissident demons, but no one wanted to try his luck against Bubba and it was all agreed upon.

CHAPTER THIRTEEN

The Dark Realm was almost finished now, and Mordread stood on the hot asphalt, shielding his eyes and looking up at the sky-scraper that would house his office. A few of the demons stood with him, trying to decide where they were to live. It looked like any major city, multi-laned highways and tall buildings glittering in the sun with their large picture windows. Bubba's Bakery sported a red and white sign and you could smell the bread baking already. Loaves of fresh breads and pastries arranged on white paper laced doilies adorned the big picture window. Mordread had to grin at that. He had never taken Bubba for that sort of demon. You never knew the nature of a person until you granted them a wish.

There were apartments and theaters, houses of ill repute, and shops opening up as the demons decided what they wanted to do. The Sultry Siren, a dark, thriving bar already had patrons and you could hear music and laughter from where he stood. There wasn't a single blade of grass, shrub, or tree. Mordread hated fairies and refused to have anything around that would remind him of them. Insolent little busybodies, they were always flitting around and poking into everyone's business and reporting it back to the Magic Realm. He despised the elves and he didn't want a thing that would call to them either. Trees had a way of mournfully pleading for help that elves couldn't resist and he didn't want them sashaying around. No lakes for the limp little water nymphs either. He looked around with satisfaction and then marched into the building to claim his right as the King.

Once on the top floor, he furnished his office and sat down on his leather chair. Leaning back with his arms behind his head, he began to make plans for the future. Things were going well, so far. Oh, there were a few scuffles over locations, the age-old fight for territory, but all in all, the Dark Realm was taking shape very nicely. He would demand tokens of power from every one for the protection he would afford them, giving him enough power to keep them well under his control. Right now, he had the doubt-lets watching the portal so nothing could get through; as fighters, they were practically worthless, but he would have stronger guards later and whole armies to wage war with. He cautioned himself to have patience and to ease into this project with careful diligence. He would make no mistakes. Any mistakes could cost him the position as ruler. His constituents were ruthless, after all, and would be vy-ing for his position.

He laughed to himself as he gazed upon the bakery. Beelzebub was his greatest concern, but good old Bubba seemed quite content making cakes and buns. That came as a big relief to Mordread. If he could keep Bubba on his side, there wasn't anyone who could stop him. He made a mental note to drop in at the bakery to compli-ment Bubba. He would make it a point to patronize him every day and get a cake or a pie. If that was what the demon wanted out of life, he would do everything in his power to keep him happy and busy. The more preoccupied, the better. He wondered if he would have any trouble from the magicals. Eventually, they would be a problem, but for now, he surmised they were probably happy that the Dark Magicals had left the mortal world. It would be less that they had to contend with, making visits to the mortal world seldom and safer for their own members. He was fairly sure he would have no trouble for a long time.

He stood looking out of the huge picture window at the pan-orama of the city. It could be New York or Chicago of the future. He glanced up at the gargoyles he had positioned on top of the building. They were vigilantly staring down at the street below. He would need cameras in the future and a security system, as well. He saw one customer being thrown out of the bar already and he laughed. Yes, this was going to be the finest of the three realms.

The mortals were suffering now with sickness and foul waters and lands; ignorance was running rampant there. The magicals were faring better with their green, leafy, grassy, tree-filled world, but then there was the Dark Realm. He took in a deep breath of satisfaction. The Dark Realm would be the finest place in which to live. Every indulgence could be found here and it would be perfectly legal, just for the taking. No more church to beat them to death with their Bibles. Men and women demons alike could live here in harmony with whatever they wished to do. Of course, he would not forget their real purpose: to cause hate and discontent among the mortals, but for awhile at least, he would enjoy his creation. Let the mortals have a short break while he put the finishing touches on his Realm. He looked at the wide streets. They had all seen the future, or at least the most powerful of the Darklings had, and cars would come in time with the railroads and planes. Just a bit at a time, he cautioned himself. The Realm would not be built in one day, but in the future, it would be grand.

He settled back down to think about a pet project of his. He had always been fascinated by the torment of the humans, but he wanted to work out a system where they tormented themselves to death. Demons were lazy by nature, and if he could just get these mortals to eliminate themselves with as little demon involvement as possible, well, it would be the ultimate accomplishment.

* * *

"So what if they have a Dark Realm? We might have known as much. After all, we left, didn't we? What makes you think they wouldn't leave as well, for a place of their own? The mortals have gone mad down there, you know. None of us were safe, light magical or dark" King Oberon said, as he gestured with one claw. "It makes no difference to us, really; we will fight them on common ground, the grounds of the mortals. With them gone for awhile, the mortals will have very few problems and we get to take a rest."

The representative from the dwarves spoke up, "Aye, that's all well and good, but now they have a chance to organize against us. Remember, it was them who put evil in the thoughts of the mortals to commit the atrocities upon us."

The Elven king spoke up, "They don't have the capacity to organize. They do nothing but backstab each other. Not a true one among them. They will never be able to organize against us. We have the advantage there. We can and have counter-acted every evil against the mortals and the land so far. Let them have their own Realm, and good riddance." He sat back down and there were sounds of agreement with him.

The dwarf still shook his head, not convinced. "We should be on our guard, in any case."

King Oberon stood up. "And so we shall be. I do not take lightly the possibilities, but I'm not looking for trouble, either. We will monitor the situation at all times. Any move they make will be very apparent to us. My fairies are everywhere. They have always been our first line of defense. We will handle the situations as they arrive at our door. I see no need to start an incident because they chose to build themselves a shelter. We did the same thing and even invited them to join us in refuge. They chose not to come. So, evidently they've changed their minds and they have created their own place to be. That does not alarm me, nor should it intimidate you." Oberon shrugged. "We are safe here. The mortals are on their own for the time being. Without the demons, they should fare very well. If they are having trouble, it is their own doing. I will not interfere in the lives of the demons. They do not interfere with us."

King Orion stood again and said, "The demons do not threaten us directly. They never have. I agree they bear watching, but that is all. I, for one, am glad for the news. It gives my elves more time to heal the land without their interference. The fairies agree. The blighted land will recover now and the people will prosper with better crops. The animals will have better grazing lands. Anywhere there are demons, the land suffers, and now, without them for awhile, it can heal. I think it's the best thing that could have happened to the land. They can't hurt us collectively, they haven't the power. We have the dragons on our side and nothing can overcome that. We have nothing to worry about." He smiled at Oberon and sat back down.

Illustra walked up to the table and was recognized. "We will enter the world again, with the demons gone. The mortals are not by nature against the unicorns. It was the demon influence that made them hunt us. We have many gifts to give them, and now we may try again."

Oberon nodded. A gift from a unicorn had become rare, indeed. It was time the people believed again and the unicorn was the vision that made people believe in magic. When the people believed, they unknowingly gave the magicals more power, and that was always in demand. He looked to Argon, who sat there trimming a claw. He shrugged at Oberon. Oberon knew the griffins didn't care either way. They were fearless and wouldn't mind a battle or two against almost anyone, mortal or demon. The news of a Dark Realm didn't interest Argon much, unless the king commanded him to attack it, and Argon knew King Oberon would never do that unless it was unavoidable.

The Pegasus had brought them the message and they had called for a summit. Other than delivering the message, and flirting with Illustra, the Pegasus didn't care about the Dark Realm's existence either. Neither did the trolls. They were happy with where they were and with what they were doing. Seldom, if ever, did they venture into the world of the mortals. Only architecture of an extreme nature, something so very new and different, constructed by the mortals would interest them.

Oberon glanced around the table for any more comments. Seeing no one else that wanted to speak he said, "Well then, we all seem to agree. We all know of the Dark Realm and we know it bears watching. It poses no threat to us, so we will simply acknowledge its existence and mind our own business. We will monitor the situation."

He gave a smile and a nod to the fairy representative, who nodded back. He adjourned the meeting and, as the clans broke up, most of them left to go back to their lands. Argon fluffed his feathers and remained until everyone had left. Oberon saw him and walked over.

"How are you Argon?"

Argon bowed. "Fine, my Lord. Everything is going as well as it can. The Griffin Forest is secure and no one has crossed the portal without your permission."

Oberon nodded, distracted, and said, "How are Greccon and Ilona?"

Argon straightened up at Ilona's name. "Well, my King. Greccon is busy with the court there, but his son, Ursan, is growing quickly and is being taught the magic of the Realm. Ilona is the same. She mixes her herbs and studies her magic. She is at an Adept level now, but she will not leave the forest. I've been keeping away the curious. Hunters, for the most part. I throw them in the ocean. You see? My temper has mellowed. Were I younger and irrational as I once was, the sharks would be fat and sassy on the bodies I would give them. Ilona asked me not to kill them, so I try not to."

King Oberon chuckled. Argon had grown into maturity and Oberon had noticed him. He had grown larger than most griffins, and was a fearless fighter, or so his trainer had told Oberon. He was now training the younger griffins to fight and Gunny had told Oberon he was the finest fighter he had ever known, far surpassing his father, Reaper. That had impressed Oberon. Reaper and he went back a long time and he had always admired Reaper's fighting prowess. He couldn't imagine anyone being a better fighter than Reaper, but with Argon's extra height and bulk, it was very possible that his strength had surpassed his father's. He liked Argon and was very comfortable talking with him. He was so much like his father that it comforted Oberon to have him around. He granted him full control of the gate and the Griffin Forest. Ilona made a great difference in his attitude, which was remarkably bad to begin with. He was glad to see it. It seemed Argon thought more rationally now, and was of an increasing intelligence. He wondered if Ilona had played a substantial part in that as well. Either way, his relationship with Ilona, strange as it was, seemed to benefit the griffin a great deal, and Oberon was thankful to her for helping to develop the best fighter in the Realm, except for perhaps Oberon himself.

As they walked outside into the courtyard, Oberon asked "And your brother, Shylock? He's now in training, is he not?"

Argon made a face at Oberon and shifted his wings uncomfortably. "That buffoon. Yes, he is in training, but keeping his mind on his lessons takes an act of God. He's much too sociable for my liking. He has to talk to everyone, flirt with the women, and trying to keep him focused is a real challenge. He would make a better celebration host than he would a fighter."

Oberon laughed. Argon's brother, Shylock, was a very gregari-

ous griffin. Chestnut bronze as the sunset, and much too happy to
be a temperamental griffin. But Oberon found him entertaining. He
always had a joke or a story to tell. The younger griffins loved him
for his playful animated nature. He could be seen a lot of the time
playing with the children - griffin, unicorn, elven, dwarf, or troll,
it didn't matter; he just loved children and adults alike. He was so
different from Argon, it was hard to believe they were brothers.
Having always been his mother's favorite, he had grown up secure
and happy. Argon, on the other hand, bore resentment towards
Shylock, but was intelligent enough to know it and overlook it.
Argon had a dark and dangerous nature, but tempered with Ilona's
love, he had learned how to put it to the best use possible. He could
have very easily been persuaded to join the Dark Realm, with his
disdain for humans. Oberon wondered if Ilona knew how much of
a key element she was in the Magical Realm.

Argon shook his head and glanced up at the dragon. "Never
fear, my king, I will make a fighter out of him if I have to rip him
apart to do it."

Oberon raised one claw. "Why do I think you would enjoy
that? Make him better, Argon, but in one piece, if you please."

He chuckled again and Argon bowed and took off to patrol the
Griffin Forest. Oberon watched as he headed towards the gate and
smiled to himself. He had every confidence that Argon would have
Shylock trained to perfection. It was just the way Argon was. He
didn't doubt that Shylock would lose some feathers and fur in the
process, but he tried not to think about it too much.

* * *

The people of the mortal world enjoyed a much more prosperous time with the demons gone. The elves, true to their word, healed
the land, making it well again. Crops flourished and sickness abated
as the water nymphs purified wetlands. The climate was conducive
to the crops and it was a record year as people rejoiced in the abundance. They harvested their fields, loaded their wagons and traded
heartily, having more than enough to sell, even after keeping what
they would need for themselves and their families. When the crops
were good, the lives and temperaments of the people improved. Of

course the church proclaimed that it was the grace of God that was smiling down on the village and perhaps it was. There was less finger-pointing now, and the execution of the innocent had stopped. With nothing to complain about, surely the witches were gone and they could now relax and enjoy their good fortune. The people were more apt to celebrate then they were to conspire against each other. Remarkably, it was a time of peace. Invaders had left them alone for a time, which further improved the people's morale. It was a time of festivals and lightheartedness. Even the church, ever watchful over its flock, could find no wrongdoings to shout from the pulpit. Six years went by and the people started to relax. Their bellies were full, their purses grew heavy with trade, and life was good.

* * *

When Illustra heard the request by Greccon for a unicorn to impress a little eight year-old girl, she responded immediately, even though she had her newborn colt, Moon Shadow by her side. She nuzzled his mane. "Well, if one unicorn will impress her, just think of what two would do, especially a handsome young prince like you."

Moon Shadow grinned back at his mother and before he knew it, they were standing in the Griffin Forest, facing two human children and a man. Moon Shadow froze, all his confidence gone. His mother seemed fine with all of this and he looked to her for reassurance.

She winked at him and nudged him forward. Mentally, she told him, *This is my very good friend, Greccon, and I would guess his son and the lady of Griffin's Gate.*

She was right, of course. Illustra was always right. The man produced a basket of apples and gave them to the girl. All conversation was lost on Moon Shadow when he saw a big juicy apple and he went to eat it out of the girl's hand. It was just a brief visit and he didn't even get to finish the apple, but he had it in his mouth when they returned to the Realm.

"Please, please, don't let me fall, Ursan." said Alyssa, as she hung out of the west tower, trying to see where the unicorns had gone into the forest.

Ursan did his best. He had a stranglehold on her legs as she leaned even further out of the window slit.

"Alyssa, I can't hold you much longer, you're too heavy. I'm pulling you back in now."

Ursan gave her a tug, and she fell backwards into him, toppling him over, and sending them both crashing onto the stone floor of the tower. Giggling, they both sat there as Alyssa tried to get all her hair out of her face. She had wanted so badly to see the unicorns again.

"Can't your father make a unicorn for me to keep? Can you do that, Mage Ursan? Can you get me a unicorn that I can keep forever?"

Ursan grinned and shook his head. "Of course not. Those were real unicorns from the Magic Realm. They weren't made up. That was the queen, too. My father told me that he met the queen of the unicorns, but I thought he was teasing me. That was Illustra, Light of the Morning Star, Queen of the Unicorns."

She sat there, her eyes wide. "The Magic Realm? Can we go there, Ursan? Have you ever been there? Has your father been there?"

Ursan smiled. "My father has, once, when he was a little boy, about our age. I have never been and I have no idea how to get there. He never would tell me how he went there, just that he's been there and about all the wonderful things there. I wish I could go, but he said it was a private place and we weren't welcome unless we were invited to go. I don't know how to get invited, either."

Alyssa frowned in disappointment. "Oh, I do so want to go there. What else did he see?"

Ursan rocked a foot back and forth on the stone floor, hoping he wouldn't get in trouble for telling her, but his father had just produced a unicorn for her and she deserved some explanation, after all. He looked into her sapphire eyes. "Do you promise never to tell another soul if I tell you a secret?"

She nodded eagerly.

Ursan took a deep breath. "Well, somehow, my father ended up in the Realm, and he was face to face with a huge griffin. His name was Reaper. Well, he told my father to climb on and he flew him to a huge castle on a hill. The King of the Magical Realm is a mighty black and gold dragon named Oberon, and he talked to him. The dragon told him that because he could do magic, he was a member of his kingdom. My father told me I was too, because I can do magic, too."

Alyssa's mouth dropped open in surprise. "That's not fair. I want to be a part of the Magic Realm, too. I'm the Lady of Griffin's Gate castle. Can't I be a part of the Magic Realm, too?"

Ursan shook his head sadly. "Can you do any magic, Alyssa? Any at all?"

She sighed and pushed her long blond curls back. "No. Not a bit."

Ursan looked sadly at her. "I guess not, then. You have to be magic to go there. I still don't know how to get there, and he won't tell me, either. It sounds like a wonderful place though, doesn't it? Maybe when I'm older, he'll tell me and I'll bring you with me, alright? If I learn how to do the magic, I should be able to take you with me."

She wrapped her arms around his neck. It was then that he noticed the stone under his right foot was wobbling back and forth with his shoe.

"Look at that. The stone under my foot is loose. Let's see what's under it. Help me move it, Alyssa."

She got up, and between the two of them, they managed to move the stone and pull it aside. It fit on a little ledge cut into the rocks. They gasped as they looked into the blackness below. Their voices echoed even louder than before. Ursan took a pebble out of his pocket and dropped it down. It made a clinking sound as it hit the floor under it. Ursan lay on his stomach and peered into the hole.

"It's not far down. I'm going down there."

Alyssa grabbed his arm. "No, Ursan. What if you get hurt or can't get back up here?"

But her concerns were too late, as Ursan dropped down to the floor below. He landed in a crouch and looked around. It was another room. A secret room that he didn't think anyone knew about. There were two tiny window slits cut into the wall that Ursan knew were not visible from outside the tower. Then he saw a doorway. He relayed all this information to Alyssa, and went through the door to a long set of roughly carved steps. They wound down the tower in a dark spiral and deposited him outside, right on the beach, but the doorway was amid bunches of sea grasses and you really couldn't see the doorway either. A secret room and a secret escape passage. Ursan's heart beat with excitement. He ran around and went back into the original door to the tower and running all the way back up the stairs, met Alyssa back in the same room and once again looked down the hole. He told her all about the hidden staircase and the outlet on to the beach.

"It's a secret room, Alyssa. It could be our secret hiding place. She wanted to see it for herself, as he just knew she would, so he grabbed her hands and lowered her as far as he could. She landed on her feet and waited for him to jump.

Excited now, he said, "It's a good place to hide if the barbarians come. We can come here to talk too, when we don't want anyone else to hear us."

She nodded and ran to look out of the windows, then started down the stairs. They ran around the tower and back up to replace the stone. It fit into the floor perfectly. There was no way to tell that it was a passage to a secret room. He took her hand and they left the tower and ran to the pond. Tired and hot from all the climbing, they threw off their clothes and jumped into the water. They splashed each other and talked more of the secret hiding place and the Magical Realm until a court lady ordered Alyssa out of the pond and escorted her back to the castle, all the time scolding her for her shameless behavior. Ursan got an evil look from the woman and he sulked. He knew she would tell and he would get a whipping from the stableman for being a bad influence on the Lady. He wished his father was there, but once again, just after visiting with the children, he had gone off with the knights into France. The stableman was harsh with his discipline, and Ursan knew he would be standing at dinner again tonight. He never understood why he was in trouble all the time. Alyssa and he had always been best friends and had always been together. He couldn't remember a time when they were apart. No one ever bothered about them before and he couldn't understand why he was in trouble for doing what they had always done. As far as he could see, nothing had changed except now he was in trouble.

He climbed out of the pond, dressed, and walked back to the castle. Sure enough, the stableman was waiting for him. Not only would he get the whip, he had to clean out the barn as well. After serving out his punishment, Ursan ran to the kitchen. He loaded up bread and cheese and a few honey cakes into a sack and ran through the forest to see Ilona. She was inside, stirring a huge pot on the fire. She smiled as he came through the door. He placed the sack on the table and stood watching her. She frowned as she saw him rubbing his back.

"Have you received another whipping, Ursan? What was it this time? Let me guess. I bet you were defending Lady Alyssa again, Ursan the Protector."

Ursan groaned and sat down heavily on a stool by the fire. *Ursan, the Protector* was the name bestowed upon him at Griffin's Gate for his fierce protection of Alyssa. At first it was a joke, but the name had stuck and he took it for his own now.

"No. I wasn't fighting for her, just swimming in the pond. I don't know what I did wrong, to be truthful, Ilona. We've been swimming in that pond, ever since we learned how to swim."

Ilona stood staring at Ursan, then smiled to herself and continued stirring the pot.

"Lady Alyssa is growing up, Ursan. I'm sure the Lord wants her to behave like the Lady she is. My guess would be that she was to be somewhere else learning to sew or learning to read and write, not off swimming."

Ursan scowled. "So why do I get the beating then, instead of Alyssa?"

Ilona laughed. "Well, I'm sure you would rather receive the whip than your Lady, right?" She sat down next to him. "Ursan, the point is that you both are getting older. You can't play together like you used to. She needs to grow up and be the Lady of Griffin's Gate, and you need to learn your magic. It isn't proper for the two of you to go off together. It is her station to marry, and it will be to someone of rank in another land. You must stay here and protect the kingdom with your magic, as your father does."

Ursan looked disturbed. "I never thought about that. I can't lose Alyssa. She is my best friend. Why can't I marry her and keep her here?"

Ilona shook her head. "No, Ursan. You are not of royal blood. Put those thoughts out of your mind. I'm sure you can stay friends, no matter where she has to go, but you must remember your place. I know she's your best friend. You two have been together for a long time, but things will change rapidly and you must accept that. You have to treat her like a young lady, not as a little girl."

Ursan stood up, his fists clenched in exasperation. "But she is a little girl."

Ilona laughed. "Not for long. You both will be changing into adults soon and your feelings will change towards her. The farther you can stay from her, the better for both of your sakes. When nature takes over, it's hard to resist. Oh dear, I'm not very good at this. Is your father gone on crusade again? He would be the best one to talk to. He should explain all this to you. Why don't we have a bite to eat together and then practice some of your magic lessons? What have you brought for us today?"

Changing the subject, Ilona was relieved to see the confused look on the poor boy's face dissolve at the mention of food. They ate cheese and bread and she poured them some tea. She felt sorry for Ursan. He was alone most of the time, with his father gone. Lord McTavish had insisted Greccon should go and help the knights in their quest, as he had Ursan to help protect the castle. Even at only eight years of age, Ursan was a true mage with amazing powers. Ilona took credit for that, teaching him patiently and keeping him company while his father ran about the world. He stayed with her more often than not, feeling more comfortable with his gift there and not being singled out as different. It was a lonely life at the castle for him. Children his age were afraid of him, except for Alyssa. Ilona knew how hard it would be for Ursan to give up his only friend, but he could no longer be as familiar with Alyssa and it not be considered an offense against the Lady. Ilona knew how the ways of the court worked, and Alyssa's reputation would have to be beyond reproach for her to be a good alliance with another land. *I need to get him so involved with magic that he has little time for thinking of Alyssa*, she thought, as she looked at the pain in his eyes as he ate. She pushed back her chair and folded her arms. She knew he really wasn't old enough for this, but she thought she'd try anyway, if for no other reason but to involve him in his magic.

"I thought we'd try something new today. Instead of the usual defensive magic, I thought we'd try some battle strikes."

He looked at her with disbelief, dropping his bread as he blustered, "Really, Ilona? Real battle strikes. I thought you said you couldn't teach me those things, that my father would only be able to teach me that. Can we really work on that, today?"

His eyes lit up as if he were a beacon and he jumped to his feet. Ilona gave him a slow smile at his enthusiasm. She had opened a door that would be impossible to close, now. He stood there, hardly able to contain himself, and she debated whether she had made the right decision. Still, he was a level-headed boy, and she didn't believe he would abuse the power she would teach him.

More sternly now, she said, "Yes, I can teach you battle strikes. I thought it more your father's place to teach you those things, but he's gone so much. Now, I must caution you, Ursan. This is a dangerous spell and not to be taken lightly or frivolously. Being responsible is the most important lesson a mage must learn. Power has its price, and the price you must pay is to learn it correctly and know when it's to be used. This is not something to show off with."

Ursan's face went from excited to concerned. "I know that, Ilona. I would never show off. I like it better when no one knows what I can do."

She nodded solemnly. "That is well, Ursan. You have an advantage when you can surprise your enemy. If they know you are a mage, they will expect a magical attack and will be ready to fend it off. Keeping what you know secret is like a weapon all on its own." Ilona got up and began to pull some books out of her book shelves, placing them on her table in front of the boy. His eyes widened with the amount of books that would be needed. She motioned him to sit down. She had thought fast and found a way to prolong his lessons for a few years. She sat back down and motioned to the books.

"First, you must learn battle strategy. It won't be easy, but if you think you're old enough to learn battle strikes, first you must learn of war. Here are some of the books I want you to read."

Ursan gasped audibly and she raised her eyebrows at him. "Is there something wrong?"

Not wanting to admit he would rather just learn the spells that could turn the course of a battle, he shook his head. She was right. If he knew nothing of battles, what good would he be in the fighting? "It will take me a long time to read all these books, Ilona, but I will. I want to be good at battle strikes. I guess you can't use them properly if you don't know why you're using them."

He looked a little disappointed at the amount of work all this would require but she saw he was still interested and congratulated herself. Ilona couldn't have an eight year-old running around with a spell that dangerous, but she could keep him busy and educate him so when he was old enough to control himself in a battle, he would be ready. She watched as he looked through the first book. She knew the writing was difficult and she did not want him to get discouraged.

"Magic isn't as easy as everyone thinks it is, is it? I know those books might be difficult for you, but I'll help you get through them. Knowledge is just as powerful as magic. One cannot exist without the other. Now, I know you can do the simple spells already, the survival spells and a bit of the weather spells, but when you are talking about destroying lives of other people, you have to realize there will be a lot more involved. Life is precious, Ursan, and for you to decide to end the life of another person is a power that must be respected. Just as all good magic brings rewards, bad magic brings pain and suffering. You have to know the difference. You have to ask yourself, *Do I have the right to kill?* Now, maybe if you don't, the enemy will kill you or your kinsmen, but is there a possibility of surrender for them or not? Would a different spell work as well without ending lives? You see, it's all very complicated, but I think you are old enough to start to think of these things. Either way, it will keep you busy enough that you won't need a whipping as often as you do now." She winked at him as he made a face at her.

He picked up the second book and flipped through it, eyeing the third and fourth book as well. "Ilona, are you just trying to get my thoughts away from Alyssa with all this work?"

The question had caught Ilona by surprise, but she showed no sign of it. He had figured out her whole plot. She lied, "Not at all, Ursan. As I said before, you won't be a boy much longer. If you are going to grow up a mage, you need to learn how to act like one, and learn like one, too. You've wasted enough time playing children's games. You have to grow up as well as Alyssa, and I suspect you are both going to be very busy learning different things. You have to concentrate on your work, Ursan. See? Already your thoughts are back with Alyssa and not on your lessons. Maybe you aren't old enough for these things yet."

Ursan looked stunned at Ilona as he hurriedly placed the four books in the sack that had contained the food. He went to the door before she could change her mind and take the books back.

"No, no, Ilona, I'm old enough. You're right. I need to get busy reading all of these. I'll come back by here tomorrow." He ran out of the door and into the woods.

Ilona stood there watching him go. It had amazed her that he had her intentions figured out so quickly. He's a smart little boy, she thought, as she heard him crashing through the woods on his way home to the castle. She thought he should learn stealth too, and she shook her head with amusement. She took a deep breath and sighed. He could have been her son. She missed Greccon. She should have married him. She was as lonely as Ursan was, she realized. Well then, they could keep each other company. She knew Ursan would have a terrible time letting Alyssa go and live the life that was meant for her, just as she had a terrible time letting Greccon go, but it was so long ago and so many years had passed since. She still loved him, she knew, just as Ursan would always love Alyssa, but some things just were not meant to happen.

A sound above her caused her to look up at the large shadow in the trees. "Argon. I'm so glad you're here. Come down here and tell me all the news of the Realm."

He dropped down out of the trees without making a sound. She absently smoothed a few of his wing feathers down as she said, "You should have been here earlier. I was giving Ursan battle lessons. I could have used your help."

He snickered. "Just tell him to kill them all, Ilona. The last one standing wins, you know. At least that's what I would have told him. It's my policy. I see you do not agree, as usual. You're such a pacifist, Ilona. If you ask me, they all deserve to die, as worthless as these humans are. Except for you my dear." He gave her a playful tug on her hair and she smacked his beak. "Isn't he a little young to be learning the spoils of battle?"

Ilona shook her head. "No. I was trying to get his mind off of a lovely little girl that he's grown to love. You know how you males are; if it's not women you're thinking of, it's fighting. I was just trying to move his thoughts."

Argon nodded. "Well, you're right there. I daresay a good battle always takes precedence."

Thinking of Greccon, off in a crusade, she agreed miserably.

CHAPTER FOURTEEN

Ilona had been right, thought Ursan, as he watched a group of court ladies making wreaths of flowers. Alyssa sat in the middle of the group, shining like the sun. They had both passed their seventeenth birthdays, and he knew his feelings for her were deeper and richer than they had been when he was eight, and totally improper considering her station. As Ilona had suggested, Ursan immersed himself in his studies. He always carried a book with him now, and he looked away from the women and buried his thoughts and attentions in his work. It was a beautiful spring day, unusually warm, and the fragrance of the masses of flowers the women entwined was distracting. He found himself glancing at them, caught up in their conversations, and not retaining a single word he was trying to read. As a matter of fact, he had read the same sentence over and over again.

The castle was in an uproar. Lord McTavish was taking a new wife and the court was preparing for the elaborate celebration that would take place. The marriage would unite their kingdom with that of the immediate north, ensuring their relief from the attacks that always seemed to come out of that territory. Lord McTavish had never met the lady, and Ursan wondered what kind of life it would be for two strangers to make that kind of commitment. Of course, he knew it was necessary; it was the same principle that kept him apart from the Lady Alyssa.

He glanced over again and this time their eyes met and she

smiled radiantly at him, and he smiled back. He gave up trying to study and, tucking the book under his arm, he got up to talk with the women. A celebration always put the court in a good mood and the women were very generous with all of their plans to decorate. He heard more of dresses and food than he wanted to hear, but his mind wasn't on the celebration, or the conversation for that matter; it was on Alyssa. It was one of the very few times he could converse with her without suspicion falling upon him. He caught a signal from her, just a slight gesture, undetectable by anyone else that might be watching. It was a little hand signal they had worked out between them to let the other one know they needed to speak together out of the ears of the court. He nodded slightly, indicating to her that he understood, wished the ladies a wonderful morning, and walked off amid a chorus of laughter.

He knew it would take awhile for Alyssa to extract herself from the gaggle of girls so he stopped by the church to find Father Murphy busy lighting candles for the mid-morning mass. The father shook out the splinter of wood and hurried over to clap him on the back.

"Ursan, my boy, can I look forward to having you join us in mass this morning? I've worked out a splendid service I think you would enjoy."

Ursan shook his head. "Not this morning, Father. I have to be elsewhere. Perhaps another time."

Father Murphy sighed. He had been trying to convert Greccon and Ursan since his first day at the castle, but they clung tightly to their ancient roots, along with Ilona. Only a handful of Druids were left as Father Murphy's conversion rate was high among the kinsmen, and he always believed that at least Ursan would convert. Ursan had studied his religious documents along with anything else he could read, but he found the father's religion too male-oriented for his beliefs. There was no mention of the Goddess or her wondrous works upon the Earth.

Father Murphy motioned out the window. "Everyone is getting ready for the marriage. Of course. I've worked exceptionally hard on this sermon, so I hope people will spare the time to come in and hear it. What do you hear of your father?"

Ursan smiled. "They've arrived back already. He's in council with the Lord right now, giving him all the news. I'll have to wait until later to give him my regards. I hear the Lady and her entourage will be arriving this afternoon. What do you know of them? Lord McTavish has been a widower so long that I can't imagine him taking a wife, especially one he has never met."

Father Murphy sat down and indicated to Ursan to do the same. "Well, I hear she is a Catholic, but her people weren't in support of this union. We've been at odds with her country for a long time. Perhaps this will calm down the discord between us. I hear she isn't a young maiden, but neither is the Lord a young man anymore. She is bringing her mage with her. That should interest you. That will give Griffin's Gate quite an advantage over the other kingdoms. I daresay they will think twice before attacking us. So that is well."

Ursan nodded. He hadn't known about the new mage. He was anxious to meet this new mage and learn the magic of the northern lands. It would give them a distinct advantage. He wished to speak with his father about all of this, but it would wait. By the time the Lord finished hearing every bit of news from the travelers, it would be late in the afternoon. He told Father Murphy that he hoped his service went well and hurried away, making his way down to walk along the shore. There was a warm breeze blowing in off of the water, and the gulls circled above him noisily. Ursan drew in huge breaths of the salty air, feeling it relax him. The wind brushed his long dark hair back and he could feel the spray dampening his clothes. He stood and took in the vast blue of the water and watched the waves crash on its shoreline. The tide was out and he saw a few gulls picking through clumps of seaweed.

He scanned the shore to ensure he was alone. Even the guards up on the walls were talking to each other, and although he was sure he had been recognized and dismissed, he walked further along the beach as if that had been his intentions all along. In his mind, he could see two happy children running to beat the waves into shore and curiously peering into shells to find their inhabitants. Remembering Alyssa's hair blowing and tangling in the wind, he tried to put all the thoughts of unlimited time spent with Alyssa out of his mind, as he could not bear it any longer. Seeing that no one was watching, he ducked into the tall clumps of sea oats and headed for the secret door. It looked like nothing more than a whole in the wall of the tower, but Ursan knew where it led and he climbed up the rough-cut stairs, spiraling to the hidden room near the top of the tower. He listened to make sure he was alone, but he could hear nothing but the surf pounding the sand as the waves came in. The gulls were still flying and he could hear them scolding each other. He sat down, leaning his back on the cool stone of the tower wall to wait. He knew Alyssa would meet with him there as soon as she could sneak away from the court. It may take awhile, he thought, but he would wait forever to have the chance to speak with her alone and unsupervised. As custom demanded, the older they became, the more separated they had to be. It was all about what was proper now, and all their conversations, strictly monitored, were polite and totally worthless as far as Ursan was concerned. He had to treat her as if he hadn't known her all his life, and she had to treat him as a servant of the court and nothing more. Gone were the days of laughter and confidences, except for right here in their hiding place where they could be themselves.

It became more of a challenge to meet here. Ursan tried to remember when they met last. It was a long time ago. It was her seventeenth birthday, and they met in the dead of night, as the day was full of celebrations for her. It was in the winter time, he thought, and here it is spring already. So precious was the time they could steal away and be together.

He opened his book and began to study. He was nearly through with the book when he sensed her presence running along the beach. Unable to move the loose stone herself, she would have to use that entrance. He heard her light footsteps climbing the tower. She burst in through the door, closed and bolted it. She threw herself into his arms. She kissed him.

"Oh, Ursan. I couldn't wait to get away. I can't stand all this." She began pacing and ranting, so Ursan sat back down, watching her move back and forth with the grace of a cat.

"I can't believe Father is marrying again. I hear the woman is horrid. She's mean, fat, and ugly. She's older than he is, too. This is just awful. And she's arriving today, this very afternoon. I'll have to be there, of course, so we don't have much time to talk, but I had to see you. Something terrible has happened. I hear she's made an arrangement for me already, to get me out of the way, of course.

I understand I'm to marry the cruel Lord of a remote drafty castle somewhere in France, if you can believe that. Now, I'm supposed to be happy about all this and smile and laugh, all the time knowing my life is over? That Lord has already killed two of his previous wives. I don't know whether he poisoned them or beat them to death, but they didn't die of sickness, or so I'm told. Things couldn't be worse." She collapsed against him.

The news hit him like a lightening bolt. She was leaving him? He put his arm around her and pulled her close. This was his nightmare brought to life. He knew it would happen someday, but he always pushed it out of his mind, never wanting to think about it.

"But this is all rumor, is it not? You haven't even met the lady. How can you know all these things?"

She pushed her hair back. He thought he saw a glimmer of hope in her cloudy eyes. "Do you think that's all it is, Ursan? Maybe you're right. I did talk with Sir Collin and he has confirmed to me, confidentially of course, that she is old and ugly, but he didn't mention the arrangement. God. I do hope it's a rumor. Father would never arrange a marriage he thought would harm me. He would have talked to me about it first, don't you think?"

Ursan nodded. "I do. Don't panic, Alyssa. I'm sure that's all it is. You know how jealous the court women are of you. They pretend to be your friends, and then they talk about you behind your back. You can't trust anyone."

She threw her arms around him and buried her face in his chest. "I can. I can trust you, Ursan. I've always trusted you. Oh, I wish all this wasn't happening. I don't want a new mother. I've managed all these years without one, and so have you."

Ursan patted her back. "Now, give her a chance. Maybe she won't be as bad as all that. You know how people talk. I heard from Father Murphy that she's bringing her mage with her. Have you heard anything about him?" He felt her head shake on his chest.

She looked up at him. "Why would we need another mage? We have both your father and you."

Ursan shrugged. "I don't know. Maybe she's more trusting of her own mage, although being mages of the court, we would be bound to her as well, once she married the Lord."

Alyssa stood up then and brushed out her dress and patted her hair. Looking out of the window slit, she said sadly, "I've got to go before someone finds out I'm missing. I hate this. I feel so much better when I'm with you."

He took her in his arms again and kissed her hair. She held him tightly and kissed him again. Then she ran out of the door and back down the stairs. Ursan slid down the wall into a sitting position once more. He touched his lips where she had kissed him. They had kissed numerous times, always little happy children's kisses, but these were different now, and his heart ached every time she left him. Who knew when they would meet again? Meanwhile, they had to act as cordially as if they were strangers. She had been there all of perhaps five minutes. He had waited hours for just a few minutes alone with her, but he wouldn't have traded those minutes for anything in the world.

Opening his book now, he decided to finish it and then go to Ilona's house and trade it for another one. It would be hours before he could speak with his father. But he couldn't concentrate on the subject. What if the rumors were true? He couldn't let her go to her death with some cruel Lord. Alyssa was too wonderful for that. If she had to marry, it should be to a prosperous Lord, a young Lord with an appreciation for beautiful women. How lucky that Lord would be, thought Ursan, and he sighed. He knew he shouldn't have feelings for her, but the truth was that he did and there was nothing to be done about it. As much as he tried, he could never fully pull apart from her. As long as he lived, he would love her.

Realizing that he, too, would be expected for the arrival of the Lord's intended, he quickly tucked the book away and went down the stairs. Checking the position of the sun, and knowing he would have to hurry now, he skirted along the outside tower wall until he reached the woodlands. He ran most of the way to Ilona's and knocked on her door. She answered right away as he brushed past her to exchange the book for another on her bookshelf. She stood there with her hands on her hips.

"You're in quite a hurry today, aren't you, Ursan?"

He looked at her apologetically and said, "I'm sorry, Ilona, I was finishing this book and I just remembered the Lord's new lady is due to arrive and I'm not ready for the presentation. My father will kill me."

She chuckled a bit. "He's home then, your father?"

Ursan could see her eyes light up as she asked. His father spent quite a bit of time with Ilona when he was home, but Ursan didn't have time to speculate about all that now. "Yes, he arrived just this morning and has been in council with the Lord. I'll tell him you send your regards, but now I have to rush home."

Placing the book in his bag, he gave her a quick kiss on the cheek and tore through the woods. He reached his father's chamber, freshly washed and dressed for the ceremony, just as his father emerged.

"Ursan. I've been searching for you. We haven't much time. The lady has arrived with much fanfare. We're to be at the castle banquet hall."

He grinned at his handsome young son and, grasping his arm, led him down the hallway to go to the Lord's banquet room. "I trust you have been well? You look a little flushed."

Ursan nodded. "I know. I almost forgot the Lady was coming today. I had to run all the way home from Ilona's. I've been reading her books. Father, I really need to speak with you of an important matter-"

Greccon silenced him with an upraised hand. "All in good time my son. We will speak over dinner. Now, let's not be late."

They took their places in the reception line. Flowers decorated the banquet hall and everyone was wearing their best. There was much talk and laughter as they arrived. Lady Alyssa wore a dress of light purple silk, with a crown of lavender flowers in her hair, and it took Ursan's breath away. She looked so beautiful. She would be the first one to greet the guests.

Greccon leaned over to speak confidentially with Ursan. "Lady Alyssa is a vision, isn't she?" He winked at Ursan, who he knew was staring intently at her. He added, "I hear the new Lady of the castle bears a very good likeness to Farther Murphy's new mule."

Ursan gasped and tried not to laugh, his eyes still on Lady Alyssa. His father poked at him.

"Ursan," he said quietly. "Perhaps you should look elsewhere."

Ursan swallowed and nodded, now turning his attentions to the rest of the visitors. His father was right; he was being a bit too bold. He trained his eyes on the door, waiting for the Lady to appear with the Lord.

The crowd hushed as Lady Anna appeared on the arm of Lord McTavish. Ursan noted that she indeed resembled Father Murphy's mule, although he thought the mule the fairer of the two. Her plump form was draped in the finest brocade dress, dark in color to match her severely pulled back, black hair. She had enough jewelry on to provide ballast in a storm, and her expression was that of someone who had just bit into a green apple. She had six ladies with her, all looking as if they had seen better days and a tall slim dark-haired man who Ursan hoped was not the mage because he disliked him immediately, as he fawned over Alyssa.

They waited their turn to pledge their service to the Lady and meet her kinsmen, who were now to be their own. When it was their turn to meet the Lady, Ursan did exactly as his father had done, expressing his loyalty and introducing himself to Lady Anna, and then he brushed his lips on the hands of her ladies in waiting. Ursan thought they had indeed been waiting a long time, and had yet more time to wait, as homely as they were. They blushed and fanned themselves just as any other lady might, and he stood to bow to Raskin the mage, as he was introduced to him. Ursan felt the evil just as quickly as Greccon did and they exchanged looks with each other. So. Now they had an evil mage to deal with. Father Murphy had a strange expression of uncertainty as he bowed, and Ursan saw his hand go to his waistline as if he had a sudden pain.

Greccon bent to speak into his ear. "Ursan, go back to my chambers. We will talk immediately."

Ursan nodded and left the room, but not before he stole another glance at Alyssa, who looked like a peacock amid Lady Anna's train of crows.

*　*　*

Raskin laughed to himself as he watched Ursan and Greccon leave. Not wanting to join the demons in the new Dark Realm, he had opted to stay behind and have a little fun. He knew the gate to the Magic Realm was somewhere around here and he was determined to find it and infiltrate the Magical Realm, bringing back information to Mordread. He had taken possession of the weak mage that Lady Anna had, even before the trip. He wanted his presence at Griffin's Gate to be a welcome one, and one that would give him full access to the grounds and castle. What better way to explore than to be a mage? Lady Anna was a spiteful, hard woman and had actually liked the change in her faltering mage. It seemed as if he had more backbone now. She would make Griffin's Gate her own, with his help. After all, she was one of his own kind.

He chose an apple from the bowls of fruit and other foods spread out on the long tables. Chewing noisily, he watched the Lady Alyssa. It was the number one mission on Lady Anna's list, to be rid of the daughter as soon as possible. A pity, he thought, as he watched her smile and dance with the rest of the women. She was probably the one thing in this whole miserable kingdom that he'd keep. She was fair and enticing and he thought maybe the Lady Anna might change her mind, or at least give her to him to dispose of. He scoffed at the two mages. They wouldn't be any trouble at all. Look how they ran away already, like hunted deer. He gazed at Father Murphy. The priest had something; he wasn't sure what yet, but he would find out. Something had alerted him to Raskin's demonic nature and he didn't think it was his cross. *All in good time, Raskin my boy,* he thought, and devoured the rest of the apple. The mongrel dogs under the tables jumped on the apple core as it hit the floor. Raskin kicked at them, sending them scurrying back under the table.

He looked at the Lord with his new Lady. He felt sorry for the poor bastard. It had to be a political marriage, he thought, as no one in their right mind would want that old mean prune of a woman for a wife. But she would serve his purpose well. She was stupid and cruel, but as long as she had her way, things would be fine. It was Raskin's job to ensure things went the way she wanted, and she made sure he knew it. He was to enchant the Lord to bend to her will. She wanted full control over that territory and the use of Griffin's Gate's defensive location to expand the northern territories southward. Now, she would have another army in which to conquer the lands she desired. She was ambitious and Raskin had to give her credit there, but he had no use for her greedy tendencies. He wanted to find the gate, and if helping her would allow him the freedom to look for it, well then, so be it. Alyssa caught his eye again as she crossed the room. He might have to get rid of her, but he would sure have some fun with her first. He hadn't had a lady that lovely in a long time and he thought he deserved a treat. He hoisted his belt and downed a tankard of ale, watching her with hungry eyes.

Father Murphy wrung his hands as he nervously scanned the crowd. His demon dagger was alerting him to a demon in the area, but he wasn't sure which new person was the demon. It had been years since the blade had sprung to life, so it stood to reason that it had to be one of the new Lady's entourage. He could feel the warm blade heat up and he could hear its hum. He hoped it wasn't notice-able to anyone else. So far, no one had acted as if they heard it. He prayed to God that it wasn't the Lady, herself. He moved around, making small talk with the celebrating guests. Stopping here and there to clasp a hand or give a blessing, all the time wondering who the demon might be. He wished he could talk to Greccon about it, or Ursan, but they had no knowledge that he possessed the demon dagger and Elijah had told him to keep it secret. Well, he could tell Greccon that he felt an evil presence and that would be the truth. Let the mage deal with the demons, he thought, but he knew it was his responsibility, too. Why hadn't the demon left, knowing full well the power to kill it was here? It worked in the church without him having to draw it out of its sheath. No, it must be a stronger demon, like the one in Father Johns. He didn't want to go through that again and he shuddered at the thought of it. Things had been so wonderful and peaceful that he nearly forgot why he wore the dagger. Now, it was very evident, and as keeper of the dagger, it was his job to find out who it was.

Methodically, he went around visiting with every new face, in-viting them to join his church and welcoming them to Griffin's Gate. When he approached Raskin, he felt the dagger actually vi-brate and he knew he found the demon. Being cautious, he extend-ed a hand and welcomed Raskin as he had the other members of the Lady's court and Raskin fearlessly took it and thanked him. His face was smiling, but his eyes were cold as he examined the priest from head to toe. Not wanting to cause a scene, Father Murphy moved on, waving a hand at one of the knights. He had found out who the demon was; now all he had to do was get rid of it, but not now and not here. The air contained enough tension with former enemies joining together in the same room. It would be a miracle to get through the night without a fight breaking out as soon as the ale was consumed. Somehow, he knew the demon knew he had a weapon he could use against it. He didn't know how he knew these things, but he did. That would make him more vulnerable, he thought. The demon would pursue him now, and in a way, Father Murphy was glad. If it was busy chasing the priest, it would leave everyone else alone. Still, it was unsettling, and once again Father Murphy found himself looking over his shoulder.

Lord McTavish put out a hand to his daughter. "Come and get to know your new mother- to- be."

Alyssa gave a deep curtsey and lowered her eyes. "My Lady."

Anna leaned over to talk to Lord McTavish. "Such a pretty young lady, my Lord. How ever did you manage to keep her here at Griffin's Gate? Lords everywhere would want her for their own as soon as they laid eyes upon her."

Lord McTavish chuckled. "Aye, it's the truth, but she's such a comfort to me since her mother's death. She's so much like my Mary." He looked at her wistfully and smiled, and she smiled back at him.

Lady Anna patted his hand. "Well, with the good Lord's blessing, I shall be a comfort to you now. Leave it to a doting father to coddle his daughter to the point where he denies her her own kingdom."

Alyssa looked alarmed and grasped her father's hand again. "Griffin's Gate is my home. I have no desire to leave it, Father, or you."

He patted her hand, and then kissed it. "I never thought of your needs, Alyssa. Perhaps Lady Anna is right. If I was waiting for you to get any lovelier, it just wouldn't happen. You should have children of your own now. Oh, I am a selfish old man."

Anna gave Alyssa a smug smile and a calculating look.

In his chambers, Greccon paced the floor, then stopped to look at his son. "We will have our hands full now, Ursan. Raskin will be out to destroy us both. Since he knows we can counteract any of his spells, he will look for other excuses to send us away. I need to talk with Ilona and have your lessons stepped up. You will need more aggressive spells now. I'm afraid that when I leave to assist the knights you will be left to deal with Raskin on your own. Maybe you should go with the knights in the future. I'm sure I can arrange that with Lord McTavish. It's nothing that you can't handle, weather spells and the like. I've never had to use any defensive magic, and the knights are sturdy enough on their own."

Ursan shook his head. "No, Father, the knights consider you their lucky charm for maneuvers. They won't accept me as a substitute. I'm not afraid of Raskin. I know enough magic now to handle the likes of him."

Greccon had to laugh at his son, puffed out like a rooster. "Spoken like a true fool. You have no idea what magic the mage has. How can you be so sure of yourself, Ursan? He's from a different land."

Ursan would not be discouraged. "And I am from a different land than his. I'd say we were on pretty even ground. He does not know my power either."

Greccon sat down and poured each of them a glass of wine. "A good point. Perhaps you are wiser than I gave you credit for."

He could tell Ursan was nervous about the situation and he thought he would be still and let the boy talk. Ursan obliged him.

"I talked with Alyssa today. There's a rumor the new Lady will try to marry her off to some cruel Lord in France. She's pretty upset about that. If Lord McTavish announces that, we have to try to convince him not to send her. He killed his last two wives."

Greccon took a slow sip of the wine and swirled it in his cup. "Ursan, you know Lady Alyssa will marry, and you know it will be to unite lands. Now, I agree, if the proposed Lord is one of a violent nature, we should try to intervene, but Ursan, you have to let her go."

Ursan made a face of despair. "I know that, Father. I've always known that. I don't have to lose her friendship, though. I rarely see her at all now, let alone talk with her, but that doesn't mean I want to see her die."

Greccon leaned over to look into his eyes. "I know, my son. She is your Lady and she always will be, Ursan the Protector. That's why you have to be extraordinarily careful now. Raskin won't come right out and blast you with a spell. He'll find other ways of expelling you from the court. It will be treason or worse, if he finds out you spend time with Alyssa alone. Oh, yes, I know. I've always known, Ursan, and I saw nothing wrong with it either. I know how you feel about her and I know she feels the same way and there isn't a thing either one of you can do about it."

Ursan's face reddened out of embarrassment and frustration. How would his father have known? He was hardly ever there. Of course, he was a powerful mage and he had abilities Ursan could only dream of at this stage of his life. It was rumored King Oberon, himself, even taught Greccon some magic. Ursan could not meet his father's eyes. He looked away.

Greccon put a hand on his shoulder. "There's nothing wrong with loving someone, Ursan. I wish circumstances were that you could have Alyssa for your own wife, but you know that is impossible. You must concentrate on your lessons. You must put Alyssa out of your mind and work hard to learn all that you can. You may save her life someday with what you may learn tomorrow. Remember that."

Ursan nodded. "You're right, Father. Ilona has told me as much."

Greccon sat back, amused. "Ilona is very wise. I'm thankful she is teaching you. Learn everything you can from her. She will be a very important person in your life someday."

Ursan looked up. "What do you see, Father? What do you see in the future for me?"

Greccon shook his head. "Nothing. You know I can't tell my own future or yours."

Ursan smiled slyly. "Alright then, what do you see for Ilona?"

Greccon clapped him on the back, laughing. "I see she will entertain an old wizard tonight. I have to go and tell her of Raskin. She will know how to train you for unexpected magical attacks."

Ursan scoffed at his father's refusal to tell him of the future. "You seem to know everything about me and Alyssa. How about you and Ilona?" he asked bravely, knowing he was crossing a line that was none of his business. But his father had a twinkle in his eye.

"No one cares about me being with Ilona. She's not a Lady in the royal sense, but she's a Goddess to me. You be careful, Ursan.

Stay away from Alyssa and Raskin, at least until we find out more about him. Agreed? I suggest you stay here in my chambers tonight, for safety. Read your new book."

Ursan nodded in agreement. "Where will you sleep, then?" His father smiled and left the room.

Greccon entered the woods carefully, disarming the magical web and then rearming it as he passed. It was a game he always played. He would surprise Argon before Argon found him. As old as he was now, and as many times as he passed through the forest, he had yet to catch Argon unawares. Each time he believed he would finally get the better of the griffin, but it was to no avail. As he reached the stream, a silent dark shadow descended and forced him to the ground.

"Really, Greccon, aren't we getting a little too old to be playing these games?" The griffin laughed. "How are you, my friend? Tell me all the news of your last quest as we walk."

Greccon rose back to his feet, brushing off the dead leaves from the winter. "One of these days, you will get old and lazy, Argon, and I will have you then. I'm afraid I have some grave news that I want you to relay back to the King. Raskin, the mage of the new Lady of Griffin's Gate, is a demon. I don't know why he's here, yet. Maybe it's to start a war or an epidemic of some sort, but he may be here to find the gate. Why this kingdom, if not for that? We are not that good of a land as far as strategy leverage, and we're too far out for the trade routes. Still, he's here now, and I feel his power is strong. I fear for Ursan."

The griffin considered what the mage had said. "Ursan has been training with Ilona. You haven't been around long enough to appreciate his power. I take it the demon knows you know about him?"

Greccon nodded.

The griffin furled his wings in a shrug. "You will just have to wait and see what his real purpose is here. I tend to agree with you, but he'll never penetrate the Realm. He'd have to get by me to do that. I have demons for snacks. And he doesn't know about me, either, so I'm one up on him already. It's good to be forewarned, but I welcome the challenge. It's been too quiet for too long." The griffin punctuated his statement with a yawn and a snap of his sharp beak.

Greccon turned and put an arm around Argon's neck. "If I have to leave, Argon, and I'm sure this demon will make sure that I do, will you help Ursan? Don't tell him that I asked; it's just that he's so full of himself at eighteen. Confidence breeds mistakes if you're not careful. I know you are not here all of the time, but I don't like this demon showing up right now. It bothers me."

Argon nodded. "You know I would never let anything happen to Ilona or Ursan, no matter what a pain in the tail he is. When I am here, I'll watch for him and the new demon. I could use a snack, and that would take care of that problem now, wouldn't it?"

Greccon laughed. "That would do it, but what with this new Lady, Argon, I feel it's going to change a lot of things around here, and not for the better, either. Ursan is afraid for the Lady Alyssa. It wouldn't surprise me if she gets married off somewhere else to get her opinions away from her father's ear. I don't know why Lord McTavish is doing this, to be honest with you. The trouble from the north is not bad enough to warrant spending your life with a horrid woman - and she is. She will be the Lady straight from Hell, if you believe in that sort of thing."

Argon trudged on beside Greccon. "There isn't a woman alive worth compromising your principals for, if you ask me. Maybe he's just grown lonely, Greccon. You humans are like that, you know. You're never happy to be by yourselves."

Greccon stepped over a fallen log. "I can't imagine being so lonely that I would marry a toad. That's it, Argon."

Argon froze, looking confused. "A toad, is it? Whatever do you mean, Greccon?"

Greccon was talking faster now. "No, no, I mean that she had put a spell on the Lord McTavish. Why else would he marry that woman? That's what the demon is doing for her. She's in league with the demon to get her Griffin's Gate. She'll bewitch him and then bring in her troops, take over Griffin's Gate, and continue south down the coast. Of course."

Argon closed his eyes, thinking now. "It's possible, I guess. It would have to be a spell of great proportions to be able to do all that. It doesn't matter to the magicals, but for you and Ilona, it may turn into a problem. Either way, I'm protecting this forest, so no

one will reach you from the woods. You may have to watch the sea.
I can help there, if I have to, but I'd be very visible then. If I were
you, I would alert the knights to your suspicions, if you can trust
them"

Greccon turned and rubbed his chin as he walked. It was clear to
him now, but he wasn't sure what he could do about it. He'd have
to train Ursan how to undo a spell like that and keep Raskin thinking his spells were working on the Lord. Greccon would check the
Lord in the morning and see if there was any enchantments put on
him. It would be a game of point and counterpoint from here on
in. Alerting the knights would just breed suspicion and possibly a
charge of treason. No, he would have to keep this between himself
and Ursan. Argon left him at Ilona's door, wishing him a good evening and telling him he was going to fly to the tower and see if he
could spot the demon for himself. He camouflaged himself in invisibility so no one would see him, except for perhaps Ursan, if he was
out and about. The demon may have the power to see him as well
and he relished the look he would see on the demon's face if he saw
him. He chuckled to himself. He would let Oberon know tonight,
but first he would try to get a look at him and see if he recognized
him. Some demons were worse than others. If the demons had just
created the Dark Realm, why did this one stay behind? Of course, if
he had the protection of the Lady of Griffin's Gate, being her mage,
he could do a lot of damage without consequences. They left the human world for the same reasons the magicals did. They were tired
of being hunted. But demons in a position of power were another
threat that the magicals hadn't thought of, and it would need to be
discussed before the world got out of balance once again.

King Oberon couldn't believe what he was hearing from Argon.

"A demon posing as a mage at Griffin's Gate? Well, if Greccon
says it's a demon, I'm sure he's right. How ignorant is the Lady to
take a demon as a mage? Does she not know what he is?"

Argon shook his head. "I doubt it. She is an evil little person,
herself. I'm sure she doesn't care if he's a demon or not, as long as
he can do what she wants him to. The real mage she had didn't have
real magic to begin with. It was all a charade, but now that he's possessed, there's real magic there now. I saw him. It's a changeling like

Mordread. He's a lesser demon, but enough to cause trouble."

Oberon sat back, thinking. "You're right, Argon. They wouldn't care, would they? They're such flimsy creatures. Well, this puts light on a new subject that the Commission will have to work on. If the demons put their own in positions of power, they will be able to do almost anything. This has reached a new level of responsibility for us. Somehow, they knew our mages were still in the real world and they've decided to counteract them with their own. It will have to be fought on a mage level then, don't you think?"

Argon nodded. "That's exactly what Greccon proposed, and I agreed with him. Oh, I'll help them if I can. If I can find that damn demon in my forest, it will be over quicker than it started."

Oberon sighed with exasperation. "Call a meeting of the Commission. Now, they will have more to deal with than blighted lands. If the demons are on the move, we must move with them or all is lost. They will have to work with the mages to identify and counteract the demonic influences that will be entering the populations. Next, it will be evil Lords and Kings."

Argon nodded. "I think they've slipped through already. I think we should take another look at the leaders for possessions. I'm afraid we've been slack, too comfortable in our celebrations. We need to stay alert as the danger will never be past."

CHAPTER FIFTEEN

Father Murphy was reviewing his church records when he heard the door crash open. He jumped up and went around his desk, into the sanctuary. The Lady Alyssa rocketed through the door and threw herself at his feet. She was in a complete state of disarray.

"Father, hide me."

He pulled her up and pointed to his chamber. "In there, quickly. Hide under the desk." He had a flashback from the time her mother, Mary, had done the same thing so many years ago. She had hidden under his desk in the monastery when the townspeople were going to burn her as a witch. He shook his head to clear it. He didn't think that was Alyssa's problem at all. He heard shouts and arguments coming from the courtyard. He walked briskly to the door as the Lady fled to her hiding place. He saw Raskin exchanging words with Sir Collin.

Raskin said, "Yes, well, I'm afraid that the Lady is now my responsibility, Sir Collin. I have no need for your protection, now or on the journey north. I am a mage, and two traveling alone will raise no alarm in the other countries, but a full army will. We will be safer on our own." He turned his back on Sir Collin and entered the church.

Ursan, hearing the fray, left the stable and hurried over to Sir Collin. "What was that all about?" He saw the knight's face was red and his expression was angry.

Sir Collin looked around. "Let's go into the pub and talk privately out of the hearing distance of Lady Anna's spies."

Ursan nodded and they walked to the tavern, which was off of the Griffin's Gate grounds. They were silent as they walked past the sentries, whose faces were unfamiliar and obviously of the new guard. Lord McTavish's wedding had taken place two months ago and already the new Lady had acquired her own troops to move in and join forces with his. Only, they didn't behave as if they were joining kingdoms and that disturbed the knights and fighting men of Griffin's Gate. They had been ordered to combine forces and strategies with Anna's troops and none of them had liked that. Her men were rude and brash, acting as if they were the new army of Griffin's Gate and not just additional troops.

Ursan could hear Sir Collin muttering to himself as they walked. They ducked into the dark tavern. It was early in the day and, save for a few traveling merchants eating their morning meals, they were alone. Ordering two ales, they took a table in a darker far corner. In a hushed voice Sir Collin began, "I don't suppose you've heard the news yet. The Lady Alyssa is to be taken north to marry in France. It was all arranged by the Lady Anna and told to the Lord today. She is to leave immediately with no ladies to accompany her and no dowry, except for the allegiance of Griffin's Gate. I'm telling you, Ursan, I don't like it. She is not even to have an escort."

Ursan looked stricken. "Surely, you would be her protection, then?"

Sir Collin set down his tankard and shook back his long brown hair. "Raskin is to take her north, alone. The roads are not safe, and I don't care if he is a mage. The Lady should have her entourage with her. Can you imagine a Lady, moving to a new land without her trappings or clothing? She is only to take her horse and clothes for the journey. Her nurse isn't allowed to accompany her, either. Look what a show Lady Anna gave us upon her arrival. You may accuse me of treason, my good mage, but this isn't the way Lady Alyssa should depart Griffin's Gate and we both know it. Raskin is a scoundrel, and no amount of talking to the Lord will convince him of that. Is he under an enchantment?"

Ursan's mind was reeling. "No. None that I can detect, and I checked on him this morning. The whole idea is absurd. How can he possibly consider sending her with Raskin? Wouldn't that compromise her, ah, purity to her new Lord? I must go and talk to Lord McTavish immediately." Ursan jumped to his feet and the knight reached out for his arm and easily sat him back down.

"It will do you no good. If he is not enchanted, then he has lost his mind. Do you see Lady Anna's troops moving in every day? She has almost as many men as we do, moving in and taking up positions in the farmer's fields."

He looked around the tavern and, seeing that they would not be overheard, bent forward to talk conspiratorially to Ursan."What knights that are still here have banded together along with the troops. We fear an attack from Anna's men. This has not been a marriage, Ursan; it's a takeover, and by God, we will not let that happen. Look at the way her men are situated around the castle and the way they've ousted the farmers from their houses. We have been at war without even knowing it and Lord McTavish be damned for letting it happen."

Ursan sat back, staring at Sir Collin. Had he been blind? Now that he thought about it, there was an unusually large number of troops positioned in the farmer's fields. Troops and equipment. They had set up tents and one word from Lady Anna could bring down Griffin's Gate. Panic struck him then and his eyes grew wide.

"My Gods. You're right. I never gave it a thought. That was exactly what my father had said would happen. Sir Collin, could you send for my father? He's off to the king's castle on some business. We have to prepare for this."

Sir Collin waved a tankard at the serving girl and she brought two more ales for them. Sir Collin flipped her a coin and smiled at her. She caught the coin and blushed, laughing and bowing to the knight. He watched her leave. "Be at peace, Ursan. We want no one to realize that we've caught onto the plan. Act as if nothing is wrong. You look like you've been kicked in the head by a horse. I've already sent Sir Lyons to the kingdom to summon your father, without the orders of the Lord or his Lady. That is enough to hang me for treason. We have to be very careful. I've also asked the farmers to volunteer in our aid should we need them, and to send their wives and children away to safety. The fighting is almost at hand. Now, for the Lady Alyssa, do you think you could foul up the weather enough to prevent them leaving right away? Once the fighting begins, little thought will be given to her trip north. I'll confide in you, Ursan. I've known you since you were a wee lad. I don't think there is a marriage proposal at all. I think the Lady is in real danger. None of our knights have ever heard of this Lord that she's been promised to, or his kingdom. We have to prevent her from leaving with Raskin."

Ursan didn't know what to say or do first. "Yes, of course, I'll blow up a gale that would stop even you, Sir Collin, but I must get to Ilona to tell her and warn her. Where is the Lady Alyssa now?"

Sir Collin smiled. "I distracted Raskin while she ran into the church. I don't think he saw where she ran, so I imagine the good Father has her tucked away somewhere. He's on our side and has no love, Christian or otherwise for the likes of Raskin. She should be safe enough with him. Once she's told him what is to be, he'll hide her for sure. Let that bastard Raskin look until he turns blue."

* * *

Raskin stormed into the church. He had looked up and down the street, and this would be the only place she could have gone. Father Murphy gave him his most welcoming smile, his arms spread wide in a gesture of peace.

"Raskin, how good of you to stop by. I wanted to talk with you about joining our congregation. Isn't it amazing? Here I was, just thinking about you and you walk through my door."

Raskin gave him an annoyed look and his eyes darted around the church.

"I have no time to talk with you today, Father. Have you seen the Lady Alyssa?"

Father Murphy managed to look surprised, as the demon dagger he wore began to hum. "The Lady Alyssa? Of course I've seen her, and a lovely lass she is, too."

Raskin was tired of the games the priest was playing. He was uncomfortable in the priest's presence. "I meant today, Father. Did you see her come in here?"

Father smiled. "I should think I would know if she came in here, Raskin. She isn't hard to miss with that beautiful golden hair, but you are welcome to look around if you wish. I have some candles to light, if you will excuse me." He walked over to a stand of memorial candles and prayed, lighting one for Alyssa's mother, Mary. Silently, he prayed her mother would keep her safe from this demon.

Raskin walked around and peered into the different rooms that were off the sanctuary. Seeing nothing, he cursed and left through the same door he had come in. Father remained by the candles a moment longer in case he was being observed, then calmly waited for his dagger to quiet. Once it went silent, he went to his chambers and barred the door. He glanced out of the window. Seeing Raskin heading for the drawbridge, he bent over, motioning Alyssa to come out. Her face was red and her eyes swollen with tears.

"My good child, whatever is the matter? He's gone now. Tell me what is wrong."

She could hardly talk and her story came out in sobs. Father Murphy was quite disturbed at her news and of the strange way they expected her to travel. No Lady could travel alone with just a mage to protect her. The story grated on his nerves. Something was very wrong here and they both knew it.

She cried, "I would rather die, Father, than travel with Raskin. He's a lecherous, disgusting man. If I am to travel, it is my knights I would want by my side, and my women to attend me. But my Lord Father will not hear me. He does whatever the Lady tells him to do. That isn't like my father, yet Ursan said he was not enchanted. Father, you must speak to him on my behalf. Perhaps he will listen to you." She wrapped her arms around the Father and continued to cry.

His face sad, he patted her back to comfort her. "There, there now, child. Of course I'll try to speak with him. The whole plan is not proper. I hear he will see no one, though; the Lady said he was not feeling well enough to visit. Have you seen him today? Is he fit enough for me to talk to?"

She shook her head which was still buried in the priest's robes. She mumbled, "No. He would not see me, not even to say good bye." This brought on a new torrent of tears. She raised her head, the tears streaming down her face. "I can't leave without seeing him once more. Yet he will not see me, what of that?"

Father Murphy frowned. That was not like the Lord McTavish

at all. He doted upon his daughter. None of this was making any sense at all and he thought he should get down to the bottom of this. "I will see your father, Alyssa. I will bring him communion. Surely I would not be denied bringing him the sacraments. If he is ill, he should receive them with all speed."

Alyssa looked hopeful at that. It was true. Her father never missed a mass or communion. She nodded her head and nervously looked out the window.

Father Murphy nodded back at her. "Have you a place you can hide from sight?"

Alyssa thought of the tower room that no one knew about. She nodded once more.

Father Murphy said, "Then go there and stay out of sight until I can speak with your father. It may take all day, knowing the Lady. Bring food and water with you and stay hidden. Alright?"

She turned and fled from the church before Raskin could come back. Entering the kitchens, calmly, she asked for a pack of food and water for traveling. Obediently, one of the cooks prepared her a pack. She hugged Alyssa and wiped away a tear.

So, she thinks I need this for my trip up north, thought Alyssa. Well, that was well enough. There would be no suspicion here. Alyssa took the pack and left abruptly. She worked her way down to the shoreline. Seeing some of Anna's men near the boats she waited, pressed up against the tower wall, until they turned towards the sea pointing at a school of fish off in the distance. Quickly, she made her way around the tower and dove into the clump of wild sea grasses that shrouded the secret entrance to the hidden room. She stood on the first step quietly, listening for any sounds. All she could hear was the waves upon the shore, the voices of the men in the distance, and nothing more. She crept silently up to the secret room and barred the door. Collapsing on the floor miserably, her tears began anew. She buried her face in her hands and prayed for help.

She didn't understand what was going on. It was not like her father to send her away so completely and not even say farewell. Alyssa knew that protocol demanded that she bring her own servants to whatever kingdom she traveled to. It should take months to pack and make new clothes for the trip. She didn't even have a wedding gown made for her yet. It was all very strange. Was she to be thrown to this Lord like a bone to a dog? Preparations needed to be made. She should have a carriage and a full escort, not merely sent off on a horse to endure the inclement weather and arrive smelling like a horse and filthy from the road. No, something was very wrong here. If she was promised to this Lord, well then she would go, but not like this. And not with Raskin. She would demand to speak with her father first. She would not leave without seeing him once more. She was the Lady of Griffin's Gate. The true Lady. Born and raised here and she would have a say in her life.

* * *

Ursan and Sir Collin were just finishing their second tankard of ale when Raskin marched in and confronted them.

"Well, if it isn't the boy mage and his knight. Talking of treason, no doubt. Where is the Lady Alyssa?"

Sir Collin smiled broadly, and Ursan gritted his teeth as he said, "Join us, Raskin. A toast before you leave. There is no treason here, just a friendly knight trying to match up this innocent mage with that experienced serving wench."

Raskin turned to look at the girl who Sir Collin had just beckoned over.

Sir Collin said, to Ursan's embarrassment, "My lovely young woman, what do you think of this young mage here? He has an eye for you, you know. Bring my friend here a tankard."

The woman laughed and stroked Ursan's long hair. She laughed again as he blushed a deep crimson. She planted a kiss on his cheek. "Aye, he is a tender boy. I can make a man out of him."

Everyone laughed except Ursan, who wished he could use his invisibility spell and just disappear. Knowing his eyes would betray them with all the hate he had for Raskin, Ursan stared down at the table.

Sir Collin jovially clapped his shoulder. "Now, Ursan, she would do you a world of good."

Raskin scoffed, "I have no time to waste on that boy's virginity. I need to know where the Lady Alyssa went, Collin, and I demand to know now. The two of you have always been her consorts, so

where has she hidden? It will do no good. The Lord has commanded me to take her north before the day is through."

Ursan felt his jaw tightening and it was all he could do not to
set the worm on fire.

Sir Collin smiled again and drank his ale. "Then I suggest you
better go and find her, Raskin. She is not our concern today, as you
told me earlier."

Slamming his hands on the wooden table and knocking into the
serving girl carrying his ale and spilling it all over him, he turned
and left, grumbling curses.

The serving girl looked after him with disdain. "How do you
like that? Here I have his tankard and he leaves without so much as
an apology for barreling me over." She turned and went back to the
kitchen, wiping her hands on a cloth.

Ursan let out his breath and Sir Collin seethed, "I will kill him
with my own hands if you do not get to him first, Ursan."

Ursan looked up at him, then. "I would prefer you kill him
with your broadsword, severing his head so I don't have to listen to
him talk. I will kill him myself if you don't."

Sir Collin smirked. "Listen, I didn't mean to insult you. I don't
want a mage mad at me. Eliza is fair enough, and for a few coins she
can be very friendly. I owe you that much for the embarrassment I
just put you through."

Ursan made a face at him. "I can't think of anything but my
Lady right now, Sir Collin. Save your coins. I have to leave and
get to Ilona's. After this is settled, one way or the other, I will buy
the next ale. Give my apologies and excuses to Eliza." He grinned
back at the knight and hurried out the door. Sir Collin finished his
tankard in silence, but he noted a look of disappointment on Eliza's
face.

* * *

Ilona marveled at how quickly Argon responded to her call. He
back-winged as he landed and marched over, a concerned look on
his face.

"What is it, Ilona? You look very disturbed."

She went to him and hugged him. "I'm afraid there will be trouble. Ursan was just here and it seems war is eminent."

She told him of Lady Alyssa's plight and the knights banding together. He had noticed the staggering amount of men the Lady Anna had brought with her and he told her he had seen more men on the move towards the castle.

Her face pained, she went on, "Greccon is not back yet from the king's castle. Sir Lyons was sent to get him, and meanwhile, Ursan is going to draw up a terrible storm. You will need to be out of that one Argon. He's going to put everything he has into it so no one can travel. He wants to wait until his father arrives, but he may have to start it early before they can move Lady Alyssa. Things had just settled down so nicely, Argon; the people were happy and healthy. Why does this all have to happen now? It's the demon, isn't it?"

Argon nodded his head. "Yes, Ilona. Whenever a demon is at hand, trouble soon follows. I want you to cast the invisibility spell over your home. I will contact Gunny and Shylock to give the enemy a warm welcome when they reach the forest. You will be safe enough."

Ilona looked crestfallen. Argon rearranged her hair with his beak. "Now, Ilona, I know you haven't been through this yet, but your mother has and I promise you, just as my father had looked after your mother, you will be fine and there's no cause to worry. It's Greccon and Ursan you are fearful for, isn't it?"

She nodded slowly. He clucked at her a bit.

"They are the court mages, Ilona, and they will be in the battle. You have taught them all you know and they will do their best. They are warriors just like I am, and they will not take cover and hide from an attack. You know that."

He lifted her chin with his claw. "Woman, you have no time to mope. You will be needed after the battle is over to heal the wounded. Use this time to prepare. You will need lots of medicines for pain and infections, and rolls of bandages. You're the only healer here. If we can bring the wounded to the forest, some of the elves may be deployed to help after it is over. I have to go prepare myself. I saw your horse, Rosey, out in the woods by the stream. I'll chase her back for you. Gather in your pets, my dear, and get busy."

She knew everything he said was true and she gave him a nod

and a weak smile. She hugged him tightly and he purred, then left. She stood there, watching him go. A few minutes later she heard his cry and Rosey shot through the trees as if the devil himself were after her. Ilona caught her and took her to the barn. Making sure both Rosey and Baron were fed and cared for, she took the long strips of willow bark that she had drying there to the house. Before entering, she closed her eyes and cast the invisibility spell over the barn and her house, making it undetectable by anyone's eyes. Only the fragrance of her preparing her herbs for medicines would give her away - that is, if anyone were able to get past three griffins. She didn't think she had anything to worry about except the welfare of her friends.

* * *

Father Murphy carried the communion in a wooden box as he always did when administering the rite to his ill parishioners. Upon crossing over to the castle, he was stopped by Raskin, who was very angry and red in the face.

"Father, I need to know where the Lady Alyssa is. We were supposed to leave for the north some time ago, and she seems to have vanished."

Father Murphy smiled to himself, but put on a face of concern for Raskin. "I don't know where she has gone. I wanted to give her a blessing before she leaves, so if you do find her, Raskin, I need to hear her confession and bless her. I doubt you will be able to receive communion on the road."

Raskin gave him an annoyed look. "We won't have time for all that, Father, unless she's found very quickly. Perhaps you will help me look for her?"

Father Murphy shook his head. "I'm afraid I can't help you right now. I'm in a state of grace to give communion to my Lord McTavish."

Raskin looked at him, furtively. "Lord McTavish isn't seeing anyone now, Father. You are wasting your time."

Now it was Father Murphy's turn to give an annoyed look. "Wasting time? My good man, to be in communion with the Lord and Savior will never be a waste of time. Lord McTavish is a devout

Catholic and will welcome me with open arms, I assure you."

Raskin shook his head. "Not today, he won't." He stormed off and Father Murphy wondered just what the mage knew that he wasn't telling. His leg burned from the dagger's warning, and he hurried along to the castle.

Upon entering the castle, he saw the usual staff going about their business. The Lord was not in his reception hall and he inquired as to his whereabouts. A solemn servant said he was still in his chambers, so Father Murphy headed in that direction. A stout guard stood in front of his door.

Father Murphy hefted his box. "Father Murphy to see Lord McTavish," he said and prepared to open the door.

The guard blocked his way. "The Lord is not to be disturbed, Father. I'm afraid I cannot let you pass. I have my orders."

The priest's eyebrows raised in puzzlement. "I am his confessor, Sir, and I'm here to bless him and give him communion. Surely your orders do not apply to me." He smiled and moved forward.

The guard planted himself directly in front of the door and shook his head. "No one is to pass."

Lady Anna exited the room then and was surprised to see the priest. "Father Murphy. The Lord cannot see you now. I'm afraid he's fallen ill. He had a very restless night and he's taken medicine from the healer. I'm afraid he is sound asleep and should not be disturbed. I can have someone summon you to come if he should awaken." She smiled sweetly and Father Murphy could see the concern on her face.

"What matter of illness does he suffer from? I did see him early this day and he seemed well."

Anna shook her head. "It came on him again after he had taken his meal. Food is not agreeing with him as it should. Now, I'm sure you have other parishioners to see, and as I've said, I'll send someone for you, should he awaken."

Father Murphy turned to leave, and Lady Anna went back into the room. The guard shifted again to block the door.

Ursan scaled the tower steps two at a time. He would be in a better position to cast a storm from the tower. Reaching the tower room, he bolted the door and stared out of the window. It was a shame to cause foul weather as it had turned out to be a beautiful day with fluffy white clouds and a salty breeze blowing in softly from the sea. He took a deep breath and put out his arms, gathering power. His hair blew about him as the air crackled with electricity. He began his incantation and watched closely as the white clouds grew darker and their bellies swelled with rain. He raised the temperature of the water and cooled the air above it. The wind began to swirl and the clouds massed into an even darker grey, gathering like a flock of sheep. He threw his head back and put more energy into the wind and lifted more moisture upwards into the colder atmosphere. The winds increased and thunder could be heard now in the distance, growing closer. The sky went from grey to green to black, now, as lightening pierced the darkness in stabbing bolts, veining out in all directions. Hail formed and clattered on the stone as the wind howled. He could see the soldiers on the fields run for cover and a few of the farmers were chasing their animals inside. The clouds split open and it began to rain in torrents, drenching the land. It blew in through the window, wetting his face. Still, he poured more energy into his work and felt the ground shake below him as thunder roared across the land. Spiraling water cyclones formed over the sea, bending and twisting as if in a dance, connecting the water to the sky in black wild threads. Even as the rain cooled him, he sweated with exertion. This was the strongest storm he had ever summoned. He heard the stones of the walls groan under the force of the wind, and it whistled in high pitches through the cracks. No one would be able to travel in this, he thought and with a sustaining spell, he lowered his arms and watched the forces of nature furiously answer his commands. He cupped his hands and drank the rain water. Satisfied that the storm would prevent anyone moving about, he sat to rest, his head in his hands.

She had recognized his voice as he began the incantation and watched in awe as the storm gathered on the horizon. She knew Ursan was calling the storm and she waited until he was through. Waiting until after the next bout of thunder, she called up, "Ursan, it's me; it's Alyssa." She heard him move from where he was apparently sitting and she saw the large flagstone move. He peered down at her and then she saw his feet sliding through. He jumped down and took her in his arms.

"Alyssa. I made the storm so you couldn't travel today. You

can't go off with Raskin. We have to talk, I've heard so many things today. I just don't know what to think."

She held him closer, shaking with fright. "I know. I'm scared, Ursan."

He removed his cloak and spread it out on the floor for her to sit on. He sat next to her and held her hands. "Alyssa, Raskin is looking all over for you. I'm glad you are here and I'm glad you hid. I talked with Sir Collin. He said the knights have never heard of this Lord that you're promised to, and you know they've been everywhere. I don't like it. Run away with me. I'll get food and water and horses, or we can travel by boat on the sea. I don't care how you want to go, but I want to take you away from here."

She wiped away her tears and allowed herself a little giggle. "Ursan, you can't kidnap me - I'm the Lady of Griffin's Gate. I can't just come up missing. They would hunt you down and hang you for that. You don't think anyone would figure out that we've left together if both of us came up missing?" She stood up and began to pace back and forth. "Come here."

He looked up and went to her. She gestured out of the window. "Look at all those farmers. If I don't consolidate us with the northern kingdoms, war will break out and a lot of people will die. I can't break a promise given by Griffin's Gate. It's no use. I can't disobey my father."

Ursan shook his head. "No, Alyssa, I don't think your father arranged this. I think Lady Anna is trying to get rid of you. I think Raskin is dangerous; he's evil. You can't go with him."

She turned and faced him. "I came here to get away from him, Ursan. You don't think I know that? I will talk with my father. I will not go with him alone. I want my ladies and a carriage. I've made up my mind on that. I will not be sent off like a beggar." She sat back down on his cloak and he sat with her again.

He held her as she cried. He pushed back her hair and kissed her cheeks. "Something is very wrong here. None of us have ever heard of a Lady traveling alone with a mage, and an evil one at that. You're the king's second cousin. I speak no treason, Alyssa, but your father is not in his right mind to send you off like that. Sir Collin is very concerned about all of Lady Anna's troops being here." He lowered his voice. "He thinks it might be war she wants, instead of combining the lands. He's put everyone on alert and he has sent for my father to return. He should be here in the morning. He'll know what to do. I wish I did. I'm supposed to take care of things when he's gone and look at this mess." He shook his head in despair.

She reached for him and they held onto each other as they had when they were children and were afraid. She thought about what he had told her. Could that be possible? Why wouldn't her father see through all of Anna's evil plots? Perhaps he was enchanted or drugged. She hadn't seen him in days and that was not like him at all.

"I will wait until your father arrives and I will go with him to see my father. Your father would never let harm come to me. He is stronger than Raskin. I just have to stay hidden until then, and you have to stay with me. I could never leave without saying goodbye to you, Ursan. I love you. Stay with me tonight?"

Ursan was torn between his desire to stay with Alyssa and what would be the proper thing to do. He stammered, "But, Alyssa, if I stay, people would talk about us and it would compromise your situation. I would be hung either way."

She looked so forlorn, and he couldn't leave her alone in the dark in the middle of the worst storm they had ever had. He sighed. "Of course I'll stay with you. I am ever at your service. You are my Lady, after all, and if you command me to stay, then it is my duty to do so." There. He had reasoned it out well enough to justify his presence there.

Alyssa was having a hard time keeping a straight face. She wished things had been different. She wished that Ursan was a Lord and that they could be together, always. He had always been there for her ever since she could remember. He was Ursan the Protector. *My protector,* she thought fondly, *my best friend, and a true one at that.* Here, he had conjured up the land's worst storm to protect her again and now he was wrestling with her reputation when they had always been together for so long. She never realized just how much she really did love him, and she always would no matter what had to happen to her. All hope gone now, she clung to him and, throwing all caution to the winds of the storm, she decided he would be her first love. She reached up and kissed him passionately. He tried to resist her but he found he could not and kissed her back.

Breaking away, he said, "Alyssa, we can't do this. It's wrong. You know we can't."

She reached for him again and said, "Ursan, all our lives, all we've really had was each other. We don't know what will happen tomorrow. I know we love each other, and we may never see each other again. And I can't think of anything that would be more right. Can you?"

Nighttime shrouded them as Ursan held Alyssa in his arms. The storm was slowing now and only a few flashes of lightening remained, illuminating the room for only a moment at a time. As he drifted off to sleep, he thought he would welcome death right now because he didn't think life could give him any more pleasure than he had received that night. He was totally exhausted and he didn't think he could leave even if he wanted to, which he did not. He felt Alyssa's slow breathing as she slept, her head on his chest, and he stroked her long hair. He had never felt as wonderful as he did right now. Realizing that he was living his fantasy, he kissed her hair and held her tighter. She snuggled closer, still asleep, and he thought that if he could freeze time, he would do it right now and stay this way forever. He fought sleep, not wanting to surrender for one minute. He would remember every moment.

The morning sun crept in through the small window and illuminated Alyssa in a warm beautiful glow. He knew she was lovely, but in the morning sun, her skin and hair glowed like a goddess. She roused when the sounds of the early morning seagulls screamed along the shoreline. She smiled and kissed him. Reality coming back to her now, she frowned. "Your father should be arriving soon. I'd better go." She pulled on her clothing and stood looking out of the window. She turned to Ursan, who was dressing.

"I can see him; he's on the way to the castle." She ran to him then and they kissed for the last time. She looked into his eyes and said solemnly, "I love you, Ursan." She left him then, taking the stairs down to the beach. They were wet and slippery and he could hear her as she descended.

Looking up, he saw that he would have to go up the tower stairs so he could replace the stone he had pulled up the night before. Instead, he reached up, catching his arms and pulling himself up to the room above. He had replaced the stone, stepping on it to make sure it was secure when he heard footsteps coming up the stairs. Why was she returning? He walked over and unbolted the door to the stairs.

CHAPTER SIXTEEN

He saw a flash of dark robes as Raskin yanked the door open the rest of the way and shoved his way in.

"You miserable cur, where is she? Where is the Lady Alyssa? I know you've spent the night with her. You will hang for treason!"

Ursan jumped back, being caught completely off guard. He had thought it was Alyssa returning and had not expected Raskin at all. He looked coldly at him, thinking how close he had been to actually being caught with the lady.

"I don't know what you're talking about, Raskin. The lady is not here. Do you see her? If she was here, you would have seen her on her way down the stairs." He went to go past Raskin to the stairs, but the mage pushed him back against the wall and drew his sword.

"I'll run you through, Ursan. I don't know what you've done with her, but you are about to die. Your kingdom is lost and your lady is mine."

Ursan pushed him away and with a glance and a nod, made the sword melt into the floor, leaving Raskin unarmed.

Raskin laughed. "So, you want a challenge, boy wizard. You dare to challenge me? This should be entertaining at best, you insolent swine."

Ursan couldn't be bothered with Raskin's insults; he was gathering power. Let the fool babble on, he thought, as he absorbed more energy, even from the stone walls. He had depleted a lot of energy creating the storm, but with the knowledge that Alyssa did indeed love him, he felt his power renew. He had to defend her once again against this mage who would have her for spite. He knew he had to kill him, and kill him quickly.

Concentrating on the magic he knew and not worrying about the amount or quality of Raskin's magic, Ursan ran over attacks in his head. He would probably have just a single chance and he wanted everything to go right. He drew in energy from the wind now, letting it wash over him from the window. He knew magic from the Realm would overpower any demon. He was a match for Raskin and he knew the demon knew it, although he persisted in trying to shake him emotionally with his constant chatter and threats. He blocked it all out as they circled each other, trying to size up each other's abilities. Ursan's eyes never left his opponent's.

Raskin flung a hand in the air, causing a loud explosion with a flash of light. Ursan just laughed. If he was trying to scare him, he would have to do much better than that. Children's fireworks were no match for the amount of energy he was gathering now. Drawing energy from Raskin's fireball, Ursan decided on an inclusion spell. Let the bastard become part of the tower!

* * *

Greccon had arrived at the castle and found it in disarray. No one had seen the lord in a few days. It seemed the Lady Anna had denied entrance to everyone that would see him. Greccon had been given disturbing news about Lady Alyssa and the possibility of a takeover by Lady Anna's troops, and had rushed home. He was going in to see the lord and no one would stop him.

Lady Alyssa saw him and implored him to take her to him as she clung to his robes.

"What do you mean - they won't even let you in to see him? That's absurd. We will get to the root of this problem right now, Alyssa" he assured her and took her arm, hurrying off to the lord's chamber. Greccon stunned the guard there and watched him collapse to the floor. They entered the lord's chamber to find him lying on his bed, fully dressed and his throat slit from one ear to the other. His bed was soaked with blood. He had been dead for some time, thought Greccon, as he helped the Lady Alyssa who had screamed and fallen to her knees. It had been murder. He wondered if it was at the hand of Anna. Greccon knew there would be war now. *Damn them*', he thought, as he looked upon the face of Lord McTavish. He had been like a father to Greccon and although his heart was heavy, he'd have to care for Alyssa now. He would grieve later.

"Alyssa, listen to me. Run to Ilona's. You know the way. Go straight there and you will be safe. It is no longer safe for you here. You are next in line for the kingdom and you will be the next one they try to kill. Run, girl - run to Ilona and don't look back."

She turned and ran for her life. Greccon closed his eyes and called Argon. "It is to be war, my friend, and Anna's troops are many. Much more than ours. We will send the wounded into the woods for Ilona to help. Get help, Argon. Even you couldn't handle this many on your own."

He was still in the corridor when he heard the call to arms. He broke into a run, disabling Anna's men as he passed them. He saw the courtyard in an uproar, men drawing weapons and people screaming. Women and children ran to the church and he could see Father Murphy yanking them in as fast as he could.

Anna's men had been told to wait for the signal that she would give, and as Raskin's intimidating spell went off in the tower, it was immediately taken as the sign to attack. Sir Collin screamed for the drawbridge to be drawn and his men began pulling on the counterweights to reel the great bridge up. They would kill Anna's men within the court first, then deal with the attack from the fields. Blood was being spilled everywhere and already the courtyard was littered with bodies. He was mounted on his horse and swung his blade as he went.

* * *

Ursan and Raskin both heard the call to arms, but they didn't rush to defend their posts. They had their own war to fight right here in the tower and neither man flinched. Ursan cupped his hands together and massed a fireball. He noticed Raskin was doing the same thing. Light shone out between his fingers. *He's just going to throw another showy display*, thought Ursan, as he began his incantation.

Raskin followed suit and the two men chanted at the same time. They threw the light simultaneously, and to Ursan's horror, he realized that they had both chosen the same spell. It would amplify tenfold. They were both struck at the same time, their bodies dissolving and melting into the tower walls themselves, on opposite sides. They would both be a part of the tower now forever. Ursan's heart sank, and he thought of Alyssa. He would be a part of the tower, and no one would ever know. He could no longer feel anything, he couldn't speak, just think and survive without being able to communicate. He would be thinking for a long time.

He could hear the shouts and cries of the fighting men below. There wasn't anything he could do now but listen to their men die as he turned into stone. He was finished, part of the structure now and he would remain that way forever. *At least I did win*, he thought. He would have given up his life to protect Alyssa. Raskin was in the same position as he was, preserved for all time, and he would never know Alyssa. Ursan smiled in his thoughts. He wished her well; he thought back to the night before, and it comforted him. He remembered thinking that if he could have frozen a moment in time, it would be with Alyssa. How little he had known the night before that he would indeed be frozen for all time. It wasn't with her, but it had been for her, and he was satisfied.

Somehow, he thought that Raskin was not. Maybe he hadn't defeated him exactly, but he had stopped him in his tracks, and he would no longer be a threat to Griffin's Gate. At least, now the other army had no mage. His father was still out there somewhere. He knew Raskin was thinking the same thing. They would be neighbors for a long time, but Alyssa was free and she was safe from him. He knew it was a waste of his talent to stop just one man, but if it had to be just one man he had stopped, he was glad it was Raskin.

* * *

Greccon yelled to Sir Collin, "Send the wounded to the woods. I have help there for them. Where is Ursan?"

Sir Collin nodded at the direction but shrugged his answer

about Ursan. He hadn't seen the young mage in the fighting. They both flinched as huge boulders began hitting the walls. Anna's men were using the catapults that they had once been so happy to have for their own. What a charade Anna had played on them. The wall held, but it was weakening. The archers were shooting, but several were falling from the wall as Anna's archers shot back at them. Sir Collin spotted a few of her archers in hiding, within the castle walls, and went to slay them. Greccon scrambled to the wall to destroy the catapult before they could get off another boulder.

After killing the archers, Sir Collin noticed the church door ajar. He rode up to it and dismounted. Father Murphy should have had the door barred. He ran in to find the priest on the floor with two arrows shot through him.

"Bar the door, Sir Collin," he gasped. "They shot at me before I could close it."

Sir Collin barred the door and ran to the priest's side. There was a growing pool of blood beneath him and he could see that the arrows had gone straight through him. "Let me help you, Father. I'll get you to the healer."

Father Murphy shook his head and smiled weakly. "No, get the women and children out the back passage to the woods. I've seen my Savior and he beckons to me." He grasped the knight's arm. "Take this dagger, Collin. It's magical, a demon dagger. The wooden box is on my desk, there." He pointed to his office chamber. "Take it and guard it well. Keep it secret. Another priest will come for it. You will know who to give it to." Blood poured from his mouth and the priest took his last breaths. "God bless you, my friend," he whispered.

Sir Collin watched in anguish as Father Murphy's eyes closed and he went to his Savior. He took the dagger, dropped it into the box and lashed it on the leather belt that held the sheath for his sword. Making the sign of the cross over the priest, he stood and made his way into the back rooms to get the women and children out and into the woods. He prayed Greccon was right, and that help waited there.

Sir Collin whistled for his horse as he guided the women and children quickly out of the door and into the woods. He jumped up into the saddle as soon as his horse arrived, and with his sword drawn, he guarded them as they ran deeper into the woods. He heard a voice shout, "This way! Hurry along, now", and he turned to see an oddly dressed man herding them along. The man made a sign of peace and he guessed he was the help that Greccon had promised, although he had never seen this man before.

The shadow of enormous wings passed over him and he turned suddenly to see a huge winged animal heading for the courtyard. He was showered with leaves as gusts of air struck him from the mighty wings. Griffins! He had never seen one before, and he prayed they were on their side.

There was a colossal crash as the castle wall broke apart and Anna's troops swarmed in like insects. There were too many of them, and Sir Collin knew the battle for Griffin's Gate was lost. He turned the horse around abruptly and rode back out, killing as many as he could, but he soon saw that there was no way they could defeat this many men. He shouted for his men to retreat to the shelter of the woods. There were very few of his men left that he could see, and he rode to cover them as they fled. He saw Greccon fighting with all the magic he could muster, but that wasn't enough, either. "Greccon! To the trees! It's over."

Anna's men began to follow and to Sir Collin's amazement, every one of her men that entered the woods were being killed and thrown back out on the battlefield by the griffins. There were mounds of corpses there, shredded beyond recognition. He knew then, if he could get the men to the forest, they would be protected by the griffins. He rode up to them and flung them on the back of his horse. Greccon made his way there too, and they watched in stunned amazement as eight griffins took care of the men that pursued them. The army that was still fighting, turned and ran as bodies of their comrades were being flung down upon them. The battle was over and Anna's surviving troops fled north, leaving the courtyard in an eerie quiet.

There was no one left alive to save and Sir Collin, holding a gash on his arm, turned his horse and followed the migration of men into the forest. Crossing the stream, Collin saw men laid out on the ground, being tended by a host of people that he did not know. His horse bolted as a griffin landed near Greccon, who was leaning against a tree and drinking water. He dismounted and watched him from a good distance away. His horse snorted and stomped. Greccon looked up and motioned him over. He tied the horse to the tree limb and cautiously walked over, watching the huge black griffin with awe.

"Don't be afraid - this is my friend, Argon. He was the leader in the attack today. I was thanking him for the job the griffins had done. If it weren't for them, we would all be pouring our blood into the ground."

Sir Collin gave a bow. "My thanks to you, and your griffins as well, Argon. It was your griffins that won the battle today."

Argon nodded at him. "Don't give it another thought. We griffins are fighters and have sat on our rumps far too long. The battle was welcomed. I'm sorry for your losses. Once my griffins have eaten and rested, we will go back and clear the battlefield for you to prevent disease. It was not victorious for either army. There are so many dead. You'd best see one of the elves or Ilona about that arm. It's still bleeding."

Sir Collin nodded and left them to see about his wound and Argon turned to Greccon. "What will you do now without a lord or a kingdom?"

Greccon shook his head. "First, I must find Ursan and Alyssa. They should be around here, somewhere. Then we will go to the king with the news of the fall of Griffin's Gate."

He watched Ilona and Tannis working together, going from one man to the next, treating wounds and administering medicines. He would have them all go to the king. There was nothing left of Griffin's Gate, but ruins and bodies. The catapults had knocked down a good part of the castle and only the church and one tower was left standing. He looked around for Father Murphy. There were so many men missing, it was hard to tell how many had survived. *All in good time*, he thought, and he sat down to rest.

Argon laid down beside him. Shylock stood in the grass near them, wiping his beak on the grass, leaving red streaks of blood behind. Other griffins landed to drink from the stream. Argon got up to talk with them and Greccon went to Ilona.

"Most of your men are alright, Greccon. Cuts and battle wounds. The worst of them will have to stay for awhile until the broken bones and deeper gashes have had a chance to heal so they can be moved. The griffins herded the horses deep into the woods. Perhaps that would be a good job for the children. They can round them up. Sir Bennet can lead them to the king. I hear there is nothing left of the castle, or their homes for that matter."

Greccon kissed her hand. "Thank you, Ilona, and thank the elves. You've saved a lot of our men, today. It's true - there is nothing left of the castle." He sighed deeply. "The Lord McTavish was murdered."

Ilona hung her head. There was nothing more she could do. "The elves are preparing food and a fire in the pasture there for your men. Let them stay the night and rest. Tannis has brought plenty of ale to help them forget. They can head out in the morning. Now, let them eat and rest. It's been a terrible day for everyone."

Greccon agreed. "Ilona, have you seen Ursan or Alyssa? I know I sent her here just before the battle started. I haven't seen Ursan at all. What of Father Murphy? I guessed it was he who had brought the women and children here."

Ilona shook her head. "No, I haven't seen any of them, although Sir Collin said that Father Murphy was shot and killed in the church. It was Sir Collin who brought the children and women to the woods." She saw the pain on his face and held him tightly. "Perhaps Ursan has taken Alyssa to safety. Argon hasn't seen him either. I asked about him, too."

Greccon nodded slowly. It did make sense to him, now. He knew his son. He would have taken her away to protect her. It did make him feel a little better although the loss of Father Murphy grieved him sorely. He went to the pasture to help Tannis with the food and the fire. Erastis, Tannis' younger brother, was put in charge of leading the children to find all the horses that had been frightened into the woods and to bring them back so the refugees of Griffin's Gate could ride to the king in the morning. Tannis had told him that Razz was exceptionally good with the horses, and the children, as well.

It was a night of uncertainty, as families worried about what was to come and the wounded moaned. Stars hid behind the clouds and the people moved about in a daze. The morning dawned clear as they prepared for their exodus.

The griffins had flown into the castle area and removed all of the bodies, taking them well out to sea, leaving only the blood soaked ground to tell the tale of the battle. Sir Collin insisted on digging a grave for Father Murphy, right by the church. In the morning, they had services to say farewell to their beloved priest, and they tossed flowers into the ocean to honor their dead before they left for the south.

Greccon checked with Argon and no sign of Ursan or Alyssa was found. They were simply gone. Greccon was sure, as he walked around the deserted castle grounds, that Ursan had fled with Alyssa and he would find them eventually. Smoke rose from the shells of burned out farmhouses and hung in the air as he bent to pick up a small piece of the castle, which now stood in ruins. Only parts of the two towers still stood, but the church was still whole. He looked out to sea and wondered where his son had gone. Surely the griffins would have spotted him by now if he were still in the area. At least he was not among the dead. Greccon turned and watched the men hitch up wagons to carry the women and children to the king. They could no longer live here without the protection of a noble and his knights. The first ship bearing Norsemen would brutally murder them all. He closed his eyes and remembered the kingdom when it was a working castle with friendly faces and children playing, dodging the horsemen as they rode by. All, gone in an instant.

He waved to Sir Collin and walked over to wish them a safe trip. "Peace be with you, Sir Collin, and may the gods protect you and your charges. I'm sure we will meet again."

Sir Collin reined in his horse. "Will you not come to the king, as well? He would welcome a mage of your caliber."

Greccon shook his head. "I'll stay and help Ilona with the rest of the men here, and then I must go and find my son. Should you see him or the Lady Alyssa, tell them to go to Ilona so she can contact me."

Sir Collin nodded and then gave a shout, and the group set off to the south down the road, still swollen with puddles of rain from the night before.

Greccon stood there for a long time, watching them until they were out of sight. His eyes turned to the towers. The east tower contained the gate to the Realm, but the gate would be unaffected by the existence of the tower. It was too far away to see it as he had when he was a child. Ursan had never discovered the gate, but now he wished that he had told him. Ursan and Alyssa could have been safe in the Realm while all this was going on, but no - Ursan would never turn his back on a fight. He scratched his head and started back to the forest. Where had Ursan gone? How did he get the Lady Alyssa away so quickly? All these thoughts ran through his mind. He would find them. He would travel north, visiting villages until he came across them.

It was two weeks before the rest of the men were able to travel, and with the last man gone, Greccon and Ilona enjoyed a meal together alone. Greccon, full from the dinner, raised his cup to her in thanks for all her hard work. "You are truly an amazing healer, Ilona. You have far surpassed even your mother's abilities. Why don't we move you to the king's land? A healer of your quality would be welcomed there."

She shook her head. "I will never leave this forest, Greccon. It is my home and the home of my ancestors."

He agreed and crossed his legs. "Of course it is, but with no kingdom here, you'll be quite alone."

She glanced up from her meal. "So, you are leaving me to find Ursan. I will miss you, Greccon, but I'll never be alone. I always have Argon. What need do I have of a kingdom when I have a griffin? Between Argon and the protection that you've put on the forest, I feel quite safe."

Greccon smiled sadly. "You're right, of course, my love. It is my guilt in leaving you that bothers me so much. Why don't you travel with me? We could make it an adventure, you and I." He raised questioning eyebrows at her.

Ilona laughed. "You men and your adventures. And who would look after my animals? Besides, the townspeople still come to me in secret for their cures. I can't leave here, Greccon. I'll be fine, really. You know where I am, and I'll always be here. You, on the other hand will be everywhere, and I wish you well. Find Ursan. It's not like him to leave without a word to anyone. He's much too responsible for that. He has to be somewhere and I'm sure you will find him and bring him home."

Greccon looked at the fire and studied the way it leapt. He would find no reason that would convince Ilona to join him in the search. He felt so alone now, with Ursan missing. It was as if Ursan was the reason for being alive. It was true that he was gone for months on end with the knights, but Ursan was always home waiting for him to return. He wondered if Ursan had felt as lost as he did right now, without him.

Sensing his sorrow, Ilona reached out a hand to him and he grasped it. "I will miss you, Greccon."

He kissed her hand and said, "With all this death and destruction, Ilona, you are the only thing that I find right with this world."

* * *

Mordread sat back at the little café table in the back of Bubba's Bakery and watched with amusement as Beelzebub prepared a tray of coffee and decadent cream puffs for them. Bubba wore a bakery chef's outfit and looked absolutely ridiculous, in Mordread's eyes. He looked around. The aroma was intoxicating. Who would have guessed that a demon could bake such wonderful treats? There were all kinds of cakes and pastries, topped with every kind of fruit, nuts, and chocolate. There were an assortment of pies in all flavors, cupcakes with mounds of swirled frosting on top, and more varieties of cookies then he had ever seen in one place, all arranged enticingly on snowflake doilies beneath sparkling glass counters. It looked as if he was doing a bustling bit of business, and the door was constantly opening and closing with customers. Demons loved desert. The whole place was antiseptically clean and so white it almost hurt your eyes.

Bubba motioned for one of his helpers to take over the counter, then made his way over to Mordread's table, placing a coffee and a cream puff in front of him. He stood there, his hands on his hips, beaming at him. "Go ahead and take a bite."

As Beelzebub watched with anticipation, Mordread did take a forkful and rolled his eyes in delight. "It's absolutely delicious, Bubba - what the devil do you put into these things?"

Bubba laughed and sat down, taking a huge bite of his own puff and washed it down with the coffee. "It's the best you've ever had, isn't it? I'm telling you, Mordread, these treats are more harmful and addictive than any of your drugs. Jacks up the cholesterol, plays hell with the sugar, clogs up the arteries, and they are perfectly legal and accessible."

He looked up to see if things were running properly at the counter and said, "I love making them, too. I've gotten a recipe right from the top for a Death by Chocolate Cake that will kill you instantly, but what a way to go! No?" He chuckled and continued to eat with relish.

Mordread had already finished his and Bubba motioned to the helper to bring him another. Mordread put up his hands in protest, but it did no good. Another cream puff before him, he watched as the helper tied a cake box with a thin red and white string.

"I've got to hand it to you, Bubba, this place is a gold mine. It seems way too pleasant to use this technique on the human population. They don't deserve to die this well."

Bubba pushed his dish away and sat back, his coffee in his hand. "It's a passion of mine. It would work, given enough time and temptation, but I've been working on something much more deadly for them."

Interested now, Mordread chewed the flaky crust. Covering his mouth he said, "Oh? And what would that be?"

Bubba looked around and bent low over the table. "Well, you know how the light magicals work. Everything is so big and grand. Well, I've come up with something so small, no one would even know where it came from. Been working on it right here in the back room, in my spare time."

His mouth full of sweet fluffy cream now, Mordread mumbled, "Well, what is it?"

Bubba laughed. "Viruses."

Mordread began to choke and Bubba pounded him on the back with a huge hand, laughing the whole time. "Don't flatter yourself, Mordread. I wouldn't waste one of my little beauties on you! I don't want your job. As I've said before, just give me my bakery and I'm happy. I just thought I'd contribute to the cause, so to speak. I know you've got demons working night and day on ways to agonize the humans. I just thought I'd do my share, too. Let me tell you about them."

His red eyes lit up with glee as Mordread set down his fork and wiped his mouth on a napkin. This time, he had really had quite enough to eat. Bubba said, "They are just amazing, Mordread. You know how you developed the doubtlets and grounders and such?"

Mordread nodded.

"Well, these have life forms of their own. They have the ability to reproduce themselves in every human cell, and the wisdom to get out and find another host when they've finished with the one they are in. I've got one that will kill them before they even know there's something wrong - no symptoms until they're dead." He sat back and smiled, waiting for approval.

Mordread's eyes were wide with wonder. "When did you find the time to develop these viruses? I didn't know you were into that sort of thing. How do you get it to them?"

Bubba waved a hand. "Well, I haven't worked all that out yet. I'm working on it, though. It should be ready in a hundred years or so, and then I'll probably put it in a rat or fleas or something like that. It's got to go into the bloodstream. The really efficient one is airborne, though. It's tiny. We can wipe out whole countries with that one. It spreads very fast. They won't develop the technology to fight those little buggers off for years. We've got it made, my man!"

Mordread smiled at Bubba's enthusiasm. "I admire your talent, Bubba. Not only in the bakery, but this idea of yours has real merit. Yes, I think we could use those viruses to our advantage. It'll help clear out the overpopulated areas. What about the light magicals? Do you think they can counteract your pets?"

Bubba refilled their coffees. "Nope. Once they get started, there isn't much they can do to stand in their way. They won't know what the problem is until it's too late. Oh, they're used to fevers and such, and they'll think it's the same sicknesses that the people have always suffered from until it's too late. They would never suspect us, anyway. As many travelers that pass through that area, they would blame it all on them. I'm telling you, it's perfect."

Mordread drank some of his coffee, thinking. It was perfect. Bubba was a genius. Everyone poked fun at him and no one really took him seriously until he got angry, but deep inside that big buffoon was a mind like a steel trap. Mordread imagined wiping out whole populations without risking a single one of his demons. Yes, the virus would be the most wonderful demon of all. Then a thought came to him. "How do you stop them, Bubba? I mean when they're through?"

Bubba lifted his cap, ran a hand through his hair, and replaced the hat. "Well, you see, that's the tricky part. I'm still working on that, too, but they can change themselves, or they lay dormant for awhile. It'll take awhile to hammer all this out, Mordread. It's just in the planning stages now, but I can do it. Won't they be surprised?"

A darkling, one of Mordread's shadowy lesser demons, slipped in through the door and glided over. Cringing out of Beelzebub's way, it bent to whisper in Mordread's ear. Mordread made a face as the darkling retreated and left the bakery. Bubba waited for the news.

Mordread said, "The war at Griffin's Gate has taken place, just as Raskin had promised. The castle lies in ruins, but Raskin seems to have vanished. Now, where would that damn demon go? He is a thorn in my side, Bubba. He's like a loose cannon. He was supposed to come right back after the attack was over. I told him to take Greccon out of the picture, and he's still there. I can't do anything with that demon! I'd better get back to my office and see if I can get a party up to find him. At least the morning was delightful, Bubba. Thank you for the coffee and pastries. I think I'll come here every morning."

Bubba smiled and got up to put several cookies in a little box for Mordread to take with him. "Don't worry about Raskin. He'll probably turn up under a rock, somewhere. He's such a coward, he more than likely ran and hid and is waiting for a chance to slip away undetected." Mordread nodded and with a wave, left for his tower.

Bubba watched him through the window, and then with a glare at his helper, which made the worker furiously start to scrub the counter, he left for his workroom. He sat at his desk, thinking about his creative viruses. The virus had been around for a long time, granted, but his new twist on these particular viruses gave him a lot of pleasure. He had all the time in the world to work on them. So what if he really did not know how to stop them once they were introduced? Who cared what happened if they caused a plague of memorable proportions? Things needed to be cleaned up there, anyway. He despised filth, and this would be an excellent way to motivate them into living in a more sanitary world. Demons had power over the life forms there, but these tiny little organisms were relentless when it came to survival. Never before had he realized that a life form so tiny could have such a will to live. He was anxious to try them out, but he would be cautious. Another hundred years maybe, or two, and they would be ready to go.

CHAPTER SEVENTEEN

Sir Collin slumped in his chair at the tavern situated in King Richard's courtyard. He had accomplished all he could and was now looking forward to a hot bowl of mutton stew and a few cold drafts. The king had been more than fair with the people of Griffin's Gate, promising them revenge on the Lady Anna and her tribe of marauders. The knights were welcomed and he found his new quarters just as comfortable as his last, but the defeat had irked him. How foolish they had been to overlook the obvious. He nodded as the serving girl brought his food and drink. He glanced around, knowing no one there. He fished out large pieces of the mutton, chewing them hungrily. It didn't take him long to finish the bowl.

He listened absently to a man in merchant's clothing as he tried to sell a book to what must be a collector of such things. The merchant was saying, "This book is one of magical things, you know of dragons and griffins. It seems very authentic and I'm only asking a few coins. I heard you collect rare books. I doubt you'd fine another such as this."

Sir Collin ran a hand over his face. The last thing he wanted to think about was griffins. It brought the battle back to the foreground again, and he closed his eyes. They were magical alright, wondrous and so ferocious beyond belief. He recalled the screams of their victims, and the blood dripping from their beaks, yet he had been so thankful for them at the time; still, they haunted his dreams at night. He drank his ale and listened to see if the vendor did indeed make the sale of the book.

The collector said, "It is a quality book, by the looks of it, but it is just fantasy. I collect books of a historic nature."

The seller looked insulted. "My good man, this is quality work. Look at the drawings. Much time and effort has gone into those pictures. How do you mean, it is all fantasy? There are more than just a few who have seen dragons and griffins and the like. It was not so long ago, and that makes it historic, then."

Sir Collin heard the collector laugh. "Aye, more than a few have seen such creatures, and more than a few have been drunk with the ale. Sensible people know better, but it is a novel little book, although of not much value."

Sir Collin was on his second draft now and smiled as they bantered back and forth, trying to agree on a price. The people of Griffin's Gate could testify to the existence of the magicals; a few of them wouldn't be here today if it weren't for the learned elves that helped put them back together again. He would say nothing, though. He was in a land so far away from where magical creatures were commonplace, and he would not stand out in a crowd. *It would be best to keep my thoughts to myself*, he thought, but he drew out the wooden box Father Murphy had charged him to protect. He ran his fingers over the lid. It felt warm to the touch and was made out of wood with a cross engraved beautifully on the top. He opened it and looked at the dagger. For something that was to be passed along, and had been for some time, it looked brand new. He tapped the blade with his fingernail and it had a ring to it. It did not resemble the metal his own blade was made of. He closed the box as the book exchange was made, and the two men got up to leave. The collector caught sight of the blade as he closed the box. The seller hurried off to spend the money he had just earned.

The collector, a stout bearded man, smiled at him, holding the book in one hand. He pointed at the box. "Ah, you must be one of the new knights from Griffin's Gate. I'm Bartrum Calbot, a collector of oddities." He extended a hand and Sir Collin shook it.

"Sir Collin, formerly of Griffin's Gate."

Bartrum pointed at the chair opposite of Sir Collin. "May I join you?"

Collin nodded and watched as the man situated himself in the chair, putting the book in a pouch at his belt.

"I heard of the trouble there," he said quietly. "I knew Lord McTavish. He was a good man, and I'll drink to his memory." He raised his tankard the girl had brought and Sir Collin joined him in a toast to the late McTavish.

Setting the tankard down, Sir Collin picked up his box to put it back in it's holder at his belt.

Bartrum sputtered a bit. "I was just going to ask about that blade. As a collector of such things, I can see it is of a strange metal. Might I look at it?"

Sir Collin shook his head. "Sorry. It's not mine, and it's not for sale. I heard you did just purchase an interesting book, though."

Bartrum sat back, a little disappointed at not getting his hands on the unusual weapon. He laughed good-naturedly. "Yes, so you overheard. It's not a very good purchase, but that man seems to find the most curious things and I like to keep him happy. Who knows? Someday, he may come up with something I can use, something interesting, such as the dagger you have there."

Sir Collin raised his eyebrows. "I know nothing of it, really. I'm to hold on to it until I can deliver it to its owner. Why would you say it has value?"

Bartrum licked his lips. " Well, now, I don't know its value, really. I said it was interesting. It almost looks Sumerian in nature. I would pay handsomely for it should you reconsider. I am sure it would not be as worthless as this book of folly I just bought." He took the book back out and set it on the table.

Sir Collin looked at it. It was written by a man named Elijah and he was surprised to see a picture of Argon. It even had Argon's name printed below his picture. He gave Bartrum a quick glance and leafed through the book. "If you'd like your money back, I would purchase this from you. It reminds me of Griffin's Gate, a place close to my heart, as you know."

The book collector played with his beard, thinking. "Well, I could include it in the price for that dagger of yours. You could have the book and quite a bit more for it."

Sir Collin shook his head. "As I've told you before, I cannot sell something that is not mine. It is the last wish of a dying priest that I care for this and see it gets to where it must go."

Bartrum frowned. "And where must it go?"

Sir Collin laughed shortly. "That's the strange thing about it. I'm not sure."

Thinking the man mad now, Bartrum gathered his worthless book and put it in the pouch. He got up to leave. "I'll think about selling the book. I'm here on most nights, being a bachelor of sorts. A man has to eat. Perhaps we will talk again." He patted the man on the shoulder and left. The poor knight must be suffering from battle fatigue, he thought as he left.

Sir Collin sat back then, wondering if that book had been a part of Glynnis' belongings that didn't arrive back on Baron when the horse bolted. Elijah. He was sure that was the name of the man she visited in the mountains. The hermit that people talked of. He knew he would buy the book if given the opportunity again, but not at the cost of Father Murphy's dagger. He would keep it until another priest came for it, as he was told, and the book collector was no priest. The purpose of the dagger was mysterious to him, but he knew it was to serve a higher purpose than to just sit on a shelf in a collector's house. He could see their conversation had generated some interest about the tavern, and as he got up to leave he covered the dagger box with his cloak.

He started for the door and someone called out, "You! Knight of Griffin's Gate!"

Sir Collin turned to find the caller. It was an elderly man by the fireplace. He stared at him. The man went on, "You were there at the battle. I hear tell of a flock of griffins that tore the men to shreds and spit them out on the northern army. Is it true? I've got me best milk cow riding on the answer."

There was laughter and a little shoving in the group. Sir Collin gave a grim smile. "Should I say, 'Aye', you would think me mad, yet if I say 'Nay', would I then be true to myself? Keep the milk cow and good health to your children, for I will not answer either way."

He turned as groans of dissatisfaction and laughter rang out. He scanned the crowd once more, hoping to find Ursan or Alyssa among the throngs of people there, but he didn't find them. As he left, he heard the old man giving an account of the battle of Griffin's Gate. He hadn't remembered it being so glamorous, just tragic.

* * *

King Oberon sat at his council. Everyone was talking at once and he found it to be maddening. He looked over at Argon, in desperation. Argon nodded and gave a war cry that would puncture the sturdiest of eardrums.

King Orion covered his ears. "Damn it, Argon, a simple 'Quiet please!' would do!" Others murmured their agreement. King Oberon sat up tall.

"Thank you, Argon. Now, as I see it, we have a lot to discuss. First, let me acknowledge the tremendous effort given by the griffins and the elves in the battle of Griffin's Gate. We are really not here to influence the outcomes of battle or discord between the lands of the mortals, however, since we've had a bond of sorts with a few of the mortals of Griffin's Gate, we felt compelled to help. Everyone there is gone now, except for Ilona, the healer. The gate is still secure, although the tower is in ruins. We do have a problem, though. We seem to be missing two mages. One is our concern, the other is not."

The council members looked around at each other. King Oberon continued, "The mage, Ursan, is missing. Normally, we could track him on the remnants of magic in the surrounding area, but Greccon was fighting in the battle and there is so much residual magic, it is impossible to separate it. The other mage, Raskin, is a demon, and he has also disappeared. As you know, Ursan is Greccon's son, and is from a long line of mages. I cannot accept that a mage could just vanish without a trace. I have the fairy folk searching for him. How is that going, Lily?"

He glanced up to look at a demure little fairy dressed all in white. She shook her head. "We haven't found even a trace of either one."

Oberon thanked her. Argon fluffed his feathers and raised a claw. Oberon nodded.

Argon said, "Greccon is going to search for him. As he is his father, chances are good he can pick up on Ursan's magic. There is also another missing piece to the puzzle. The Lady Alyssa of Griffin's Gate is also missing. Now, considering the affection the lad had for Alyssa, odds are good he has fled with her to protect her."

Lily flicked her wings and was recognized. "But we would have seen them somewhere. We have fairies everywhere. They could not walk down a road without a fairy noticing, and they certainly couldn't hide in the woods without a sprite seeing them, either."

Argon nodded at her. "Yes, my dear Lily, but you have no fairies on the sea. Even though none of the griffins saw a boat that day, chances are that they took off on a boat and will head south, not wanting to end up with the leftover army. Alert your fairies to the ports. Even the Mer people wouldn't have seen them unless they fall overboard, so they must be on a ship or boat." He swallowed and looked at Oberon and shrugged. "At least, that's what I think."

Oberon glanced up at the council. "No idea is folly. We have two mages and a lady missing. Now, I'm not asking for a search party, but we can transfer information about these missing people and that's just what we'll do, should we find them."

Illustra looked very concerned. She loved Greccon and she knew Ursan was his pride and joy. If only she could think of what she could do to help. An idea came to her, an awful idea, and she tossed her head. Oberon recognized her. "My lord, Can we contact the Dark Realm? Perhaps Raskin has captured them both and is holding them hostage. I know it's a stretch of an idea, but could we contact them?"

Oberon shook his head. "We don't have to, my dear. They have already contacted us. Mordread alerted us this morning he would like his mage back, thinking we were doing the very same thing. Of course, we aren't, so we're all back where we started, I'm afraid."

King Orion stood up, dressed in a dark green robe. "My elves treated all the wounded. Greccon said he had sent the lady to Ilona's. She never entered the forest, and neither did the two mages. No matter how hectic it was, my sentries are sharp and they would not have gotten past them. Another interesting point was that all three of the missing people's horses were in the stable when Shylock drove them into the forest to protect them. If they left by horseback, they had to procure horses other than their own."

Kelton, the large amiable troll stood up, at Oberon's nod. "Listening to everything, it seems to be a disappearance of a magical nature. If they used a transport magic, the three of them could be anywhere. Perhaps they left to avoid the fray?"

Argon shook his head. "There is no love between Raskin and Ursan. They would not agree on anything. Ursan is no coward and has been trained in battle magic. At his age, he was just itching to try it out, I'm sure." He scratched behind an ear tuft. "Although, I think you are on the right track. The scenario is all wrong. Besides, Ursan and Raskin would be on opposite armies, and the lady was told to flee."

Brodrick the dwarf stood up. "My men are in every tavern, selling our wares. No one has seen them. Without food or water, they would have to stop at an inn or tavern, sometime. A lady couldn't travel far without comforts."

Illustra snorted at that and it looked as if there was going to be protests from the female members of the council. Oberon was not in the mood for that. He cleared his massive throat. "That is your opinion, of course, Brodrick and your dwarves could be of monumental help in this crisis. No one can travel long without provisions. Of course, we are talking about mages, and they are quite capable of conjuring whatever they need, right down to the horses. I am confident they will show up somewhere. Let's all stay on top of any information we receive and I am to be notified immediately."

The council broke then and Oberon sighed. Argon was still there, arguing some point with Illustra. Oberon said, "Where is Greccon now, Argon?"

Argon gave Illustra a playful poke and she nipped at him. He went over to Oberon. "He's on the road, much to Ilona's dismay. He said he would go on a pilgrimage until he found Ursan. He's quite devastated, as you could imagine. It was his only child. He feels responsible for Alyssa as well, and he's confident Ursan took her away to save her."

Oberon absently stared out of the window. "He may be right. At least, I hope he is, but what about Raskin? He's an unsavory demon. Kelton is right, I think. Magic had something to do with it. It's too odd that no one anywhere, including fairies," He paused and looked around quickly before he continued, to make sure Lily had left. "And you know how nosy fairies are. You can't make a move without them watching you."

Argon growled a response. "What if they went to another time?"

Oberon laughed, joined by Illustra. Argon looked annoyed. "What's so funny?"

Illustra swished her full tail at him. "Only dragons can move through time, Argon. You know that."

Argon, not to look foolish, responded, "Of course I know that. That's your basic dragon 101 along with eating only rocks, but it doesn't always hold true, does it? We all moved through time to get here using a gate and we're not dragons... and Oberon likes spaghetti when he's in human form. What if Ursan's magic went wrong? His and Raskin's, combined? He's just a young mage. Something terrible could have happened. They could have blown each other up, along with the lady, who was sure to be at Ursan's side. Now, that's possible, isn't it?"

Illustra gasped, horrified, and Oberon looked sad but thoughtful. "It certainly is. Gods! Here we are thinking logically, and we all know magic is fickle. Well, let's exhaust the obvious first, and then we can speculate on the disastrous possibilities. Illustra, my dear, don't look so stricken. You, out of all my magicals, should have the most hope. That's what unicorns are all about, isn't it?"

She looked over her shoulder as she turned to leave, her head held low. "Only in fairy tales, and you know how those fairies are." She walked out of the castle, her hooves scraping on the stone floor.

It was a sad sound, thought Oberon. There was nothing worse than a sad unicorn, and he hated the sight of it. Argon could be right, and Ursan, Raskin and Alyssa dead. Greccon could go on searching forever. A magical catastrophe was possible, even likely, when the mage was young and inexperienced, but Ilona and Greccon had taught Ursan well, and he should be beyond mistakes like that; yet it was possible, especially under stress, and a battle was just that. If only someone had seen him. Everyone he talked to, all the searching he had done, revealed nothing. No one had seen him at all that day. Alyssa had been seen by Greccon and told to go to Ilona and she never made it there. Raskin had been seen at the castle before Greccon had returned from seeing King Richard, but no one had seen Ursan that day at all.

Oberon watched Argon take flight, soaring high overhead now, and turning east towards the gate. He would check the forest and make sure Ilona was fine, now that she was alone. Oberon blew out a huge plume of fire in frustration. His talk with Mordread had left him with a suspicious unsettling feeling, as if Mordread knew more than he was telling him. He was down a mage too, and Oberon thought he might be more cooperative, but he felt as if he were hiding something. He prattled on about a bakery and new projects that he didn't want to talk about, and seemed as if he could care less about his missing mage. *He probably doesn't care*, thought Oberon. Since when did Mordread care about anything but himself? He shrugged it off and tore at a boulder in his bed chamber. It was granite and it was good. He pulverized the rock between dagger-like teeth, crumbs of rock dropping to the floor. He would eat, then think on all these problems again.

King Orion walked back through the woods and was met by Razz, his youngest son, who fell in step with his father. It took double steps to keep up and when Orion saw that, he slowed to a pace Razz could match.

"What's wrong, Father?" Razz's emerald green eyes clouded as he sensed his father's mood.

King Orion stopped and stared at Razz as if he had never seen him before. This startled Razz and he stopped walking and met his father's eyes in wonder.

"Razz, you were there. You never miss a thing. I want you to take a moment and think of anything that you think was unusual that day in the forest, when the battle of Griffin's Gate was taking place. Can you do that?"

Razz rubbed his nose and thought for a moment. "Everything was unusual. A battle at Griffin's Gate is unusual. Having so many people in the forest is out of the ordinary, too. All the griffins being there was different."

King Orion smiled encouragingly. "Yes, yes, that's all true, go on."

Razz closed his eyes so he could picture it all clearly in his mind. "Having so many horses in the woods wasn't normal. And the ship off of the coast was never there before, either."

King Orion grasped his shoulders. "A ship, you say? What did it look like, Razz? Can you remember? It could be very important."

Razz nodded. "I saw it from the top of the large oak tree. I had climbed up to watch the fighting. It was out quite a bit, but they had row boats and one was rowing back to the ship. It was a galleon, I think, with red and white sails - with a red falcon on it, I think. The bow of the ship looked like a dragon head was on it. No one else saw it while they were fighting."

King Orion sat down and Razz sat next to him. "Norsemen, I think. I'm not sure. All I know is that I thought it strange because no one knew about it, yet they were rowing back to the ship, which means they had been at the castle earlier. I bet they stole something, didn't they?"

King Orion's mind was racing now. An attack from the barbarians at the same time as an attack from Anna's men? Why only one boat rowing back? If they were attacking, there would be more than several. "Are you sure you saw only one boat going back?"

Razz nodded. So, it was a small raid for food or goods. One boat would slip in under the guard's gaze, pilfer a few supplies and take off again. It had happened before, but not in broad daylight. Although, seeing a battle raging, it would be a perfect time to steal. What if they stole Ursan or Raskin, or dear gods no, Alyssa? He turned to his son again, who was herding ants into a line. "Razz, did you see how many people were in the boat?"

Razz dropped the blade of grass he was using and thought again. "Four or five, with a big bundle in the front."

Orion slapped his leg and sent Razz on his way, telling him to go and cheer up Illustra and then he ran back to the castle with the new information. Why hadn't he asked Razz earlier? Children always know everything, and everyone forgets to ask them.

Shylock saw King Orion running and winged in for a landing, narrowly missing his head with one of his wings. Orion stopped and ducked.

Shylock folded his wings. "Sorry. Why are you running, my king? Do you want a ride to the castle?"

King Orion jumped on Shylock's back and they took off. He shouted what Razz had told him. Shylock shouted back as he flew, "Damn, I did see that ship, but I thought it was one of Lady Anna's. I thought that was why so many men were there. A Viking ship, you say? Would they have taken Ursan and Alyssa?"

Orion said, "I don't think they would take the men, but the

lady, for sure. They're known for kidnapping women. Oh, good
gods, this is horrible. I'd bet a field of flowers, they took Alyssa, and
with all the fighting going on, no one noticed."

Shylock landed and King Orion slapped his rump. "Thank you,
my friend."

Shylock bobbed his head. "I think I'll fly off and find Argon.
I wonder why my meticulously efficient brother didn't notice a
Viking ship with big red and white stripes off of the coast? You'd
think, with his eyes, he'd see something as big as that. I saw it, I just
didn't know it didn't belong there. But warrior that he is, Argon
should have known. He's going to hate the fact I saw something
that he missed." Shylock suppressed a sinister chuckle, but his gloat
was too obvious.

* * *

Sir Collin made it back to his quarters unscathed, even though
he would have bet money someone would try to relieve him of the
dagger. It wasn't that he didn't trust Bartrum, he just didn't trust
anyone at all. He told one of the pages to prepare him a hot bath,
and he was looking forward to it, but he wanted to hide the box first
in his room. He pulled it from his belt, thinking he should have the
tanner make him a pouch for it. The way he was carrying it now, it
would get soaked and have to endure all the elements, unprotected.
He remembered the greed in Bartrum's eyes and wondered exactly
what he had been put in charge of.

He set it on a low desk by the bed and lifted the lid. He caught
the sight of movement and drew his sword out of reflex. There was
no one there. Yet again, he saw something move towards the window. Dark forms that moved like shadows, only faster. He thought
back to Father Murphy and his last words, "It's a demon dagger."
Were those demons, running to get out of the room? Did that little
dagger have that much power? He lifted it now and felt how well
balanced it was. Its hilt was a black, shiny cross. He stood up and
slowly walked around the room, holding the dagger out in front of
him. More shadows, and a humming noise from the dagger itself.
He bent his ear to make sure, and indeed, the sound emitted from
it. It grew warmer as he walked. Once he had encircled the room,

the dagger ceased its humming and the hilt cooled off. The room seemed brighter and all the feelings of dread and suspicion had left Sir Collin. He put it back in its box, gently, and closed the lid. It was amazing. He actually ran at least five demons out of his room with that dagger. So that is why the blade was so coveted? It had to be magical, he thought, so why would a Catholic priest be in possession of a magical blade? Well, it was of no concern of his why Father Murphy had owned this blade; his problem was who should he give it to? Meanwhile, he could see it was a handy little dagger to have around.

He took the box and placed it under the bucket that stood in the corner, disrobed, and went to have his bath. He sat in the hot tub of water, a luxury afforded to knights, and he took full advantage of it. He closed his eyes and felt his muscles relax. He couldn't remember when he had taken his last bath. It had to be before all the trouble at Griffin's Gate. Of course, he would serve King Richard. He had no problem with that, but Lord McTavish had such a way about him that made you feel as if you belonged at Griffin's Gate, and that you were a special person. Here, he was just another knight. When jousting began, he would prove his worth. He had been undefeated at the festivals at home. He wished things had remained the same, but he knew they never did.

He worried about Ursan. He could care less about that rat, Raskin. He supposed he had herded the lady Anna off to safety at some point. Ursan would be one person he would call a friend, and he didn't have many. At least, none he trusted, but you could trust Ursan. He didn't know how he knew that, but the mage seemed like the kind of person you would want for a brother. Orphaned at an early age, Sir Collin knew how valuable it would be to him to have someone he could trust. He knew Greccon would search until he had an answer, and whenever he could, he would look for Ursan, too. He thought if he found Ursan, Lady Alyssa would be there as well. He knew Ursan was in love with her; hell, everyone knew, and he thought it must be hard on the man to know he could never have the one woman he loved. He hoped Ursan had taken her away. Now, with everything lost, he could have his lady. He deserved that, Sir Collin mused. *Well, I deserve someone too*, he thought, but he could never bring himself to be vulnerable enough to have a lady of his own. At least, one that cared about him and not the coins in his pocket. Maybe here, he would have a chance at a normal life. Most of the ladies at Griffin's Gate had been spoken for and there were very few who weren't already mothers.

He scrubbed his face. *I guess I'd better get clean before I entertain any of those notions.* He smiled for the first time since the battle and ducked his entire head underwater. Tomorrow, he would have a pouch made for the dagger box and see about repairing his horse's tack. He was going to have a fresh start here and so was his sturdy steed, Thor. Now that he had had a hot meal, a few drafts and a hot bath, he craved sleep, and sliding his dagger box next to the bed, he went to sleep; and for once, his hand on the box, he did not have dreams that disturbed him. He wondered if he could let the dagger go. It comforted him, somehow, driving away demons and giving him hopeful thoughts. Perhaps he should keep the dagger for his own, but in his heart he knew that when the priest came for it, whoever it was, he would give it over gladly. He kept his promises and he was an honorable man. He was just determined to live long enough for someone else to appreciate that fact. The longer he lived, the harder it was to stay alive. Either times had gotten worse, people had gone mad, or he was just getting too old to fight and enjoy it like he used to. He'd have to draw his sword on a daily basis now, where he remembered he'd have to oil the blade to keep it from sticking to the sheath. He used to draw it out just to look at it, but now it seemed it never stayed in the sheath long. Times were getting crueler. He wondered if he could get that book collector to sell him that book. Not only did he wish to read it, but he thought he'd return it to Ilona. He was sure it had belonged to her mother. He believed in magic, now. After the battle of Griffin's Gate, a lot more people believed in magic, too.

CHAPTER EIGHTEEN

When Alyssa left Greccon, she did not run to the forest as she was told, butt instead, she circled around to go back to the tower. She was so distraught, she couldn't think. Now that her father was dead, she turned to the only person she had ever turned to in times of trouble. She would find Ursan. He would protect her and get her safely to Ilona's home. She knew she couldn't trust anyone else. Greccon had said Anna's men would kill her. She was too frightened to go anywhere on her own. Yes, she would find Ursan and he would save her. She was shaking from head to toe as she slid down to the beach and carefully skirted around the tower to find the hidden entrance. She had pushed through the large overgrown weeds, when she felt a sharp pain in her head and the world went black.

Alyssa awoke to find herself swaying. At first, she thought she was dizzy, that she had fainted from fear, but as she opened her eyes, she found that she wasn't in Griffin's Gate anymore. A hand flew to her head where she had a rather large knot. Someone had hit her from behind. Terrified now, she looked around at the gathering of men who were staring and laughing at her. They were talking in a strange language she didn't understand. The swaying feeling she had came from the rocking of the ship below her on the waves. As they came closer to her, she screamed and buried her head in her arms as she had done as a small child when she was scared.

A shout made her look up to see a tall brawny man pull the men out of the way. He stood there, his hand on his sword. He talked to several of the men, then directed what had sounded like questions at her. She cried and shook her head. She had no idea what he was asking her. The crew surrounding them laughed again. The man with the sword bent down in a squatting position and asked her something very softly. All she could do was stare at him. She had never seen hair in such a deep red color, and his face was concerned as she stared up into slate blue eyes. "I don't understand you. I speak the language of England."

This time it was he that looked puzzled, and he glanced around at the crew for help. Some laughed, some shrugged, and some shook their heads. No one could understand her. They were calling him Dorn. She guessed he must be the captain of the ship. At least he had on a medallion and the rest of them looked to be a pitiful bunch of pirates. Tears came in earnest as she speculated her chances of survival. Dorn stood up and put out his hand to help her up from the deck. She took his hand and then startled at the chorus of laughter and whistles it produced. What choice did she have? At least he had kind eyes and didn't look as barbaric as the rest of the crew.

After three miserable days at sea, during which she felt sick most of the time, she finally stopped crying. Dorn had placed her in a corner of his quarters. He tried to talk with her several times, but to no avail. Most of the time, he just stared at her. He had offered her food and water. She had managed to drink some water, but the food was unappealing to her as she fought down nausea. She had never been on a ship, and she thought if she could survive this journey, she would never willingly board another one. She had no idea where she was going or what fate had in store for her, not that it mattered. This was certainly no worse than having to marry a Lord who would be cruel to her, if he had even existed.

She thought back to what Ursan had told her. None of the knights had ever heard of that Lord and she would certainly rather be here than with Raskin. She would never see her home again, she knew that, but what would there be left for her to go home to? Her father was dead and she would never do Lady Anna's bidding. She was confident Lady Anna killed her father. She would miss Ursan and Greccon, but it seemed as if she would be starting a new life, frightening as it was. At least Dorn had not abused her; on the contrary, he seemed genuinely concerned for her well-being, and just as frustrated as she was that they couldn't seem to understand each other. He left her alone for long periods of time, but always returned to see if she was alright. He wouldn't let any of the crew near her and she was thankful for that. He made no effort to touch her, but sat for hours talking to her in a language she could not comprehend. He had offered her his bunk, and when she shook her head in fright, he sighed and gathered up his blankets and arranged them on the floor for her comfort.

On this day, he returned carrying a green and yellow parrot. He held her wrist steady and transferred the parrot from his arm to hers. He pointed to the bird and said, "Kie."

She smiled for the first time since she had been brought on board and gingerly touched the bird's head. Kie lowered his head as she scratched. Dorn sat down on a bench anchored to the floor to watch her interact with the bird. Kie was a rather large parrot of some sort, and she found he loved the attention she was giving him and made no motion to bite her. He bobbed his head and made various noises and she giggled as he strutted back and forth on her arm.

Dorn smiled to see that he had finally given her something that would make her smile. He handed her one of her plates with food on it and pointed repeatedly from the plate to the parrot. She nodded and picked up a piece of flatbread and handed it to Kie. The parrot chirped happily and held it with his foot, contently biting off portions and eating them. When Kie was through, he held out his foot to her and she handed him another piece.

Dorn nodded happily at her. "Alyssa, Kie." He pointed at the bird and then back at her.

"I can keep him? Really?" She put out a hand and stroked the bird. She didn't really know if the bird was a gift or not, but she thought she would enjoy him as long as Dorn would let her. He was a beautiful bird and very friendly. It took her mind off of her situation and she forgot how queasy she was. All her attention was on Kie now.

The bird pulled at her hair, sending her into fits of giggles and Dorn laughed easily, thrilled that he had brought a sparkle to her eyes. He had lost his wife and his newborn son at the same time, years ago, and had not taken another wife. His heart had been broken, and only now did he feel any interest. His crew, short on rations, looking for merchants and finding none, had pilfered the kitchens at Griffin's Gate for food and making their way back to their boats, had happened upon this woman and had brought her back as a gift for their leader. He found her fascinating, even though he had chided his crew that they were not pirates, just tradesmen, and they should never have taken the girl. He knew he should have ordered his men to take her back to the shore, but he could not bring himself to do it. It was an omen, and he felt that this girl was meant for him. If only he understood what she was saying. His heart melted when he looked at her. He had never seen hair so golden or eyes so blue. He wished they had met under more reasonable circumstances, as he could tell how frightened she was of being there and how sick the sea made her. Things were looking up now, he thought, as he watched her playing with the parrot. He would have her for his own, but not by force. He had all the time in the world and without the ability to speak his language, it would take time for her to trust him. He had bought Kie in the islands further south as a lark, but now he could see his purchase would reward him with the lady's favor. After watching the two of them get acquainted, Dorn stood up to leave and instruct his crew. He would head north now.

Alyssa, seeing that Dorn was leaving her, sadly offered him Kie to take back, but she smiled as he indicated to her that she was to keep the bird. She hugged the bird to her chest and the bird purred with contentment. Dorn laughed and left his cabin, closing the door behind him.

Kie helped Alyssa immensely. Now, she never felt as scared or alone. She talked incessantly to him and was surprised when he tried to talk back. When she slept, he tucked his head under his wing and sat right by her. She saw that one of his wings was deformed which explained the reason he did not fly away. She laughed at all his clownish antics and they became very attached to each other. Dorn watched this whole process with satisfaction. He was amazed when Kie mimicked her speech, and watched with interest. He had learned her name and a few of her basic words, but as she taught Kie, he was paying close attention and before long, he understood more and more of her language. At least, enough to talk with her on an elementary level. On mild nights when the sea was calm, he would take her above deck and walk with her. He pointed out the dolphin and the shark to her and she watched with wonder. She let him hold her hand and stroke her hair as the wind blew it about her. The crew would tease him and heckle from time to time, and Dorn would laugh and trade insults with them, but he would never let them near her and they kept their distance.

Alyssa heard shouting on deck one morning and she crept to the door to see the sails being lowered. The crew was moving around quickly, securing the sails, and it seemed as if they were at a port in a strange country.

Dorn came in briskly. "Alyssa, come with Dorn."

She nodded and they closed Kie in his cabin. Kie was annoyed that she left him and as Dorn helped her off of the ship she could hear him squawking loudly in protest. "Kie?"

Dorn shook his head. "No. We come back."

She nodded, trusting Dorn now, and followed him into the seaport. Everything looked strange. The vendors were there as they always were at ports, but the goods were different. There were a lot of furs and food stuffs that she did not recognize. The people spoke a different language, but it was one that Dorn spoke fluently as he bargained for the goods he needed. A few of the merchants knew him by name and she guessed this was a port he visited frequently. A few of the merchants motioned to Alyssa with raised eyebrows and Alyssa would have given anything to know what Dorn had said about her in reply. At least he looked at her, smiling, and nodded at them and a few clapped him on the back, laughing and talking very excitedly. Dorn wanted her to find warmer clothing and tried to make her understand they were going to a very cold place. She laughed as he purchased her trousers and boots lined with fur. Heavy clothing was bought for her and she wondered where they would be going that one would need such apparel. He turned her around to face the other way and she could only guess he wanted to surprise her with something, but he wouldn't tell her. He took on a lot of food and ale for the crew and they made their way back to the ship. He was busy loading the stores and she went back to their quarters to change into the heavier clothing, thankful for the privacy so she could wash. There usually was little water on board that could be used for more than cooking and drinking, but while they were in port, it was plentiful. She looked at the robes she once wore then again at her new outfit. She became totally transformed. The Lady of Griffin's Gate was a person of the past. She looked more like a man in the trousers and boots. But they were warmer and there were heavier cloaks of fur that she could only hope she wouldn't have to wear too often, but the air was getting colder the further north they traveled, and she was thankful.

Kie tugged at one of her boot laces and she remembered she had something for him, too. She took out a pouch of nuts she had insisted on having for Kie, and Dorn had nodded and purchased them for her. Kie was delighted with the treat and sat there happily cracking them with his sharp beak and eating the nut meat with great relish, tossing the shells as he finished with them.

"Kie, you are a messy bird." she said, as she laughed. Kie was only momentarily distracted from his treat long enough to turn his head to look at her and say, "Messy bird." Then he chirped happily and held out his foot for another one.

It took most of that day to load up the ship's stores and she could see men were repairing rips in the sails and replacing worn ropes with new ones. She walked around the deck with Kie on her shoulder, watching the people in the port and the crew as they worked. She had been on board for over a month now, she guessed, and she had resigned herself to that kind of life. She was no longer sick, although they went through some storms that she thought surely would capsize the ship, only they never did. She was fascinated with the sea life she could watch from the rail, and had been allowed to help the crew with the cooking, and they had nodded with approval at some of the dishes she had made. They accepted her as Dorn's woman now, and she accepted it herself, and was not unhappy about it. He treated her well and he was gentle and kind to her. She found him charming, and felt fortunate to have this life instead of the torture she would have had at the hands of Anna and Raskin. She wondered if Ursan was looking for her. She realized no one would know where she had gone. She had been kidnapped and carried away from her home and she would probably never see it again. Thoughts of Ursan haunted her, but she pushed them away. Of course she loved him and she should have let him spirit her away so they could be together, but that was all in the past now, and she knew in her heart she would never see him again, or anyone else from home. They had traveled so far now. She didn't know where they were, only that it was turning so cold, much colder than the winters in her home. She had bought some skins to make Kie a little enclosed nest to keep him warm, as he constantly tried to get close to her skin now, climbing into her clothing for warmth.

Dorn had bought her an exquisite necklace of gold he put on her and tried to make her understand he wanted her to be his wife. She had blushed and nodded shyly. She had grown to love Dorn and wanted him by her side. It took awhile for them both to understand they both were together forever now, but when they were sure they understood, the cook threw a huge party on the deck that night and the crew drank so much ale that they were worthless for days.

Being a good Catholic, she wondered what Father Murphy would say to their marriage agreement without the proper rituals, and she prayed God would favor their union anyway. It was real enough to them, and as they stood together on the deck looking at the stars that hung so low in the sky she asked him, "Dorn, where is your home? Where are we to live?"

He looked at her with surprise and patted the rail of the ship affectionately. "Home is here; we go everywhere. I show you all places, my Alyssa." He smiled at her and she smiled back. That was fine with her. She found she loved the sea and she loved to travel and visit the ports. It would be a good life for her.

* * *

Argon swallowed the fish whole. In between gulps, he asked, "So, my dear, what do you hear of Greccon? Has he found Ursan yet?"

Ilona shook her head in dismay, but she lit up as she said, "He didn't find Ursan, but he did come across Elijah in the high mountains. All this time, we thought him dead. Greccon said he is old and frail but he still writes his books and makes his drawings. He didn't know about me until Greccon told him. Now he is sad he will never see me."

Argon turned his head, quizzically. "You don't want to meet him? You could travel there, you know. It would be quite a journey, though, and I don't recommend you go there alone, but I know the way."

Ilona shook her head. "No. My home is here. I never knew him and it would be an awkward meeting, don't you think?"

Argon shrugged. "I suppose. I guess you've learned everything you could about him through his writings. Your mother had all of his papers, didn't she?"

Ilona said, "Yes, I've read them all, too. A few of my favorite books are missing, though. I think the murderers took some of Mother's things when they attacked her that day on the road. If I recall correctly, one was a book with a picture of you in it. I hear Elijah talked to King Oberon on a regular basis. My mother said she met the king several times at Elijah's house, but that was before he became king. Anyway, I'm glad Greccon found him and he hadn't died. He still writes and that's important. I wish my mother was still alive. I think she really loved Elijah and was saddened by the thought that he had died. I wish she knew he was still alive, even if she is not."

Argon nodded and stretched out in the sun. "Well, I certainly hope it was an attractive picture of me in that lost book. How many years has it been now since Greccon left?"

Ilona stopped to think. "I would guess it's been over five years now since the castle was lost and still there's no sign of Ursan or Alyssa."

Argon trimmed a claw as he thought. "I don't believe Alyssa is with Ursan. There was a ship that day offshore near the tower that no one seemed to pay much attention to. Razz saw a small boat leaving the coast with a bundle in the bow. It was the Norsemen, and they are known for taking women and children. I don't think we will ever see Alyssa again. I can only hope that they would take her for their own and not kill her. They are said to be brutal, but then again they may have taken her to improve their bloodlines. They've done that, too. If she is with them, they've taken her to the top of the world to the cold country. It takes months to get there by ship. It's very far away. They spend years on the sea. None of our fairies have spotted her yet, so she must still be on the ship. I just can't believe the ship had escaped me completely. Shylock saw it, but he thought all of Anna's men had come in it. I was in the front lines by the woods, so I don't think I would have seen it from there. Shylock was engaging the enemies on the field, so he was closer. He's never going to let me forget it, either."

Ilona took a seat on the grass and put one arm over Argon's back, sighing heavily. "Things have turned out so horrible, haven't they, Argon? I've walked around the castle ruins and I remember when it was such a happy place. Now, it's just eerie, haunted, almost. Even my horse shies from riding in there. I had to leave her at the forest's edge and go in on foot. It feels odd to me, as if there was still life there. You can almost hear people talking and horses trotting along and yet the air is still and the creepers grow up the remaining walls. Birds nest in the cracks as if it had been vacant a long time. If you go there in the morning, it's shrouded in fog and it looks so empty." She put her head down on Argon's wing.

He turned his head to look at her. He hated seeing her so forlorn. "It's just mist from the sea. I fly through that portal in the west tower several times a day, Ilona, and it's just a broken down castle, nothing more. It's probably the doublets and synthasites, Mordread's nasty little demons, that are giving you that impression of the castle. I think you are lonely. You miss Greccon. When is he returning? By the look of you, it can't be too soon."

She made a face at him and pinched his side. He flinched and chuckled. "I already know the villagers think this whole place is haunted and that's to your advantage, Ilona. You needn't fear being alone here, but you are your worst enemy. I hate to see you like this."

Ilona sat up and a tear rolled down her face. "Argon, I don't think Greccon is ever coming back. He travels west now. He keeps going further away from me."

Argon decided to change the subject before Ilona got herself deeper into depression. Glynnis had done the same thing over Elijah, but she at least had Ilona to keep her sane.

"You will be too busy to worry about Greccon, soon. Rumor has it that Mordread is planning some sort of a plague. People will start coming to you for a cure." He held up a claw at her expression. "Now, before you start in on me, that's all I know. I don't know what kind of disease, but he's obviously not satisfied with the amount of people that are being burned or hung for little more than sporting a scar. I hear they're developing new weapons as well. He has demons flooding the church, and now, more than ever, reasonable priests are turning into finger-pointing zealots and more people are being accused of crimes against the church. He really wants them to go crazy. I do know King Orion will be sending you all the help you need should something break out like that. The elves are working right now on medicines that should counteract whatever the bastard comes up with."

Ilona got up, pacing and thinking. She looked quite annoyed. "Why can't he just leave the people alone, Argon? It's the same thing. They come up with evil and we counteract it with the good."

Argon broke out laughing. "It's always been that way, Ilona. It's a balance, don't you see that? That's what life is all about." He snatched her hair and tugged at it as she paced by and it made her smile.

"Do you know, Argon, you are the only one I can count on to make me feel better even if I'm in the worst possible mood. Here I'm going to have a plague to contend with, Greccon will never come back, just as Elijah had never returned to Mother, Gods only know if Ursan and Alyssa are even still alive, and I'll probably never see them again either. I feel as alone as I've ever been and here you are pulling my hair like you did when you were little. How do you do it, Argon? How do you stay so optimistic all the time? You seem to always be in a jovial mood and nothing seems to bother you in the least, unless you are hungry."

They both felt the sudden tingle of the protective web and their eyes met. Someone had entered the forest with evil intentions.

"Get inside, Ilona, and stay there." Argon lifted his massive wings and was airborne within seconds.

Ilona returned to her house and barred the door. It wasn't an hour before she saw Argon back-winging to land in her yard and she opened the door to run to him. "What was it, Argon?"

He grimaced. "Just a man with a bow and arrows. A hunter, I presume. Anyway, he'll have a good long swim to shore now and wonder how he had ended up in the drink." He shrugged. "I guess that's why I'm so optimistic, Ilona. I get to take out all my aggres-

sion on idiots. I wonder how long it will take them to finally realize that there is no hunting in this forest? I have no use for these
people, Ilona. I would much rather just kill them, but you soften
my heart, my dear. I keep thinking that this person or that one
will have a heart as pure as yours is, and they may do some good
in this world. I hate to say it, but more often than not, I am sorely
disappointed. I really don't hold out much hope for your world.
No matter how many times we intervene and try to steer them in
the right direction, they would rather listen to Mordread and his
demons and turn on each other instead. I don't know what the
answer is. It's a choice they make, and they inevitably make the
wrong choice every time. It's basically hopeless." He slumped and
collapsed on the green grass.

Ilona looked down on him. "Did I say you were optimistic? I
take it all back."

He glared up at her. "Sorry. I guess I was a little harsh. I guess
I would have felt better if I could have shredded that man, but I
promised you that I would just get rid of them and not kill them.
You know, I'm sorry I made that promise. I really am. It's instinc-
tive, you know. I have all I can do not to just snap off their ugly
little heads."

Ilona started to laugh and Argon joined her. Ilona caught her
breath and sat down again beside him. "And you wonder why they
choose evil over the good? My dear feathered friend, I hate to in-
form you but you would do the same thing if given the choice.
You're a magical, and you are not supposed to think that way at all,
and yet you do. Admit it."

He yawned. "I'm a griffin, my dear, and I will admit only to
that. I may be a part of the Realm, but I'm a griffin, pure and simple, and we are not known for our gentle ways and amiable sunny
dispositions. How else would you have me? Do you think I could
get rid of these intruders by kissing them and wishing them well? I
think not." He got up and pranced delicately around her.

"Maybe I should read them a sonnet and sit them down to tea
and explain to them the value of life and of the land. Perhaps we
could chat and they would leave better people than they had been
to begin with. Do you think that would work?" He bent low to
look directly into her face with his huge golden eyes. "No. As I said,

and I will hold to it, I would rather rip their ugly little heads off."

She grabbed his beak and kissed it, laughing the whole time. He gave her a sideways look, said, "You are hopeless, Ilona." and took off above the trees. He could still hear her laughing at him as he climbed higher. She was annoying, but she was his best friend and always would be. His love for Ilona would last through the centuries, and they would never be alone.

Ilona felt much better after visiting with Argon. She loved that egocentric griffin with all her heart. If it weren't for him, she was sure her life would have been over a long time ago. She faced prejudices from the village and every time something went wrong, it was her that they pointed their fingers at. Argon had thwarted many an assassination attempt on her life and she was frightened to leave her home. She had no friends left and she spent her time alone with her animals. She cared for anything she found hurt in the forest, and made her medicines and read her books over and over again. It was a lonely life and she pondered if she should have gone with Greccon on his quest. She knew times would only get worse and she kept busy making medicines for fevers and infections. She'd spent the morning scouring the forest for the type of plants she needed and the afternoons preparing them. The only bright spot of the day was when Argon would visit. They would argue every time over anything at all, but she knew she could not live without being near him, even if it was only for a few hours here and there. He was pompous and insufferable, but he was loyal and trustworthy too, and they had bonded so long ago that nothing would ever come between them and they both knew that.

CHAPTER NINETEEN

Elgin looked down at his grandson's puzzled face and tried not to laugh.

"Because, Titanion, evil and good have always existed. You can't have one without the other. It's as if you wouldn't know you were warm if you hadn't experienced being cool.

"Yes, but that part about Bubba's Bakery, Grandpa - that wasn't really true, was it? You made that all up, didn't you?" Titanion looked boldly at Elgin. He had been listening to tales for years on end and some of what Grandpa was telling him couldn't be true and he knew it.

Elgin blew out a cloud of smoke. "As I live and breathe fire, every word I've told you is true. That's why you are here, my boy; not to humor an old dragon, but to learn your history. Now, why would I fill you with fantasies? I understand that old Beelzebub still has his bakery and he's very talented in that field. Not only can he make a cake that is light and fluffy, he can also make diseases that are dangerous and appalling."

Titanion scowled. He was sure Elgin had made that one up. He had been there for decades, learning from him. Illustra had been right; his mother had sent him off to his grandfather as soon as he was old enough to talk back to her and stir up trouble. Oberon didn't even have to talk with her again on the subject. Baby dragons reach that insolent age a lot faster than she realized, and she found him precocious and very hard to handle. So, it had been time to fly him off to Elgin, who was more than delighted to have his handsome young grandson with him.

Titanion took a few bites out of the pile of minerals his grandfather had put before him, thinking about all the stories he had been told. Shards of the rocks fell from his mouth and dropped to the floor, making an echoing noise in the large spacious cave. "What about the viruses? Did he ever infect the people with them, or did the elves come up with a cure?"

Elgin nodded. "What year is this?" He scratched his head. "Well, no matter. Either he did or he will, causing a plague of epic proportions. Many will die before it runs its course. It was devastating. I believe he used rat fleas to spread its deadly path all over Europe. When the rats left the ships, it went from country to country. He put a lot of thought into it, I'll give him that. Even the elves couldn't stop it, as hard as they tried, or will try, whatever the case may be." Elgin scratched his head again. It was so hard to keep track of time. He had been both forwards and backwards in time and he pretty much knew the outcomes of the stories he had just told Titanion.

"So, what did the demons try after that?"

Elgin frowned at his grandson's apparent fascination with demons. He would much rather he embrace the Light magic, but he would hear it all, both good and bad. *Little boys are just like that*, he thought. *They want sensationalism, and the more gruesome, the better.*

"They will continue to torment the people with evil rulers, incurable diseases, terrorist attacks, and poison the environment which will kill a lot of people, as well. Then they will start wars on top of all that. They stay busy, my boy."

Titanion looked sad. "Have you told my father all of this? Does he know?"

Elgin nodded. "Of course he knows. He knows all this because he listened to his grandfather, just as you are listening to me. Dragons know everything because of our ability to transcend time. We are the oldest residents of this Earth, and we live forever. Why do you think he organized the Commission? They try to stay on top of the evil plots against humanity."

Titanion sprawled out on the cave floor and watched a condor fly past the cave's mouth. He turned his golden eyes back to his grandfather, who was half asleep further inside the cave.

"Grandpa? Did Sir Collin ever give the demon dagger to another priest, or did he keep it for himself?"

Elgin thought for a minute. "A priest did come for it and he gave it to him. I think the priest went to Ireland with it, and then it went over the ocean with a group of immigrants. It is a magnificent piece of work, that sword. Its blade is sheathed at the tip with obsidian, the sharpest rock you will find. Its edge never dulls, no matter how long it's used, and its cross hilt is made out of the same thing. The dagger will eliminate the demon and make it so he can't come back into the world. It's a mastery of ingenuity; it will locate demons and hum. It was created by magicals and priests alike and there is no other like it. It was forged with dragon fire at temperatures that are still immeasurable. The dagger generates the warmth of the light, even if it's kept in darkness. It's an important weapon. It will become instrumental to the Magical Realm."

Titanion nodded. He just knew Sir Collin would never let him down. He liked the knights although he had never really seen one. He had never been allowed to visit the mortal world, even though he had begged Argon to take him with him when he went to visit his human friend, Ilona. Argon said that unless he had permission to go, and it was given directly to him by his father, he would not let him go. He didn't think the mortal world was safe for children of the Magical Realm, or at least not the ones who looked a lot like dragons. His father said he could not go either, as it was no place for a young dragon. Dragons were too rare and important to take such risks. He loved being told the stories, but he did so want to see things for himself. To think he could fight a battle alongside of the knights and blast the enemy with his fire was a dream he wished would come true. He knew he was fearless and ready for war, if only the adults would let him. He was in the mortal world now with Grandpa, but they seldom left the cave and they flew so high you couldn't see the ground.

"Grandpa? Did we really live in the mortal world with all the people, before?"

Elgin looked incredulous. "Didn't I just tell you the whole story of the Realm? Of course we did. I live there still, as you well know. People are just not ready to accept us, Titanion. They think we're monsters or worse, make believe. We just don't belong in their world anymore. It isn't safe. They have weapons now that could destroy us. I know I said dragons live forever, but that's only if we aren't killed. We'll never die on our own, but we are still vulnerable. No one will take a chance with you, young prince."

He watched with amusement as Titanion pushed rocks to the edge of the cave and let them fall, hanging out of the cave mouth to see where they had landed. Elgin could feel the boy's eagerness to join the real world and was saddened by the fact he would have to remain in the Realm with Oberon. He doubted if he would ever have the chance for any adventures as the rest of them had. Well, it couldn't be helped. This lad could become king one day, should something happen to Oberon. His son's love for the real world might be his undoing, one day, and then little Titanion would be King of the Realm. He loved talking to him and telling him everything that he knew. It made him feel young again.

"Whatever happened to Sir Collin after he gave the dagger up?"

Elgin nodded. "Let me see now, Sir Collin... I believe he went on a crusade to the Holy Lands. I'm not sure what happened to him after that, I'm afraid. I'm sure he was victorious, though. He had a rare gift for battle. One of the best knights I've ever seen. Yes, I remember now; he went on a quest for the Grail with a group of other knights. They'll never find it because it doesn't exist. He gave up the quest as he got older, but I'm sure he settled down with a wonderful woman and had a family. "

"And Alyssa? Did they just sail around and around or did the ship ever land?" Elgin got up and watched the rocks fall with his grandson.

"Oh, they traveled for awhile, visiting wonderful exotic ports. I think Dorn even bought her a few more parrots to train, and then settled down in Nova Scotia, I believe. She gave him four handsome sons. Two of them became explorers. She lived a better life than any she would have had in Europe. It was just a twist of fate that saved her. She didn't have all the finery she would have had as a Lady of court, but she was happy enough and that's all that really matters, isn't it?"

Titanion agreed and then asked if the evil Lady Anna had been killed or captured by the king.

"I didn't say, did I? Well, you know, she wasn't a real lady to begin with."

Titanion scoffed at that. "I'll say. She slit her own husband's throat. That's no lady, if you ask me."

Elgin frowned. "Yes, that was such a shame. I liked Lord McTavish. Well, anyway, as I was saying, she wasn't a lady. Actually, she wasn't a person at all. She was a demon sent with Raskin to bring about the downfall of Griffin's Gate. Mordread thought if he could capture the castle, he could find the gate to the Realm. He never did, thanks to the griffins. Anna's army fled for their lives. Anna went back to the Dark Realm. It's a shame that Griffin's Gate didn't survive. It was one of the kingdoms that was thriving. Mordread knows the magicals surrounded the kingdom, but he never found the gate. He didn't care about the destruction. He'll live to regret that."

Titanion flew out of the mouth of the cave, circled in the air and back inside, over and over again. Elgin grinned. The boy never rested. *It was a good quality in a dragon*, he thought, as he watched him. As soon as he was finished teaching him, he would go to Queen Illustra to learn compassion and hope, then off to Argon for battle training. He would spend time with all of the represented magicals there to learn all that he could from them. *He was growing too fast*, thought Elgin. Soon he would be as arrogant as his father, but then, that was a good quality for a dragon as well. He would enjoy Titanion as long as he could. He was a smart boy, attentive and skeptical at the same time. He is very much his father's son, and he watched curiously as Titanion dug a large hole in the floor, Flinging rocks everywhere, and then flopped down in it.

"I have to learn to fight and Argon will teach me, but who am I supposed to fight, then? In the Realm, no one really fights each other. It's boring there most of the time. I'll never see any real fighting where I can show everyone how ferocious I am."

Elgin laughed. "You would do well to learn all you can from Argon. He's the best fighter I've ever seen, be it griffin or dragon. He's very skilled, cold and calculating in his warfare, yet intelligent and complex in his personal life. He makes wise decisions. You can keep the skill he teaches you, and should you ever be in a position to use it, you will have it then. No one's future is guaranteed and you never know when it might be needed. You are next in line for the throne and you must be all things to all people, magical and mortal."

Titanion rolled over and began to scrape the side of the cave with his claw, as he blew smoke out of his nostrils. "There's too much to remember, Grandpa. I don't think I can do all that. It's too much."

Elgin rubbed Titanion's head with a claw. "It seems so, doesn't it? Never fear, young prince. When the time comes for you, everything will fit into place and you will be a glorious ruler, as your father is now. I'm proud of both of you."

Titanion jumped back up and paced. "I'm glad, Grandpa. I really am, that you're proud of me, but I have done nothing to make you that way. All I do is sit and listen and try to learn. I need to get into some action to show you how much of a real dragon I really am." He blew out a sizeable flame. It reflected off of the cave wall and he had to jump back to keep his nose from being burnt from the backlash.

Elgin grinned. "You might want to make sure you have enough clearance before you shoot out a flame, my boy. Fire has a power of its own and you have to learn and respect that. Aim out, not towards anything, unless of course you intend it to catch on fire."

Titanion lowered his head and looked chagrined. It didn't seem that he could do anything right. He was restless and driven, but he didn't know what to do about it or what he really wanted to do at all. Elgin sat down and seeing the restlessness in his grandson as he had seen so many times before in young dragons, said," You are so impetuous, young prince. There is much to learn before you are ready to forge out on your own. In time you will be able to do what you want and go where you will, but you need to know what you are all about first. You need to know where you came from, why you are here and what you can and can't do, and to learn to do well the things that you can. You can't just go around fighting and burning things up for the sheer joy of it. There is a certain responsibility that goes along with might. We dragons have known that from the beginning and have been teaching this very same thing throughout generations of dragons. Now, it's your turn to learn before you act.

What good is all you can do if you haven't a clue as to why you are doing them?"

Titanion sat down and twitched his singed nose. "I know, Grandpa, but it just takes so long to learn everything. I won't be able to do anything until I'm too old." he whined miserably. "I have to live in the Realm, and be polite to everyone, and I don't feel like a real dragon. You know? Now if I could burn a village or rip apart a demon, I would feel so much better."

Elgin shook his head. "You would need a reason to burn a village, wouldn't you? And I'm afraid, young prince, that you wouldn't know a demon if it had you by the tail. I know how you feel though; believe it or not, I was young once too, a long time ago. I recall I felt the same way you do. I had to wait to grow up, too. It isn't easy is it? So you see, it's your patience and willingness to learn that I am so proud of you for. It's the hardest part to have to wait to really live the way you want to."

Titanion took a deep breath and emitted a cloud of smoke. "Do you think we will ever be able to live in the same world with the mortals? The magicals, I mean, all of us, like we used to do and be a part of the same world? I know you do, here in this cave, but you aren't really a part of the mortal world, unless they find you, that is. What would happen then, Grandpa?"

Elgin had been expecting that question. The magicals had always wanted to live with the mortals and the mortals dreamed of the magicals, but if and when they ever merged together, it would be disastrous, just as it had been before.

"I guess that if the mortals find me, I shall have to go to the Realm with the rest of you magicals. Until then, I'm quite comfortable here in my cavern in the sky. As far as the magicals in the real world, well, a lot of them are already there. The elves, mostly, resembling the mortals as close as they do, and they are vital to the mortal world. King Orion has his hands full keeping track of them. They take positions in the healing world, fighting disease, and in the environmental cause they are essential. They travel worldwide, or at least they will when the time comes for it. They will work side by side with the mortals and help them all they can. The mortals could never survive on their own. The fairies are there and always have been, or they would all starve to death and have no oxygen to breathe. The dwarves deal in the mineral trade and in big business. They know the value of a coin and will control the financial aspect of the civilizations. The trolls are masters of architect and will help in the building of sturdier shelters to protect them from the elements. They also have a flair for artistry, and all of your breath taking structures we have today or will in the future will have the mark of the trolls on it for sure."

Titanion waited for him to continue, but he stopped talking and stretched out on the cave floor. "Yeah, but what about the griffins, unicorns, and dragons?" He tapped a claw impatiently. He wanted to know what part he would have to play along with everyone else.

Elgin opened one golden eye at him and yawned. "The magicals that do not resemble mortals will remain in the Realm. Now, the griffins protect the gate, but they rarely go beyond that. I'm afraid we would not be welcome in the mortal world. The others are, only because they are thought of as mortals and the mortals do not know the difference. If their true nature were known, I'm afraid they would be persecuted much as they were before. It was the unicorns and the griffins that suffered the worst then, and they would be reluctant to go back. Illustra makes an appearance from time to time to mortals she deems worthy and she is good enough to grant gifts to them if she so desires, but she is very cautious. You see, Titanion, in the Realm you are respected and life is good for you. Out here, you would be hunted and killed. I am fortunate enough to have been here so long that I'm just a legend to the people who live directly below on this mountain. They think I'm an omen, a sign from their Gods, so I make a show of it every fifty years or so, enough for the legend to survive from one generation to the next. They will protect me here. I'm on sacred ground as far as they are concerned, and I must be protected. Oh, I suppose when science catches up with the people here and someone can prove that there really is a live dragon living here, I'll have to go. Once the shroud of mystery is broken, it will be time to leave. Right now, they think I control the good and evil in their lives and they respect me for it."

Titanion blinked a few times. "So you have to be a legend to be safe?"

Elgin chuckled. "Sort of. They have to fear you for it to work.

You see, that is part of the problem. People have to react to fear before they will respond. It's not enough for them to do the right things yet. I haven't gone far enough in the future to see if they will evolve into more reasonable beings. If I had to guess, I would say that they wouldn't learn until it was too late and they've destroyed everything. Even with all the help of the magicals, their greed and wastefulness will do them in. Now, let me just get a short nap in here, and we'll talk more when I've rested. Try to stay young, Titanion; getting old is not fun."

Elgin nodded off to sleep and Titanion went to the mouth of the cave to look out. It started to snow again and he flicked out his tongue, catching the icy flakes. It never snowed in the Realm and he wondered why. He found it fascinating. A gust of wind blew a cloud of snow in all over his face and it felt good on his sore nose. He thought his future didn't look very grand. It seemed he would be stuck in the Realm without much hope of doing anything exciting. He turned, watching his grandfather snore. He wondered if he could find a cave and become a legend to mortals. It wasn't fair to be a dragon and have to hide away from everyone. There had to be room for dragons somewhere.

There was before, he knew. They would rescue their fellow magicals and pretty damsels in distress, and fight for their kingdoms. It was hard to believe they weren't welcome anymore. He flew out into the frigid air and it felt good. He did a few circles, feeling the snow slide off of his wings, then landed back inside the cave. He looked down the mountain for a long time, watching the grey clouds gather above and below him. He glanced furtively at Elgin who was deep in sleep now and decided he would be back way before his grandfather woke up.

He flew out, circling lower and lower. He could see small huts off in the distance. When he tried to land, he found that snow was slippery underfoot, and he slid down the rest of the way, plowing up snow as he streaked along. He gave a cry of delight as snow went everywhere. He knew he was much too close to the huts as he skidded to a stop through the tree line. He couldn't help but look around in amazement. He was in the real world now, and not just in his grandfather's cave. He looked back up and found he couldn't see the cave from where he landed. It was much too high up for that. Smoke came out of the huts and he understood that real mortals were living there and then a frightening thought occurred to him that if he was seen, they would try to kill him. He rested there only for a moment, breathing heavily, his heart pounding so hard he could hear it in his ears, and then he flapped his enormous wings, leaving behind a dragon snow print below.

In one of the small huts nestled in the Andes mountain pass, little Marta stood by the door, frozen, watching the dragon in the snow. She remained perfectly still, since dragons ate children. Her father told her if she wandered off and away from the house, a terrible dragon would swoop down and snatch her up, taking her away forever. She was only four years old, but even being so young, she did not believe what her father had told her was real. There was no such thing as dragons, yet there was one right there, in the snow. As blue as ice and snorting smoke from his nose. She could see his dagger like teeth and curved sharp claws as he sat in the snow, looking right at her with big golden eyes. As soon as he left, she ran to her father.

"Poppa. I saw one. I saw a real dragon in the snow, right outside the door. He was blue and he had sharp teeth and huge wings."

Her father laughed and scooped up the child, offering her some of his hot coffee to drink. "Yes? You see then what I tell you is the truth." He couldn't help glancing out of the door. "So, where is this terrible dragon, Marta?"

She put her arms up in the air. "Well, he flew away. Up there, through the trees."

Her father nodded, smiling. "A blue one, you say? I seem to remember the legend saying it was a red dragon that protects us and steals children. This must be the snow dragon, eh? Maybe we should look for one every time it snows. Are you sure it wasn't red?" He was having fun with her now and he winked at her mother, who sat sewing by the fire, shaking her head in amusement.

Marta shook her head vigorously. "He was as blue as the ice. Light blue and covered with snow."

Her father smiled, leaned back in his chair, and drank his coffee. "Well, then Marta, you will either have good luck, or at least you have a vivid imagination."

Titanion had a little trouble negotiating the currents of air as he climbed higher in his panic not to be seen, but he had been seen by the little mortal. He had looked right in her eyes and had seen the fear there. She didn't seem to be happy to see a dragon at all. She was scared to death and he knew it. He knew because he had felt the same way himself.

He skidded into the cave and shook the snow off of his wings. He wasn't going to tell his grandfather. He'd get in trouble for sure. He plopped down to dry. Not only was the snow cold, it was wet too, and his body temperature turned all the dampness into steam. He tried to get his heart to stop pounding in his chest. He'd have to make it look as if he had been there the whole time. For a brave ferocious dragon, he had experienced enough of an adventure for one day. *Grandpa is right*, he thought, *I'm not ready to face the real world yet. I didn't know what to do. What would I have done if that mortal ran out and grabbed me?* He shook again and closed his eyes in submission. He didn't know anything yet. He had been in the real world less than an hour and already he had been frightened. The Realm was safer for him as he knew how everything would respond to him. They all knew him there and no one had ever looked at him the way that little mortal did, and she was just small. They had bigger mortals out there that would try to hurt him. Exhausted by the stress of the flight and from the predicament he had been in, he fell fast asleep, safe in the sky cave of his protective grandfather.

Elgin knew his brazen young grandson had decided to explore and although he held his breath until he came back safely, he said nothing. Titanion's demeanor spoke volumes about what had happened. He had lost the desire to act without thinking first, and that was a big lesson to learn. He wondered what had happened to the boy, but he was content to know Titanion had learned something from it. He seemed more willing to listen and asked incessant questions.

Elgin thought it might be better to bring him back to the Realm for awhile so he could work off some of his pent up energy and frustrations. Perhaps a few lessons with Argon would be appropriate now. He couldn't risk any harm coming to the prince. He could never face Oberon or God forbid, Harmonia, should something harm their son. He told Titanion in the morning they would go back to the Realm for a time. Elgin said he wanted to chat with King

Orion again and he always enjoyed Illustra's company. It would be a vacation of sorts for him. He didn't want Titanion to think he'd done anything wrong, after all; the boy was just curious to learn, but the stakes were too high in his case. He brought his best gemstones out for a hearty breakfast. Titanion relished sapphires and he told his grandfather they were his favorites. He gobbled them all up. His grandfather laughed. The boy's appetite was insatiable, but then so was Oberon's at that age.

"Grandpa, you never said what happened to that evil Raskin."

Elgin turned around. "I didn't? Well, after eight hundred years of being captive by his and Ursan's spell, I'm afraid he came back and caused a lot more trouble. Finish your breakfast, boy; we have a long flight and you'll need your energy."

Titanion finished chewing, his sparkling teeth full of sapphires, then licked up the crumbs on the floor. "And Ursan? Whatever happened to poor Ursan? I really liked him."

Elgin nodded "Yes, well, he too, was trapped for as long as Raskin. None of the magicals could figure out how to free him from his own spell. They could have if it were just Raskin's spell he was under. Ilona was the one who assumed he was in the wall. She did a bit of scrying when she thought she could pick up on his magic around the tower walls. Even your father couldn't help a mage trapped under his own spell. No one could figure out how he had managed to do that until we found out Raskin had been there with his evil magic. The same spell was cast by both mages, contained in the confines of the tower and it intensified ten fold, sealing them both away for what we thought would be forever. Somehow it leaked out about the duel in the tower and it became a legend in town. It remained that way for, as I've said, eight hundred years."

Titanion regarded his grandfather with wide golden eyes. "You said you thought he would be trapped forever. Does that mean he got out of the wall? If Raskin could escape, then surely Ursan could too. Did they, Grandpa?"

Elgin sighed and saw the sun climbing in the sky. He said, "So many questions, Titanion. Let's go. It's a long flight. I can tell you everything that happened on your way home. Let's take off now and once we've reached enough height, why then we'll have a little sky talk.